THE UNEXPECTED PLAN

LEDDY HARPER

.

For my unicorn and my lobster…

PROLOGUE

Brooklyn

"BROOKLYN!" my bestie, Nellie, squealed from across the room, momentarily pulling me from my thoughts of doom. "Get over here."

She frantically waved me over to where she stood, where three hunk-a-burning-love drop-dead-gorgeous men stood. But they did nothing for me. The love of my life had managed to rip up, stomp on, and scorch my heart to smithereens.

All men were now dead to me.

Dead.

Chase and I had gone from *I love you and want to spend the rest of my life with you* to *we need to take a break to figure things out*. There were no warning signs. No fights. How could things have ended so rapidly? There'd been nothing wrong. We'd just had dinner with his parents last week, for crying out loud!

As cliché as it sounded, we were perfect together. Absolutely perfect. I'd mentally picked out my wedding dress, bridesmaids' dresses—Nellie would, without question, be my maid of honor. And flowers...peach and white. I was just waiting for the ring—which I'd already described in subtle hints.

What woman didn't already have the three Cs picked out for their dream diamond?

Who was I kidding? Obviously our relationship hadn't been perfect, but I still had no idea where things had gone wrong. All the typical reasons of rejection coursed their way through me while lightning bolts struck my internal sanctuary, leaving my soul utterly decimated.

As I stared at my best friend, I knew I'd have to move my ass and go to her side, or she'd never stop waving her arms like a lunatic. Then again, Penelope Fields was certifiably insane; it was one of the many reasons I loved her so much.

"Brookie," she hollered again, her boisterous tone alerting me to just how far ahead she was in the drinking department.

I wondered if I should just give in and numb my senses. After all, I had mentally reserved all day tomorrow to wallow. It only made sense to do so while hungover—multitasking never hurt anybody.

"Hey, Nells." My fake go-to smile felt as plastic as Barbie's tits as I inwardly screamed, *get me out of here!* I grabbed the full shot glass from her, not caring what was in it, and downed it in one gulp. My cheeks burned as the liquor lit my throat on fire. I tried to think of it as a good pain, but it was gross. "What the hell was that?"

"Liquid courage." Nellie beamed, and upon closer inspection, I realized she wasn't as blitzed as she'd first appeared. She was simply in full-blown flirt mode—even though I desperately needed supportive-friend mode.

She caught my glance and immediately signaled the other two members of our crew to head back to our table. And just like the close friends and self-proclaimed besties we were, our posse met back at the booth we had snagged shortly after getting here. We usually had a blast on a night out, but tonight, I'd brought along heavy baggage. It weighed me down, kind of like trying to walk through quicksand in high heels while wearing a ball and chain tethered to my ankles, hindering me from having much—or *any* fun.

As we took our seats, Nellie swung her arm around my shoulders and pulled me closer on the wooden bench. Without needing to be told, she just got me. She knew when I was down, sometimes even before I did. That's why she'd suggested going out tonight in the first place. Heartache was the absolute worst.

I gulped down water, still battling the fire that scorched my throat.

"So...this is fun." It was supposed to be a joke, but the tears that leaked from my eyes drowned any ounce of humor from my statement.

"I'm so sorry, babe. He's a dick. He doesn't deserve you." Nellie stroked my arm in that comforting way she always did when I needed it. She'd always been my security blanket—she preferred to call herself my Xanax, but I never thought that made much of an endearing nickname.

"He really doesn't. There are other fish in the sea." Mady never understood the correct timing to use her singsong voice. Normally I'd laugh or have a witty comeback for her lame one-liners, but tonight, I just wanted to bury myself in a pile of blankets and never come up for air.

"I have to use the restroom." Julie hopped up from her seat and stood next to the table. "Mady, care to join me?" There would no doubt be a loving, friendly confrontation in the ladies' room over the inappropriate timing of my clueless friend's encouragement.

These women were my pack, and as such, we all took care of each other. Which was why I wasn't bothered by Mady's level of support; I knew her well enough to understand that was just her way of having my back.

Turning to the only other person at the table, Nellie, I huffed and wiped away an errant tear. "I know there are other men out there. I swear, I do, but none for me. He was it. The one. And we only have one lobster."

"Yes, and I'm yours. How many times do I have to tell you to stop giving that title to someone else?" At least her feigned offense brought a smile to my face—very small and, likely, unnoticeable to the untrained eye, but a smile, nonetheless. "Sweetie, I know it's hard to see this right now, but maybe he wasn't the one. Sometimes things don't work out for a good reason. We just have to sit back and wait for that reason to show itself."

I adamantly shook my head. We were meant to be; she just couldn't see that. "Did you suspect that there was anything wrong with us? With our relationship? Like, was the writing on the wall and I just didn't see it?"

Mady and Julie rejoined us, preventing Nellie from answering. There was no way they'd been gone long enough to even make it to the bathroom let alone use it, but before I could question them, Mady said, "We ordered an Uber. I thought maybe we can go back to my place?"

Her question seemed to be for both of us, except she kept her wide eyes aimed directly at Nellie. As if that wasn't strange enough, Julie had gone pale. Those reactions were induced by more than alcohol.

Things only became weirder from there. Nellie craned her neck and peered over my head, then fumbled through her purse and hurriedly threw two twenties on the table. "Yup. Sounds good to me."

Her suspicious behavior provoked me to sneak a peek over my shoulder to see what had garnered her attention. Instantly, my body grew numb. My limbs rejected every signal of movement my brain tried sending. My heart immobilized. The atmosphere was eerily quiet as my gaze locked on *him*.

"Oh my…" My hand went to my mouth as vomit taunted my esophagus, threatening to make its way to the surface. I swallowed profusely, urging it back down.

"Come on, let's get out of here." Nellie yanked me from my seat and practically dragged me through the exit.

4

My three friends huddled around me on the sidewalk. I buried my face in their embrace for what felt like hours until our Uber pulled up, and before I knew it, the four of us were squished in the backseat.

"I'm ordering pizza; hopefully it'll arrive shortly after we do. This situation calls for major junk food. Do we need to make a pit stop at a gas station for anything else? Wine? Chips? Chocolate? A crowbar?"

I shook my head while they continued to discuss what all to purchase at the corner store—which sounded a lot like things one would need to dispose of a body.

The entire car ride was a blur. One minute I was sandwiched between Julie and Nellie, and the next, I found myself being shuffled inside and my coat removed. A wave of thankfulness washed over me. I was incredibly lucky to have such compassionate friends. We'd been through many breakups, although none of them mine. Sure, there'd been Joe Blow in ninth grade and Joe Schmow in eleventh, but they hadn't been serious. Not like Chase. Chase had been my one chance at happiness.

"Okay, who's gonna start?" Julie popped a cheese puff into her mouth and began to chew. "Can I just say she's not that pretty?"

"I agree." Mady nodded and broke open the tub of ice cream, then handed out three spoons. The four of us dug in.

"She's beautiful," I argued. "She's everything I'm not. Stunning, outgoing, sophisticated. I'm not sophisticated." I held up my spoon as if to prove my point.

"You're gorgeous." Nellie elbowed me before scooping up another mouthful. "She's got nothing on you."

Nellie had always admired my thick brown hair that hung past my bra strap, light skin tone, big green eyes, and many other attributes of mine she said she wished she had. And I knew I wasn't ugly. However, there were many differences between *that* woman and me.

"You guys are beyond nice, but come on! She obviously has

5

something I don't." My tears had momentarily dried and anger began to stir. "We broke up less than a week ago, and he's already with someone else?"

"Maybe they weren't together. Maybe they met at the bar. Like a one-night hook-up." Julie looked so sincere, it made me want to believe her.

"Nope. I recognized her," I finally stated.

They all gasped and turned to look at me.

"She's his assistant. Not to be confused with a secretary—he constantly corrected me on that detail—but administrative assistant. And, apparently, champion horn blower!"

Julie spit out a little ice cream as she laughed. It wasn't a secret that I detested giving head. It was a fact this group wouldn't ever let me live down. And that had been eleventh-grade Joe Schmow's fault. He'd held my head down and practically drowned me in his cum my first time.

"No way!" Mady exclaimed and sat forward. "That was Heather? The infamous suck-retary?"

I nodded mutely.

"Oh, wow. We'd joked about this—her secretly plotting to steal your man—but what a hussy to actually follow through!" Nellie and I *had* spoken of this, but mainly because of the long hours he'd worked lately. Never in my wildest dreams had I imagined it would actually come to fruition.

"Doesn't Chase work at AdCorp?" Julie asked, scanning the room until someone verified her claim. "As in…the same company that Nellie's brother works for?"

"Yeah, but I don't think they know each other. I've never heard Chase mention him."

"It's okay…they don't have to."

"They don't have to for what? Where are you going with this, Jules?" Nellie asked cautiously with her gaze zeroed in on our friend.

"I have an idea." Julie's dark eyes sparkled, a sinister grin tugging at the corners of her mouth as she rubbed her hands together like she had some evil genius plan brewing in her head. "Why don't we secretly plot to get Chase back?"

"Yes!" I squealed and clapped. "Let's get him back!"

Hope blossomed in my chest.

Although, it quickly died when Nellie shoved me back with one arm and put herself between Julie and me as if she were rescuing me from a stray bullet. "We don't want Chase back. He's a dog!"

Julie tsked and shook her head. "No, not get him back like that. I mean get even. Give him a taste of his own medicine by taking Heather away from him so he knows how it feels."

"Oh…this sounds fun!" Mady's eyes lit up like the sky on Fourth of July.

I waved my hands in front of their excited, devious faces. "I hate to break it to you all, but I don't think Heather bats for the other team. I'm fairly certain she likes dick…a lot."

"I wouldn't be so sure of that; she's with Chase, isn't she?" Leave it to Nellie to be the one to accuse my ex of having a vagina. Although, there was a very good chance they were all thinking the same thing; she was just the only one to verbalize it.

I rolled my eyes and groaned. "What I'm trying to say is…how are we supposed to pull that off if we're all women?"

"Not us, silly. We'll have to find someone." Julie licked her lips. "Someone hot. Someone irresistible."

"Where the hell would we find anyone like that?" I challenged.

Which was the wrong thing to do, because a split second later, Mady exclaimed, "Corbin!"

We all burst into laughter—well, everyone except Nellie. Julie, Mady, and I had gossiped about Corbin Fields over the years. I mean, who doesn't fantasize about their friend's hot older brother? But actually doing something with him? Gross. It was more like a drunken fantasy that would never amount to anything.

"No way!" Nellie finally weighed in. "Not my brother."

"Oh, come on, Penelope. It's perfect. They work together, and since they don't know each other, Chase would never suspect anything. Plus, Corbin would do anything for you. All you have to do is ask—the worst he can say is no." Julie knew he'd never tell his baby sister no; hell, we all knew that much.

"I refuse. Not to mention, there's no way he'd go along with it. He takes his job very seriously. This would be crossing a line. Brother or not, I can't ask him to bring some personal vendetta to work…one that's not even his own."

"Oh my God." Realization smacked me in the head. "What if they have a no-fraternization policy? Holy hell… Chase might get fired."

The idea of him not having the job he'd worked so hard to obtain almost killed me. If he lost his job, he wouldn't be able to support the family we were going to have when we finally got back together. And we all knew we'd get back together…okay, so maybe I was the only one, but that didn't make it any less true.

Mady clapped her hands and bounced up and down excitedly on her knees. "That gives Corbin the 'in' he needs. Doesn't Chase report to him?"

"Not really," I clarified. "They're in two different departments."

"This could still work," Julie mused.

"Absolutely not." Nellie got up and began to pace.

If Corbin could keep Chase from being fired… "I'm beginning to warm up to the idea."

This could potentially kill three birds with one stone: keep Chase from losing his job, make Chase experience the level of betrayal and hurt he'd made me feel, and at the same time, breaking them up so we could get back together. It really was a genius idea.

"Brooklyn Miller, you've got to be kidding me." Nellie gawked at me.

"Think about it. You're his little sister; he would do anything for you." I grabbed her hand and looked at her pleadingly.

"Just like I'll do anything for you?" She sighed, and I knew she was coming to our side.

"This is just what I need, something to take my mind off this horrible breakup. And what's better than revenge?"

CHAPTER 1

CORBIN

"THERE'S no way on God's green earth I will let the two of you rope me into one of your schemes again." I focused back on the neat pile of papers in front of me and then shot my sister a glare. "You've gone crazy!"

"Not crazy, just desperate. She's like a sister to me, Corbin. Which means she's kind of like your sister, too, if you really think about it. And I haven't even told you our plan yet. How can you say no without hearing me out?"

"Grow up. You two aren't twelve anymore. I've been manipulated into helping you with things in the past, but not anymore. We're adults now. Let's act like it. Drag some other poor sap into this charade of yours."

"Okay, but imagine if this were *your* best friend. And he was distraught. Wouldn't you do anything—and I mean *anything*—to make him feel better?"

God had blessed my sister with the biggest brown eyes. Eyes that pulled you in and made you want to rescue her. And every time I did, I ended up getting stuck in situations I couldn't even remember agreeing to. I'd fallen under her puppy-dog spell before and suffered the consequences, but now a full-fledged adult, I refused to fall for the sibling-in-distress call again. The big-brother mentality was hard to ignore. I mean, naturally, I wanted to swoop in and save her. But I'd been there, done that, and I didn't care to go back.

There was the time her new kitten managed to climb all the way up one of our prize palm trees. The fireman who ended up rescuing both of us had said it was twenty-plus feet. Not to mention, our parents had to chop down their beautiful and expensive Sylvester Palm due to the damage caused. I remembered exactly how expensive it had been, because I'd spent my summer working off every fucking penny to replace it. Not to mention, the teasing I'd endured from my buddies.

Then there was the time both girls had decided that adding soap to our outdoor pool filter would be a good idea. They'd come shrieking upstairs to my room when the bubbles had reached the second-floor windowsill. That had been deemed my fault as well because I'd agreed to "watch" them while my parents went out to dinner—thanks to Nellie's promises that they'd be good and were practically old enough to watch themselves.

No, not falling for her doe-eyed routine again.

"Nellie, you need—" The ringing phone on my desk cut off the speech I'd mentally prepared. "Hold on." I held up one finger to my sister and answered the call. "This is Corbin."

"I need you to get a handle on this situation with Motto. Pronto. I'm sending you an email that needs immediate attention." My boss's not-too-happy voice bellowed in my ear.

I wrangled my computer mouse and opened my email. "I see it. I'll get right on it, sir." I quickly set the phone in the cradle and returned my attention to the computer screen. I needed to figure out how to respond, and quickly.

"Corbin—"

"Nellie, can it. My boss just notified me that the head honcho of our most lucrative account is pissed. They're threatening to pull out of the new ad campaign contract if we can't come up with something to entice them to stay. Apparently, they aren't too happy with the project assistant they've been dealing with, so I need to contact them immediately to smooth things over before we lose the account. Can we finish this another time?"

She started to respond, but I didn't bother listening to what she had to say before grabbing the receiver and punching the button for my assistant.

"Hey, Em. Can you get Mike at Transition Motto on the phone, please?" I turned my attention back to my longwinded sister while still holding the receiver to my ear. Talking over her, I said, "Nell, I need to fix this."

"But I need you to help me with something. Just this one thing."

"Spit it out...*quickly*." Then I held up another finger because Mike came on the line. "Mike, this is Corbin from AdCorp."

"Listen, I'm sorry, but I'm done. I'm serious this time."

"I understand you're unhappy with your current ad campaign, and I'd really like to make this right. How can I help get this project back on track for you? I'd really hate to see you go."

"Have you seen their concept?"

"Not personally, no." That never sounded good to a client, but approving campaign pitches was no longer my job. Unfortunately, most of the contracts I'd dealt with prior to my last promotion didn't seem to understand this.

Mike rambled in my ear about all the things he *strongly* disliked regarding the concept while Nellie chattered from across the desk. It was a good thing I'd learned long ago how to ignore her and pretend she wasn't speaking—especially because that girl didn't know where her off button was.

After some wheeling and dealing, I was able to smooth Mike's ruffled feathers and obtain his agreement on giving things another try. By the time I'd finished with all the calls I needed to make, I felt like I'd slain a dragon.

"Corbin, did you hear me?" Nell brought me back to the present.

"Yeah, I heard you." I hadn't heard a word, but was it really important? Probably not. I had just evaded an entire conversation, and she hadn't even noticed.

"Okay, so drinks on Friday at the Round Up?"

"Friday?" I mentally checked my schedule. If it would appease her, I could easily go for one drink. "Yeah. That should work. Six thirty?"

"Great." Nellie hopped up from her chair and kissed me on the cheek. "You're the best brother ever."

I smiled as she left. I truly loved her, but God, she could be a champion pain in the ass. How could someone make your life hell while making it worth living? She was a conundrum, no doubt.

RUNNING LATE WAS part of my mantra. Why arrive early when you usually ended up waiting for the other party anyway? It made no sense to me.

Of course, this was not my way of doing things at work. My tardiness mainly affected my personal life, which had been the issue with my past and current relationships. Girlfriends were usually a problem. Work came first, romance second. If they couldn't deal with that, then there was no future. Thank goodness for my secretary, Emily. She'd saved me more times than not by remembering important dates and sending appropriate gifts on my behalf.

My on-again-off-again girlfriend—currently off—was perfect for me. Lindsey adhered to the same work ethic, so she didn't mind when I chose work over her. The current problem was that *she* had chosen work over me. Mainly a life-changing promotion she'd worked her entire career to achieve. Unfortunately for me, it was in a different state, and I wasn't prepared to give up my position at AdCorp to move. So, for the time being, Lindsey and I were apart.

I was meeting my sister at Round Up, which was a hole-in-the-wall barbecue place that doubled as a bar. They had killer drinks and even better happy hours. Although, I'd probably missed happy hour since I was so late.

"Corbin!" My sister spotted me and waved me over.

But my attention went straight to the woman seated with her at the table. For a split second, I felt like a schoolboy all over again —racing heart, clammy hands, obsessively worrying if my hair was a mess or if my shirt was wrinkled. But the longer I stared, the more familiar she looked…then I recognized her, and I immediately felt strange for having the hots for someone who I'd always viewed as another sister to me.

"Hey, Nell." I kissed her on the cheek and then turned to the dark-haired beauty next to her—her life-long best friend, Brooke. "Hey, Bridge. Long time no see." Rather than give her a kiss as well, I offered a smile before sitting down. Damn, she had really… well, *grown up* since the last time I saw her. Too bad I couldn't remember how long ago that'd been. It was hard to tell considering I'd heard about her constantly, thanks to my sister bringing her up at dinner every Sunday. Although, staying current with her life hadn't prepared me for just how much she'd changed since the last time I actually saw her in person.

I wasn't sure why she was here, but I'd decided not to ask. I certainly didn't want to make it sound like I wasn't happy to see her. Then again, I didn't want to admit just how happy I *was* to see her. For fuck's sake she looked good.

"Why must you continue to call her that? You know that's not her name." Nellie seemed more irritated than Brooke over the childhood moniker I'd given her.

"There are lots of Brookes and Brooklyns in the world, but as far as I'm concerned, there's only *one* Brooklyn Bridge." I winked at her and then watched her cheeks flame with heat. Oddly enough, that lit a fire in the pit of my stomach.

I looked Brooklyn over—inconspicuously, of course—and suppressed a groan. She had cleavage, and her hair practically draped her shoulders like a thick, dark curtain. The word *goddess* didn't begin to describe her beauty.

"So, *Bridge*, what have you been up to?"

That question induced a glare from Brooke. She hated the nickname I'd christened her with during childhood. I'd originally done it to piss her off after one of the charades they'd tangled me into, but it had stuck. And I couldn't stop using it now, even though it had been years since I'd seen her. She didn't look like the Bridge I'd known before, but the reaction the nickname produced was invaluable. It still worked.

"You should probably ask what we *haven't* been up to!" They both giggled, though where my sister's sounded genuine, Brooke's seemed to be filled with nerves more than anything.

Deciding to turn my attention elsewhere before I made this entire evening uncomfortable, I scanned the drink menu; suddenly alcohol seemed like a necessity. Truth be told, I didn't really know too much about Brooke's life anymore, other than what Nell shared, so I was a bit stunted on conversation topics.

"So, how's work?" I asked Brooke without actually looking at her. If I got trapped in her pale-green eyes again, I doubted I'd ever find my way out of that sexual labyrinth.

"It's fine. It's not really a job, though; at least not one that your family would accept."

Based on what Nellie had told me—granted, I'd never really asked—Brooklyn was currently doing an internship toward becoming a teacher. Her degree had taken her longer to obtain because of her childhood. Her mom had worked two or three jobs at a time to help her with her community college education, and Brooke had to take breaks from school in order to work when her mom had fallen ill. There was no one else. No father. No siblings. Just Brooke and her mom.

And now it was just Brooke.

It had taken her longer than most to finish her bachelor's degree because of the hurdles placed in her way, something that my family—namely my parents—couldn't seem to grasp. Nell and I had each attended four-year prestigious colleges and graduated during the customary time period it took to earn a degree—

with honors, no less. We also both immediately landed paid internships, and once they concluded, we began working in "impressive" jobs. That was all according to my parents, anyway. But let's be honest, it's who you know, not *what* you know, and my parents were able to provide those connections for us.

I couldn't care less how Brooke achieved her dream. In fact, I was more proud of her for overcoming her struggles and still continuing along her path. But I still thought of her as the pain-in-the-ass kid sister I never wanted. She was a flat-out nuisance. Granted, now she was more of a knock-out nuisance, but that was neither here nor there.

"You know I don't feel the same as my parents, right? I think I've proven that time and time again." The sincerity of my tone made the tense lines of her face smooth away until a slow smile spread over her lips.

"I know," she said quietly. "How have you been? Is your job still going well?"

"Yes." Thanks to the server's perfect timing, I was able to end it there with a long pull of my drink. I didn't understand why talking to her was so hard. Taking another gulp, I chalked it up to the fact that I wasn't used to conversing with this version of Brooklyn. This was a grown woman, not the kid sister I was used to.

Seriously, how long had it been?

"Any hooter," Nell interjected, breaking the silence. "We've all gathered here to discuss a plan. One that is absolutely ingenious and perfect in every single way!"

"You've got to be kidding me." I shot her a look of disbelief. "I feel like I was brought here under false pretenses. You said we'd get drinks and catch up."

"Catch up on the plan. Duh!" Nell rolled her eyes. "I sat in your office and told you about this. You agreed by continually nodding, and you even pointed your finger at me during the good parts."

"I did no such thing!"

"Yes, you did. I'm still amazed by your multitasking skills. You were on a phone call, addressing an email, *and* carrying on a conversation with me…all at the same time! Crazy!"

"Maybe you think it's crazy because it absolutely did *not* happen. I clearly told you to wait a sec and didn't hear a word you said."

"Unbelievable!" Nell threw her hands in the air, then turned to Brooke. "I knew he'd back out like the pussy he is."

"First of all, I'm not a pussy. And secondly, just because you work for Dad's company and can pawn off your duties doesn't mean we all can. Some of us have to work for a living, and that phone call could've turned into a career-changing event."

"I'm not saying it wasn't. I guess I just misinterpreted our conversation. I really thought you were listening to me."

"It's fine. Whatever. Just know this *plan,* or whatever it is, is finished."

Her nose crinkled while she studied her napkin, which was indicative of a few tears being shed in the near future. *Fuck!*

"Look, Nellie, it was a long shot anyway." Brooklyn patted her friend's hand in an attempt to make her feel better. "And it's actually fine. Maybe we'll come up with an even better strategy. You know if we put our heads together we're nothing short of awesome."

"Yeah." Nellie offered a small smile, but then her bottom lip slightly quivered.

"Fine. I'll do it." *Fuck me!* That little twerp always knew how to pull at my heartstrings. And I let her do it. Every. Single. Time.

"You don't even know what *it* is yet." Nell smirked.

"I have a feeling you two will fill me in."

"Oh, we will! You're absolutely going to die when you hear it!" My sister laughed as she rubbed her hands together vindictively. "Chase will never know what hit him!"

CHAPTER 2

BROOKLYN

TO SAY I felt uncomfortable was an understatement.

Nellie had a way of twisting the truth to fit what she wanted to hear, so I shouldn't have been surprised. And I guess I wasn't. But it didn't stop me from wanting to descend deep into my seat, or beneath the table and disappear. At first, the scheme had sounded perfect, but now that the cat was out of the bag about Corbin not really being on board, and we'd have to present it to him from the beginning, my stomach was in knots.

"Corbin, if you don't want to do it, I understand."

"I thought we've worked past that point," he snapped.

Nellie shot me a look that clearly said, *do not rock the boat*, even though we were already on the verge of sinking.

"Okay. Well, since we're going to be here a while, should we order dinner?" I suggested.

"That sounds amazing, but I have to get going." My bestie got up and started to open her wallet to pay for her drink.

"I got this," Corbin assured her.

"Thanks, bro. I'll catch you next time."

I gawked at her while she quickly hugged Corbin, then me. And she was gone. Poof, completely disappeared before I knew what had happened. What the heck? She just left me with her brother. Alone. To explain everything. What a bitch!

"Guess it's just us," I said, sounding like a complete buffoon. For whatever reason, I found it nearly impossible to talk normal around him when Nellie wasn't here. It was beyond awkward. I made a mental note to kill my best friend once I made it through this dinner.

"Cheers." Corbin gave me a smile and held up his drink.

He didn't seem to have a care in the world, so why should I? I held up my glass and clinked his before taking a sip. I sometimes had a tendency to make more out of a situation than was there, so I needed to ignore the nerves that ransacked my system and just enjoy dinner.

"Tell me about this scheme the two of you have concocted."

"Well…I guess you know my boyfriend broke up with me."

"No. Not really. I didn't even know you had a boyfriend, so perhaps you should start at the beginning."

The waitress approached our table and took our order for dinner. Considering this could go either way, we ended up ordering a few appetizers to share. No sense in getting a full entrée if he'd tell me to forget the plan five minutes into our conversation.

"The beginning?" I asked once the waitress had refilled our drinks.

"Sounds like a good place to start." He offered a kind smile, and I felt my body relax even more. This wasn't so bad. Maybe he'd be easier to talk to than I'd expected.

"Hmm…" I tapped my chin, wondering which beginning he'd meant; clearly he didn't want the entire story from the first day we had met. "Well, Chase, my boyfriend, and I were together for two years—two amazingly perfect years. We used to talk about the future all the time, to the point that we had our entire lives mapped out, down to how many kids we wanted to have. But then he dumped me out of the blue, no warning at all. I mean, we've always gotten along great, never having any issues whatsoever."

"I kind of find that hard to believe," Corbin stated, butting into my storytelling.

"You find what hard to believe?"

"Well, you said he broke up with you, which makes him your *ex*-boyfriend, so there had to be issues somewhere. You don't just break up with someone for no reason. You may not have seen it coming, and I'm sure it took you by complete surprise, but there had to be signs that he was itching for a break. Maybe you just didn't see them."

To my sheer mortification, my eyes begin to water. Anytime I thought of the love of my life no longer with me...it killed me inside. And having to explain it to anyone, let alone my bestie's brother of all people, made the pain worse. Add in the mortification of crying at a sports bar, and I was ready to call it quits.

"Oh, hey. I didn't mean anything by that." He reached across the table, but before he could cover my hand with his, he pulled his arm back to his side, as if the thought of touching me skeeved him out. "I'm an asshole. Just ignore me."

"It's okay. You're probably right." I sniffled. "But I seriously didn't know of any issues, and we never discussed anything that supported that argument." I squared my shoulders before continuing. "He said he loved me. Said he wanted to spend the rest of his life with me. I had no reason not to believe him. You know? So when he suddenly dumped me almost two weeks ago, it hit me hard."

"You poor kid." Corbin patted my hand like a child, which made me pull mine back this time and hide it under the table. Kid? He was only four years older than me.

"Yeah, well, the kicker was last week. My friends took me out to cheer me up, and we saw him. Only he wasn't alone. He was with another woman. They were very familiar with one another. I instantly recognized her, but it took me a minute to place her. She's his assistant."

"Okay. That makes things awkward."

"Yeah. And to make matters worse, I think they were seeing each other before we broke up."

Leaning back in his seat, he slouched his shoulders and let out a long huff. "So what is it you think I can do for you?"

"Well...Chase works at AdCorp."

He sat upright, his eyes practically bugging out of his head as he stared at me in disbelief. "He does? What'd you say his name is? Chase?" When I nodded, he shook his head with a sigh. "Are you wanting me to fire him? If so, I have to be honest with you, Bridge; I don't have that kind of authority."

"*No, no, no.* Nothing like that at all. That's just it...I *don't* want him to lose his job."

"Well, good. You don't have anything to worry about, because he won't."

I huffed and tried to explain better. "I'm worried about a no-fraternization policy and—"

"Let me just go ahead and put your mind at ease now." He leaned forward and completely captured my attention with his blue eyes. "AdCorp doesn't have that policy. The closest thing is a rule about reporting relationships to HR, but that's just to cover their own asses. The best I could do is look into it to see if he's made the relationship public, but I've got to be honest with you, Bridge...even if he hasn't, they'll just make him report it."

"Oh." I covered my face with my hands, feeling a little embarrassed and maybe slightly disappointed. I didn't want to get him in any trouble, and I certainly didn't want him fired. But knowing he could cheat on me with his assistant and get away with it made me a little sick to my stomach. "I didn't mean anything like that. I just wanted to get back at him a bit."

The waitress delivered our appetizers, and we made the normal conversation, like "oh, that looks good" and "I'll try one of those." After we each had our plates filled with what I liked to call tasters, I took a deep breath and continued with what I'd been saying prior to our food being served.

"I mainly thought—well, my friend Julie thought—that we should give Chase a taste of his own medicine, which Nellie and I agreed was a good idea. That led to us all concocting this strategy of you hitting on Chase's assistant and making her leave him for you." This hadn't even been my idea. Julie had devised it, Mady had jumped on it, and then Nellie had taken the proverbial baton and run with it. Now I was left holding the flaming stick with no one to pass it to.

"Excuse me?" Corbin's hand over his mouth muffled his laughter. "Make her leave him for me? How on earth do you expect me to accomplish something like that?"

"Maybe pay her extra attention and flirt a little? You don't have to sleep with her or anything."

"Well, thank goodness for that." He continued his laughter, only this time, he didn't try to mask it. He belted it out, and it made me want to curse Nellie for leaving me here alone. Meeting with him tonight had been her frickin' idea anyway. I went along with it because it sounded good, but I wasn't selling it the way she could have. Instead, I came across like a salesman with zero knowledge of the product I was trying to deliver.

"This isn't coming out right. I can't explain it well enough."

"Oh, I think it's coming out just fine. I completely understand." He winked at me.

My cheeks burned red hot, and when the heat moved down my neck, I was well aware that every inch of my visible skin glowed crimson. *Great. Just great.*

"It's not like you're currently dating anyone, right?" After saying that, I wanted to stick my foot in my mouth—hell, *both* feet!

"Are you hitting on me now, Bridge?"

"God, no!" I desperately wished I could slip under the table to hide.

"I'm just teasing you. I know you aren't interested in me." He took another swig of his beer and then signaled the waitress. "So how do you suggest I steal this woman away?"

After the waitress cleared some of our dishes, I continued. "Her name is Heather. She's thirty-something and has three kids. I honestly can't see the attraction." I shrugged, unable to believe my own lie that rolled off my tongue. Of course I saw what drew him to her. She was frickin' gorgeous. *Blonde bombshell* came to mind when picturing her in my mind's eye.

"Are you kidding? Older woman? Built-in family? Who wouldn't go for her?" He chuckled and threw his hands up. "I'm kidding, Bridge. Chill out. I'll do it, okay?"

I spent the next forty-five minutes telling Corbin everything I knew about the woman who had stolen my man. I recalled conversations I'd had with Chase regarding his assistant and repeated the essential facts. Things she liked, things she abhorred.

He patiently listened, and I thought I caught him studying me intently a couple of times, but that couldn't be right. He'd never liked me as a friend—or even a person for that matter. He'd never kept it a secret just how annoying he used to think I was, and I wasn't delusional enough to believe he no longer felt that way.

Once I'd finished listing all the details I could remember, I sat back and waited for his response to the verbal vomit I'd just hit him with.

"So when should I start fucking with her?"

I almost spit out my mouthful of wine and then snickered. "Wow, you certainly don't waste any time."

"What's the point? You know Nell won't let me sneak out of this one. I might as well *get 'er done* so I can put this to bed. And I don't mean literally."

I bit my tongue to stave off my laughter. "I really think that sex should be the end goal. It'd be the ultimate payback. I mean, if Chase catches the two of you in bed together, it would be perfect. Don't you agree?"

"Bridge, I am absolutely *not* sleeping with her. I have to be honest, things with my girlfriend might be on hold right now, but they will pick up again—they always do. This is just how things with Lindsey and me go; we keep each other on the back burner, waiting for the right time to reconcile. It's what works for us."

"I see, so you don't want to sleep with her because you still love your *ex*-girlfriend?" I totally understood this, because I was truly, madly, deeply still in love with my ex. But that didn't stop me from giving him a hard time. "Sounds like a rather...*frustrating* way to live if you ask me."

"No. We're not together, so we can sleep with whomever we please. I just don't want to lead someone on, especially someone in the office, and then complicate things by sleeping with her; it's morally wrong in my opinion."

The humor that had warmed my stomach a moment ago had faded, which meant I needed to switch to water because I'd had too much wine.

What he said made perfect sense, but I couldn't believe he had morals. It made me realize just how much I didn't know about Corbin. I only remembered him as the gangly teenager who used to rescue Nellie and me from situations we'd found ourselves in.

"How are you, Corbin?" My words came out sincere and bordered on caring.

"I'm good." He chuckled, shaking his head at the way I'd hijacked the conversation and turned it around about a hundred and eighty degrees. "What brought that on?"

I shrugged and studied the table, tracing invisible lines with my finger. "I don't know...I guess I finally realized that I don't know very much about the grown-up Corbin, only the teenage version I remember from my childhood."

"I feel the same way, but that's kind of how life is. We grow up, people move on. Then life gets busier and busier, and you lose touch. You meet different people, form new circles of friends."

"Yeah. Do you still hang out with any of your high school buddies?" I surprised myself by how invested I was in his answer. It was like I really wanted to know all about him or something. So strange.

"I do. But not often. Most of them have moved due to job

offers they received, and several have started families. I'm just not there yet. I don't know if I'll ever reach a point in my life where I'll be ready to be a family man. My career doesn't allow for it."

If that wasn't the go-to excuse for any commitment-phobe, then I didn't know what was.

"Really? I find that hard to believe. Especially in this day and age. People telecommute, have part-time jobs, do whatever they need to make things work. I still can't believe how nice it was for my school to allow me to switch to online courses when my mom became ill. It allowed me to continue, even if it wasn't the way I would've preferred had things been different."

"Yeah. That had to have been tough." It was his turn to study the table. "I'm really sorry about that, Brooklyn. Really sorry. You were dealt a shitty hand."

"I don't think I've ever heard you say my actual name before." I offered a small smile and then immediately felt awkward. It had almost been a bit flirtatious. What the hell was I doing? I wasn't ready to flirt with another guy, let alone Corbin!

I pushed my wine glass to the side and started sipping water.

"It's a nice name, but Bridge just suits you. I don't know... Initially, I used it to piss you off, and then it stuck."

Corbin still sported the genetically pleasing traits he'd had in high school, minus the gangly teenager part. His face was chiseled, while still managing to look approachable and soft. He'd always been a kind person, one who would help the underdog or go out of his way to make others feel included. The complete opposite of his parents, even though they'd raised him to be the same way.

"Do you still see your mom and dad?" I decided a subject change was in order.

"Yeah, just not as often as they'd like. I've been avoiding them the last couple of weeks due to my recent breakup. They want Lindsey—my ex—and me to get married and be the dynamic power couple they've always dreamed of. But that's not my end goal."

"What is your end goal?"

"I'd like to be happy." His eyebrows raised, and he scooted away from the table. I doubted he'd meant to be that honest.

"Isn't that what we all want?" I tried to smooth over his ruffled feathers, and then decided on yet another subject change. If this continued, we'd end up discussing the inflation rate of foreign currency. "My internship is going great. I'm at a local elementary school and the kids are amazing. Did Nellie tell you about my plans after my student-teaching is over?"

He shook his head and moved closer to the table again.

"Well, my life-long goal is to be an administrator. But I want to be one who makes a difference in kids' lives. I want to be the one they remember when they're old and grey. Reliving their youth by telling their grandkids about the teacher or principal that made a difference in their life because they went that extra mile and truly cared about them as a person. Know what I mean? I had a teacher like that, and I'll never forget her."

"Yeah, I did too. I think that's very admirable of you."

I shrugged. "It's just how I really feel. There are so many children out there who don't have the support they need at home, and they have no one else to turn to. Some turn to drugs, alcohol, gangs, abusive boyfriends, but why not school? I want school to be a safe haven. Somewhere they can feel sheltered and free to trust."

"That makes sense." Corbin looked like he wanted to bolt, but I couldn't understand why. I spoke from my heart and he appeared completely freaked out.

"Oh, look at the time." I should really remember to make sure I'm wearing a watch when I check my wrist and say that. "I need to get home, and I'm sure you have things to do as well." When I reached for my purse, Corbin immediately put his hand over mine. The warmth I felt was completely unexpected and made my heart skip a beat.

"I've got this," he insisted. "I've really enjoyed catching up with you. It made me reminisce and think of all the good times we had. The least I can do is buy your dinner…if you can call this dinner." He snickered and gestured to the half-eaten appetizers and empty glasses that still littered the table.

"It's my favorite kind."

We quickly exchanged numbers, and he promised to text me on Monday to let me know how the initial contact with Chase's blonde bombshell went. I'd enjoyed myself, just talking to him, that I'd almost forgotten what the initial plan had been.

Outside of the restaurant, he kissed me on the cheek after walking me to my car. I found myself watching him walk down the block back to his office.

That was when I identified these feelings I experienced—sorrow and helplessness.

Corbin didn't have anything going for him except his job. And that was no way to live.

If only things were different, I thought. I could give him many things to look forward to beyond his nine-to-five. Unfortunately, things weren't different, which meant I couldn't give him anything other than this plan to occupy his time.

CHAPTER 3

CORBIN

MONDAY MORNING STARTED off with a bang.

The incompetent guy who'd been in charge of our Transition Motto campaign had fucked it up yet again. It was time to let him go and reassign the contract. Better yet, I'd probably just take over the account. It got tiresome dealing with inept people. This guy obviously didn't care about his job, and I'd had to spend the entire morning and most of the afternoon cleaning up his mess and ironing out the creases. So when my sister called to check in, I wasn't in the best mood.

"Corbie!" Her cheerful greeting and obnoxious nickname grated on my very last nerve.

I grunted in response. It was the best I could offer. If I said *anything*, it would've been rude.

"I'm just calling to see how your weekend was. You didn't work the entire time, did you? Please tell me you did something fun." Nellie's mothering tone held worry, which erased a couple degrees of my irritability.

"Yes. I had to work all weekend. And this morning has been a complete clusterfuck."

"Wow. You sound like you're in a mood of all moods today. Guess you haven't had time to check in on Heather, Chase's hussy of a secretary." Her singsong voice smoothed my annoyance, but her statement angered me. What did she think I did all day, anyway? Twiddle my thumbs and sing showtunes? She worked for my parents, so she basically had a free pass to do whatever the hell she wanted all day long, while I constantly had to work my fucking ass off cleaning up other people's messes. *Infuriating!*

The plan was for me to eventually take over the family company, so I'd made the unpopular decision to work elsewhere until that time. Mainly to gain experience before tackling that undertaking, because I didn't want anything handed to me—not to mention, I prided myself on my job. I couldn't say the same for my sister.

"Nell, I don't have time for this today. It's been a shitshow." I kept my voice monotone and tried not to lose it with her. It wasn't her fault I had complete morons working downstairs, nor could I expect her to understand what I had to deal with on a daily basis.

"Oh." The disappointment in her tone knotted my stomach, but only slightly.

I held back my usual big-brother-to-the-rescue response and only somewhat caved. "Listen, I promise I will follow up, but I might not get to it today. Your friend has probably texted you a thousand times, fishing for information, but I don't have any."

"Yeah. Brooke's texted me." Her heavy sigh tugged at my heartstrings. "I just hate it when she's so down. She's like a part of me, so when she's down, I'm down."

"Yes, I know. And when she hurts, you hurt. I get the gist. Are you going to Mom and Dad's for dinner this Sunday? I missed it last night."

"I went last night. Thanks for ditching me. It sucked big time. They wanted the scoop on you and Lindsey. I didn't know what to tell them, so I said I thought you were working things out."

"Nell, you know that's not true. In fact, I doubt we'll get back together."

"I've heard that before." Yeah, her and everyone else.

"No...this time may be for good. I mean, we can't really get around the several-hundred-mile distance. I'm not moving there and giving up my career. Not for anyone. And I highly doubt she'd give up her dreams to come back here." As much as I hated to say that, considering Lindsey was the only woman I'd ever loved, I couldn't see any way around it. I held out hope that we'd make a go of a long-distance relationship, but who knew what would happen.

"Well, you know that I've always thought Lindsey was *it* for you. Hell, everyone thinks so. You guys are a match made in heaven, status-wise. And you'd definitely earn brownie points with Mom and Dad if you at least tried to make it work."

"I'm not marrying someone in order to earn points, Nellie. I'll marry someone who understands me. She just has to be understanding of my career." Which was why Linds and I were perfect for one another. "But sometimes things don't work out. Look at Bridge and her Prince Charming...she was convinced they were perfect together, and then she found out the dickwad was cheating."

"Yeah, well...you love Lindsey, and she'd never cheat on you." She couldn't be more right about that.

"Exactly. Why cheat when we can break up every other year?"

Nellie huffed through the line, and I could tell she was getting tired of my pessimism.

"Maybe love doesn't exist." I shrugged, even though she couldn't see me. "And if that's the case, I'll just enjoy bachelorhood for the rest of my life. My friends don't seem to enjoy marriage; all they do is complain about their wives and kids. No thank you."

"Are you done with your moment of absolute stupidity yet?"

I grunted, then turned my attention back to the computer screen and began typing an answer to latest issue that had popped up in my inbox.

"Can you just go scope out Heather and then send Brooke a short text?"

"Fine, but that's all I have time for. Okay?" Outwardly, I

agreed, but inwardly, I started to devise a plan of my own. I could just say I went and had an initial conversation with her, and no one would be the wiser.

Within ten minutes of saying goodbye to my sister, a text came through. I'd just hung up with one nuisance, and another one popped up. Bridge couldn't even wait two seconds before questioning me if I'd made contact.

Bridge: Just wanted to check in on that date you're scheduling.

I quickly typed out a reply.

Me: I'm meeting with BB (aka: Blonde Bombshell) on Thursday for drinks. Should have info for you by Friday. TTYL

That should hold her off for a bit, and I still had plenty of time to find this Heather person and ask her out. I could even use work as the reason for such a meeting. It would be easy.

Bridge: Thank you for your support. You're a great friend!

That made me feel like shit. I'd lied and received a heartfelt compliment for it. But I still planned to act on it. Before I could respond, she sent another text.

Bridge: Maybe we should meet on Friday to chat after your rendezvous?

Me: LOL Sure, that's fine.

Bridge: Same place?

Me: Works for me.

Bridge: Perfect, see you then.

And it was settled.

Now all I had to do was find Heather.

I didn't even have a chance to finish my thought before Peter barged into my office and demanded answers regarding his dismissal. My assistant followed him in all flustered. "I asked him to wait, Mr. Fields." The use of my last name depicted how bleak this conversation would be.

"It's all right, Emily. Can you close the door and stay for a minute?" I wanted her to bear witness to what I had to say to Peter, since emotional people had a way of turning things around later on when their memory failed them.

By the time Emily escorted Peter from my office, it was past five o'clock, and most of the employees had started to head home. I was tired and still had two reports to finish, not to mention, I'd started my morning at six. I was done. I'd scope out this chick tomorrow.

It could wait one more day.

BRIDGE: Just wanted to wish you luck on your date later.

It was Thursday morning, and I still hadn't taken the time to find Heather. In my defense, I'd been assigned two more accounts since Peter's departure. And who knew how long it would take human resources to find someone to replace him. So, in the meantime, it was my job to pick up the slack. It's not like I minded, though. Working under pressure was how I thrived. It gave me energy, and driving myself at such a fast pace provided a boost of adrenaline. Addicting and rewarding were the final results.

If it weren't for Brooke's text, I would've forgotten all about the date I had yet to schedule. I'd had every intention of going down and scoping this chick out. Time just hadn't been on my side this week.

At ten in the morning, I got off my ass and hoofed it downstairs. We had two floors in a skyscraper downtown; my office was housed on the top, and I always took the stairs. Elevators were for old people and the gas they passed. I swear, they always smelled like stale farts.

I made it downstairs, and what usually happened, happened. People flagged me down to say a quick hi, to find out how I'd been, to ask a random question about God only knew what project. And that's why I stayed holed up in my office and never ventured down to this floor. It's not that I was a loner; I enjoyed people. But I couldn't get my job done if my day wasn't focused without mindless interruptions. I just didn't have the time for it.

I discretely asked one of the employees to point out Chase, since AdCorp had more employees than I could keep track of, and I'd never met half of them. When Brooklyn had mentioned that he worked here, there was no way to know if I'd even seen him before.

"How's it going, buddy?" He greeted me with a firm handshake.

Being in my position meant everyone knew me, regardless if I'd never laid eyes on them before. It'd taken a while to get used to it. For the longest time, I questioned my sanity, wondering if I was suffering from early onset Alzheimer's or something, because even though they spoke to me like I'd known them for years, I couldn't recall a single time I'd even passed them in the hallway. It seemed this Chase character was no different.

This business was more about who you *acted* like you knew instead of who you *actually* knew.

"Great." I smiled and gripped his hand as if I were tightening a bolt, establishing dominance. "How are things with you, Chase?" I found great pleasure in watching his eyes widen, likely wondering how I knew his name.

"Oh, you know. The job has its ups and downs. But that's to be expected. What brings you down to this floor?"

"Well, I recently had to let go of an advertiser from my team, and HR seems to be taking forever to find me a replacement, so I thought I'd meander down here to see if I could offer them a few names to help speed things along. Do you by chance have anyone in mind who might want to transition to the big corporation level?"

"Follow me, and I'll see if I've got anyone to give you." As if this had been my plan all along, he led me to his office, which would give me the opportunity I needed to scope out my prey.

When I rounded the corner, I spotted his administrative assistant's desk perched outside a solid oak door with an engraved nameplate in the center that read Chase Kramer. It made me laugh, imagining the guy from *Seinfeld* being Brooke's ex.

There was just one problem—the desk out front was empty.

"Where's your assistant? Give her the day off?" I asked. With a wink, I nudged him with my elbow and played up the friendly banter. "You must not be busy enough down here, huh? Hopefully that means you'll have several names to offer."

"Oh, she took an early lunch to run errands or something." He waved his hand as if it were unimportant and continued to give me a tour of his space. It was grandiose, but not as nice as mine. He still hadn't made it all the way to the top of the ladder—that would be a while.

Or never, if he keeps dipping his pen in the company ink.

I made a few more pleasantries and then finally escaped back to my office—without any names of employees to offer HR, not that I really cared. That guy dripped sleaziness, and I fought the urge to call Bridge to tell her she was better off without him. Seriously, even after touching him, I felt like I needed to wash my hand.

Maybe seeing Brooklyn again after all these years had done something to me. That thought escaped my mind before I could reel it back in and allow it to make me stop and think. *Brooklyn Bridge.* She'd been a cute kid with the sprinkle of freckles across her upturned nose.

Nell was the ringleader and head troublemaker in their dynamic duo, but Brooklyn didn't just go along with Nell for the hell of it. They truly cared for one another in a way I'd never felt for anyone. Well, I loved my sister, but she was family. You sort of had to love your family. Bridge and Nell weren't family, yet they were closer than most siblings I knew. In fact, I didn't know any sisters closer than they were. Their bond was unbreakable.

It made me curious as to why I hadn't found someone like that. I'd had buddies growing up, and sure, we'd had each other's backs. When I made the move on Jill Shackle in tenth grade in hopes of giving up my V-card, Scott had covered for me. In eleventh grade, when I had pulled a prank on Mrs. Peabody, the dreaded chemistry teacher everyone hated, Frank had given me an alibi. But it wasn't the same.

What was I missing?

I made a decision in that moment to hunt down Heather and have at least one drink with her…for Brooklyn's sake. Then, I shot Brooke a text to thank her for wishing me luck on the current non-existent date.

Me: What time are we meeting for drinks tomorrow?

Bridge: How does 6 sound?

Her response was immediate, as if she were sitting impatiently by the phone, which made me feel bad for making her wait. I texted her that I'd be there and made a mental note to be on time.

For some reason, I didn't want to keep her waiting for anything else.

CHAPTER 4

BROOKLYN

BONE TIRED DIDN'T COME CLOSE to how I felt.

Teaching first grade wasn't my favorite, but it had definitely opened my heart. These kids were precious and just ate up attention. I'd only started my student-teaching gig six weeks ago, and it had taken mere moments for me to fall in love with each and every child.

The school where I'd been placed had been the perfect start. Since I'd gotten behind in my schooling, I'd taken a couple of accelerated classes in order to finish my program early and wasn't even slated to begin my internship until the fall. This had been the only position left; it was as if it had been set aside for me because no one else wanted it. I was twenty-five years old and considered the ancient one.

In our school district, this site held the spot for highest poverty rate, and every child in attendance qualified for the free lunch program, which meant money was scarce. But what they lacked in monetary means meant they were worth ten-fold in my eyes. Their sweet smiles greeted me every morning, which made my day. And when their grateful gazes locked on mine at lunchtime—I always ensured they each got a little something to take home for a snack later on—it filled my heart to the brim.

Chase hadn't ever understood my compassion for these kids. I'd tried numerous times to explain it, but he couldn't grasp the agony of going to bed hungry or scrimping enough money to buy the bare necessities.

A little boy named Johnny had confided in me one day after his stomach began to growl so loudly that the class erupted in laughter, forcing him to run from the room in tears. I followed him while the other teacher stayed behind. After a few questions and gentle prodding, I'd learned he didn't get to eat dinner. Ever. I couldn't even begin to imagine going to bed hungry every day. I'd struggled financially, especially after Mom had fallen ill and I'd taken over her care, but things were never that bad. And for a child to have to deal with a burden of that magnitude was hard for me to fathom.

Even after explaining to Chase all the changes I'd implemented and how the excited faces had melted my heart, he still didn't get it. I'd taken it upon myself to talk to the lunch lady, and she started ordering extra food from the district. Not much, just an apple or an extra package of crackers. But at least I'd made a difference, only I continuously wished I could do more.

There was Sarah, who had holes in her shoes and didn't own a pair of socks. Little Greg couldn't brush his teeth until he came to school, because toothbrushes and paste were a luxury his family couldn't afford. I'd procured donations from a local dentist for them, and it was now part of our morning hygiene routine.

All of that made days like today worth it—days when I had to meet someone after work with green paint in my hair and the remnants of permanent marker on my cheek. I'd practically scrubbed my cheek raw before giving up. I really wished I could've gone home to clean up before meeting Corbin for drinks, but time hadn't allowed for that, and I feared that if I asked for more time, he would decide to reschedule. It'd already been a week since I last saw him; I didn't desire to wait even longer.

My *only* desire at the moment was to sit down and put my feet up. If I could rub them, that would be heaven. In fact, I would totally pay someone for a five-minute foot massage. They were beyond sore. I had been chasing, running, standing, and kneeling all day long. However, regardless of how tired I was or how badly my feet hurt, I still couldn't wipe the huge smile off my face.

Because I was about to see Corbin again.

Actually, I was both nervous *and* excited about that. I was about to find out information regarding his first meet-up with Heather. I wondered if he'd found her as attractive as Chase obviously had. A stab of regret coursed through my gut. Why did Chase have to be so stupid and cheat on me? It had ruined everything.

Doubt creased my brow as I thought of all the ways I'd fallen short. I hadn't been enough for him. Part of me wanted to move on, but the other part knew I'd never find someone better. He'd been the one for me. It was Chase who I'd planned my future in its entirety around.

The second I spotted Corbin sitting in the booth, every thought of Chase drifted away, and surprise faltered my steps momentarily. Nellie always joked that he was habitually late. And I wasn't. Not today. Which meant he was downright early. By, like, ten minutes.

He met my gaze, and his lips burst into a genuine smile. My aching cheeks alerted me to the fact that I sported one that matched. However, something felt off as I gave him a quick, awkward hug when he stood to greet me. I couldn't put my finger on it, so I took a seat across the small high-top table and perused the menu while he made the appropriate small talk.

Once we placed our drink order, we sat there for a few silent seconds. Realistically, it was less than a minute, but it dragged on and on, feeling more like forever.

"Well, don't keep me in suspense. How was it?" I nervously cleared my throat and messed with the small square napkin the server had left as a placeholder for my glass. I suddenly felt desperate for that drink. Anxiety bubbled in my stomach and threatened to burst through my abdominal lining.

I scooted forward on the stool to get closer to him until I was on the edge of my seat. Literally.

"It was okay." Corbin shrugged.

That's it?

"Dude, I'm going to need more than that." I chuckled to make my tone sound lighthearted, because apprehension continued to gnaw at my insides. At least the trepidation kept me from feeling silly for calling him *dude*.

It was at that moment the waitress decided to serve our drinks.

"Cheers. Happy Friday." He held up his glass and awaited my clank. "How was work today?"

"It was good." I couldn't keep the smile from taking over my face. I loved talking about my job, loved it so much I hadn't even realized he'd completely changed the subject. "Those kids have completely stolen my heart. I'm going to hate leaving them."

He took a sip of his beer. "I'm confused…by kids, you mean your students, right?"

"Yes, but they're so much more to me than that. Each one has made an imprint on me that I will carry with me forever. I'm the one who's supposed to be educating them, but instead, I feel like *they're* the ones teaching *me*." I shook my head in disbelief, because it was true. Little people weren't meant to educate adults. But they did. Some of them were wise beyond their years due to the experiences they'd been subjected to.

"If they're your students, why would you have to leave them?"

"Oh, I didn't mean right now. I'll have to leave them in June because my internship will be over. This is the last class I need to obtain my credential. I'm beyond excited for all the studying to be over, but it's bittersweet."

"I get that. I just can't imagine kids having that much of an impact. I think of them more as little shits."

I laughed out loud. "I know. In fact, I thought that exact same thing. You'd have to experience it to believe it, I guess."

"Well, I'm intrigued. Give me an example."

"Okay. Let me see…" There were so many stories I could draw from. I wanted to find the right one, yet nothing came to me. My brain was tired; it had been a treacherous day. "Well, the school I currently teach in has a very low poverty rate. And those kids deal with so many daily struggles. They've been through so much already in their short little lives. Way more than I have, that's for sure. It's inspirational to see how they navigate through. I don't know."

"I think I understand. It's just that I have nothing to compare it to. My life definitely hasn't been a struggle. I mean, there's the normal stuff—it hasn't been all rainbows and butterflies."

Laughter filled the air; his words brought a memory to the surface. "Remember when Nellie and I persuaded you to help us find the end of the rainbow so we could locate that pot of gold? We wholeheartedly believed we'd find it and be rich."

"You didn't convince me. I knew there was no pot of anything at the end." His eyes danced with amusement as he continued. "That was another scheme where I should've dug my heels in and said no. I've now learned that *no* is a complete sentence."

"Except when it comes to Nellie."

"Yeah, that's true." He appeared almost wistful as he played with his napkin beneath his drink. "We only had each other. The entire time we were growing up, our parents weren't really there. They both had their careers, and it was well-known that they always came first—we came second." He let out a grunt, but I waited through the silence, not wanting him to lose his train of thought. "I guess if I think about it, that's why I am the way I am."

"What do you mean? You're nothing like your parents." That was preposterous. His parents were stuck up; all they cared about was financial worth and social standing. That had never been important to him, at least it hadn't been when we were younger.

"Not in the sense you're probably thinking, but I am. Work always comes first and my relationships second. *All* relationships…including friendships." Deep lines formed across his brow, and his lips practically flattened when he pressed his mouth into a straight line. "It started to get to me yesterday when you texted. And it seems like I can't let it go."

"How did my text get to you?" Until last week, I hadn't seen Corbin in years. I didn't understand how I could've somehow unearthed emotion of this magnitude.

Our conversation had suddenly switched to a deeper level, but it didn't seem odd. I just wasn't sure how to handle it. We'd been friends through Nellie; talked through Nellie; seen each other *with* Nellie. All without ever engaging in meaningful conversation. It was weird that so many of my early memories of Nellie were laced with Corbin, and yet he'd remained such a small part of my life.

"Because it got me thinking…mainly about you and my sister —well, your friendship. You guys have always been so close. I mean, Nell is ready at a moment's notice to lay on the train tracks and flag down the conductor for you. And you'd do the same for her. Where does that kind of loyalty and kinship come from? I'm stumped. I've totally missed something, and now I'm an old fucker void of meaningful relationships in my life." He let out a soft chuckle. "That sounds more pathetic than it did in my head."

"I think I understand." I reached my hand over to his, and he instantly cupped it. I was the little spoon to his gargantuan palm. Our eyes met, and I saw something I'd never seen before. Well, that's not true. I'd seen it whenever he looked at his sister. *Tenderness*.

"You have this friend who would do anything for you. What does that kind of superpower feel like?"

I almost giggled, except he appeared genuinely perplexed. "Siblings or not, you have the same with Nellie. I think you're being way too hard on yourself, Corbin. I mean, seriously. You aren't even thirty. You're not supposed to have everything figured out." I tried to take my hand back, but he held on to it a few seconds more. Thankfully, before the gesture caused my heart to seize, he finally let go.

"I guess."

"Look, you don't have that kind of relationship with your parents. It wasn't modeled for you, so it's hard to grasp. But you've seen glimpses of it during your lifetime. Now it's up to you to learn from what you've seen and implement what *you* want into *your* life. What do you want?"

Each word that whispered past my lips seemed to only confuse him more. I couldn't tell if he was baffled or angry. I hoped it wasn't the latter, because an angry Corbin wasn't a fun Corbin. And I should know; he'd been angry at Nellie and me so many times over the years I'd lost count.

"I've never been asked what I want. I've always just done what's expected of me. The end goal is for me to run my parents' company after I garner enough experience, which is something I insisted on. I guess that's the only time I've ever stood up for myself to my parents, when I demanded they allow me to gain outside experience before joining the family business."

It wasn't a secret that his family ran the most successful ad agency in the state—or maybe even the region. It probably hadn't sat well with his parents that he worked somewhere else first. I always kind of wondered why he'd done things that way. Now it made sense. He held a lucrative position, something he'd earned all on his own.

"Yeah. That must have been hard to stand up to them. They probably didn't handle that well."

"Oh, that's an understatement. My inheritance was in question for a while until my grandmother stepped in as the voice of reason. They've always been hard to please."

"I can relate. They've never warmed up to me." I grimaced because it was still a hard pill for me to swallow. My best friend's family hated me—even Corbin had joined in at times.

"They don't hate you. They're just standoffish, and that's because they truly don't know you."

"And they don't care to, either."

"That's probably true." Genuine amusement curled his lips

and sparkled in his eyes. "Why don't you join us for family dinner on Sunday? Give them a chance to get to know you?"

"No way." I shook my head animatedly while laughing beneath my breath. "No way would I just show up for dinner." Nellie had tried to get me to go a million times, and my answer was always the same. I'd given in a handful of times over the years—and not since Corbin had moved back to town—but I mostly tried to avoid awkward encounters.

"Why?" He seemed sincerely puzzled.

"Because, Corbin, I don't belong there—a fact that's been shoved in my face more times than I can count."

"I don't remember you ever coming to a Sunday dinner."

"Well, not lately, but I used to all the time when Nellie still lived at home." Cue gigantic eye roll. Why wasn't he getting it? He seemed seriously mystified, but I hadn't imagined his parents' feelings toward me. They'd made them crystal clear, on more than one occasion.

"Just come with me."

The way he said that made me stop and study him. Come *with* him? Like a date? Or friend? Or...what the fuck was he thinking?

More importantly, what the fuck was I thinking even contemplating it?

CHAPTER 5

CORBIN

AS SOON AS the sentence was out there and I saw the look on her face, I wanted to rewind time and take it back. *Shit*. That wasn't what I'd meant. Being with her had made me feel so comfortable, and she was familiar. She should be there. *That's* what I had meant.

"God, Bridge. Don't take it the wrong way. I meant as a friend...as in, Nell would love to have your support around our parents." I took a long swig of my beer and snuck a peek at her over the bottle, hoping she'd drop the argument and agree to join me.

I mean...join *us*. As in Nell and me.

"I get it. But the answer is still no."

"What have you got to lose?" I shrugged as I took another healthy swig. The amber ale made its way down my throat and numbed the uncomfortableness I'd brought forward by complete accident. What a dumbass. Suddenly, inspiration struck. "I triple dog dare you!"

A burst of laughter peeled past her lips, and I wondered if they'd always been such a soft shade of pink. I guess I'd never paid this much attention to her mouth before. Then she garnered my attention in another way when her tongue peeked out, licking away a drop of wine, before she said, "We haven't played that game in forever. In fact, I think the last time was the three of us at your parents' house. I can't remember what Nellie dared you to do."

"I do." I'd never forget it.

"What was it?" Brooke's innocent question was about to cause major embarrassment—*for me.*

"Nellie dared me to call the library to ask if they carry a dictionary that translates British to American." And I'd stupidly asked for another dare, since we were allowed to turn one down. "Then, when I refused to do that, she dared me to spank you."

"Oh, that's right!" She laughed and clapped her hands. "Damn, that hurt. You spanked me hard."

And I had. It was mainly because when I'd started spanking her, it had done things to me. I grunted before responding, "So, will you think about coming to dinner on Sunday?"

"I will, but I have to be honest…I probably won't come. It would be too awkward."

"It's in two days. If you plan on coming, I need to let my parents know. Their staff has to set an extra setting, and you know all the hoopla that goes with it."

"That's exactly why I'm not going."

"My parents don't hate you. I have no idea why you think that." They had their issues, but I highly doubted they would've disliked Brooklyn. Now, they thought very little of her mom for being a single parent working multiple jobs just to pay the bills, but I would be willing to bet they'd never put that on a child. "Be honest, if they hated you, do you think they would've let you come over as often as you did?"

"Well, if we're talking honestly, they weren't always there, so they didn't always know when I was over."

"Trust me. They knew." My parents had an uncanny ability to know all the goings on at the Fields' residence. "But, since you're obviously having a hard time digesting the idea, we'll agree to table the discussion for now. How's that?"

Brooklyn rolled her eyes and practically gave me the middle finger by avoiding my question and changing the subject. "So, tell me how the date with Heather went."

Just when I thought I was in the clear, she circled back to the purpose for our meeting here tonight. It was time for me to come clean. "Well, we didn't actually meet up. I guess she was out with the flu all week. When you texted yesterday, I thought I could still squeeze in a drink with her. But it didn't work out." By the time I'd finished work for the day yesterday, everyone on Chase's floor had gone home. But I wasn't about to tell Brooke that I'd dropped the ball. The flu made for a much better excuse.

"Why didn't you just cancel tonight then?"

"I guess I should've, but it slipped my mind until this afternoon, and then it was too late. I guess I didn't think you'd be so disappointed."

"I'm not. Really. I just think it's funny you didn't cancel." She shrugged before the waitress came over with our refills. We both ordered a cheeseburger and fries and moved onto other topics of discussion.

Our conversation flowed, and we laughed so hard my cheeks hurt. God, if I said that out loud, I'd sound like a total pussy. But it was true. And that kind of baffled me. I had no earthly idea that little Brooklyn Bridge and I would get on so well. She was so easy to be around, and she wasn't hard on the eyes, either. I found myself not wanting the evening to end, but you can only drag out a meal for so long. After our cheeseburger plates were practically licked clean and the bill was on the table, I reached for it.

"I'll get it." Bridge went for it, but I was quicker.

"No, I'll get it. I insist, especially since I led you here under false pretenses."

"You truly did."

That smile. I'd never noticed how it lit up her entire face. I wanted to ask her out again. I don't think it was a romantic interest per se, but I couldn't help wondering how she'd taste, just one taste. One touch of her lips...her tongue on mine. I leaned forward, but she quickly jumped up from the table, her eyes wide with surprise and something else—fear maybe? I had to think on my feet before she bolted, and I never saw her again.

"You have a little smudge on your cheek." I stood and joined her. Then I took my napkin and ran it across the side of her face. She had a mark on her cheekbone, and when she'd backed away from the table, it had hit the light, catching my attention for the first time all evening. Thank God I'd spotted it, because how else was I supposed to cover my impromptu move to kiss her.

"What is it?" She tried to look at the napkin with a heavily furrowed brow.

"Looks like marker." I disregarded her embarrassment and smiled at her cute groan.

"Perks of being a teacher. I didn't have time to go home and shower before meeting you. I thought I had covered it well enough…guess I didn't." She strung her purse strap casually over her shoulder and took a step back. "Anyway, thanks for drinks and dinner."

Damn her for mentioning a shower. Now I couldn't stop picturing her naked and sudsy.

I did my best to shake off the images that plagued my mind, deciding to hold onto those for when I was alone. "No problem. Just promise me that you'll think about dinner on Sunday?"

All I got was a very short, tight nod, and then she turned and hightailed it for the door.

What the fuck was that green paint all over the back of her shirt?

MY MEET-UP with Brooklyn had tanked. There was no other way to describe it.

It had started out fine; our conversation had flowed, she'd laughed at my jokes, and I found myself talking about things I hadn't thought about in years. Hell, she'd even reached across the table and touched my hand, which had been such a sweet and genuine gesture. But it hadn't been a date. Our meeting was on the pretense of updating her on the progress of the plan. And I had failed the Heather mission miserably.

Last night, there had been undeniable attraction between us. The electric currents in the air were palpable. Brooklyn had developed into a beautiful woman, and what was even better was that she didn't know it. She came across innocent and naïve, but she had a body made for sin. Just the thought of her sinful body caused my balls to tighten and my stomach to knot with the onset of arousal.

Instead of following the outline of the original plan, I decided to put my own spin on things and picked up my phone to dial Nellie.

"Hey, big brother. What's hanging?" She dissolved into a fit of giggles on the other end.

"Just the usual."

"You never call me, let alone on a Saturday. So what's the reason? Do you have a scandalous update on Heather?"

"Heather?" Is it bad that I momentarily forgot who that was? "Oh, no. She ended up having the flu, so we haven't met up yet, but I met Bridge for drinks last night, which was fun."

"That's just weird. Why on earth would you meet her for drinks when you hadn't scoped out the target?" The irritation in her voice carried across the line.

"I had every intention of meeting Heather prior to meeting Brooklyn, but like I said before, she was out the entire week." She hadn't been out the *entire* week, just the one time I'd meandered downstairs. But if I admitted that, I would look like the procrastinator I'd been. Let's face it, drinks with Heather hadn't been my first priority, and it wouldn't be for a while...now that I had another objective in mind.

"Well, that sucks. When do you think you'll get a chance?"

"Hopefully on Monday." Then a lightning bolt struck, and I suddenly knew how to convince Brooke to come to our parents' house. I'd use Nellie, just as she'd done to me time and time again. "But I need something first."

"What is it?"

"I was thinking that Brooklyn must get pretty lonely. I tried to invite her over to the 'rents house for Sunday dinner, but she wouldn't budge. Maybe you could try? It would be nice for Mom and Dad to see her again."

"Are you on crack?

"No, I haven't done that since second grade," I deadpanned.

"That's not even funny. You always say things to show your sense of humor, but instead, it shows you don't have one, Corbin."

I rolled my eyes, even though she couldn't see me; she didn't know what she was talking about. I was a funny motherfucker.

"I've tried *so* many times to get her to come to Sunday dinner," she continued. "She's convinced Mom and Dad hate her. I always tell her they don't, but she's stubborn. They know I'm good friends with her, and I love her as a sister, so that makes her important to them, too. They haven't always been around when we were growing up, but they cared."

"Okay, the thing is, I think the three of us should reconvene and see if maybe we can up the ante and come up with a different strategy." I currently had no idea what that was but hoped it would come to me before Sunday evening.

"I'll try. But Brooklyn's pretty determined on this topic. Maybe if I dangle the Heather carrot, she'll accept."

"Well, I have all the faith in the world that you can persuade her, Nell. After all, convincing people to do what you want is what you do best."

I PULLED up to the gargantuan building I'd called home for the first eighteen years of my life. I hadn't lived there in more than ten years—since leaving for college—but I still felt nothing when pulling into the driveway. It literally felt no different than parking in front of my doctor's office.

Going back to my childhood home wasn't ever exciting. I'd say it was more or less habitual. It was simply a place I'd spent my childhood years, not a home like every other kid I knew had. I really had no emotional ties to any part of it—it was nothing more than a big house on a lake surrounded by acres of green rolling hills. My high school friends had jokingly nicknamed it Fields of Dreams—a play on words with our family surname—but even that bit of nostalgia didn't tug at my heartstrings. It wasn't that I'd had a bad childhood or anything; by all accounts, it had been fairly normal. My disconnect was basically due to the coldness the actual structure possessed; you can only have so much warmth in a house that size.

Nellie joked that I had a black soul, and sometimes, I sincerely wondered if I did.

Per usual, I ran about fifteen minutes behind, and a quick scan of the cars parked along the circular drive told me Brooklyn wasn't here. That meant she wasn't coming. Disappointment smacked me across the face, leaving my mood rather heavy. Honestly, my reaction surprised me. I'd wanted her to come, *hoped* she would, but never in a million years did I think I'd be upset if she didn't. Let down, sure. Possibly a little annoyed or discouraged. But not disheartened like I was.

I must've gotten my hopes up at the prospect of Brooklyn being here; that was the only reason I could think of as to why her absence left me so miserable. I came to this event—and that's what it was, an event, nothing like the "family dinner" my parents tried to play it off as—every week. And every week, I sat through each course, listening to Mom and Dad go on and on about work, Nell occasionally chiming in. Honestly, the two or three hours I spent here felt more like twelve, and I guess I'd started looking forward to having someone here who'd help the time pass by quicker.

Yeah…that's what it was. My despondence was nothing more

than a selfish reaction to having to endure the next few hours without a distraction. It wasn't about Brooklyn, per se. I could've invited my boss and still been upset if he hadn't shown up.

I opened the front door without knocking and headed down the hallway toward the formal dining room, where I knew my parents and sister were gathered. However, halfway down the hall, I was attacked by someone coming out of the guest bathroom. Okay, so *attacked* wouldn't be the right word, but I was definitely surprised, and I may or may not have jumped a little. But once the shock of having someone leap out at me, elation replaced the sorrow that had plagued me since pulling into the driveway—Bridge was here after all. With as quickly as she showed up in front of me, I didn't have time to sort through my emotions; I roped my arm around her waist and pulled her in for a friendly hug before I could stop myself.

"I didn't see your car outside, so I thought you changed your mind and didn't come."

Brooklyn patted my back and then pulled away. "I came with Nellie."

"Oh, yeah?" I turned to walk with her. "Are you planning to get drunk or something?"

She rolled her eyes and huffed a quick laugh. "No, my car has a flat tire, and I haven't had a chance to change it yet because I needed to get ready to come here."

I scanned her simple sundress quickly and then returned my attention to where I was going. The last thing I wanted to do was run into the wall because I was too busy checking her out. Plus, I didn't really want her to catch me checking her out.

"Well, I think you look very nice. It seems your time was well spent."

"Corbin Fields…I think that just might be the first compliment you've ever given me." A smile lit up her face, which surprisingly did me in. My stomach dipped at the sight of her innocence.

The urge to wrap her up in my arms and protect her from the world was a feeling I didn't recognize—except when it came to my sister. Which kind of made sense, because like Nell had said, Brooklyn was like my little sister, too.

That was a crock of shit, because I didn't have one brotherly thought when it came to Brooklyn. In fact, it was quite the opposite. It was like I'd been teleported back to high school, because for some reason, I couldn't control my reactions. I shoved my hands into my pockets uncomfortably.

"If you want, I can swing by after dinner and change your tire for you."

"That's really sweet of you to offer, but it's okay. I can get it." She let out a long sigh and stilled a few feet from the open double doors that led into the dining room.

I knew the cause of her hesitation, and it had nothing to do with her flat tire. The fact that she seemed anxious to walk into a room with my parents told me she hadn't seen them yet. That meant she'd gone straight to the restroom after coming inside.

"It'll be okay. Come on, let's get this over with." I grabbed her hand and pulled her to the dining room with me. There was something exhilarating about walking in together, hand in hand. However, Brooklyn quickly slipped hers from mine as soon as we crossed the threshold.

Nell and my parents were already seated at the long ten-person table, which had five place settings. When they had dinner parties, it could stretch out to seat as many as forty.

My parents got up and came over to greet us. In my peripheral vision, I saw Brooklyn take a step backward. My mom rushed forward and enveloped her into a warm hug. Brooke went stiff, and I could tell that my mom noticed, but thankfully, she didn't say anything. Mom had way too much etiquette to call someone out like that.

"I'm so glad you accepted our invitation, dear. It's been too long." She patted Brooklyn's hand while beaming at her with a bright smile covering her face. I knew my mom well enough to know it was a sincere grin.

It took considerable effort to keep from pointing out that

Brooke hadn't accepted my mom's invitation but mine, because Mom hadn't invited her. I had. Then again, she wouldn't be my mother if she hadn't taken the credit for everything.

My parents sat at either end of the table, Nellie across from me. There was an empty place setting on my sister's right, and disappointment flooded my core, which soured my mood. I really thought she would've been seated next to me, even though that didn't make any practical sense. She was Nellie's best friend, not mine. I hadn't seen her in years until a week ago. Now it felt as if she'd always been by *my* side instead.

"Tell us how your work is going, dear." My mom gestured to the server to fill our wine glasses. Sunday dinner was formal as far as serving and manners were concerned, but etiquette went out the window when it came to our conversations. Every topic had been unearthed at this dining room table. Although, most were initiated by Nellie or me trying to get each other in trouble with a myriad of confessions.

One of the most embarrassing was the topic of my virginity, and if I'd done the deed.

Brooklyn's face lit up, like it had when we'd discussed her work a couple nights ago. She waved her arms animatedly as she described the students she worked with and how rewarding it was. She'd just downed her second glass of wine and the waitstaff quickly refilled the burgundy liquid. I wanted to shout at him to slow it the fuck down and fill her water instead. I'd had drinks with her twice now, so I knew her well enough to call her a light-weight. She never finished more than two drinks when we'd gone out. And that had been nursing them over hours, not downing them in a mere five minutes.

Boredom covered Nellie's face. She tried to look interested, but she had probably heard her friend tell the same story a million times.

"I just feel completely fulfilled, and nothing I've ever done in my life has made me feel half as good. I truly love it and know I made the right decision in continuing through this arduous process. There'd been so many times I'd wanted to quit for numerous reasons. But I persevered and stayed the course. Now that I'm so close to the finish line, I sometimes want to spread my arms open wide and sing from the mountaintops like Maria Von Trapp in the *Sound of Music*." She giggled, and then her cheeks flushed in embarrassment. She looked around the table apologetically before grabbing up her third full glass of wine.

My heart stopped at the sight, and I suddenly felt grateful for the truth serum she'd consumed. I had never witnessed so much passion for something. Part of me was envious because I wanted to experience what she had found in her career. Part of me was astounded that work could be thought of as fun and adventurous. Those were certainly not words I would've ever used to describe my career. But the part that was hardest to come to terms with was the pride. She'd come such a long way and fought so many battles to arrive where she was today. And she wasn't bitter at all.

We had good idle conversation throughout the remainder of dinner. My parents were openly happy to hear about her achievements, no matter what Brooklyn thought. Nellie and Brooke demonstrated their lighthearted banter, which was still as alive today as it had been years ago. I observed the evening and felt like a spectator, and that's when it hit me—I was only a bystander of my life. I had no real connections to anyone. I still hung out with the same guys from high school and college, but those friendships lacked depth. My life held no true meaning.

My parents excused themselves after we finished dinner to leave us kids to have dessert. It was comical the way everything fell into the same routine, yet nothing felt familiar.

I didn't belong.

CHAPTER 6

BROOKLYN

THIS EVENING HAD BEEN WAY MORE enjoyable than I'd initially thought it would be. Corbin had stayed quiet almost the entire night, but I chalked it up to him being tired. However, the later and later it got, the more dazed he looked.

"Corbie, are you on crack?" Nellie snickered, and I mildly joined in.

He offered a small smile, and that's when I knew something was definitely up with him. In the past, he'd always provided a witty, albeit stupid, comeback for Nellie's snide remarks, so the fact that he only smiled—if you could even call it that—was incredibly alarming.

"I'm going to the kitchen to get more vanilla ice cream. Be back in a sec!" Nellie raced out of the room as if her underpants were on fire. She really should stop leaving me alone with her brother if she knew what was good for her.

"Are you okay, Corbin?" Concern laced my voice. I didn't know why I cared all of a sudden, but I did. Although, I ignored the confusing emotions that ran through me in order to hear what he had to say.

"Yeah. Fine. You?"

"I actually had a pretty good time." I offered a shy smile and tipped my head toward the table to hide my burning cheeks. Damn, why was it suddenly so hot in this room?

Corbin threw his napkin on the table and abruptly stood. "Take a walk with me?" He held out his hand while I sat there like a bump on a log, not knowing how to respond.

It was just a stupid stroll, but that wasn't why the red flags were blatantly waving in my face. I knew Corbin would never let anything hurt me, not in a million years. He didn't have it in him. He was too good. But something flashed in my brain to stay put.

"Suit yourself." His arm went limp before his dejected strides took him toward the side exit.

I knew that door well because it was the one we always snuck in and out of as kids. I hadn't expected all the nostalgic memories tonight, but ever since I'd arrived, the flood gates had opened, and they'd poured right in. Blame it on the wine or the laughter we'd shared during the meal. Before I could second and third guess my decision, I leapt up and joined him on the stoop outside.

"It's a beautiful night," I whispered, taking a seat beside him on the ornate garden bench. I wasn't sure why I kept my voice so low, it just seemed right. The evening air had grown dark with night and the usual suspects offered their singsong chirps. "When I was younger, I never stopped to admire the beauty of this place. Of course, I used to think how magnificent it was, but that was due to the wealth and prestige this place holds. Not the nature that's so obvious to me tonight." Peacefulness cloaked us along with the starry, purple sky.

"I don't fit in here," Corbin softly uttered, then sighed.

Unsure if I'd heard him correctly, I took his hand, and he allowed it. "What do you mean?"

"You guys all had so much fun this evening, laughing around the table. I didn't feel like I belonged."

"I'm sorry if you felt left out." I exhaled. "Several of our friends have accused Nellie and me of living in our own bubble, regardless of who else is around. We tell inside jokes only we know and forget about everyone else. We just have that connection, and sometimes, it makes others uncomfortable."

"That's not it." He shook his head adamantly, stood, and began to walk toward the lake.

I jumped up and began to chase after him, trying to keep up with his pace—which was nearly impossible. He was a foot taller than me, and while I wasn't short by any means at five-foot-six, he had the height to make anyone feel tiny. But everyone in his family was tall—a curse Nellie constantly complained about. At five-nine, she could've been a runway model, especially with those long, slender legs and lean figure. Sure, when I wore heels, we were the same height, but where she was flat, I was curvy, and where she was sexy, I was frumpy. Okay…not frumpy, but certainly not worthy of being a Victoria's Secret angel.

"Are you trying to outwalk me? Because if you keep up this stride, you're going to leave me in your dust." I tried to jab his sense of humor but only earned a grunt, even though he did slow a bit.

The lake was beautiful at night, all shimmery silver above the water and mysteriously dark beneath the surface. Nighttime had always been my favorite part of the day. I'd always felt like I could escape into the darkness and nothing could hurt me. It also gave me time to think, allowed me to be alone with my own thoughts. I'd written some of my best papers for school during the midnight hours, especially when Mom had been sick. That had been tough. And no matter how many times I told myself she was in a better place now, if I let too many thoughts creep in, I would cry.

God, I missed her.

I must've been too lost in my thoughts, staring out over the glassy top of the lake, because I gasped when someone grabbed me from behind. He effortlessly spun me into a wall of muscle, where I buried my face into his chest and started to cough incessantly; there was a good chance I had swallowed a fly when Corbin startled me.

"Shit, Bridge…are you okay?" he asked while gently patting my back the way one would when someone choked on food.

My coughs immediately turned to hacking laugher, which was interrupted by hiccups. Between the wine and the hilarity of the situation, I pressed my hands against the hard planes of his chest and dropped my head back, my fit of giggles and breathy hitches escaping into the night.

"Being scared is supposed to get rid of hiccups, not cause them." Humor filled his husky voice, causing me to clench my thighs together. But nothing affected me as much as when he took my face in his hands and blew a long puff of air into my open mouth.

"What was that for?" I asked while keeping my head cocked back, my face close to his.

"I just thought it might help the hiccups go away."

My fingers curled into his button-up shirt, gathering a decent grip on him so I could pull him closer. I closed my eyes at the sound of his soft exhale, seconds before yielding lips met mine. Surprise had turned to amusement, which then quickly became heated desire at the feel of his tongue.

My arms looped easily around Corbin's waist, and I leaned into him. I held all the doubt and red flags at bay. I didn't want to stop, so I wasn't going to listen to anything but the sensual awakenings that raced through my body. His lips were soft, especially for a guy—softer than anything I'd ever experienced before—and it didn't take long until the kiss deepened. I couldn't even tell which of us took it to the next level. Hell, maybe we both did simultaneously.

His tongue was warm and smooth as he glided it along mine. I eagerly met his advances and then brought forth my own. The way he encouraged me showed his expertise and pulled several moans from my chest. I was borderline ready to hump his leg if he didn't do something to relieve the ache that had developed between my thighs. I'd never experienced something that produced this many jolts to my system.

Only one thing was absolutely certain: I wanted more and felt like I'd do anything to obtain it. I quickly began to unbutton his shirt in a desperate attempt at removing it, and the closer I got to the last one, the harsher he gripped my hips. I wasn't sure if he held onto me so tightly to restrain himself, or if it was his way of encouraging me to continue. Either way, as long as he didn't let me go, I was good with it.

Although, it would've been better had he used his hold on me to grind me into him.

As soon as I had his shirt open, I slipped my palms up his torso over the thin tee he wore beneath the collared one until I had my fingers interlocked around the back of his neck. I used that as leverage to pull him impossibly closer, finally pressing my front against his.

Holy. Shit.

If I thought his mouth had lit a fire within me, nothing—and I mean *nothing*—compared to the inferno caused by his massive erection against my lower stomach. Had I been able to focus on anything other than that, I would've heard myself moan in sexual hunger.

Corbin Fields would be the death of me.

At least I could definitively say that I was capable of being turned on by someone other than Chase. Which was both good and bad news. Good news because I'd convinced myself that I'd be a lonely old cat lady if he never came to his senses about us, but bad because the simple thought of my ex had the same effect as being doused with a barrel of artic water.

I immediately pulled my face away, though I was smart enough not to drop my arms or take a step back. At least I still possessed *some* common sense—based on the way I'd practically mauled him like a dog in heat, I wouldn't dare say I had very much.

"I'm so sorry, Corbin," I panted while frantically trying to read his expression in the glow from the moon. "I have no idea what came over me."

He flexed his fingers so that they dug a little deeper into the meaty parts of my hips, his breathing raspy and ragged. "Could've been all the wine you pounded back during dinner. But I can't let you take all the credit for this—after all, it wasn't like I did anything to stop it."

With a rushed exhale, I dropped my forehead to his chest, my arms still wrapped around his shoulders, fingers locked behind his neck, and closed my eyes. It seemed I was full of bad decisions tonight, because that one move did nothing but deepen the hole I'd begun to dig for myself. After releasing all the air from my lungs, I now had to refill them, and since my face was pressed against the front of his body, my sense of smell became consumed by whatever cologne he had on.

I never remembered him smelling this good. I was a sucker for cologne, and he wore one that complimented him completely. It made me want to bury my nose further into his shirt and breathe all of him in, so I did. Either there was more than fermented grapes in the wine tonight, or Corbin Fields had a way of impairing my self-control. Based on the fact that I couldn't seem to stop myself, regardless of how mortified I knew I'd be once I stepped away, I figured it might've been both.

"What cologne are you wearing?" I wasn't sure if he could hear my question beneath the hedonistic moans that flooded my voice, but I didn't care. I also didn't stop sniffing him…I mean, I'd already gone this far, why stop, right?

His laughter rumbled his chest and seeped out into his words when he answered. "Cool Water for men. I take it you don't like it?"

"*Don't like it*?" I pulled my head back and stared at him in shock, though that didn't last long. Reality hit me with the waves of humor that slipped past his smiling lips, bringing with it a level of embarrassment that I had wished would drown me. "Oh, you were being sarcastic."

Damn, I needed a straw so I could suck down half the water in the lake. I would need that much to sober me. Oh, who the hell was I kidding? I needed to tie a cinderblock to my ankle and jump in. Not only would it counteract the alcohol, but it would also solve the issue of my humiliation.

"Hey…" He lifted one hand, trailing his fingers up my side over my ribs, while holding me against him with the other. "Whatever's going through that pretty head of yours, stop it. I wasn't making fun; I thought your reaction was cute."

Cute. Exactly what every girl wants to be called after trying to seduce someone.

But before I could groan in complaint, Corbin lowered his head to the side of mine, brushing my cheek with the stubble that lined his. I had to admit, it was slightly awkward with the drastic height difference, yet not enough to put on the brakes. Then again, I wasn't the one craning my neck so far just to keep from separating our bodies. I was just the one who stood there while Corbin buried his face in my hair—he likely tried to reach the crook of my neck, but without stepping back to bend over, the side of my head was about as far as he could go.

With his lips next to my ear, he hummed and asked, "What shampoo do you use?"

What came out of my mouth next was, without a doubt, the product of his deep timbre reverberating around my ear drum, which sent shock waves directly to the pit of my stomach, and in turn, released a flood of molten lava between my legs—and into my panties.

"I don't think you're smelling my shampoo, Corbin. I ran out of time to take a shower before coming here, so I wiped down the valuables with a washcloth and doused myself with body spray, my hair included."

Kill.

Me.

Now.

Apparently, the heavens heard my request, because a split second later, Corbin's lips were on mine again, I felt as if I had floated out of my body. Sparks flew behind my closed lids as I drifted closer to the pearly gates. But before Peter could grant me access, the heat of hell licked its way up my inner thighs and scorched my aforementioned "valuables" when he palmed my breast with one of his impressively large hands.

I sucked his tongue and moaned in pleasure as his thumb found my hardened nipple. And when his careful touch turned into an unexpectedly harsh pinch, I rolled my hips into him, grinding myself against the rock-hard bulge in his pants, desperately seeking relief. Craving more. I was drugged from his kisses, out of my mind with need. My brain void of thoughts and reason, I only had one goal in mind—to make him touch me.

I loosened the buckle on his pants just enough to slip my hand between the waistband of his khakis and the warm skin over his abs. He moaned into my mouth when I grazed his hard dick with my knuckles. His grip on me grew rougher, which I took as a green light to keep going—not that I'd been waiting for one. But the instant I felt his heat against my palm, not quite getting my fingers wrapped around the thick shaft—but enough to verify that he did, indeed, have a *very* thick shaft—an invisible defibrillator shocked my heart and brought me back to life.

"Corbin! Brooke! Where are you guys?" Nellie's shrieking broke us apart faster than an infestation of herpes at a brothel. "I found the vanilla ice cream!"

As if I were a cat with a canary in my mouth, I took off. The last thing I needed was to get caught with my hand down my best friend's brother's pants…by said best friend. Nellie could forgive a lot, but I would be willing to bet that would be beyond the scope of her forgiveness.

"Bridge, wait a minute." Corbin tried to race after me while securing his pants, but I'd gotten a hefty head start—thanks to the fact that I didn't have to waste time redressing.

Thank goodness I knew all the shortcuts and ways to get around this property. I'd left my phone and purse in the car, so I high-tailed it to the gate that ran along the perimeter of the front of the house. I figured I'd just tell her that I'd gone outside to wait on her. That seemed totally plausible…and not at all questionable.

Hearing Corbin's steps behind me, I jumped in the passenger seat of Nellie's car and slammed the door, securing myself inside. The dome light had just switched off, cloaking the interior in darkness, when a body came crashing down across the hood. It scared the bejesus out of me, and I screamed before flinging the door open again.

"What the hell was that for?" I shouted, then looked around to make sure I hadn't garnered the attention of anyone I didn't want to bear witness to this humiliating moment. I could've convinced Nellie that I had gone to the car to wait for her, but I doubted I'd be able to come up with a compelling excuse why her brother was sprawled out on the hood, out of breath with his shirt unbuttoned and his belt halfway undone.

"I was trying to keep you from leaving." His chest heaved from either the exertion of running after me or having the wind knocked out of him.

With only one foot on the driveway, the other still on the floorboard of the car, I glanced between the passenger seat I'd just jumped out of and Corbin a few times. Then I deadpanned, "This isn't my vehicle. I wasn't even behind the wheel. And the engine's not on—not to mention, I don't have the keys. What'd you think I was going to do…Fred Flintstone it out of here?"

He stepped to the side, moving away from the front of the car but not coming to me, and blinked a few times while staring at the open door, seemingly dumbfounded at the lack of thought he'd put into his grand gesture.

"I see what you mean. But you didn't leave, so I'd say it was justified."

Laughter bubbled up from my chest, and in an instant, the tension that had suffocated me ever since Nellie had interrupted our thoughtless moment of sexual gratification eased. My shoulders immediately relaxed and the knots that had riddled my stomach were long gone.

Corbin must've noticed my lighter disposition, because he moved closer, stopping when only a few feet and the car door separated us. "Seriously though, why'd you run off like that?"

"You really have to ask? Was I the only one who heard your sister come outside?"

He peered over his shoulder at the front of the house, and then faced me again. "Bridge, it was dark, and she wasn't anywhere near us. There was no way she could've seen us, let alone what we were doing. I'm willing to bet she didn't even know we were back there."

All I could do was shake my head. I had no idea what to say other than, "I didn't want to take the chance of getting caught."

While that wasn't a total lie, it hadn't been the primary reason for my escape. And for some reason, it felt like he knew that. Thankfully, though, he hadn't questioned me or pressed for more. Instead, he mindlessly buttoned his shirt, head slightly tilted to the side, and said, "I just need to know one thing. Okay?"

My heart rate accelerated, but that didn't stop me from letting him continue.

"Did you enjoy yourself?"

However, that was the *last* thing I had expected him to say. It had caught me so off guard that I couldn't keep the rolling laughter from escaping, filling the quite night sky with the lilting sound of my amusement.

"I'll take that as a yes." His smile filled his words.

When the humor finally slowed to a soft rumble, I said, "Yes, I did. But you're my best friend's brother, and she'll fucking kill me if she finds out. Or worse, she'll kill you."

Corbin took one more step toward me, larger than the others, and closed the distance between us. The only thing in his way now was the door that he grabbed onto, his hands practically on top of mine. He rubbed his thumb over my knuckles and commanded my attention by staring into my eyes.

"I was actually talking about dinner. But it's good to know you enjoyed dessert, too."

My face flushed with heat so intense I wouldn't be surprised if he could see it beneath the moonlight. But thankfully, he didn't wait around for a response—or say anything else. Instead, he patted the top of my hand, told me goodnight, and turned to head back to the house.

Part of me wanted to stop him, but with as fried as my brain was—thanks to the wine, as well as the unexpected desire he'd filled me with—I decided it would be best to let him go. I'd already humiliated myself enough for one night; there was no need to add to it.

I fell into the seat and waited for Nellie to find me, wondering if it had all been a dream.

I never did things like that...*ever*.

But there was something about Corbin this evening that had compelled me to take action.

I had no idea what would happen next, but I was too busy recalling the feel of his lips to care.

MONDAYS WERE MY FUN DAYS. Screw Sundays. Those were the worst, because it was the day before returning to work. Mondays were way better. And I definitely needed today. Every other week, my girls and I met at Donovan's, which was an old Irish Pub located smack dab in the middle of town, central to all of us. It'd been our tradition for the past four years—since we'd all turned twenty-one—and I hoped it never ended.

I had arrived first, which wasn't unusual, but this time, it wasn't to ensure we had our regular table. Today, I'd gotten here early because I didn't want to sit alone at home, lost in thoughts of the night before. It was bad enough that every second of my time with Corbin in his parents' back yard had played in my mind on repeat ever since he'd said goodnight before walking away, leaving me in the unfamiliar erotic state between mortification and sheer bliss. I couldn't risk losing myself in the fantasy of Corbin Fields, only to then have drinks and dinner with Nellie.

When I spotted Julie coming my way, a devious smile spread across her face, I realized they were all going to ask me about the status of Heather and Chase. And I didn't have anything to tell them. Hell, I hadn't even thought of it until now.

My, how quickly things slip my mind when my thoughts are filled with...*other* things.

I grabbed my phone and held it in my lap to discreetly type a message to Corbin. He had texted me this morning to ask how I felt, but I ignored it. I couldn't figure out how to respond, and I didn't care to embarrass myself so soon after the last time. Now, I couldn't tap the letters to form a sentence fast enough.

Me: *Hey. Hope you had a great day.*

That was so lame, but I couldn't think of anything else. It made me incredibly uncomfortable to text him, so I quickly sent another one.

Me: *I'm meeting the girls for drinks and have nothing to tell them about you and Heather. Can you provide me with any updates? Did you see her today?*

Nellie startled me before taking the seat beside me and giving me a quick hug. Thank God she didn't notice the phone in my lap. She wouldn't have let it go until she thoroughly read my texts, and I wasn't sure how to explain why Corbin had asked me how I was feeling this morning.

With Julie and Nellie at the table, we were just missing Mady. I prayed he would text back before our fourth musketeer arrived; they wouldn't let more than five seconds pass before hounding me for an update...an update I couldn't give without Corbin's response.

"Hey yourself, girl." I grimaced. *That wasn't awkward at all. My*

67

secret is totally safe. No it's not. She totally knows. "Today was super busy at work. We started state testing, and all the kiddos had to partake. It took forever to get them settled down enough to concentrate on that long-ass test." That had sounded customary. It was something I'd absolutely say on any other day.

Fuck. I need a drink.

Thanks to Corbin, I was on the verge of becoming an alcoholic!

My phone vibrated between my legs, and it made me jump a mile.

"You okay?" Nellie looked worried, which made my guilt quadruple.

"Yup. I swear. Busy day."

Mady decided to show up in that moment, which momentarily let me off the hook. While they were all preoccupied with greeting each other, I took the opportunity to check my phone.

Corbin: I see how it is. First you use me for your own sexual gratification last night, and now you're using me to get info for your friends. Keep this up and I might start making you earn it LOL

Fuck me sideways! I didn't know what I'd expected him to say, but it wasn't that. I thought we'd pretend it didn't happen. Apparently not. And now, thanks to his teasing, I had to sit next to his sister and pray she wouldn't notice my flaming cheeks. Or bouncing knee. There was absolutely *no* way I could explain his text.

Me: You're making this hard.

Corbin: Then I guess we're even. You made something else hard last night.

Sweet baby Jesus. I clenched my thighs and tried to think of anything to get my mind elsewhere. How could words, just plain old words, have that kind of effect on me?

Me: Please, Corbin…just give me something I can tell them to hold them over for now. I'm literally sitting right next to Nellie, so no more talking about last night. Unless you want her to stab me with her butter knife.

"What's going on with you?" Nellie eyed me with intense scrutiny, as if she could read my mind by staring at me.

"Nothing. Why? I don't know what you're talking about." *Smooth, Brooke.*

"You're acting weird." She turned to the others and said, "Guys, isn't she acting weird?"

"No I'm not. You are." Just then, my cell buzzed beneath the table, calling her attention.

"Give me your phone. You're being sneaky, like you don't want me to see something. Are you talking to Chase?" With lightning speed, she grabbed the top of my cell and gave it a yank.

Panic lit within as I attempted to keep the device clutched firmly in my grasp. She could *not* see that message from Corbin. My life flashed before my eyes as she got the upper hand. She knew all of my passcodes. I'd never had anything to hide before now.

"Would you two quit it?" Julie looked at us like we'd each grown two heads. "What are you fighting over?"

I grunted as I almost regained control of *my* phone.

"I know how to solve this." Mady perched herself high in her chair and leaned across the table to pluck the device from Nellie and me. The color drained from my face as she looked at the screen. *Please be on lock mode*, was the only thing I could manage. I would've never been able to foresee what came next. Mady dropped my cell into the glass of ice water in front of her.

"What the hell, Mady!" I gawked and then sat with my mouth open for what seemed like forever before grabbing it out of the water and trying to dry it with my napkin.

"That played out so much better in my head." She shrugged. "You two wouldn't let it go, so like the mom I am, I took the toy from the children who can't get along."

69

"What are you talking about?" Nellie asked. "You're not a mom!"

"Yeah. But we're all girls, so we have that mom gene. You know?"

I couldn't help it. I didn't know if it was the tension I'd been doused in all evening or what, but I began to laugh uncontrollably. Mady had long ago been dubbed the dumb blonde of the group. And it made matters worse because her family had emigrated from Italy, and there wasn't one blond hair on her head, or anywhere else for that matter.

"To Chase being a complete asshole!" Julie held up her glass and patiently waited for us to follow suit.

I had never been happier to discuss my ex. And oddly enough, his name didn't make me sad. In fact, it didn't make me feel anything.

Maybe Corbin was the distraction I needed.

CHAPTER 7

CORBIN

"EMILY! GET IN HERE!" I roared through the closed door. I didn't care if I sounded like a lunatic.

"What is it?" My assistant stood in the doorway, her arms crossed and eyes lit on fire, but she didn't come any closer.

"I need that memo," I spat out, then I stood and began to pace. Like a madman. I knew my actions were intolerable, and I seemed on the verge of a psychotic break, but I couldn't help myself.

"You mean the one you just dictated? How about giving me more than five minutes to type it up for you?" She turned around and firmly shut the door behind her, without even waiting for my response.

I grunted before sitting back down at my computer. I'd been a total asshole all week. I knew my demands were unreasonable, my mood was insufferable, and my attitude sucked, but I needed a scapegoat to take out my frustration. I hadn't heard from Bridge since Monday, after I'd sent her those teasing texts. I'd thrown caution to the wind and had gone for it. Stupidly. In my defense, though, I thought she would've known I was only giving her a hard time, nothing personal. Apparently, I was wrong.

Dammit! I'd never felt this undone before, especially over a couple dumb texts. Maybe I was losing it. My assistant was definitely going to have me committed. She was probably dialing the asylum as I sat here twiddling my thumbs.

This was how I'd been all week. I needed to pull my shit together or I'd end up losing my job. I mean, that wasn't entirely true. I'd pretty much been able to stay afloat this week, but I didn't know how much longer I'd be able to carry on like a puppy pining away for his mommy. I was a total pussy! Even I had to admit it.

My phone chose that moment to ring, and I welcomed the distraction. But when I ended the call, the distinct chirp of an incoming text jolted me out of my chair. My keyboard and mouse went flying, but all I cared about was my phone.

> **Bridge**: *I finally got my phone back! What a loooong week. Meet me for drinks tonight? I really need to talk to you. Xxx*

I read and then re-read her words five times. Then I wrote a message and erased it, only to re-type it another five times before ultimately pressing send.

> **Me**: *Yes. Same place? Round Up?*

> **Bridge**: *Sounds good. See you at 6pm. Or is that too early?*

I looked at my watch; I'd still have to wait all goddamn afternoon.

> **Me**: *Perfect. See you then.*

My heart seemed lighter, and my mood instantly improved. I wanted to get up and dance. Then I became immobile. I'd been an asshole. All week. I needed to fix things. Firstly, with my assistant, who'd been with me through more bad times than good. This was one of the bad.

I looked up the local flower shop I patronized. Well, Emily

usually did on my behalf, but today I was going to have to put on my big-boy pants and do it myself. I added a hefty spring bouquet for Emily to my cart and asked for it to be delivered by two in the afternoon. I wrote, *from the asshole behind the closed door,* and thought that sounded good enough.

I didn't want to dive too deep into my feelings for an actual apology. This would suffice.

Then I decided to let her leave as soon as her bouquet arrived. Since it was Friday, she could get a head start on the weekend, and I could bang out some work before meeting Brooklyn. Not to mention, it was only a few hours early. Emily deserved it after my emotional week-long tirade.

I used to send Lindsey flowers every other week to let her know I was thinking about her—then again, I did that because I worked so much and would go days without much more than a few texts to remind her that she still had a boyfriend. The last time had been a congratulatory bouquet to her new office. Needless to say, it felt weird to be buying flowers for someone else.

The phone rang, and I abandoned my keyboard to answer. While talking, I quickly finished my flower order and paid extra for a speedy delivery and then turned my attention back to the phone. Thanks to Nellie, I'd perfected the art of multitasking.

By two in the afternoon, the flowers had been delivered and a happy Emily had pranced home for the day. All was forgiven, but the main attraction of the day still lay before me—dinner with Bridge. I went back and forth between feeling anxious and happy. It was a mixed bag of emotions, and I couldn't put my finger on how I truly felt.

I threw myself into work and tried not to think about the impending meetup, but it was nearly impossible. I managed to make it through most of my inbox and signed nearly everything requiring my attention before I checked my watch for the twelfth time in ten minutes. It was only five thirty. It only took five minutes, if that, to walk to the place, but I couldn't make myself wait any longer. I had to leave now. I set all the completed signature files on Emily's desk to deal with on Monday and then gathered my things to leave.

The entire walk to Round Up, I tried *not* to anticipate what would happen. I tried to study the people around me or slow down enough to window shop, but I failed miserably. I quickly found myself in front of the pub and took a deep breath before stepping inside.

My eyes instantly found Bridge at a corner table located in the back. She studied the drink menu and, as if she felt my gaze, looked up. Her eyebrows knitted together, and her mouth hung half open in bewilderment. Did she not think I'd show? Or maybe my prompt arrival threw her off?

Her confusion made my steps falter. I mean, I didn't expect her to jump up from the table and throw herself into my arms or anything; that shit only happened in movies. But I figured she'd at least greet me with a smile—even if it was small—not confusion.

"Hi. Did you order drinks yet?" I sat down across from her and realized her mouth still gaped, her face seemingly frozen in time. "Is something wrong?"

"I—I just wasn't expecting *you*." Her voice was quiet and laced with tension; it made me want to bolt.

"I don't understand. I received a text from you…" There was obviously some big mistake. I fought the urge to show her the text to prove I'd received it.

"But I didn't." She shook her head, her brows still knitted together. She took her cell out and studied it for a minute. "Is your number…" When she rattled it off, I knew instantly it was mine.

"Yeah, that's me."

"But it's listed as Nellie's." As if to prove her point, she handed me her cell and, indeed, my number was listed under my sister's name.

"Huh." I had no earthly idea as to why or how that had happened. And then I remembered something. "You mentioned that you just got your phone back. Did you get it fixed or something?"

"I actually got a new one, but it took forever because I had to send it off to the insurance carrier and then wait until I received one back."

"Well, the same thing happened to a buddy of mine a couple years back. He had to get a new one, too. And when he downloaded his contact information, all the names and numbers got jumbled. It was a mess."

"Are you serious?" Bridge's wide eyes and arched brows made me laugh.

"Completely."

"That's insane. In this day and age? They can't figure out something that simple?"

"Guess not." I shrugged. "What happened to your phone anyway? Why'd you have to get a new one"

She rolled her eyes with a hint of a smile playing at the corners of her mouth. "When you texted me about how I had made something hard"—the sparkle in her eye nearly made it hard again —"Nellie tried to see who I was talking to, and to keep us from arguing, one of our other friends took my cell and dropped it into a cup of water. Don't ask. So really, if you think about it, it's all your fault."

Feeling like a dick, I sat with the unopened menu in front of me. I'd resigned myself to the fact that she'd probably ask me to leave and quickly call Nellie to meet her instead. I fought the disappointment that slowly began to creep in.

"Well, since we're both here, we might as well eat something. Right?" She giggled and then opened her menu again. "I seriously can't believe this. Maybe it's fate or something that we have dinner tonight."

"It does seem surreal." This evening just might turn around after all.

"So, what did your friend do? To get the contact information corrected. Please don't tell me I have to go one by one and correct them all. That will take me forever! Not to mention, it will be nearly impossible since I have none of them memorized."

"He just set it back to the factory settings and then started all over again. Thankfully, everything downloaded correctly the second time. It made for some funny stories, though. Because his mom got texts meant for his girlfriend and so on. We still tease him about it."

After the waitress took our order, the air around us seemed more relaxed.

"I'm sorry that I showed up instead of my sister. I can call her quickly and ask her to join us if you want." I only offered that to make her feel better, but I secretly wanted her to say no so that I could have her all to myself.

"Nah, she probably already has plans. I've been talking to her back and forth all week using other people's phones, so she knows I'm not MIA. She just doesn't know I got mine back. But I'll text her when I get home and fill her in on what happened. She'll probably think it's hilarious. That girl seems to find the humor in everything."

A trait I didn't possess, and to be honest, I had no idea where she'd inherited it from. Certainly not either of our parents—they wouldn't know humor if it smacked them in the face. For me, I found irony much funnier than jokes, but not my sister. Just about anything could amuse that girl. And now that I thought about it, I remembered Bridge had always been the same.

"To be honest with you, I thought you were ignoring me all week because of my texts Monday night." I wanted to add that there was no way she would've avoided me after our rendezvous in my parents' back yard on Sunday, but I figured that might've taken things too far.

She broke out into laughter, shaking her head. "I'll admit... they took me by surprise."

"I just want you to know that I was only teasing."

Her high cheekbones tinged pink, and her smile fell slightly, turning into more of a shy grin than the curve of laughter from before. "I know. I guess I wasn't expecting it. I'm still really embarrassed about what happened."

"Don't be." I reached across the table and covered her hand with mine. "I mean it, Bridge, there's nothing to be embarrassed about. You had a lot of wine that night, and it wasn't like I'd done anything to stop it from happening. Everything's fine, okay?"

She shrugged and turned her attention to her lap. "I really don't want anything to change."

"Good, because neither do I. Nothing has to change. We have so many ties between us with my family. Even though you aren't close to my parents, they still care about you. And it seems like most of our childhood memories are interwoven. One make-out session won't change that." One very hot, intense, wet-dream worthy make-out session.

"Yeah. I guess you're right." She lifted her gaze and offered a small smile. "I'm really glad you're here, though. I've been dying to know what all has happened with Heather, but I didn't really have a way to find out. Not to mention, I wasn't sure how things would be between us, and without a phone of my own, I was nervous to reach out."

Heather had been the *furthest* thing from my mind all week, but I couldn't exactly tell her that. How was I supposed to explain that I hadn't been able to think about anything other than her lips or the feel of her body pressed against mine? Or that her silence all week had driven me batshit crazy?

"Well, since I hadn't heard from you, I wasn't sure if the plan was still on, so I haven't done anything about it. I was waiting to talk to you first." Yeah, that made sense. Totally believable. She wouldn't question it at all.

The waitress dropped off our drinks and a basket of chips, causing Brooke to pull her hand from mine. And after a quick sip of her soda—it was not lost on me that she hadn't ordered an alcoholic beverage—she cleared her throat and leveled me with a stare. "Oh, it's still on. Like Donkey Kong."

I practically spit out my beer, not at all expecting that to have come from her. "Can I ask you why you are so adamant about keeping this plan going? I get that he hurt you, but what are you wanting to gain from this?" I silently prayed she wasn't about to tell me she wanted him back.

Her pink tongue slipped out and slowly ran along her bottom lip while she peered over my shoulder in thought. It was such a small gesture, but it was hot all hell. "I guess I just want him to know what it feels like."

"Which I totally get, but why's it so important to ensure that happens?"

"He stole my entire future from me, Corbin. He needs to know that, and no matter what I say to him, he'll never get it until it happens to him. He'll never understand how it feels until he falls in love with someone, plans to spend the rest of his life with her, makes her his whole world like I had done with him, and then loses her to someone else."

I mulled that over in my head for a moment; I could see her point, though that didn't mean I was suddenly on board with it. "So what is it you hope will happen? Like, how would this play out if everything went the way you wanted it to?"

"I hope she makes him happier than he ever thought possible, flips his life upside down, becomes so ingrained in his existence that he doesn't know where he ends and she begins. I hope he goes broke buying her a diamond ring, gets down on one knee, plans the entire thing out to a T. And then I hope she cheats on him…like he cheated on me."

The conviction in her voice felt like a punch in the gut. This Chase guy really did a number on her, and while I'd already known that he had hurt her, I would've never guessed she was as broken as she was. It made my heart hurt. And it made me want to do everything in my power to make it right—just not the way she wanted. I agreed that her ex shouldn't get a happy ending after what he'd done to her, but right now, my concern was making sure *she* got her happily ever after. That *she* got over the hurt he'd caused. All without recreating the same devastation for him.

Getting revenge on him might've been her goal, but it wasn't mine. My goal, as of this very second, was to make her see that he had done her a favor by letting her go. There were so many men out there who could make her happy, treat her right, never hurt her the way Chase had, and all I wanted was to help her see that.

Too bad that guy would never be me.

But that didn't mean I couldn't show her what she was worth.

"How was work today?" I decided a complete change of subject was in order, because no matter what I said, I'd end up pushing her away. And no matter how temporary I knew this thing between us was, I wasn't ready to close the book on it yet.

I also knew if I got her talking about her work—a very safe topic—she'd talk for hours without a problem. I didn't knock her for that, because I could listen just as long. The way her face lit up as she discussed students intoxicated me.

Hell, *everything* about her intoxicated me.

I was so fucked.

CHAPTER 8

BROOKE

THIS EVENING HAD NOT TURNED out as planned. But sometimes, those were the best kinds of experiences—once you learned to let go and allow things to happen.

I was not the type of girl who "let go" easily. I'd learned to roll with it better than I used to, though; life lessons will do that to you. If someone would've told me that Corbin Fields would show up tonight instead of Nellie, I would've laughed in their face. Yet here I sat with Corbin across from me. *Not* Nellie.

Life had a weird way of showing you who was boss.

I definitely didn't have control of what happened in my life, and things like this continually came up to remind me of that fact.

When Corbin had asked about my work, I inwardly did a happy dance. Whenever I spoke of my students or my job, he didn't have to fake interest. He truly cared. Or he was one hell of an actor—which I *highly* doubted.

"Today was unexpected. I guess this evening speaks volumes of how many surprises were in store for me." I'd already told him the story of Mady dropping my phone in my glass of water. He thought that it hysterical. I still didn't, but I loved the girl. She'd been there many more times than a stupid phone could count.

"Luck of the draw, I guess." He held up his glass and chuckled when I overly clanked it with mine. It had become sort of a thing between us since our first meet-up for drinks. Not that I kept track of these types of things or anything.

We'd just finished eating and were taking the last sips of our drinks. I had successfully won the fight and paid for dinner, considering he'd covered the last two...again, not that I was counting.

"Ready to go?"

I wasn't, but I couldn't tell him that. I'd had so much fun hanging out with him that I wasn't ready for the night to end. But it was a Friday after all, and there was a good chance he had plans —by himself, most likely, but plans were plans, no matter how many people they involved.

However, rather than say anything, I nodded, grabbed my coat, and pulled my purse over my shoulder.

"What movie should we watch?" His question caught me off guard and made me pause.

I stood on the sidewalk, just outside the front door of the pub, and stared at him in confusion. I had to have misunderstood him, but the way he regarded me, a devious smirk brightening his blue eyes, told me otherwise.

"Did you change your mind already?" he asked, his head cocked to the side.

"When did we decide to watch a movie?"

Corbin huffed dramatically, reminding me of his sister—it didn't happen often, but when it did, it took me by surprise—and said, "While we were eating. We had an entire conversation about what we were doing after we ate."

I would've definitely remembered that, although it seemed he had a way of making me feel like I'd lost my mind. Last weekend had been a prime example of that. "Oh, yeah. I recall that now. But if my memory serves me correctly, we agreed you'd pick the movie."

Two can play this game.

"Funny, I don't think that's how the conversation went."

"You wouldn't, because we never made plans for after dinner. But good try, buddy." I wagged my brows and fell in step next to him along the sidewalk. "Although, now that we *have* made plans, you get to pick the movie."

He hummed to himself while glancing off into the distance, as if he had to put a lot of thought into which title to choose. "Well, romantic comedies are out. And so is anything with graphic sex scenes. We don't want to tempt ourselves or anything." He winked at me, and I found myself giggling. He *was* funny, even though I'd never admit that to him.

"That pretty much leaves us with nothing, so I guess I'll see you later," I teased.

"Have you seen *Aquaman* yet?"

I stopped abruptly and waited for him to look my way. With a scowl, I said, "Ew, no. I'm a Marvel fan through and through." I curled my lip in disgust. "Pick one of the *Avengers*, and I'll agree to watch a movie with you. Anything else, and you can watch it by yourself."

He blinked at me, a mixture of shock and awe covering his face. "You're a Marvel girl?"

"Is there any other way to be?"

"Be still my beating heart!" He grabbed my had and practically ran down the sidewalk to a tall building two blocks down. The animation that colored his every move had me laughing the entire way.

From the moment we left Round Up until we made our way off the elevator at his condo, we took turns rattling off Marvel trivia . I couldn't tell if my vast knowledge impressed him, or if he was just happy to finally have someone to talk superheroes with. Either way, I'd enjoyed every second of it. It was funny because it was the only interest Nellie and I *didn't* have in common. She hated all things comic book with a passion.

"Did you know there's a new untitled Marvel movie coming out?" I asked him, still excited over the news. "It's featuring Black Widow."

"Yup. I can't wait to see it. With my work schedule, I don't have a chance to visit the theatre very often. Are you already reserving me so we can go together?"

"No, Corbin." I laughed, hoping he couldn't see through my lie. In reality, the thought of seeing it with him on opening day filled me with giddiness. "Did you know that *Captain Marvel* was planned out from the beginning? Like back to the very first *Avengers* movie, but not a lot of people remember it even being mentioned."

"I don't remember that!" Corbin admitted as he unlocked his front door. He lived in a high-rise on the twenty-second floor, and his number was two twenty-two. I found it oddly amusing.

"Was this a coincidence?" I pointed to the numbers on the front of his door.

"Actually, no. Two is my favorite number. When I was looking to buy a place, this building hadn't been finished yet, so they were selling the units at a lower price—some pre-built special that a lot of new places offer. I think it's to fill them up so the developer isn't stuck with a bunch of empty condos. Anyway, there were only a few left, this being one of them. I picked it based on the numbers, sight unseen. It could've been a shithole and I still would've bought it simply because of all the twos. You have no idea how excited I was to find out it wasn't the size of a shoebox."

I couldn't believe Corbin had taken a leap of faith like that. He didn't seem the type.

As we entered the main living area, I was instantly impressed. The views from his condo must've been astounding during the day, but at night, they bordered on spectacular. The city lights went on as far as the eye could see, and I found myself mesmerized by them.

He went over to the wall next to the TV and pushed a button. Rows upon rows of DVDs appeared before my very eyes. It was like magic. "I had this installed when I moved in. DVDs have lost their appeal to many, but I treasure my collection. Especially my

Marvel movies." He pointed to a row dead center, and I was in awe. He had every single one.

I plucked a title off the shelf and smiled with excitement. "*Thor* is my favorite."

"*Thor* it is then," he said as he took the DVD from my hand. "Why don't you go make popcorn while I put the movie on and light a fire? It's gotten chilly." It was clear that no one had been here all day; without a source of heat, the air held a bite that had prevented either of us from removing our coats.

Following his directions, I found the popcorn and put it on to bake; it wasn't long until I became hypnotized by the sound of the kernels popping away. It played in the background as I daydreamed of spending evenings just like this—in complete comfort with someone I enjoyed. Apparently, I'd gotten so lost in my thoughts that I jumped when Corbin came up behind me and began to rub my arms.

"Do you feel any warmer?"

"Yes, thank you." I moved out of reach. There wasn't anything inappropriate in his actions, but it made the butterflies dance in my stomach. And I needed to ignore that feeling. He was my best friend's brother. Nothing more.

I got the hot bag out of the microwave and poured the buttery goodness into a bowl Corbin had put on the counter. He poured two glasses of red wine and expertly carried them into the living room.

The sigh escaped my lips before it registered.

"You okay?"

"It's just so serene. The city lights through the window, the warm fire, and the gigantic movie screen—because that television is big enough to pass as a theatre rendition. If I lived here, I would never leave!"

"I'm actually not home very often. Most of my free time is spent at the office." He chuckled and then pointed to the ottoman. "Pull out a blanket if you're still cold."

We established our boundaries by silently placing a throw

pillow between us. It didn't take me long to forget about the awkwardness of being so close to Corbin and get into the movie. I couldn't even say how many times I'd seen it—countless. But it still held my attention, and I swear I always picked out something I'd never seen before. Although, I had to say, the best part was having someone to talk about it with. He was the first person who seemed as interested as I was in the mythological aspect of Thor.

When we finished the movie, I wasn't sleepy in the slightest. My earlier exhaustion had dissipated, and if anything, I felt invigorated. "Do you want to watch the next one? If you're tired, I can take a raincheck."

"No raincheck necessary." He got up to switch the discs over, and I realized I hadn't spoken to Nellie all day. We usually didn't go long without texting one another, and I didn't want her to think something was wrong.

I grabbed my purse off the floor and pulled out my cell. But before I could do anything else, Corbin snatched it from my hand and tsked, shaking his head. "No phones allowed."

"I'm just going to send a quick text to Nellie. I don't want her to worry."

"You guys are so co-dependent it's ridiculous." His tone was light, yet it struck a chord.

"I don't think so." I tried to hold back the attitude, but it had seeped into my words anyway. "I get it, Corbin—Nellie could do better than me for a friend. But guess what? It doesn't concern you, so your opinion doesn't matter. I refuse to defend our friendship to anyone. I mean, wasn't it enough to pester us when we were younger?"

"Hey, hold on. Where the hell is all this coming from?"

"It's like you're always putting us down." I seemed to have reverted back to my teenage self. But rather than cry like I would have when I was twelve, I got angry. It was amazing how much strength one person could find when they felt like the whole world was against them. "You may see it as codependency, but I see it as respect. You may think we're always up to something, but really, we're just trying to help the other out."

"Will you let me explain?"

I nodded. Not trusting myself to speak for fear of rivers flowing down my cheeks.

"You and I are grappling to find our footing because this is different. A lot of times you witnessed the sibling relationship between Nellie and me. Hell, you were even part of it. It was my brotherly duty to give *both* of you a hard time. I *do* respect you guys and what you have. Fuck! If I'm honest, I envy you at times."

"You envy me? Why?" That made no sense. "For what?"

"Because you two have this awesome kinship; you have someone to talk to when you need it. Someone to stand by you, no matter what. Who wouldn't want that?"

"I don't understand, Corbin...you have the same thing."

He laughed. Like, tossed his head back and howled at the ceiling. "With who?"

"Uh...Nellie? Your ex? And you've told me you still hang out with your old friends from school. I mean, I don't presume to know everyone in your life, but I assume you have people."

"Sure, I can call my sister anytime I want, except the dynamic between me and her isn't the same as it is for you two. And just because I still see the guys I'd gone to school with from time to time doesn't mean I can depend on them for anything."

It wasn't lost on me that he'd left out his ex.

"You always seem to leap to the wrong conclusion because you're so hell-bent that you don't fit in. You *do* fit in, Brooke. More than you realize. For instance, you didn't want to go to my parents' house for dinner last weekend because you had convinced yourself that they don't like you. They love you, yet you're blinded by self-doubt. After all you've accomplished, how can that be?"

"I don't know." And I didn't. Despite my close friendship with Nellie, it had always hung over me. And hearing him point it out didn't help. If anything, it exacerbated the doubt. And uncomfortableness.

"Believe in yourself, Bridge. Believe in your abilities." He leaned over and took my hand in his. His words touched me, but they also brought about questions—questions I wasn't sure I wanted the answers to. Part of me wanted to point out that he, too, needed to abide by his advice.

"I'll try," I promised.

"Okay. We'll leave it at that." He awkwardly patted my hand, since he'd been holding it too long.

I laughed and then turned back to my cell, determined to contact Nellie. "Can you give me your sister's number, please? I swear, this ordeal makes me want to memorize the numbers of everyone I frequently call."

He typed in his passcode and then threw the device at me.

"Ouch!" I exclaimed half-jokingly as it hit my thigh. Then I quickly looked up her info and sent her a message—from me— explaining that I got my cell back and we'd hang out tomorrow.

Corbin tossed his phone onto the ottoman and sat back on the couch. When I wasn't looking, he snatched mine off the cushion between us.

"Hey, what are you doing?" I practically jumped on him. My screen was open for him to look up anything, and the image of Mady and Nellie fighting me for the same thing replayed in my mind.

"Settle Down, Bridge. I'm just going to help you reset your contacts and make everything right in the world again. I'll tell you when you need to do your part."

My back hit the couch and I feigned pouting, but I quickly grew tired of the act as the movie played on. I'd gotten so sucked into the action that by the time he was ready for my part, I mindlessly entered my password and gave it back.

While he worked on my phone, I curled into the corner of the sofa and continued to watch the movie. There was something about seeing it on his big screen in his living room...next to him...

that made it so much better. I couldn't explain it, nor did I want to.

I grew lost in the visions of Chris Hemsworth swinging around that massive hammer while his long hair blew in the air behind him. Damn he was hot. Although, the guy next to me had his own appeal—one I couldn't ignore no matter how hard I tried.

"Okay, all done. Check your contacts." He scooted closer and leaned over me, now situated between my thighs and hovering over my torso. I wasn't sure why he needed to be so close, but I didn't question it.

Nor did I ask why he brushed the hair off my face.

I just moaned while taking a moment to enjoy his touch.

"Don't do that," he grunted, sounding as though he were in pain.

At that point, I realized his breathing was coming out in short pants. "Are you hurt?" I asked, feeling confused over the scenario that played out before me.

"No, I'm fine." He was either lying or hiding something.

His mouth was close to mine, and I felt his girth against the inside of my thigh. And suddenly, I couldn't even remember what movie we were watching. All I could focus on was his closeness... and his body heat that warmed me from the inside out. Then I remembered how good last Sunday had been. I would've done anything in that moment, because I'd fallen deeply under his spell.

Before I could deliberate anything more, I did something I normally wouldn't. I grabbed either side of his face and pulled him to me. Once his mouth met mine, I felt complete. That feeling I'd been craving came back full force. A sense of calm wrapped around me like a comforting blanket. My lips grew tingly, and I opened them to trace his with my tongue. It was bold, but my move only brought additional pleasure. His hot lips moved in tandem with mine, and I began to suck his tongue. Sucking wasn't my thing, but this was the second time I got caught up in the moment and lost myself, doing things I normally didn't.

He toyed with the waistband on my skirt, and I stiffened.

"Do you want to stop?"

"Oh, God. No," I stated between pants. "Don't stop."

His mouth met mine again, and I lost all thought.

His hands caressed the length of my body, and it made me arch deeply into him. My skirt gathered around my waist from the twisting, but I didn't even care. He lined up his massive bulge with my entrance and began rolling his hips against me through my thin panties. I cried out and began to meet each thrust, which hit the spot it was supposed to.

"Fuck! I want to bend you over my knee and spank you. You're so bad, you're good. I can imagine my cock moving in and out of your wet pussy." He put his hand behind my head so that it didn't hit the armrest. "Are you wet?"

"So wet…" I couldn't believe I answered him, or the hedonistic tone that came from me. My cheeks flushed with heat, although it wasn't from embarrassment. It was because my orgasm was reaching the point of no return, and I didn't know if that was okay. I didn't even know what we were doing, but I never wanted him to stop.

"Would you squeeze me when I'm inside you? I bet you would, because you're a bad girl who does amazing things. My cock would stretch that tight pussy. Wouldn't it?"

I reached the top of pleasure mountain, and his dirty talk propelled me over into pulsating bliss. He brought his face close to mine and kissed the tip of my nose.

"Are you okay?" he asked me softly.

I hummed, and then I heard his reverberating chuckle. I must've closed my eyes, because I couldn't see his face, and my body was so warm I could no longer feel him against me.

Then my phone dinged. And the warmth that had coursed through me turned to fuzzy tingles. The kind that consumed you during that in-between state of sleep and wake.

At that point, I became fully aware that I had fallen asleep on the couch, but I was so mortified, I refused to open my eyes. There was no telling if I had voiced any part of my dream. Something told me I had, because as I ran through the entire situation in my head, his asking me if I was okay had definitely happened in real life.

I wonder if he'd believe I had died in my sleep.

Then his phone began to ring, which had given me the break I needed. Saved by the bell!

"I'll be right back." Without waiting for a response, he was off the couch, and the soft padding if his footsteps indicated he was on his way out of the room.

His place had an open concept, so his voice carried. From my spot on the couch—where I hadn't moved from, nor had I opened my eyes—I could hear his side of the conversation. And he didn't sound happy.

"Linds, I don't know."

Lindsey. As in his ex, Lindsey?

My eyes flew open, and I frantically searched for an escape route. I seemed to always end up in sticky situations, mostly with Nellie, but this one took the proverbial cake. Luckily, my shoes were on the floor next to the couch, so I quickly slipped them on and prepared myself for my exit. After a quick glance behind me to make sure I hadn't caught Corbin's attention, I snatched my purse and jacket off the back of the sofa and hurried to the front door as quietly as I could.

I felt like a thief in the night.

Although, before I could make my escape, I heard Corbin say, "I'm glad you enjoyed the flowers," and it made me freeze in place, mere feet from freedom.

He sent her flowers?

Before or after I'd had my hand down his pants last weekend?

The answer didn't matter. I had to get out of there.

I yanked open the door, not caring how much noise it made.

"Bridge, wait!" Corbin shouted behind me. Followed by, "No, I'm not alone."

That did it.

I was done.

I ran to the elevator and punched the down arrow harder than necessary; I was fairly certain I had jammed my thumb, but that was the least of my worries. My foot tapped anxiously in the hallway as I waited for the cart to arrive and take me away.

"Bridge. Let me explain." I heard the words, but I couldn't see him. I looked for the stairwell and thought I would go down twenty-two flights of stairs to avoid him if I had to. But luckily, that wasn't necessary. The elevator chose that moment to show up and save me from the sheer mortification of facing Corbin Fields.

CHAPTER 9

CORBIN

I PACED the living room floor with my head in my hands. What the fuck had happened? This evening had been effortless, better than I could've imagined. Then everything went to shit when Lindsey called. I hadn't heard from her in weeks, and then, of all the nights she could've called, it just had to be this one.

I needed a plan.

That's when I spotted it.

Brooke's cell phone, lying in plain sight on the ottoman.

She'd forgotten it during her hasty exit.

I'd barely taken a step after grabbing her cell when my doorbell rang, and a smile instantly stretched across my face. She may have run off like a bat out of hell, but now that I had something she needed, she'd have to talk to me.

Brooke didn't wait for me to open the door all the way before barging past me, arms crossed, face painted in a crimson shade of anger. Normally, that color on her cheeks meant she'd done something cute and embarrassed herself, which automatically made me smile, but not this time. This time, it caused me to chase after her while my stomach did somersaults.

"Where's my phone?" Her voice wavered as she frantically

searched the couch where she'd been asleep just a few minutes ago.

"This one?" I held it up, but then quickly hid it behind my back when she lunged for it like an animal attacking prey.

She grabbed at my arms and followed me in complete circles as I turned to keep her from getting it. It reminded me of when we were kids and I'd taunt her and my sister by taking something they were playing with. If not for the vicious way she growled at me, I would've found it comical. Actually, the growling only made it funnier. The tears lining her eyes, however, did not.

"Bridge... Brooke..." I assumed her anger had stolen her ability to hear me, so I wrapped my arms around her, pulled her to my chest, and whispered into her ear, "Brooklyn...hear me out."

With my hands behind her, she couldn't reach her phone, and with her face pressed into my shirt, she couldn't speak—well, she could, but it would've been muffled and unintelligible. At least she seemed to recognize this, because she immediately calmed, giving up her fight.

For now.

I wasn't stupid enough to think she wouldn't try again once I eased up.

"I'll give it back. I promise." I relaxed my arms just enough to pull away and look at her, though I refused to release my hold on her. Not until I knew for certain that she wouldn't go all Billy-Badass on me again. "The only thing I ask is that you listen to me. Give me two minutes. Can you do that, please?"

She stood before me, a storm brewing in her pistachio-colored eyes. I had a feeling there was little I could do to hold it at bay. So I needed to explain things quickly before the huffing and puffing returned.

"Fine." She may have given in, given me what I wanted, but the defeat that hung heavy in that one word offered me no sense of victory.

I stuck her cell in my back pocket and motioned toward the living room. "Come sit on the couch."

Brooke's defenses came back so fast it practically gave me whiplash. The walls she erected around her in that split second filled me with panic, fearful that, this time, they wouldn't be as easily penetrable. That was only reinforced by her crossed arms and clipped tone when she said, "Corbin, spit it out. I said I'd listen, not sit and converse."

"Okay." I began to outline my speech in my head and recite it at the same time. At work, I could do this on the fly, but this was entirely different. She wasn't someone I was trying to pitch a campaign to, nor was I attempting to sell her on an idea that would benefit me. Although, I hoped more than anything that this conversation would end in my favor. "It all started this morning. I had a shit week and wasn't very nice to my assistant. I decided to get her flowers to apologize for making her put up with my mood."

"What does this have to do with me?"

"Well, when I ordered the flowers, I must've inadvertently sent some to Lindsey as well. I used the same florist I've always used, so the only thing I can come up with is that all of Lindsey's information was on some auto list. I had no intention of sending her flowers. I swear."

The corners of her lips twitched, a smile forming past her fight against it. Though, for the life of me, I couldn't figure out what she found so funny. I wanted to ask, but all I could do was stare and wait for her to clue me in on the joke I clearly wasn't privy to.

Finally, she shook her head and dropped her arms, her disposition much lighter now. "Again, Corbin, what does that have to do with me? Do you think I'm upset about you ordering your girlfriend flowers?"

"*Ex*-girlfriend," I corrected.

She waved me off and rolled her eyes in amusement. "Semantics. I don't care who you buy what for, so I'm not sure why you felt the need to explain all that. Or why you're acting like it's a big deal."

"Oh, uh…" I scratched my head, wondering if I'd somehow made a big deal out of nothing. But then I remembered how fast she'd fled after Lindsey called, and how angry she seemed when she stormed back in. There was no way I had imagined that. "If you weren't upset about the flowers, then why did you leave?"

Heat seeped back into her cheeks, yet this time, it was the hue of shy embarrassment—my favorite kind. "Because I felt stupid."

"Why? What happened to make you feel that way?"

Brooke turned her attention to the couch and held out her hand, rolling her wrist while gesturing to the spot she had occupied during the movie. And suddenly, I understood. Until now, I hadn't considered it a possibility, mainly because she'd been asleep, and the chances of her recognizing what she'd said while unconscious were slim to none.

I'd had no intention of bringing it up, but now that she had, the subject was on the table and ready to be discussed. "Are you referring to drooling on my couch? If so, it's fine, Bridge. That's the beauty of leather—wipes right off." I stepped closer and lowered my voice. "Or are you referring to what you said while you were asleep?"

Her eyes widened, and her gasp caught loudly in her throat.

"If so," I continued in the same hushed tone, "you have nothing to worry about."

She groaned and bowed her head, hiding her face behind her hands. "Oh God," was the other thing that came from her, and she must've repeated it a dozen times. When she finally dropped her arms, she refused to look at me, so I placed a curled finger beneath her chin and lifted her gaze to meet my eyes.

"I'm serious, Bridge…you have nothing to be embarrassed about."

"That's easy for *you* to say. You're not the one who unintentionally verbalized your wet dream."

Hearing her call it a *wet dream* made my dick twitch. I was so turned on I had to take a moment to compose myself, knowing if I tried to speak too soon, I'd sound more like a phone-sex operator with his hand in his pants than a friend.

I wasn't even sure if men *could* be a phone-sex operator, but that wasn't the point.

"Bridge…" I cleared my throat and tried again. "It's really not a big deal. You didn't say much, so really, you have nothing to worry about."

"Well, I must've said enough for you to know about it."

It was obvious she was prodding for information, wondering what all she'd uttered while asleep. I hadn't planned to give details, but if that's what she wanted, then who was I to deny her? "Honestly, all you said was 'don't stop.' You moaned a couple of times and shifted a little on the couch. That's it."

Her head fell back as a barking laugh escaped her lips. "In my opinion, that's enough to crawl into a hole and die. I'd ask if we could just pretend it never happened, but considering this would be the second thing in less than a week that I'd rather forget, I'd saw my luck may be running out."

"Nah. Plus, I'm sure there will come a time when I'll need to even the score and ask you to forget something I did or said. So you're all good." I reached into my pocket and pulled out her phone. "Anyway, here's this. I'm sorry I held it hostage, but I didn't like the way you bolted earlier, and I was desperate to make things right."

"Thanks," she said with a smile before dropping her cell into her purse. "And I'm sorry for running out of here like that. Believe it or not, I really enjoyed myself tonight. I can't tell you how nice it is to finally have someone who loves Marvel movies as much as I do."

I wasn't sure if I should push things and ask, but I decided to throw my balls against the wall and do it anyway. "Well, you did fall asleep during the second one. Do you want to finish it?"

"I really appreciate the offer, Corbin, but I think I should probably get home. I already fell asleep on your couch once, don't want to risk that happening again. Not to mention, I don't even remember what part I fell asleep. Let's just save it for next time, and we'll start it back from the beginning. Sound good?"

I nodded and offered her a hug. "What are your plans for the weekend?" I asked as I walked her to the door.

"Tomorrow is set aside to do nothing but grade papers—my teacher delegated that fun job to me. And on Sunday, I have a campus beautification day at school. I'm not particularly fond of gardening, so that will be tough. Hopefully, I'll get assigned a paint brush."

"That doesn't sound like fun."

A small smile curled her lips. "It's not bad. I was going to see if the girls wanted to join me, but with how hectic my week was— seriously, not having a phone is like missing an arm...or two—I never got around to asking them. Which is fine; I'm sure there will be other adults there I can hang out with."

"I'll come with you." I hadn't even completely thought it through before offering. I didn't particularly enjoy manual labor, but for some reason, painting or gardening sounded fun when Bridge mentioned it. Even though her statement had been peppered with complaints.

"You?" She eyed me up and down.

"Yeah...*me*. What time should I pick you up?"

"Um." Confusion looked sexy on her. "Well, I guess you can pick me up at eight; the shindig starts at eight-thirty." She turned to leave but stopped and poked my chest with her pointer finger. "It'll more than likely get messy, so make sure you dress for the occasion. And *be on time*. Please."

"I'm always on time," I teased, enjoying the grin that rounded her cheeks.

"Sounds good. See you Sunday!" she called out as she stepped into the hall.

I grabbed my keys from the hook next to the door and followed behind her. After locking up, I turned to find her standing with her fists perched on her hips, eyeing me with curiosity. "What? Did you seriously expect me to let you walk back to your car alone? At this time of night?"

"Corbin…it's less than two blocks away."

Brooklyn was a fool if she thought she could convince me to let her walk by herself. "Exactly, so stop acting like I'm going way out of my way by going with you. Come on," I said, taking her hand—and then holding it so it at least looked like I'd taken it on purpose, rather than by complete accident.

"Who's going to walk you home?"

"*Pfft.*" I pressed the down button for the elevator while giving her the side-eye. "Nobody's stupid enough to mess with me. This physique screams *I'll kick your ass.*"

She quirked a brow, pointing to my shirt. "In those clothes? *Puh*-lease. If anything, you look like an easy target." The elevator doors opened, and she released my hand to step inside. Giggling to herself, she added, "And let's be real, Corbin…if anything will be screaming, it'll be you—when *you* get *your* ass kicked."

"Go ahead, make your jokes. But you forget I've studied the art of karate."

"Yeah, you did. When you were, like, ten. And from what I remember, you made it to…what was it? The yellow belt?"

It was hard as hell to keep a straight face while listening to her soft waves of laughter roll past those curled, kissable lips. "Second degree yellow. It's basically a black belt."

"Don't worry, Bruce Lee. I'll drive you back. We wouldn't want to take the risk of you going to jail for manslaughter after karate chopping someone for looking at you the wrong way.

This should be fun.

BRIDGE HAD TEXTED me her address, and when I pulled up to the curb, I let out a low whistle—it wasn't much to look at. Located in one of the seediest parts of town, the neighborhood's homes were almost all in disrepair. As I sat idled in front of her house—afraid to put my car in park—I couldn't help but notice that one of the shutters only hung on by the bottom corner, and the weeds were so overgrown they reached the bottom of the first-floor windowsill.

Before I double check to make sure Google Maps hadn't sent me to the wrong place like it had a tendency of doing, I saw Bridge bouncing down the front path toward me. She was either running from a murderer, or she was part of the rare breed of people who woke up cheerful.

"Morning!" She fell into the passenger seat, and her chirpy tone did *not* go unnoticed. She handed me a travel mug of coffee and a blueberry muffin wrapped in a napkin. "Sustenance."

"Wow, I didn't expect to get breakfast out of the deal." The muffin looked moist, like it had just come from the oven, but considering the time, I doubted that was true. "Did you warm them up?"

"No, please…don't insult me. I got up early and baked them this morning. I live with an elderly woman who has a hard time looking after herself. You can probably tell by the outside that she struggles to get around." Brooke pointed to the house we continued to sit in front of.

"Yeah. I have to admit it looks a little beat; I'm not going to lie."

"That's what happens when you age and can't keep up with things."

I shifted the car into drive and slowly pulled away from the curb. "How'd you end up living here? Do you know her or something?"

"Well, I know her now, but no, she found me online while looking for a roommate. She offered me free room and board if I cleaned and cooked her meals. And I couldn't exactly turn that down; it's the perfect way to afford my latest venture—student teaching. I don't get paid while completing this portion of the program, which makes it hard because it's impossible to hold down another full-time job while simultaneously doing all the coursework. So, instead of taking out an additional loan to cover living expenses, I opted to live here and do odd jobs around the community, like run errands, babysitting, and housecleaning to cover what I need."

I never thought of myself as spoiled, but stories like hers made me feel overindulged. It's not that I overspent. I owned a nice car, a beautiful condo, but nothing over the top. Granted, my family home was a bit extravagant, but that didn't have anything to do with me or how I lived. I worked hard for what I had and didn't depend or use family money whatsoever. Seeing where Brooklyn lived definitely gave me a lot to be appreciative of.

"Are you okay?" Bridge asked before taking a small sip of her coffee.

"Yeah, I'm fine. Why?"

"You just got really quiet. Did I upset you?" Her brow furrowed in worry.

"Oh, not at all. You just gave me a healthy dose of reality, is all." I let out a long sigh before continuing. "Sometimes I forget that situations like these exist—that people struggle, and some don't have the means to fix what's broken. It's not that I take things for granted. I'm not explaining this accurately."

"You are. Don't worry. I get it. It's one of the things Nellie and I have struggled to see eye-to-eye on. I'd say she's more spoiled than you are, but that's not how I'd describe her at all. Your parents did a good job. They exposed you to the real world, and you have many experiences to draw from. But we're both from different worlds, Corbin. And no matter what you were shown, you didn't live it. Living it makes all the difference."

"Yeah, you're right. I guess I'll never be able to change it."

"You can't change the past, but you can change who you are now. Take today, for instance. You don't volunteer for things. It's obvious you're a bit outside of your comfort zone." She dramatically eyed my outfit. "And the fact that you're squirming in your seat during this discussion speaks volumes." Bridge laughed out loud, and I hated to admit it, but she was right.

"Okay. You got me. But do I at least get points for showing up today? And might I add, at the butt crack of dawn on a Sunday, no less?"

"Oh, you get points, buddy. More than you know." She offered me the biggest smile, and my heart swelled. I wished there was a pause button on life for moments like this, when I wanted nothing more than to live it in forever.

When we arrived at her school, Bridge jumped out of the car, not at all waiting for me. For a moment, I wondered if it embarrassed her to been seen with someone like me. There were no instructions or words of preparation. She simply hopped out of the car and ran.

I placed my empty coffee cup in the middle console before stepping out, taking my time as if to say her sudden absence didn't bother me—it did.

"Miss Brooklyn!" Several students ran across the lawn toward Bridge. Meanwhile, I stood about five yards behind her and halfway wondered if I should duck and cover because they weren't slowing down as they got closer.

When they threw their arms around Bridge, she automatically lowered herself to their level in order to return the hugs. If I didn't know her, I would've assumed she had kids of her own.

"Hi, Garrison," she practically cooed and pinched his side. "How's your tooth?" As soon as she finished the question, he opened his mouth and proudly showed her an empty spot. "Did the tooth fairy come last night?"

He shook his head animatedly.

"Oh, she'll come tonight. I'm sure of it. Is your mom here?"

"She's over by the purple paint." Garrison turned and pointed behind him.

"We get to paint our grade level purple!" the little girl who'd latched herself to Bridge's right hand exclaimed.

"That's exciting, Polly. I know that's your favorite color. Do you want to help me get checked in?"

She nodded eagerly, and I followed the two skipping girls in front of me to what I smartly guessed was the greeting or assignment station. That, and the big "check in here" sign helped.

"Hey, Brooke." The lady behind the table greeted her and then threw me a smile. "Do you have a preference of where you want to be today?"

"*Please* pick our group. I'm *begging* you!" Polly jumped up and down while tugging on Bridge's arm.

I had a hard time containing my smile. The little girl's excitement was contagious. I remembered being young and finding the little things in life thrilling.

Brooke turned to me and asked, "Do you care what we do?"

Remembering what she had said the other night about not being fond of gardening, I took this as my cue to say, "Anything other than planting flowers in the sun."

Her smile let me know she'd recognized my motive.

While Bridge finished checking in with the women, I took inventory of our surroundings. My parents had sent Nellie and me through public education, but we'd lived in a very affluent neighborhood. The schools were equipped with the latest furnishings and technology. Our secondary campuses were so expansive they were often compared to elite colleges. I had never been associated with the likes of this one. These buildings seemed like they were held together with duct tape and super glue. Peeling paint adorned the outside walls, the grass was overgrown, and the planter boxes currently housed weeds.

In my opinion, this place should've been condemned a long time ago.

Hordes of people gathered around to obtain their job assignments. Excited chatter occupied the courtyard, and everyone seemed to know the direction they were headed and what task they'd been given. Things appeared to be very organized, and I knew firsthand from my job at AdCorp that this held importance when coordinating a project of this magnitude.

"Okay. It seems that we've been unanimously recruited to the purple area." Brooklyn handed me a brush and roller, keeping a set for herself. "I just need to speak to Garrison's mom for a sec, and then we'll get started."

I nodded and followed her to our designated station. Signs adorned each wall, indicating which paint was supposed to be used where. This hallway belonged to the second grade; it seemed that a different color was selected for each grade level. They went in rainbow order. I couldn't imagine that palette combination working, but I guess we'd have to wait and see. Bridge approached a woman, whom I assumed was Garrison's mom, and spoke with her for a minute. I hadn't meant to pry, but when I saw Bridge take some money out of her front jeans pocket and hand it to her, I couldn't look away. The woman hugged her and then wiped her eyes. I couldn't be sure from where I was standing, but it appeared the woman was crying.

Everything about today was new territory for me.

"What was that all about?" I asked Bridge once she returned.

"Garrison said the tooth fairy hadn't visited him yet, which means his mom probably didn't have the money. She's a sweet lady, but she recently lost her job and has been struggling to get by. I gave her a couple bucks to help. It wasn't much, but hopefully, it'll keep Garrison's faith in fairy tales. He's been drawing pictures of quarters under his pillow for days. I wish I could do more, but I don't want her to feel like a charity case. I remember that feeling, and it's not a good one."

Damn anyone who'd ever made her feel that way.

I found it odd that she believed she hadn't done much. She'd accomplished more in the short time since we'd reconnected than most people achieved in their entire lives. I don't think Bridge had any idea how special she was. But I did. For the first time, I truly saw her for the remarkable person she'd become.

When I had left for college, Brooklyn and Nellie were only fourteen. There was no telling then just how either of them would turn out, but I had to admit, I never expected Bridge to be *this* person. I was proud of her, yet I didn't have a clue how to express that without belittling her. So instead, I decided to keep that to myself, choosing to show her rather than tell her.

Our group began the process by laying out the tarp. Then the adults taped off all the trim so we didn't paint anything purple we weren't supposed to. Bridge was a kid magnet, so she was constantly surrounded by a circle of hovering midgets. But I didn't mind. I found myself transfixed by their conversations. They would shuffle between somewhat-deep conversations to some of the silliest things I'd ever heard.

She would periodically check in with me by touching my arm or cracking a joke to make me laugh, all while managing the kids and parents who stopped by our station to visit. She handled it like a pro and never missed a beat.

I was amazed at how a little purple paint could teach such significant life lessons.

CHAPTER 10

BROOKE

BY THE TIME we had the hallways painted, and the other groups had finished outside, I took a moment to admire all the hard work that had been put into fixing up the school. It was obvious the kids were proud of themselves, proven by the way Johnny smiled at me with violet streaks on his face.

Attempting to wipe the color from his cheek—and failing to remove any of it—I laughed and shook my head. "I think you got more on your face than you did on the wall. How did you manage that?"

"Because the guy above me kept drippin' it on me!"

Corbin glanced over his shoulder, his wide eyes making him look like a kid who'd been caught with his hand in the cookie jar. When he faced me again, I couldn't contain the fit of giggles that shook my shoulders—he was equally covered in the lilac hue.

I laughed so hard my sides ached. Since Corbin was so much taller than everyone else here, he had taken the higher areas, which was good, but poor Johnny had to work below him.

"I understand how Johnny became a casualty, but how did *you* get covered in it? There was no one above you." The muscles in my cheeks burned from the unrelenting smile, no thanks to Corbin's guilty expression.

"I have no clue." He shrugged, which made me giggle harder.

It was a perfect picture—pristine Corbin covered in *purple* paint. I'd warned him against wearing nice clothes, considering I'd bet his wardrobe cost more than I made in a month, but he had assured me multiple times that he'd be all right. And despite how many times I'd suggested it, he hadn't worn grubbies. Maybe he considered his outfit paint worthy? Either that, or this was his first experience doing manual labor. My money was on that theory.

On our way to the parking lot, I spotted a little girl named Carly diverting Corbin's attention. It moved me because he had knelt down so he was eye-level with her. It didn't matter that he'd seen me do that exact thing earlier. It meant something because he'd noticed. And he'd applied it because he cared.

The more time I spent with him, the more things I recognized.

And the harder it would be to keep from catching feelings.

"That's my favorite part. You did a great job." And if he kept talking to my students like that, I'd be head over heels before we drove away.

I followed his line of sight to a wall near the entrance, where Carly pointed her tiny finger. All the trellises were covered in a different color and rehung with care, now adorned with growing jasmine and honey suckle. It brought tears to my eyes to see how hard every single person had worked, especially the children. I knew they'd just created a lifelong memory, because I would never forget this experience. Ever.

The thought of spending every day here with these sweet children made my heart swell.

I knew the probability of staying in this school as a first-year teacher was strong. Since it was located in a less-than desirable part of town, many permanent teachers would never accept a position here, let alone apply for one. Or if new teachers did, it would only be to get their foot in the door, and they'd immediately transfer after their tenure.

"I'm blown away." Corbin's voice startled me out of my thoughts. It was only then that I realized Carly had run off, and it was just the two of us. As we made our way down the sidewalk to the parking lot, he pointed to a small strip of lawn surrounded by a white picket fence to the side of the building. "What did they do over there?"

"Some of the older kids came up with a great idea to plant a vegetable garden in hopes that it could eventually bring fresh food to our lunch tables."

"I didn't know you could do that. I thought all the food had to come from some approved distributor. One of the women in the office does nothing but complain about the strict rules her kids' school has for bringing snacks to class."

"That's true—for the most part. But there was a grant program available, and our school had been picked. The bad part is we still have to wait for the seeds to sprout before the next phase begins. I'm just excited for the day when all that hard work pays off, so the students will have a more nutritional lunch while they're here. It's true what they say…it's harder to eat healthy on a tight budget."

"Who takes care of it? I can't imagine a bunch of five-year-olds know how to care for a vegetable garden? Although, I'm sure it would end up teaching them about responsibilities."

It was a good thing he walked a step ahead of me, otherwise he might've mistaken my quiet laughter as making fun of him. "A group of parents—who have green thumbs—formed a garden club. The school added it this year as an extra-curricular activity for the fifth graders. They've been working on it for weeks and were finally able to put the finishing touches on it today."

"I'm impressed," he said as he opened the car door for me to get in.

I waited until he got situated behind the steering wheel before asking, "Did you see our pumpkin patch?" knowing that would only impress him more.

He whipped his head to the side to stare at me with wide eyes, his hand frozen mid-air near the ignition button. His shocked expression was priceless. He acted like I'd just told him we had built a spaceship for a field trip to the moon.

"It's in the back behind the soccer field. Years ago, the school had used bungalows, kind of like really small mobile homes, for their classrooms. But when the area got bigger, they had to do something to house the growing population, so that's when they got the building. Apparently, the sheds were then moved to the back field since it was unutilized property, but they've been gone for ages. Since then, it's just been an empty lot waiting for someone to come in and make something of it."

"And out of everything, you guys decided on a pumpkin patch? Is this a school or camp?" The awe in his voice assured me that he didn't disapprove of the idea, but rather, he was impressed and maybe slightly jealous of the students here.

"Well, it's not like we have a bunch of sports in elementary school, so we had no need for a baseball or football field of that size. When the idea to utilize some of the space was brought to the table, one of the other teachers mentioned how we could benefit from a pumpkin patch. This way, the school can make some extra money in the fall by opening it up on the weekends as a fundraiser," I explained.

Corbin cast his gaze out the window behind me at the building adorned with bright-white trim, the neatly trimmed lawn with sod added in those hard to grow places, and planters filled with flowers of all colors. "I'm completely amazed at what all you guys have done to this place. Looking at it now, no one would ever believe the stories you've told me about struggles these kids face. You should be proud of yourself for giving them such a wonderful start to life."

Not being one who handled compliments well, I skirted past his praise, offered a small smile, and said, "Next weekend some of the parents are meeting to paint the blacktop. We've never had hopscotch or dodgeball squares. The kids won't know what to play first at recess."

"It's amazing. Truly. I don't think I ever expected this much of a renovation." Corbin started the car, but he hesitated before shifting out of park. "Should we grab a bite to eat?"

"Don't you have dinner with your parents tonight?" I hadn't had a chance to catch up with Nellie since our regular girls night out on Monday, so I had no idea what their family's plans were, but tonight was their regular Sunday meal.

"No. My parents are out of town this week. Are you fishing for another invitation?"

"Definitely, not." I playfully shoved his arm, hoping he hadn't seen the grin that fought to curl my lips.

"So? Dinner?"

My mind drifted through the events of the day. We'd gotten to the school fairly early, and it was now mid-afternoon, so no wonder we were half-starved. But while grabbing a bite with Corbin sounded like the perfect way to end our day, I wasn't sure if it was such a good idea. Growing up, a few of Nellie's girlfriends had intense crushes on her brother. They'd arrange sleepovers just to be around him—gangly teenager or not, he was older than us, which automatically made him cool and hot. But I had never been like that. I'd go to their house to see Nellie, not Corbin. Maybe that's why Nellie and I had become such fast friends, because I never cared about her brother.

Until now…

"Where do you have in mind?" As if his choice of restaurant was the determining factor.

"Anywhere with a burger and basket of fries. How does that sound?"

My stomach chose that moment to growl, which pretty much answered for me.

"Awesome. I know the perfect place," he said as he backed out of the parking space.

"DO you mind grabbing a table while I use the ladies' room to wash up?" I asked while he held open the door for me to enter the restaurant.

"Oh, I just assumed we'd eat like this. Thought it was our new tradition after the last time." Corbin made himself laugh at my expense by reminding me of how I'd met him Friday night with green paint smeared on my outfit. "Yeah, no problem. When you come back, I'll take a turn."

Corbin went ahead and placed our drink order while I was in the bathroom, so after we swapped places, I used the opportunity to text Nellie. Ever since the whole phone debacle, I'd felt disconnected from her.

Me: Hey, Nellie Mellie who's not smelly. LOL!! Hope you're doing okay. I miss you!

I opened the menu, and my mouth literally watered at the pictures on each page. With as hungry as I was, and with how delicious everything looked and sounded, there was no way I'd be able to settle on one thing with closing my eyes and just pointing.

My phone pinged and my cheeks stretched into a smile.

Nellie: I thought you died! Lol What the heck have you been up to? We have so much to catch up on. Wanna meet up tomorrow? Since we had girls' night last week, it'll be just us.

Me: Yes!!! Same place???

Nellie: Yup. I'll be there. Hang onto your bra straps and get ready for the ride. I have so much to tell you!

Me: Can't wait!

I set my phone on the table and went back to browsing the menu but was quickly interrupted when my text alert went off again. Apparently, a week with very little communication was too much for Nellie, because all the message said was: "I miss you." I'd barely gotten the screen unlocked to tell her—again—that I had missed her when another text came through. It was enough to make me realize that the first hadn't been from Nellie at all, but rather, Chase.

Chase: *I need to see you.*

I couldn't respond. My body was numb and my mind raced. I still pined for Chase, but things had changed. When he'd broken up with me, I'd gone through a lot of emotions that mirrored grief. My first response had been to fire off questions, desperate for answers. What had I done wrong? Why is this happening to me? Then I'd been in full-fledged denial. I knew he'd come back to me. He would realize his mistake and come rushing back to my open arms.

The anger that came next had taken me by surprise. I hated him. For everything he'd put me through—for the dreams he'd allowed me to dream, for the love I'd given and for the time I'd lost. Now, over the anger stage, I found myself void of all emotion concerning Chase. Part of me wanted to block his number, and part of me wanted to send an angry response. But in the end, I decided to wait before sending anything.

I needed time.

"You're deep in thought." Corbin chuckled as he took his seat across from me. "Sorry that took so long. I had to email something for work."

"No problem."

Corbin wrapped his long fingers around the cold mug filled with beer. I hadn't even noticed the waitress drop them off. It made me wonder just how deep into my thoughts I'd gone to not have noticed someone walking up to me and setting a glass in front of me.

"Part of me had wondered if you'd fallen asleep sitting up," he teased with a sheen of beer glistening on his upper lip.

"No. Although I probably could've. Today took a lot out of me."

"Is everything okay?" Empathy laced his voice, and concern etched his face.

"Yeah...why?"

"Don't do that." Deep lines creased his brow as he leaned against the edge of the table, getting as close to me as he could. "We were both on cloud nine when we got here, and now you look like you've lost your best friend. Is that what it is? Did you and Nellie get into it?"

"No." I shook my head and made myself smile, fighting to change my outward emotion. Fake it until you make it, or something like that. I needed to pull myself out of this fog. "I think the day just finally caught up with me." I took a hefty sip of my diet soda, desperately wishing it were alcohol instead.

"I don't know how you do it, Bridge. I mean, there were kids and parents up your ass all day, and you still managed to complete that project. How do you do all that at once? It seriously left my head spinning."

"I don't know." I shrugged and then let out a forced giggle. "I guess it must be quite different compared to your daily grind. Not that I paint for a living, but the kid maneuvering and juggling are definite parts of my everyday routine."

"But seriously, that experience goes beyond exhausting. You were everything to everyone. How do you do it?" His brows knitted together in question. His obvious disbelief lightened my mood a bit.

"It comes naturally, I guess, from growing up with a single mom. As you know, she worked several jobs at one time in order to keep a roof over our heads. In response, I took on more of the household chores."

The mention of my mom made my emotions rush forward, which turned my mood melancholy. And that, coupled with the unexpected text from Chase, left me feeling wrung out. I needed a change of subject to compose myself from the tirade of notions that ran through my head.

"I can't believe the work grind starts back up tomorrow. Today feels like a Monday."

"I agree. Normally, I don't mind going to work, but after last week, the thought of going to the office in the morning has me wishing for a vacation."

"You mentioned on Friday that you had a bad week, but you never elaborated. What happened that made it so awful?" Oddly enough, I was genuinely interested in what he had to say.

"We recently had to terminate one of our project managers, so I've taken up his slack. It makes for long days and endless weeks," Corbin explained. "Which, to be fair, is something I do regularly anyway, but adding more on top of my already full plate just means even longer days."

As the chatter continued, I started to zone out. It wasn't something I did often; I usually paid attention when someone spoke. But hearing him talk about his schedule for the week did nothing but remind me of how hectic mine was looking to be. I'd agreed to meet up with Nellie tomorrow—which was the *least* stressful of my plans—and then I had to drive my roommate, Gladys, to her appointments on Tuesday and Thursday. On top of that, I still had to fit in my daily household chores and schoolwork.

Anxiety clawed at my throat, and I fought to retain my composure. My chest struggled to lift with each breath as I suffocated beneath the weight of the world. It had been forever since I'd experienced an anxiety attack—it'd been shortly after my mom had passed away—and the last thing I wanted was to have one here, in front of Corbin.

It made me want to do one thing.

Run like hell back into Chase's arms.

CHAPTER 11

CORBIN

IF MONDAY MORNING was any indication of how the rest of the week would go, I might as well throw in the towel. Work had become stressful since losing Peter, but now that we'd acquired another high-profile account, things had gone from bad to worse. I didn't reach maximum capacity very often, but if something didn't give, I would definitely explode.

And at a quarter after four, I became that much closer to detonating.

As if I didn't already have enough on my plate, guess who decided to show up? My darling sister. Nellie always managed to find a way to make my bad days worse. So, her arrival immediately added tension to an already taxing situation.

"Corbie!" She squealed. And after giving me a squeeze that could be categorized as a hug, she perched herself in a chair opposite me. The desk didn't seem like a big enough barricade.

"I don't have time today, Nellie." I really didn't.

"What crawled up your butt and died? It must've been nasty!" She gathered her purse and stood to leave. Somehow, my sister knew how to make me back down, and that's exactly what her teenage attitude did.

"Nell, wait. I'm sorry. I've had an awful day, and I just don't have time for any shenanigans at the moment." I gestured to the chair and offered a half-smile. It must've pulled at her heart-strings, because she took her seat again.

"That was uncalled for. Seriously." She huffed after settling in—which was never a good sign. I hadn't wanted her to get *settled in*. I wanted her to get on with her purpose for being here so she could leave.

"Listen, I know you don't have the stressors of a job—"

"Corbin Fields. If you make me sit through another tirade of how I do nothing but skim off the top at our parents' company, I swear to God, I will gut you."

"Are you suddenly a fisherman?" I smirked because her remark was so off the wall.

"No, I'm a pissed off sister whose brother can't take a hint. I'm so done with you. I *do* work hard. You have no idea what I do. You never take the opportunity to actually sit down and have a conversation with me. You just assume I need something or want you to fix a problem. Well, how about you take a minute to ask me how I am before assuming the asshole big-brother role?" She straightened her skirt and then crossed her legs.

"Okay. How are you?" I had to fight—very hard—not to roll my eyes. Her attempt at a hissy fit deserved applause, but I knew she was full of shit. She *never* came to see me just to say hi. She *always* needed something. *Always*. Without fail.

I just had to wait for it.

"Well, I'm fine. Thanks for asking." She huffed again.

"Great. What can I do for you?" I continued signing the documents in front of me and thought for the hundredth time today that these documents should be digital. Why did we have so much paper? Such a waste.

"Well, since you ask…what did you do yesterday? Like, all day, and then for dinner."

There it was. She was here to dig. And I would happily grab a shovel to help her—then use the hole to hide her body. I would kill her if she inserted herself into my relationship with Bridge.

Not that we had a relationship; it was more of a friendship with an asterisk next to it. And that asterisk had yet to be defined. If Nellie interjected herself into it, she would fuck everything up before I had a chance to explore whatever connection Brooke and I had.

"Community service. Part of my work here at AdCorp is to involve myself in the community and see which ways I can give back to the place in which we live." I'd never know how I was able to get all that out without laughing. It was ridiculous. And regardless of what I thought of my sister, I knew she was too smart to buy it.

"That is such a crock of shit." Nope, she didn't fall for it. *Dammit*. She pointed her finger at me in an accusatory manner and said, "You did it to earn points with Brooke because you're trying to get into her pants. Don't deny it!"

I dropped my pen, stared at her with wide eyes—hoping I was a better actor than I used to be—and slapped a hand over my chest in feigned shock. "I'm appalled that you'd think I'd do such a thing."

Apparently, my acting skills hadn't improved since I was a teenager trying to get out of trouble with my parents, because she simply rolled her eyes and pursed her lips. "Why else would you volunteer at an elementary school? You hate kids. Even worse, you *loathe* manual labor. There's a reason you're behind a desk, and we both know it."

"She needed help, so I offered." It was the only thing I could come up with on the spot, and I realized there was a good chance I was digging my own grave instead of hers. "Really, Nell...you're making a much bigger deal of this than it is."

"Oh, yeah? How'd you know she needed help?"

"She told me." That seemed like a reasonable enough answer...

Until she asked the one question I hadn't bothered to contemplate. "When did she tell you she needed help? Are you two talking a lot now?"

Fuck. The hole I'd dug was now waist high, and I wasn't sure I'd be able to safely get out of it. "We met up on Friday for drinks to discuss my progress with Heather. You know this. It was your idea to get me involved, remember? So don't be upset with me for talking to your best friend behind your back."

Her lips twisted while she mulled over my response. At least there was hope that she believed that one. I wasn't sure if she knew about the glitch in Brooke's contacts, and I worried that if I divulged too much information, I'd wind up making this interrogation worse. So instead, I decided to leave it at that and see where she took it.

"Just keep your hands to yourself, Corbin."

"My intentions are honorable, Nell. I think of that girl like a sister." Now that it seemed I had gotten her on my side, I took a sip of water to combat the dryness left behind by the fear of being caught.

"Really? Hmm, well, that's rather concerning."

"What is?" I asked between sips.

"That you think it's okay to stick your tongue down your sister's throat. Kind of makes me never want to give you a hug again just in case you try to make a move on me."

Some of the water made its way up my nose and down the wrong pipe, causing me to choke and clutch my chest. I fought to regain control after the coughing fit from hell, and then immediately regretted it—dying would've made all this end so much quicker. I frantically went over my options as I struggled to breathe. Bridge would've never told Nellie what had taken place at my parents' house last week. So it was safe to say she didn't know anything. I had to remain cool and give her nothing to go on.

Nellie could read me like a book, so I needed to become indecipherable.

"Yeah, that's what I thought." She regarded me with her top lip curled in disgust. "You're so gross. The least you can do is keep your dick in your pants when it comes to my best friend."

"I don't know what you're talking about, Nell."

"Oh, sure you do. Where did you and Brooke disappear to after dinner when I went to get more ice cream?" If she knew the answer, she wouldn't have waited over a week to say something, which meant she was going off suspicion.

I still had a chance to save this.

"We went outside, don't you remember? I'm the one who told you she was in the driveway waiting for you. Where is all this coming from anyway?"

"Yeah, and I thought it was odd then that she'd sit in my car without saying bye to anyone." She lowered her brows and scooted a little closer to the desk, as if studying my expression. For the first time in my life, I wished I was vain and had a mirror in my office. "After I found more ice cream, I went looking for you guys. I went out back, thinking you might've taken a walk."

"But you already know we weren't out there."

"Do I? Because, you see, right after I called out for you guys, there was a lot of rustling in the grass. It was loud enough to catch my attention, so I stopped and listened, wondering if it was you two. And then, when I got back inside, I found you in the dining room—even though you weren't there a couple of minutes earlier—and for some reason, she was sitting in the driveway waiting to leave."

"I wasn't in the dining room when you first checked because I walked Brooke out to the car. She said she'd had too much wine and was feeling sick. So I took her outside, and she figured it would be best if she just waited for you to drive her home." Damn, maybe I was better at lying than I thought. Either that, or I only possessed that skill when I had something major to hide.

And keeping Nellie from finding out that her best friend had drunkenly come on to me was pretty big, Though, not as big as finding out I hadn't done anything to stop it from happening. Thank God there was no way for her to know just how badly I'd wanted it to keep going.

Nell squinted and pulled her lips to the side; it was her way of assessing a situation, something she'd done since she was a little kid. It was also the sign I needed to relax. If she truly didn't believe me, she would've had a completely different reaction. When she looked like this, it meant she was done arguing. At least, it meant she didn't have anything to come back with, whether she *actually* believed what was said or not.

"Okay, fine, but I still don't understand why you have to spend so much time with her. You can easily catch her up on Heather via text. Hell, even a phone call, although even that seems too close to the line for comfort."

"Nellie, you're being ridiculous." It was time I sprinkled a little truth into this to make her settle down. "I'm not sure if you know or not, but after she got her phone fixed, all of her contacts were messed up. She texted me thinking she was texting you."

She hummed and narrowed her gaze, lips pursed, eyes scrutinizing. "Seems a little strange if you ask me. It's a little too...*convenient*."

"Whatever, Nell. Believe what you want. It's the truth. Ask her yourself if you don't believe me." My patience was running out. Not only was I drained from having to come up with lies off the cuff, but then having to defend the parts that were *actually* true had damn near pushed me over the edge.

My attitude must've convinced her, because she sat back with her elbows on the armrests, her posture more deflated than a moment ago. This was the tricky part, because while, yes, I had gotten her to her listen, that didn't mean I could relax. I had a very small window of opportunity. I knew my sister better than anyone, and if she were given too long to think, she'd come up with seventy-seven rebuttals that would extinguish all the work I'd done to get us to this point. So, I didn't give her time to mentally run through any questions.

"Since it didn't take long to fill her in on the Heather front, we ended up bullshitting for a while, which is when she told me about the project at her school and how she'd meant to ask you and the other girls to go with her but never did because she didn't have a phone. So, I offered to go with her, for nothing more than to lend a hand and keep her company."

It seemed I had her attention as she intently listened to me explain.

"We had fun—*as friends*—and yes, we went to dinner afterward. But nothing happened. No goodnight kiss, no hanky-panky. My dick stayed in my pants the entire time. I took her home, and that was the end of it. You're making a mountain out of a molehill."

"And you're not leaving anything out?" Her voice, small yet laden with worry, practically cracked my chest wide open. She desperately wanted to believe me, that much was obvious. I just hoped the guilt that threatened to strangle me wasn't as easy to see.

"Have I ever lied to you, Nell?" I noticed her shoulders rise the tiniest bit, so I answered for her. "No. I never have." *At least, not until today.*

She lowered her gaze to her lap, and I knew that, even though I had deceived her, I'd successfully managed to win her trust. Hopefully, this would be the end of her suspicions. Side-stepping the truth while looking into her eyes had left me feeling like the biggest piece of shit, and I wasn't sure how many more times I'd be able to do it. But if Bridge and I had any shot, I had to put the kibosh on Nellie's interference.

I just prayed I could figure out things with Brooke before having to lie to my sister again.

"So, what's going on with Heather? I haven't heard anything else about it."

Well, shit.

Looks like my lying days weren't over quite yet.

"There's really nothing to report. It's only been a couple of weeks, so I haven't been able to do much more than lay the groundwork. It's not like I can just waltz up to her and ask her to cheat on her new boyfriend with me—especially with him standing right there." Yeah, that sounded truthful enough.

Her brows arched as annoyance painted her face. "How long do you plan to drag this out?"

"I don't know. This was *your* diabolical plan, in case you forgot. I'm simply going along with it. If you want me to throw caution to the wind and just go for it, tell me, and I'll do it. At least that way we can put an end to this charade." The thought of not having any reason to see Brooke caused my chest to tighten. I wasn't ready for that. "But keep in mind, if I do that, there's a good chance she'll shut me down, and then your friend won't ever get what she wants."

"Yes, I get that. But you haven't even gone out with Heather yet, have you? I'm not saying rush to the finish line, but come on, big bro; you have to do *something* to put the thought of you in her head. If you want to make her cheat, you must think like a cheater."

"Oh, and you know how cheaters think?"

"Don't be ridiculous." She rolled her wrist, dismissing me with a quick wave. "It's called research. Trust me, I didn't come to you for help without thoroughly looking into what it would take to succeed as such a task."

"You didn't think I could get her to stray?"

Nellie's laughter echoed off the walls of my office. "Be real with yourself, Corbin. I'm not saying you're not a good-looking guy—God knows I've lost many friends because of their stupid obsessions with you—but you've got no game. You lack swagger."

Ignoring what she'd said about losing friends over me, I focused on the subject at hand. I could worry about the other part later. "Then why ask for my help if you didn't think I could do it?"

"I never said I didn't think you could do it, just that I had to do a little research before asking you. I had to know the subject— her motives, who she is as a person, her morals and ethics—to see if it would even be possible to make her cheat on Chase with you." She held up a finger to silence my argument. "Which, you should be happy to hear, she's totally cheatable. She clearly has no morals *or* ethics, so that works in your favor."

"Wow, Nell...I'm so glad I took time out of my busy schedule for this visit. Really, we should do this more often," I deadpanned. "I seriously can't hear enough how inept I am at getting a woman...unless she's immoral and a bit of a floozy, that is."

"Don't be so melodramatic." She pulled her purse strap over her shoulder and stood. "It wasn't meant to be an insult. You're just a really good guy, who happens to have been in a relationship with the same woman for, like, a hundred years. And there's nothing wrong with that. No one expects you to be Rico Suave."

The phone on my desk buzzed, and Emily came through on the intercom, saving my ego from becoming even more battered and bruised. "Your four-thirty appointment is here."

I clicked the button and replied, "Thanks. I'll be right out." Then I turned my attention back to Nellie. "As much fun as this has been, I've got to get back to work."

"I have to meet Brooke for dinner anyway." She shrugged with a smile.

Fuck! I needed to contact Bridge before she met up with Nellie. My sister had a knack for discovering inconsistencies, no matter how subtle—I blame the *Highlights* magazines from our old pediatrician's office—and then picking them apart until she had the lies separated from the truths. That was something I couldn't risk happening with Brooke.

"Thanks for clearing things up," she said with her hand on the door handle. I hadn't even realized she'd moved away from my desk. "Although, I still don't think you need to spend so much time with Brooke. You can update her just as easily through texts."

Before Nellie could open the door, a large burly man barged in and pushed past her, saving me from having to finish that conversation. As much as I wasn't looking forward to this meeting, I'd be lying if I said I wasn't relieved he was here.

"Sir, if you'd just wait one moment..." Emily was on his heels, but I doubt a steel wall would've stopped him. He'd been after me ever since Peter had left the company, but with countless other clients who came before him, he had to wait his turn. And it didn't seem like he appreciated that too much.

This was the last of Peter's accounts, and I needed to smooth over things so he'd stay on with AdCorp. "It's all right, Em. I was just about to come get him anyway." I excused my assistant, only then noticing that Nellie no longer stood in the doorway. She must've gotten the hint and fled. Escorting him around the glass partition that separated the conference table from the rest of my office, I said, "Stan, nice to see you. Would you like something to drink?"

"Oh, uh…sure. Yeah. Water would be nice." His demeanor softened as he took a seat at the table. And after I got us both a drink, I sat across from him. This was an impatient man, but thanks to my father's parenting style, I was familiar with the likes of Stan McClure. I knew how to win them over.

Just as long as I didn't accidentally call him Stan Manure.

He didn't need to know what we all truly thought of him.

Due to Nellie monopolizing my prep time, I had to wing it, which meant the meeting was short and sweet. He was easily soothed, thank God, because I didn't have any fight left in me after my sister's impromptu visit. Most nights, I didn't leave the office until six or seven, and after throwing something together that resembled dinner, I was lucky if I sat on the couch in front of the TV by nine. Tonight, however, I didn't think I could make it that late. I was ready for the day to end.

My phone vibrated on my desk, and that's when it hit me. Brooke! I hadn't had a chance to send her a message before she met with Nellie.

The only thing I could think about was what my sister had said about losing friends.

I'd never be able to forgive myself if Brooke lost Nellie because of me.

CHAPTER 12

BROOKE

AS SOON AS I caught sight of Nellie sitting at a table in the middle of the room, I clumsily pushed my way through the crowded area at the front of the restaurant. I'd been looking forward to seeing her all day, and no amount of elbows to my ribs would wipe the smile from my face. I'd missed my bestie!

"Hey," I greeted her. "Thank God you got us a table. This place is crazy busy!"

I had expected her to jump up and wrap her arms around me like she always did after going this long without seeing each other. But that didn't happen. In fact, she didn't even bother to get out of her seat. "Yeah, I heard someone say they've got live music tonight. I guess everyone decided to get here early and grab a table. I went ahead and ordered you a glass of wine." She pointed to the glass across from her.

The hairs on the back of my neck stood on end and sent a shiver down my spine. Something was up with her, and worry started to set in. "What's wrong?" I set my purse on the empty seat between and pulled out the other chair to sit across from her, which allowed me to study her face.

"Nothing!" Her smile appeared manufactured. But she created

doubt in my mind when she went on to say, "It's just so busy in here I'm afraid if I get up, someone will take my seat."

That was plausible.

Except I knew her. And she was definitely hiding something.

We'd gone through periods where we would spend tons of time together, and then others where circumstances wouldn't allow for it. One of the times where our friendship had come second was when I was with Chase. We had discussed it, and we both agreed to never let that happen again, but we also understood that situations would arise, and life happened. It wasn't something we needed to stress over; no matter what, neither of us would allow anything to negatively affect our friendship. Even so, it still made me sad that we couldn't spend as much time together as we used to.

"If there's nothing going on, why do you look like your favorite vibrator just kicked the bucket?" At least that earned me a genuine smile.

She waved me off and shrugged. "Well, I did just have an interesting chat with my brother. So, maybe I should be the one asking you what's going on."

As far as I was concerned, there was nothing to tell. I mean, there was *something* to tell, sure. But Corbin and I had agreed to pretend it never happened, so that was a moot point. Still, I had no idea what Corbin had told her. Or rather, what Nellie had managed to pry from him. I fought the urge to pull my phone out and text Corbin so I wouldn't put my foot in my mouth.

God was on my side, because at that moment a man bumped into our table, sloshing my red wine all over my skirt. I jumped up, the wet fabric sticking to my inner thighs providing quite a jolt to my system.

"I'm so sorry!" The man turned his apologetic, wide eyes my way. It didn't take long to see that the wiggling toddler in his arms was the reason for the accidental bump.

"It's okay." My irritation immediately receded as I gave him a sympathetic pat on the arm. Considering I was surrounded by overly active children all day long, I could recognize a frazzled adult from a mile away.

"Your skirt!" Nellie exclaimed, obviously paying no mind to the cause of the incident. "You'll never get that out."

"It's not a big deal, Nellie." I didn't want the man to overhear her and feel even worse. Then again, I couldn't expect her to understand the level of humiliation he likely felt. She'd never been around kids and, as far as I knew, didn't plan to be around them anytime in the future.

Thankfully, she kept her thoughts to herself and handed me several napkins, which I used to smooth out my skirt. Although, they didn't really do much to help; they instantly shredded due to the liquid. But then it hit me—this was my opportunity to get away from the table and reach out to Corbin. I let out a dramatic sigh and said, "I'm going to go to the ladies' room and try to take care of this."

"Yeah, you should. I'll order you another drink. Some people just don't have a clue!" She was obviously more irritated than I was, but I had already dismissed it and moved on. The only thing on my mind was texting Corbin.

I quickly locked myself in one of the small stalls and opened my phone.

Me: What all did you tell Nellie? I'm at dinner with her and I'm freaking out!

Within ten seconds, bouncing bubbles appeared on the screen, and I immediately calmed. He wasn't away from his phone.

Corbin: Don't worry, she doesn't know anything. She was fishing for information, but I didn't give her any.

Me: Phew! Okay. Thanks!

I tossed my phone back into my purse and exited the stall.

After diluting the wine on my skirt and then doing my best to dry it under the hand dryer, I made my way back to the table where Nellie already had a fresh glass waiting for me.

"I got them to replace it for free," she said while handing it to me once I reclaimed my seat. "Although, it's a good thing you came back when you did, because I was about to drink it for you. What happened? Did you fall in?"

I grabbed a chip from the bowl in the center of the table and scooped up some salsa. "Nope. But I can tell you that using the dryer for anything other than hands is damn near impossible." I shoved the chip into my mouth and asked, "So, where were we?"

I was hoping she'd be so appalled by my talking with my mouth full that she wouldn't remember what was said prior to the wine-in-lap fiasco.

Unfortunately, that wasn't the case. "You. And Corbin."

"What about us?"

She followed suit by taking a chip and dipping it into the homemade salsa. "You know, all the time you've been spending together."

"Again, Nellie...what about it? You know he's been filling me in on his progress with Heather." Maybe if I forced her to divulge exactly what it was that she knew, I could avoid oversharing the truth.

Nellie sat forward with her palms flat on the table. "Come on, Brooke. Be real with me. Pretend for one minute we're not talking about my brother. Is there anything going on between you two?"

I wasn't foolish enough to fall for that. She may have thought she wanted the truth, but we both knew that if I told her, nothing would ever be the same again. She'd made no secret over the years about how much she hated it when her friends would hit on Corbin. And until now, I'd been one of the very few who hadn't crossed that line. Our friendship would be in the toilet if she knew about the inappropriate thoughts I'd been having about him. It'd be in the sewer if she found out the things I'd actually done to him in real life.

I took a sip of wine and then cleared my throat. "Why on earth would you think that? Is it because we've been hanging out? Well, let me put your mind at ease. There's absolutely nothing going on between Corbin and me. You have nothing to worry about."

She pushed away from the table, sitting in her chair like normal, and my heart rate began to return to a more regular rhythm. That was, until she said, "Then what happened at my parents' house last weekend?"

"What do you mean?"

"You and Corbin disappeared. Where did you go?"

This would've been a fantastic time to know exactly what Corbin had told her earlier. I made a mental note to ensure that we had our stories straight next time—*before* being confronted about it. Then I reminded myself that there wouldn't *be* a next time. It would've been nice if I didn't have to keep reminding myself of things I should've already known.

Hell, it would've been even better if I just didn't do anything to begin with.

Especially where Corbin was concerned.

"We went outside. You should know, that's where you found me, isn't it?"

She glanced around the crowded room, likely comparing her assumptions to what she'd been told. When her eyes met mine again, I could tell she still wasn't fully convinced, which made me sad. "Did you guys go in the back yard?"

Where was the "phone a friend" option when I needed it?

"Not that I remember." That was the best I could do.

Skepticism clouded her brown eyes. "So there's a chance you did but forgot?"

"I don't know, Nellie. I had a lot to drink that night. No, I don't think we went to the back yard, but the last thing I want to do is inadvertently lie to you because I was drunk and might not remember everything I did or said."

There were times I wished I could forget that evening, forget the things I'd done and said to Corbin while under the spell of alcohol. But if I were being honest with myself, I hoped I'd never forget a second of it, because drunk or not, it was one the hottest nights of my life, no matter how embarrassing it was.

"Rather than beat around the bush for whatever answer you're looking for, why don't you just ask the question. We've never played these kinds of games with each other, so why start now?"

"You're right." She met my stare, and I immediately recognized the agony and turmoil that swirled in her chocolate orbs. "I guess I'm just paranoid that you'll end up falling for my brother and then I'll lose you."

"What do you mean you'll lose me? Why are you even worried about that? You'll never lose me, Nellie." I reached across the table and placed my hand over hers.

"Growing up, I'd gotten used to all of my friends having crushes on Corbin. Granted, he never paid any attention, and if he did, he was more than likely annoyed by it. But that doesn't change how I felt. Then you came along, and even when he was around, or when we had to get him to help us cover something up, you never looked twice at him. You've always been *my* friend, Brooke. And as much as I'd love for you and my brother to date and get married so we can be sisters for real, I just know what happened when you were with Chase, and I don't want that to happen with Corbin."

Suddenly, it all made sense. She was worried that our friendship would come second to my relationship with her brother, and after feeling like she came in second place behind Corbin in all aspects of her life, I could see why the idea of it happening with me would bother her.

I leaned forward and made sure I had her undivided attention. "Listen to me, Nellie…you never have to worry about that, Got it? Trust me, I understand what you're saying and why you're concerned about that happening, but all you're doing is working yourself up for no reason."

"So you honestly have no desire to be with him?"

"Hell no!" God, I prayed that was convincing. "Eww, that's just gross. He's like my brother."

"Interesting…he said the same thing about you. Well, that he sees you like a sister, I mean. Not that you're like a brother to him." Her laugh helped to ease the tension between us. Unfortunately, though, I was still on edge, and I doubted that would go away anytime soon.

"Well, shouldn't that be enough to calm you down and make you stop obsessing over something that isn't even real?"

"Yeah, it should. But if I'm being honest, I don't think I'll completely relax until this whole scheme with Heather and Chase is over." She ate another chip, but unlike me, she waited until she'd swallowed it before speaking again. "I just can't stand the fact that he gets to see you more than I do."

"I get it, but that's only because my phone was broken last week. It won't be like that for the rest of the time he's trying to woo her."

"For the love of God, Brooke…never say *woo* again. Got it?"

I almost spit out a mouthful of wine when she made me laugh. "Yeah, got it."

"All right, now that we've got that taken care of, let's move on."

"Oh my God, I thought you'd never suggest that." Life was always so much simpler when we could be our goofy selves with each other. Which would come to a screeching halt if she ever found out about Corbin and me.

I'd decided right then and there that she could never find out. No matter what, I'd take it to my grave. And beyond that, it could never happen again. As much as I'd enjoyed being around him, and regardless of how well we got along or how much we had in common, things could not continue between us. Being around each other was too risky; not to mention, Nellie had made it clear just how much it bothered her that we had spent time together.

I liked Corbin. More than I should.

But I cared about Nellie more.

So, right then and there, I made the decision to only communicate with Corbin through texts, and only about the Chase situation.

"Oh, before I forget…" Nellie snapped her fingers, breaking me out of the trance my thoughts had me under. She wiped her mouth with her napkin and then pushed the bowl of chips to the side, signaling that she was done with them. "Did you have dinner with him on Friday night?"

There it was—the surprise attack. It was a classic move. Make your victim feel safe, lead him to believe that danger had passed, and then, when he least expects it, pounce. In a way, I felt betrayed that she'd pull this trick on me. Then again, I guess I deserved it. After all, I had kind of lied to her.

"Uh, yeah. I did." The only way out of it would be to tell the truth, crossing my fingers that Corbin hadn't gone rogue and lied about something he didn't have to lie about. "I got my phone back that day, and I sent you a text, asking if you wanted to meet up for drinks. Well, I had *meant* to text you, but all the names and numbers in my contacts were all switched around, Apparently, there was some glitch when I tried to sync it the first time. Anyway, I guess it mixed up yours and Corbin's numbers, so instead of texting you, I'd accidentally texted him. I had no idea until he showed up."

"That's what he told me, but it just seemed too weird to be true." In a strange twist of fate, that appeased her, as well as effectively ending all talk of Corbin.

She finished her drink and raised her hand to signal for another, obviously ready for one she could enjoy. You could only appreciate a glass of wine so much when you're on edge thinking your best friend and your brother are hooking up behind her back.

"So, tell me, how have things been with you at work?" I wasn't hungry, but that didn't stop me from grabbing another chip. If Nellie wasn't going to finish them, then I might as well.

No sense in leaving food behind that would end up being tossed once we left.

"Eh, same old bullshit story, different day. But I don't want to talk about work. How are you doing? I feel like I don't even know how you're feeling with the whole Chase thing anymore."

I hated the predicament I was in. This was the person I'd told everything to since I was twelve years old. We'd seen each other through countless breakups, the death of my mother, career changes, and triumphs. Yet I couldn't tell her something as simple as how I was handling the breakup—mainly because her brother had been the only reason I was getting over it as well as I was.

Rather than go into all of that, I decided to confide in her with something else. "Chase texted me. I don't know what to do about it, or if I should do *anything* about it. He said he misses me and that he needs to see me."

"*What*? Are you kidding me?" With her back ramrod straight, she leaned forward. "What the heck did you say? Are you actually thinking of seeing him?"

"No, I'm not kidding. I haven't responded, and I don't know." I gave her the answers in the same order as her questions. This was how our conversations were supposed to be. I could manage topics like this, even though it was hard bringing Chase's name up and talking about him this way.

"So what are you going to do?"

"I have no idea, Nellie. If this had happened a couple of weeks ago, I would've responded right away and told him where to find me. Then I would've jumped into his arms and forgiven him for everything, likely even excusing it as an accident on his part. If you would've told me last week that he'd reach out and say he misses me, I would've laughed and gotten the middle-finger emoji ready to send back to him. But now, I honestly can't say what I want to do."

"Do you miss him?"

"Kind of." And that was the sad truth of it all. "But I think I miss the idea of him most. You know? But more than anything, I just want answers. If we never get back together, that's okay, but I need closure. I need to know why he left."

She patted my hand from across the table. "You say that now, but I don't think there's anything he can say that'll make you feel better. Whether he tells you the truth or he lies to your face, it's going to hurt and leave you feeling no differently than you do right now."

"Yeah, you're right. I figured I'd leave his message unanswered for a few days, and then see how I feel midweek. If I respond, I'm going to need a lot of strength and willpower." I no longer knew if I was talking about Chase or Corbin.

"Well, I know what you can do to take your mind off of him. You should go out with us for St. Patty's Day. A bunch of us are getting together downtown to drink and watch the parade. It'll be a lot of fun, and after the month you've had, you deserve a night of green drinks and lucky clovers."

"That's not this week, is it?"

She nodded. "Well, technically it's on Sunday, but that's less than a week away."

"Damn, a week without my phone and calendar really screwed me up. I feel like I haven't truly recovered," I joked. While, yes, I'd been lost without my device, more than anything, I believe it was spending a weekend with Corbin that had messed with my head the most.

"So will you forget about it being a school night and come out with us anyway?"

She was right; I needed an evening of carefree fun with my friends. And St. Patrick's Day had always been one of my favorite holidays. So rather than come up with a hundred reasons why I shouldn't go, I nodded and said, "Yeah, I'll be there."

"Yay!" Nellie clapped, and the excitement on her face fooled me into believing that everything was right with the world again. "Oh, you should go ahead and plan to have dinner at my parents' house that night, too. They're doing the traditional meal—corned beef with potatoes and cabbage. That way, we can just ride down-town together."

That sounded like an awful idea.

Hopefully, I'd be able to find a way to finagle my way out of that before Sunday.

CHAPTER 13

CORBIN

BROOKE HAD SUCCEEDED in ruining me.

It was Thursday, and I hadn't heard a peep from her since Monday night. God only knew what nonsense my sister had filled Brooke's head with. Brooke and I had sent a few texts back and forth at the end of their evening together, so I knew she'd succeeded in calming Nellie's suspicion. But instead of rejoicing and continuing our newfound friendship, the line of communication between us had gone silent.

I checked my phone for what seemed like the millionth time today and outwardly sighed in disgust. I'd turned into a girl. It made me think about all the conversations I'd overheard between Nellie and Brooke when we were teenagers. I'd be on my way to the kitchen, and as soon as I'd hear their voices coming from the breakfast nook, I'd stop and listen, hoping for a nugget of something I could use to hold over their heads in the event I ever wanted *them* to do something for *me*. Which had turned out to be a waste of time, considering they never talked about anything worthwhile. They mostly fretted over so-and-so not calling, or whether or not *he* had noticed their new hairstyles.

At least that thought succeeded in putting a smile on my face. A small smile, but a smile all the same. It reminded me of how I'd casually stroll into the kitchen, grab an apple, and lean against the counter while they waited for me to leave so they could finish their conversation. Of course, I never left. Instead, I'd offer them a bit of unsolicited advice that only an older brother could. I'd explain to them that guys didn't care about hair, and how if a guy wasn't calling, it meant they should forget him and move on. In fact, I distinctively remembered assuring them that guys didn't sit around staring at their phones waiting for girls to call.

If this wasn't life laughing at me, I didn't know what was.

That settled it. I'd turned into a silly teenage girl! Brooke had demolished all rational thoughts from my head. I couldn't believe that I'd thought last week was bad; I should've waited. Because last week had nothing on this one.

Why won't she text me back?

Fuck!

I'd heard from Nellie a few times since her dinner with Brooke, so I knew she didn't have a clue that there was anything between Brooke and me—unless Nellie had decided to be cool with me, considering I was her brother, yet on the outs with Bridge. Although, that wasn't likely; if she were to blame anyone, it'd be me, and I highly doubted she'd keep me in her good graces instead of her best friend.

Seeking reassurance that I hadn't done or said anything wrong, I scrolled through the messages again. I refused to even admit to myself how many times it had been, but I knew it had to be a lot because I'd practically memorized them.

There were the few that we had exchanged at the start of Monday evening, when she'd reached out to ask what all Nellie knew. After telling her not to worry, she'd thanked me, and then I had sent one more, asking her to let me know when they were done so we could talk about it. I couldn't tell anymore, but from what I remembered about that night, it had taken her ages to read that one. However, she did as I'd requested and texted me after she'd gotten home.

Bridge: I don't know how I managed it, but I was able to convince her that we hadn't done anything.

That text had come through just before nine on Monday, and since I'd spent all evening with my cell in my hand, I hadn't made her wait for my reply.

Me: Well, I can't imagine that would've been hard to do considering we haven't done anything...unless I'm just forgetting something.

I'd made sure to add a winky-face emoji at the end, just in case it had gone over her head.

It hadn't, and she'd continued the conversation for a few more texts.

Bridge: Exactly. Nothing happened. LOL. But seriously tho...she has very strong feelings about the two of us hooking up.

Me: Trust me, I know. She didn't bother holding back her opinion of it when she came to see me this afternoon. Which is a good thing we haven't hooked up, huh?

Bridge: Yeah, it is. It's also a good thing we never will.

I'd been on the verge of responding when another text had come through.

Bridge: Well, it's been a long day and stressful night. I'm going to head to bed now.

Me: Ok, me too. Goodnight, Brooklyn Bridge. Sleep well.

I'd waited and waited for her to say goodnight, but when she hadn't sent another message, I'd set my phone down and tried to get some sleep. That had been the start of my sleep-deprived week. I had spent half the night tossing and turning, worried that something had happened at dinner that would interfere with the relationship we'd started to develop, and the last thing I wanted was to lose it before finding out what *it* was.

The next morning, I'd decided to test the waters.

Me: I hope you have a good day with all the little monsters. Stay clear of the green paint. And permanent markers.

It hadn't come as a surprise that she didn't respond, yet it bothered me just the same. Which was why I had decided to try again that evening when I got home.

Me: I just realized I have no life. After watching one movie with you on my couch, I now feel lonely anytime I sit down to watch TV. Thanks for ruining one of my favorite pastimes.

But still, I hadn't heard anything back. In fact, she hadn't even read them. Both messages—the one from that morning, as well as that one—had remained unread until the next day. I knew this because I had obsessively checked. I'd halfway wondered if she turned off her read receipts, although I wouldn't have a clue why, but thankfully, that theory was proven wrong just before noon. And as soon as I'd noticed that they had gone from "delivered" to "read," I decided to try again.

Me: Did your phone take another swim? If so, I'm hoping it wasn't in a toilet this time. And just in case your contacts are all messed up again, this is Corbin.

Me: Fields.

Me: You know…Nellie's brother.

I'd hoped that would've at least made her laugh, which in my mind, would've increased the odds of a response. Yet again, I'd gone the rest of the day without so much as a peep from her.

I'd decided earlier today that I would leave her alone. It wasn't even the end of the school day, but I hadn't texted at all. I mean, she hadn't bothered to answer any of them, so there was no need to continue pestering her. She was purposefully ignoring me. Yet I had no earthly idea why.

It was a good plan, and I'd stayed strong all day—despite constantly checking my phone. Then five o'clock hit, and my strength had withered away. Except now, rather than desperate and down, her silence had lit a fire inside. So I returned to her messages—for the millionth time since waking up this morning—and hacked out a text.

Me: *Hey...how's everything going with you? A lot has been happening here. And if you'd answer my fucking texts, I could update you on the fucking plan. The plan that you came up with by the way. The one where I'm stuck doing you a favor, yet you're fucking ignoring me.*

Scratch that. If she hadn't responded to nice messages, there was no way in hell she'd answer that one. So, I deleted it and started over, deciding that maybe it was time to use her plan as bait. If she didn't want to talk to me about normal shit, then I'd have to get her with the one thing she truly wanted—information about her ex.

Me: *I thought you'd want an update on the Heather situation. Finally made some progress...we met last night for dinner. Then I took her home and fucked her like I had paid for it. I'm surprised that girl can even walk straight today.*

I laughed at myself and started over...again. It needed to be believable.

*Me: I just wanted to let you know that I've made progress with Heather.
Let me know when you've got a sec to discuss it.*

My thumb hovered over the send button as I read and re-read it a dozen times. I couldn't come up with anything better, so I finally gave in and sent it as is.

Then I sat and waited.

And waited.

After a few minutes of staring at the word "delivered" beneath my message, my office phone rang, making me practically jump out of my seat. My brain was wired in all different directions and all led back to my text screen. I finally relented and shoved it in my top drawer, hoping I'd be able to concentrate on something else.

"Hi. How's my favorite brother?" Nellie's familiar voice brought a welcomed smile to my face.

"I'm your only brother."

"I know. But you're still my favorite."

"Well, thanks for that. I've had a hard week." Naturally, I couldn't tell her why my week had been so difficult. I couldn't even drop hints, because she'd fill in the blanks herself, and by morning, she'd have at least three people convinced that I was impotent or something equally as ridiculous.

"That sucks, but lucky for you, I know the perfect way to cheer you up! You know St. Patty's Day is on Sunday, right? And you know they do the parade downtown every year? Well, I think you should go with me!" The fact that she was inviting me to go somewhere with her—somewhere public—was enough to make me leery. She didn't just randomly call and invite me to things.

"Why? What's in it for you?"

"*What*?" Her exaggerated surprise did nothing to sell me on her innocence. "I can't believe you'd suggest such a thing, Corbin Fields! Can't I ask my big brother to spend one of my favorite holidays with me without having some ulterior motive?"

I laughed into the receiver; I couldn't help it. She really was funny when she wasn't trying to be. "No, you can't. Well...maybe you can, but you never have in the past. In fact, you rarely even call without a purpose that somehow only benefits you."

"That hurts. Maybe I wanted to spend some quality time with you."

"Downtown? Around a bunch of drunk people? While a loud parade is going on in front of us? That's your idea of *quality time*? Nah, I think I'll pass. But thanks for the invite." It would've been a lie if I'd said the thought of getting out and actually doing something with other people didn't appeal to me, but it would take more than that to get me to agree.

"Okay, fine...I want you to go because I'm worried about you." That certainly succeeded at tugging on my heartstrings. "I don't want you to spend the evening all alone—or worse, working. Not to mention, we'll be at Mom and Dad's for dinner, and you know they'll try to convince you to hang around for mint chocolate chip ice cream, or any other green-colored dessert. I'd be saving you from a night of Irish cream and coffee in front of the fire while Dad points out all the ways they're better than AdCorp and how you're wasting your time at the wrong company."

I couldn't argue with her about that. She did make a pretty valid point, but still, it wasn't enough to get me to agree to go. "I appreciate your concern, but I'm a big boy, Nell. If I'm ready to leave, they won't be able to make me stay. Why don't you stop wasting our time and just tell me the real reason you want me to go with you. Is it because none of your friends will entertain your childish need to drink green beer and watch trucks decorated in paper-mâché drive by?"

"Just because your friends don't like to hang out with you doesn't mean that mine are the same. They're all going to be there. We've been planning it for weeks."

"Then why is it so important that I go, too? It's not like we hang out in the same circle or anything, so why would you think I'd want to spend my evening around a bunch of gossiping girls?"

The merry-go-round she'd dragged me onto with this had started to give me a headache.

"Fine." She let out a huff. "I need a designated driver."

And there it was.

The ulterior motive she claimed not to have.

"And none of your friends can do that for you?"

"Not without driving out of their way. Plus, it would just be weird to have them come pick me up from Mom and Dad's. I figured it made the most sense for you to drive me since you'll already be there for dinner. That way, we can leave as soon as we finish eating, and my place isn't too far from yours, so it wouldn't be out of your way to take me back home."

"Nell, be serious for minute…driving you downtown and then back to your apartment *is* going out of my way. None of that is on my drive home from dinner." I opened my desk drawer to check that I hadn't accidentally left my phone on silent.

And as soon as I mentally accepted that Bridge hadn't responded, Nellie finally gave me a reason to take her up on her offer. "Please, Corbie! Brooke won't come to dinner, so she can't drive me, and I *really* don't want to drink water all night."

I had to take a moment to compose myself, not wanting to sound too eager. After all, Brooke and I had just gotten her to calm down on that front, so I didn't need to risk raising any more red flags where we were concerned.

"Oh, Brooke's going? I didn't imagine that would be her thing." We hadn't ever spoken about it, but based on the things she'd told me during the few times we'd hung out, she wasn't the type who enjoyed big crowds like that. So it genuinely came as a surprise to me that she planned to attend the parade.

"Yeah, I finally got her to agree. She's never gone in the past, always had plans with Chase instead. But now that they're not together, and some of the students at her school are in the parade, she said she'd come." The excitement in my sister's voice was contagious, which meant I had to try extra hard not to sound so eager to take her up on her offer.

"Her students will be there? Isn't it a school night?"

"Not *her* students. I think she said it's the fourth- or fifth-grade class. Or both. I can't remember. When she starts talking about kids, I zone out. But, yeah, they have a float this year, and I guess she wants to show support for all the troublemakers regardless of what class they're in." She must've been bored talking about Brooke's students, because she immediately switched topics by whining, "Please, Corbin... Come for a little bit, and if you don't have any fun, we'll leave, or I'll see if someone else can give me a ride."

"No, thanks." I feigned a yawn—for dramatic effect, of course. "I have no desire to be the only responsible adult amongst you and your band of misfits. Also, the sight of green beer makes me sick. I don't even know how you manage to stomach that stuff."

"Fine. I didn't actually think you'd say yes anyway. But hey, it was worth a shot; am I right?"

Dammit. I hadn't meant for her to give up just yet. I only needed her to try one more time so it wouldn't sound like I had agreed as soon as she mentioned that Brooke would be there. But now that it seemed like she was giving up, I'd have to take matters into my own hands.

"I guess I can give you a ride." I sighed loudly, hoping it gave the impression that I'd caved due to her little guilt trip and nothing else. "But if that green beer makes you sick in my car, you're detailing it for me. Got it?"

She squealed and said, "Got it! Thanks, Corbin!"

"Don't thank me yet. I didn't promise to stay all night." Only long enough to make Brooke talk. She might've been able to avoid responding to my texts, but she wouldn't be able to get through the entire evening without answering my questions.

And the one I needed the most was why she decided to start ignoring me out of the blue.

All I had to do was figure out how to get her away from Nellie long enough to make her talk to me.

Suddenly, for the first time in my life, I found myself looking forward to St. Patrick's Day.

WE'D BARELY MADE it out of our parents' driveway when Nellie's phone rang. At first, I groaned, not too keen on the idea of spending the entire drive listening to her mind-numbing conversations with her friends. But that quickly changed when she turned the radio all the way off, which had allowed me to hear the muffled voice through her earpiece.

"You can't back out now, Brooke! I've already told all the girls that you'll be there." Nellie's words sent a boulder spiraling to the pit of my stomach.

I glanced between my sister and the road, trying to eavesdrop as much as possible. The only reason I had even agreed to go was for the chance to see Bridge. If she changed her mind, then there was absolutely no point in being there.

"Maybe it's the battery; have you tried to jump it?"

I couldn't withhold my smile when I faintly heard Brooke say, "With what? I'd need another car to do that. But no, I don't think that's the problem. It's been running funny for a while."

I nudged Nellie, trying to gain her attention. "Does she need a ride?" I practically mouthed, wanting to remain as quiet as possible. Based on the radio silence I'd gotten from her all week, I doubted she would've allowed Nellie to pick her up if she knew I was driving.

She shrugged but then said, "Don't worry about it. I'm on my way to come get you."

"You don't have to do that," I heard Brooke say through the line. "You'd be backtracking."

"It's fine. I promise. Just be ready in"—she glanced at the time on the dash—"fifteen minutes. Twenty tops."

It wasn't until I heard Bridge concede that I realized I'd been holding my breath, waiting for her response. If she hadn't agreed,

I didn't know what I'd do. I doubted my sister would've appreciated being dropped off at a curb with directions to find her own way home. But luckily, that didn't have to happen.

For the first time in my entire life, I was thankful for Nellie's ridiculous need to sing in the car. If not for her belting out the off-key lyrics of annoying pop songs, I might've gone insane. Granted, the sound of nails on a chalkboard would've been better, but at least it served as the distraction I needed to make it to Brooke's house without blowing through a red light and winding up in an accident. Losing myself in thoughts of seeing her was enough to take my focus off the road.

Nervousness danced through my system, and the butterflies in my stomach decided to kick up their heels as I pulled along to the curb in front of Brooke's house. I'd been anticipating this for three days, yet now that it was here, now that she was this close, I couldn't remember what all I had planned to say. I'd be lucky if I made it to the end of the night without vomiting on my shoes—or worse, hers.

Nellie jumped from the car as soon as it was in park, leaving me alone with my thoughts. But those went out the window the second Brooke stepped outside. Not only because this was the first time I'd seen her in a week, but because her reaction at seeing me left my heart in my throat, cutting off my air supply, which made having any thought practically impossible.

Brooke's steps faltered when her eyes met mine, and her chest heaved as if she struggled to find oxygen outside. I could relate, because I needed to remind myself to breathe as well. How could someone have such a strong effect on another person? Never, in my entire life, had I experienced both heartache and adoration at the same time. I wanted to ease her fears, wanted to beg her to speak to me, to tell me what was wrong, but more than anything, I just wanted to hear her voice.

Something had happened Monday night, I just wasn't sure what. And now that I'd seen her with my own two eyes, watched the way she hesitated near the front door, reluctant to come to my car, I was sure that, whatever it was, I hadn't made it up in my head. There was a slight twinge of relief knowing that—even if it left many questions unanswered.

I could see that Nellie was saying something, just like I could see Brooke's eyes bouncing between her friend and where I sat parked along the curb. But I had no idea what they were talking about or what the holdup was. I could guess it had something to do with Brooke trying to change her mind about going, which wasn't something I'd allow to happen.

Suddenly, finding my strength—or my balls, whichever you wanted to call it—I unbuckled myself, opened the driver's side door, and put one foot on the pavement, just enough to pull myself out and talk to the girls over the roof of my car. "Come on, you two. I don't have all night."

There was a chance my harsh tone might've sent Brooke running in the opposite direction. However, I'd taken the risk, and it proved to pay off. Her shoulders deflated as if a weight had been removed—either that, or she'd felt defeated—as she made her way down the front lawn. If it could've been called that. More like a patchwork of weeds and dirt.

I had no idea how to handle being stuck in a car with her without the ability to discuss anything I wanted to, but at least I had Nellie to be the buffer until we got there. It also helped that Brooke had taken the backseat, which kept me from having to drive with her right next to me.

"I think not, Nell. I told you I would drive, but that doesn't mean I'm going to play chauffeur. You can talk to your friend just as easily from the front seat as you can back there," I said when Nellie tried to follow Brooke into the back.

She huffed, though she didn't argue. Meanwhile, Brooke remained quiet, neither of us offering any type of greeting other than briefly making eye contact in the rearview mirror. I worried that Nellie would take note and question it, finding it odd that we suddenly acted like we couldn't stand each other. But that would require her to remove herself from their bubble to pay attention to anything around her.

Nellie had herself turned in her seat to face Brooke, who sat behind me, before I pulled away from the curb. As much as I wanted to pay attention to their conversation, it didn't sound like anything that would interest me. The only thing I cared about was finding an opportunity at the parade to pull Brooke aside without Nellie catching on. That was enough to occupy my mind during the drive—which, with Brooke in the car, had felt a lot longer than it was.

"Corbin!" Nellie shouted in my ear, making me jump and jerk the wheel.

"*What*?" I glanced around the parking lot, to make sure no one had seen me swerve, and then elbowed my sister. "You don't need to yell. You're literally right next to me."

"Sorry." She giggled. "I'm just excited. Do you think we can find a spot near the start of the float precession? That's where we're supposed to meet up with everyone."

"Considering the entire town is here, I wouldn't imagine so. There's a good chance everyone has the same idea you do. I'll just be happy if I can find a spot without having to parallel park." I had worked hard for this car, and I'd be damned if some drunken idiot sideswiped it and drove away.

"*Corbin*!" Nellie shrieked again while stretching her arm across my body to point at something through my window.

This time, I let out several expletives underneath my breath and pushed her away. "What the hell, Nellie? Do that again, and I'll drop you off right here and go home."

"I was only trying to tell you that guy was pulling out, and it's a good parking spot." She threw her hands in the air and then mouthed the word *asshole* over her shoulder, as if I couldn't see it.

Luckily, I'd slammed on the brakes when she screamed in my face, which had saved me from passing the spot. Giving my sister the side-eye, I shifted into reverse, backed up a few feet, and then cut the wheel to pull into the space. "Look at that...and I didn't even have to go deaf to get it."

Once we were all out of the car, both girls went skipping ahead, leaving me, their designated driver, to find my way to *their* group of friends alone. If getting the chance to talk to Brooke hadn't been so important to me, I would've turned around and left their asses.

In fact, the night wasn't over. If Brooke continued to ignore me, I might change my mind.

Who the hell was I kidding? I'd waited all week for this opportunity.

I wouldn't leave until I had answers, one way or another.

CHAPTER 14

BROOKE

I COULD'VE STRANGLED my best friend for not informing me that Corbin would be here. The only reason she was still breathing was because that would've meant I'd have to explain to her why that bothered me so much. If only she knew that the one thing that would crush her, also happened to be the one thing that saved her life tonight.

Ever since dinner with Nellie almost a week ago, I'd decided to keep my distance from Corbin. At first, I didn't think it would be too difficult, especially since it wasn't like we were all that close. Sure, we'd hung out a few times, had drinks together, and I'd gone to his place to watch a movie—something Nellie could *never* find out about—but all that had taken place in a matter of three weeks.

We weren't *friends*. Close acquaintances as best.

Oh, the lies I tell myself.

But that was neither here nor there. It didn't change the fact that he was *completely* off limits. I'd always known Nellie's feelings regarding her friends and her brother; it'd been a constant complaint when we were younger, as well as in college when her roommate had asked him out. Truthfully, I should've known better; I shouldn't have needed to hear her objections last week to realize that he and I had blurred the line she'd drawn when we were kids.

Unfortunately, Corbin made it more difficult than it had to be. I knew we'd have to discuss it eventually—I mean, I'd gone from talking to him fairly regularly to completely ignoring him—but I needed time to figure out the best way to explain without making it sound like I was into him. The only problem was, he refused to wait. I'd caught him stealing glances my way all night, and if he kept this up, it wouldn't be long before Nellie noticed, and I doubted he'd want that to happen.

If so, then *he* could figure out how to explain it to her.

"Oh my God, Brooke..." Mady came barreling through the tipsy crowd, out of breath like she'd either run a marathon or had just seen a ghost. "I thought I just saw Chase and his hussy of a girlfriend."

I jumped out of the lawn chair I'd been perched in all night and immediately scanned the crowd around us, which wasn't easy considering at least half the town had chosen this same spot to gather. It was prime real estate as far as something like this was concerned. Not only were we near the start of the precession line —which had given us the perfect view of the floats as they drove by, providing no one stood in our way—but we were also in spitting distance from a beer tent.

"Don't worry, though." She patted my arm and took a seat in the folding chair next to Nellie. "It wasn't him."

Nellie regarded her with a furrowed brow and scrutinizing eyes. "Then what was the point in telling us that you thought you saw him if you already know it wasn't Chase?"

"Oh, to explain to Julie why I don't have a drink for her." Mady brought her plastic cup of green wine to her lips—they'd added color to almost every drink imaginable, and since we preferred wine over beer, it was a no-brainer.

All eyes moved to Julie, who sat on the other side of Mady, completing the small arc of our semi-circle on the side of the road.

She blinked at our ditzy friend and said, "You went to get us *both* a drink. How does thinking you saw Chase equate to you only coming back with one for you? That doesn't make any sense, Mady."

"Sure it does. I thought I saw him and figured I'd defend Brooke, so I threw the drink in his face." Somehow, Mady was the only one who didn't see anything wrong with that. While we all snickered and grinned, she continued to sip her wine, completely unfazed by her admission.

Julie sat forward and clasped her hands together, elbows propped on her bare knees. "Let me get this straight. You went to get us both drinks, and on your way back, you thought you saw Brooke's ex with his new girlfriend, so you threw *my* drink at him?"

"Yup, that's what I said."

"Guys?" Julie's pleading eyes scanned our small group, desperate for help.

Nellie, being the self-imposed leader of our tribe, stepped in. "At what point did you realize it wasn't Chase? I think that's the most pressing question at the moment."

"Oh, when he asked me what my problem was."

"And what did you do then?"

Mady narrowed her gaze on Nellie as if the answer should've been apparent. "Well, obviously I was mortified, so I told him I thought he grabbed my butt. Then I left."

This had to be a joke. Mady wasn't known for doing or saying the right things most of the time, but even she should've been able to recognize how ridiculous that was. "And he just let you walk away?"

She waved me off and casually rolled her eyes. "He was wasted, don't worry. I doubt he even remembers it. I wouldn't be surprised if he's standing over there wondering why his shirt's wet. Not to mention, the way his girlfriend—or whoever she was —glared at him, I think it's safe to say something similar might've happened to him before."

Well, if she'd gotten away with it, there was no point in pressing the issue.

Except, there was still one problem Julie wasn't ready to put it to rest quite yet. "Fine, whatever, but back to the drink situation. If it was your decision to douse him in wine, why did it have to be mine?"

"Oh, I didn't even think about that. Want me to go get you another one?"

At this point, it was clear Julie had given up. She slouched in her chair and sat with her arms crossed, staring at the floats as they creeped by, likely trying not to laugh at our friend. Mady did a lot of stupid things, but it was hard to stay mad at her.

"Speaking of Chase…" Nellie turned my way, though her eyes looked past me to the guy on my left. "It's been weeks, Corbin. When are you going to actually do something about this little plan of ours? It's kind of hard to get revenge when our accomplice won't get off his ass and do what he's supposed to."

Even though I could only see him out of my peripheral vision —because I refused to look at him, knowing how weird he'd make everything—I saw his hands go up, defensively. Then he said, "Hey, don't get pissy with me. I'm doing my part."

"Then why haven't we gotten an update?"

"I tried to tell Brooke about it last week, but she must've been busy."

Instantly, I felt both sets of eyes on me. Nothing was worse than being caught in the middle of a sibling squabble, especially when neither of them were *your* siblings. This was one of the very few times I was thankful to be an only child.

Luckily, Nellie didn't make me speak up. "Don't put that on her. You could've just as easily called and told me. Brooke had a bad week, which makes it even more important to know your progress with Heather."

It was like a horrible train wreck. I knew it was coming, but I couldn't stop it.

"Chase had texted her that he missed her." As soon as those

words escaped Nellie's lips, Corbin's eyes burned a hole in the side of my head. "But when she responded, he said he hadn't meant it, that he only said it because he was drunk. The bastard has to pay, and right now, you're the only one who can make that happen."

"Don't worry, Nell," he muttered softly, emotion heavy in his rumbly tone. "I'm handling it. But these things take time, especially since she's still his assistant, which means there are only so many opportunities to speak to her away from Chase. Her desk is literally right in front of his office. It kind of eliminates the element of surprise if he knows what I'm doing, don't you think?"

"Whatever, Corbin. So tell us...what's the latest?"

He was quiet for a moment, then he cleared his throat. "I mentioned grabbing drinks sometime, and she said that sounded like fun."

"*That's it*?" Nellie practically shouted.

"Like I've said before, Nell, I can't just go at her full-force. It's a process. I had to put the idea in her mind, and now that it's there, and now that I know where she stands, I can move forward. I plan to run into her at the end of the day sometime next week and complain about how stressed I am, then see if she'd like to take me up on my offer."

"Great. Glad to hear it."

It was obvious that Nellie didn't have a comeback for him. He'd effectively shut her up, which was good since I was tired of discussing Chase. I appreciated the latest update; although, I had to admit, I was a little bothered that I had ignored his text days ago when he'd reached out to tell me about it. But truth be told, I wasn't sure how I felt about it.

That was something I'd have to thoroughly contemplate when I had a moment to myself.

Luckily, Julie put an end to our conversation by asking Nellie to go with her to get another drink. At first, I was grateful for the interruption, knowing that it meant the topic was at least tabled for later. But once Nellie walked away, leaving me alone with Corbin, I instantly regretted the reprieve.

Granted, I wasn't *alone* with him, considering there were still a few members of our group nearby, as well as the hundreds of random people who milled about. But without Nellie being the babysitter, it damn sure felt like it was only the two of us.

"Why won't you talk to me, Bridge?" His pleading tone brought me one step closer to cracking.

And I couldn't take that chance. "Like I explained the last hundred times you've asked tonight, I will, but now's not the time."

Since arriving, he'd tried countless times to corner me, taking every available opportunity to get me alone so he could find out why I'd stopped returning his texts. As much as I wanted to give him those answers, knowing he deserved that for his own peace of mind, there was no way Nellie would leave us alone long enough to have that conversation from beginning to end. And I didn't care to discuss it in segments.

With his hand on my cheek, he turned my head to face him. "I've told you a billion times not to exaggerate." The smile on his lips kindled a fire in my soul and draped a curtain around us, separating us from the rest of the world.

That was, until he spoke again.

"Then can you at least tell me why you ignored me all week?"

I wrapped my fingers around his wrist and lowered his hand, removing his warm touch from my face. There was an instant loss, but I chalked that up to the chill in the air. "Listen, Corbin, we'll discuss all of this when there's time."

"What do you mean by *all of this*?"

It seemed I was only making things worse. "It's nothing."

"Clearly it's something. Did I do something last Sunday? Did I say something?"

I held up my hand in front of his face. "No. It's not anything you did."

"Then *what is it*, Brooklyn?" The pleading in his voice matched the despair in his eyes as he held my stare, and it reminded me of desperation I'd felt when trying to understand Chase's reasons for breaking up.

My lips parted, and my lungs filled with air while words began to come together in my head. But before they could make their way to my tongue so that I could ease his mind, Mady's loud gasp caught our attention.

"What happened?" I asked, worried by the sight of my friend's wide eyes and gaping mouth. My initial thought was that Nellie had returned and caught the moment between her brother and me, but as I frantically glanced around, I quickly learned that hadn't been the case. Then I wondered if maybe she'd overheard our conversation, causing me to hold my breath until she put me out of my misery.

"Julie's taking Nellie home."

I waited for more, but Mady didn't offer anything else, leaving me even more confused than before. "Why? Is everything okay?"

She must've gotten a call from one of them, because her phone was still in her hand, the screen lit up and unlocked. "I guess her shirt got caught on the fence and ripped it wide open. Now everyone can see her tits." She flicked her gaze to Corbin and added, "Sorry for talking about your sister's tits."

"But Corbin drove her here, so why is Julie taking her home?"

Mady shrugged, slipping her cell into her back pocket. "I'm assuming because she doesn't want her brother to see her fun bags." Again, she glanced at Corbin and said, "Sorry for calling your sister's tits *fun bags*."

Ignoring the gravelly groan from my left, I quickly tried to sort out what this meant. "Okay, I get that. But hasn't Julie been drinking?" She was, after all, the one who'd asked Nellie to go with her to get another cup of green wine.

"Oh, Julie didn't drive."

The groan turned into a husky chuckle, yet I ignored that, too. "Then how is she taking Nellie home?"

"Jack and Diane drove us, so they're going back with them." It wasn't Jack and Diane; their names were Jake and Dana, but Mady was horrible with names. They were Julie's neighbors. Great couple, and really nice people—anyone who wasn't bothered by constantly being called the names of one of the most famous *little ditties* were automatically good people in my book.

If they drove them here, then… "Are you going with them, too?"

"That's the thing…" Nothing good ever came after that when Mady uttered those words. "Nellie told me she'd give me a ride home."

"Just now?" I asked at the same time Corbin said, "Of course she did."

"We got ready together at her house, but my car is at my place. I called Nellie earlier today to see if she could give me a ride home, and she said that was fine. Otherwise, I would've had to get my car and then go back to Julie's before getting ready."

Corbin didn't let me say anything else before asking, "If Nellie was supposed to drive you home, how's she going to do that if she's leaving with your other friend? Not to mention"—he held up a finger—"why would she offer to do that if she wasn't even the one who drove here?"

"Oh, yeah…I can see now how that's a problem."

God bless her soul.

"That's fine." Corbin huffed. "I'll drop you off. Where do you live?"

Knowing Mady would probably recite her address rather than give him general details of the area, I chimed in to save him from further frustration. "She lives near you, actually." And then relief swept over me. I sighed before adding, "You might as well take me home first."

Rather than say anything, he started to fold up the chairs, which we discovered we had to take with us since they were Julie's, and she wasn't here. I had to admit, I was grateful things had worked out this way. Not only had I gotten out of having a conversation with Corbin, but having to haul half a dozen lawn chairs all the way back to his car did nothing but piss him off, which kept him from trying to make small talk along the way.

Unfortunately, that relief didn't last too long.

I should've known his lack of response regarding my suggestion of him taking me home first would've come back to bite me in the ass. At the time, I was thankful that he hadn't argued with me about it. I'd assumed that meant he agreed with the idea; either that or he was too irritated to oppose it. However, it turned out that he'd simply ignored me and decided to do what he wanted anyway—which was to drop Mady off first.

"Good, now we can talk. You don't have any more excuses," he grumbled as we pulled away from Mady's apartment complex.

Little did he know, I didn't need an excuse not to talk to him. I proved that by leaning against the door with my arms crossed, not saying a single word.

"Really? That's how you want to play this?"

"I'm not *playing* anything, Corbin. I don't appreciate being cornered and forced into having a conversation I'm not ready to have."

Coming to a stop at a red light, he turned to face me, though I refused to look at him. "Then when will you be ready? I'm in the dark here, and all I want to know is what happened. I just need to know why you suddenly stopped talking to me. The only thing I can think of is that I've done something terrible to upset you, yet you tell me I haven't. I'm literally lost here, Bridge."

It was clear I wouldn't be able to get out of this without an actual conversation, and there was no way he'd let me continue to postpone it. Not to mention, the more I angered him, the less likely things would end well in the long run. So, I sucked it up and gave him what he wanted.

"Nellie has *really* strong feelings about you getting involved with any of her friends, but especially her close ones. Which includes me. I refuse to risk losing my friendship by even talking to you."

The light turned green, which forced him to take his eyes off me.

Thank God.

"She literally said she doesn't want you talking to me? At all?"

"Well, not those exact words." And this was why I didn't want to get into this with him until I was ready. My mind was all jumbled since I hadn't had the opportunity to really sort through it all.

"Then why have you been ignoring me?"

"Corbin, can we please do this another time?" I rested the side of my head on the window, my emotions too high to mask if I tried to continue this conversation. "I've had a few drinks tonight, and I'm worried I won't be able to explain it properly."

He huffed, but just as I thought that he might have conceded, he said, "Can you at least try? Please? I don't understand."

"Ask your sister."

"I don't want to ask her. I'm asking *you*." He was angry, and if his tone hadn't given that away, the sudden braking and quick turn of his wheel did. "If you don't want to be around me anymore, that's fine. Just give me the courtesy and tell me why."

That about broke my heart. "No, Corbin. It's not that at all."

"*Then what is it?*"

I didn't do too well with men raising their voices. It wasn't like it scared me, but since I wasn't raised with a male figure in my life at all, it felt foreign. Anytime it happened, I shut down. And that's exactly what I did with Corbin. He was angry, and while I understood why, I wouldn't be able to give him answers until he calmed down.

When he stopped talking, stopped pressing me for answers, I began to relax a little, and the icy shell that had kept me in a frozen state for the last several minutes started to thaw. Until he pulled into the parking garage of his condo.

"Why are we here? I thought you were taking me home."

He shifted the car into park and flung his door open, all without saying a word.

"Corbin?" I asked as I pulled myself from the passenger seat. As much as I wanted to stay where I was and refuse to follow him upstairs, there was something unimaginably creepy about a public garage at night, no matter how nice the neighborhood was.

But still, he didn't say anything. Instead, he stomped toward the elevator, leaving me with no option but to follow behind. Which I did, begrudgingly. And the entire ride up to his floor, down the hall, and into his place, he remained stone-faced and silent.

I'd never seen him like this, and I had to admit, it was a little intimidating.

He left me next to the front door and headed into his kitchen. When he came back, he handed me glass of water. "Drink this, and then we'll talk," he said as he made his way to the couch.

It seemed I wouldn't get out of this until he got what he was after. And while I didn't want to give it to him, I realized it was either that or completely ruin everything between us. Between the two, I wanted that the least. So, I took a seat next to him on the sofa and steadily drank my water until the glass was empty.

My heart pounded, and my hands grew clammy, but I knew the longer I dragged this out, the worse it would be. I just needed to suck it up and get this over with. Shifting on the cushion until I was somewhat comfortable, I cleared my throat and prepared myself to offer him the answers he sought.

"I don't think Nellie has a problem with us *talking*, just as long as it's more of an occasional thing. And from what I gathered by what she confessed last week, I think she meant texting more than actual talking. She's just not comfortable with how close we've gotten."

Corbin leaned back and took a deep breath. When he turned to face me, it was clear that he'd calmed considerably. "I know all of that. It sounds to me like she had the same conversation with you as she had with me earlier that day. But what I don't understand is…if she doesn't have a problem with us texting, then why have you ignored me all week?"

"Because I don't trust myself with you." There, I'd said it, and there was no way to take it back now. So rather than obsess over what that meant to him, I decided to keep going until I'd gotten it all out. "If I'm not sticking my hand down your pants, then I'm dreaming about it."

Shit. I hadn't meant to get *that much* out.

"And we both know it's only a matter of time before it blows up in our faces," I continued, hoping that if I kept talking, he'd forget about my confession. "Nellie's not only my best friend; she's like a sister to me. And I don't think I could bear it if I lost her."

"You don't have to lose her, Bridge."

"If we cross that line, yes, I will."

He scooted closer, and even though I knew I should've backed away, I couldn't. He'd moved so close to me that I could feel heat radiating from his body. Time stood still, and I closed my eyes to commit his warmth to memory. One I could draw from in the coming weeks. "The only way that'll happen is if she *knows* that we've crossed a line. She doesn't have to know what goes on between us."

"I'm just not willing to take that chance."

"But what if we both want to explore whatever this is between us? Should we risk losing out on something great just because she doesn't think she's comfortable with it?" His eyes held mine, and I found it impossible to look away.

"And what if we *do* explore this, realize there's nothing, and then I lose her anyway?"

"You don't know that will happen." His warm palm moved from the cushion between us to my knee, where the heat spread up my leg and settled in the needy space between my thighs. "And if we realize that we don't really have anything between us, it's not like she has to know that we'd done anything."

Suddenly, his words smacked me in my face. As if they were just letters mashed together to create sounds until now. But now, they were words. With meanings. Put together to create something I hadn't contemplated. "Are you saying..." I shook my head and tried again. "Are you saying that you're interested in me?"

He dropped his head and let out a husky laugh. "You're just now figuring that out?"

"Well, how was I supposed to know if you've never said anything?"

"How about this..." He moved even closer, his words becoming less sound and more breath on my lips. "Does this let you know what I want?" He punctuated his question with a kiss, then traced it along my bottom lip with his tongue until I opened for him.

Before I knew it, I was on my back, his body over mine, my fingers twisted in his shirt.

This was definitely *not* how I saw this conversation going.

CHAPTER 15

CORBIN

SHE DIDN'T PUSH me away. She didn't put an end to our kiss. She gave no indication that she felt uncomfortable. And I couldn't have felt more invigorated. More determined. More...*grateful*. Because ever since that night two weeks ago in my parents' back yard, I hadn't been able to think about anything else.

Her soft lips.

Her body pressed against me.

Her tongue dancing with mine.

I never believed this would happen, that I'd get to feel her like this again. And now that the heavens have given me a second chance, I didn't hold back; I let go. Giving in to shear abandon, I lost all thoughts and self-control. Nothing else mattered. Except what was in front of me...or under me.

"Corbin..." Brooke moaned into my mouth, though it was unclear if she were urging me on or hitting the brakes. She hadn't released her death grip on my shirt, and she'd made no move to push me off, but there was something in her tone that made me hesitate. It was clear when she repeated, "*Corbin.*" This time, it was filled with a little less moan and a little more fear.

I broke the kiss but only pulled my head back far enough to

look into her eyes, not allowing her the space to move away without pushing me off. "What is it, Bridge? Did I read this all wrong? Do you not want this as much as I do?"

Her smile reached her eyes, which settled the nerves ransacking my system. "No. You didn't read anything wrong. In fact, this is what I was dreaming about last weekend when I was here. Just like this. You leaning over me"—she rolled her hips into mine—"grinding against me."

Feeling more secure and determined, I lowered my face to hers and covered her mouth with mine. But this time, she actually pushed me away with her hands against my chest. Not far, just enough to make eye contact again.

"Oh, God. I'm sorry, Corbin." Even though she had her hands covering her face, the humor in her tone was evident. "I'm just having a hard time separating this from the dream I had in this exact spot last week."

I wrapped my fingers around her wrist and removed her hand from her face, and then I did the same with the other. Pinning her arms to the couch cushion above her head, I held myself over her and watched in awe as she stared back at me. "Doesn't seem like such a bad thing to me. Wouldn't that make this a *dream come true*?"

Her smile lit a fire in my soul. "Yes, it does, but it keeps pulling my mind away from what's going on right now. I can't stop comparing this to my fantasy, and it's preventing me from staying in the moment."

"Well, there's only one way to solve that." I pulled away from her—all the way—and tugged on her arms until she was no longer lying down. And when I noticed the confusion in her eyes, I simply smiled and stood, dragging her with me.

She squealed when I bent down and draped her over my shoulder, but that quickly turned into a fit of flirtatious giggles when we began to move away from the couch...to my bedroom. I didn't bother turning on lights or closing the door. I made it to the foot of my bed and dropped her onto the mattress, on her back, with a bounce. Which succeeded in completely silencing her.

With the help of the moonlight drifting in through the large floor-to-ceiling windows, I admired the desire blazing in her wide eyes, as well as the hedonistic way her chest heaved. It was clear she was full of anticipation—just like me.

"Is this better?" I asked as I leaned over her, helping her scoot to the top of the bed so that she could get comfortable with her head on a pillow. "Or did you fantasize about being with me here, too?"

"I won't lie...I have thought about this, but considering I didn't really know what your room looked like, it was hard to picture it." She raked her hands down my sides and began to toy with the waistband on my jeans. "So to answer your question, Corbin...yes, this is better."

Her soft gasps and moans filled the room as I trailed light kisses from her neck to her chest. But when I slipped my hand beneath her shirt, my palm meeting the heat of her skin, her gasps turned to pants, and her moans grew louder. Sitting back on my haunches, I finished lifting her shirt until I had it over her head, and then I fell back over her to slide my hand beneath her, needing to free her breasts from the confines of her bra.

There was something about the way she looked at me that made me want to commit this moment to memory. While she never took her eyes off mine, her legs around my hips never relenting, it was clear that she was plagued with hesitation. Possibly fear. But it wasn't until she placed her hands on my chest and tried to pull her arms together in an uneasy way of covering herself that I realized what that hesitation was about. And it was enough to put me at ease knowing it had to do more with herself than what we were about to do.

"Don't do that." After unclasping her bra, I brought my hand to her front and began to softly run my fingertips down the center of her chest, around the curve of one breast and then over the slope of the other. "Don't hide yourself, Bridge. You're so beautiful. So goddamn beautiful. I've imagined this countless times, but nothing compares to actually seeing you."

The moonlight danced along her skin and made her body glow. My God. Part of me wanted to stay just like this while I spent hours admiring her beneath me, but there was another part of me that needed to explore *all* of her. And the longer this went on, the harder that part of me became.

I quickly pulled my shirt over my head and tossed it to the side, not caring where it landed. Because when we were finally skin-to-skin, I couldn't be bothered to think of anything other than how amazing it felt to feel her like this.

For some reason, in this moment, emotion bombarded my senses, leaving me raw and vulnerable. Don't get me wrong, I had experience with women. But this was different—*way* different. I just had no idea why. I couldn't pinpoint what it was that made my heart beat faster, caused my lungs to constrict, making it hard to breathe, or fried my nerve endings so badly that my legs shook as if I were stranded in the icy tundras of Antarctica without clothes. Whatever it was, it seemed only Brooklyn caused it.

The most important thing to me was making sure Bridge didn't feel taken advantage of. So rather than roll her skirt up to her hips and pull her panties to the side like my desperation wanted me to do, I unfastened the front and then slid off the bottom of the bed, pulling her skirt, along with her underwear, down her legs. And while I'd had many fantasies of her thin fingers working the button on my jeans until they were pooled at my feet, I was too eager to make that happen...*this time*. Instead, I quickly removed them and my boxers myself, kicking them to the side, and then eagerly climbed back on the mattress until I was once again on top of her.

In an instant, my lips were on hers, her tongue moving with mine between our mouths. I had one hand twisted in her hair while she explored my body with hers. At first, she delicately stroked my chest with her fingertips, but once the kiss grew more fervent, so did her touches. She raked her nails down my sides, and then swallowed the groans that came from the sensation of each scratch. But as soon as she made it to my waist, she abandoned the path she was on and moved one hand toward my lower abdomen, right where my raging erection throbbed for attention.

Attention that she gave it without pause.

She wrapped her fingers around my length and began to carefully caress it as if this were her first time handling a dick. It felt so amazing that I had to break our kiss, but I didn't pull away. I pressed my forehead to hers, our lips so close they continued to touch with each frantic breath we took, and held myself above her while she stroked my cock.

Her thumb swirled around the crown, and it almost made me come, which was ridiculous. I never lost my cool that soon. But there was just something about the way she touched me—or maybe it was because *she* was the one touching me—that threatened my stamina. Either way, I closed my eyes and allowed myself to enjoy what she was doing to me, all while praying I'd at least make it until I was inside her.

Luckily, I didn't have to worry about that, because she lifted her hips and lined up the head of my dick with her entrance. My eyes shot open at the initial feel of her heat, and I realized I hadn't done anything to prepare her for this. I hadn't thought about it until now, and even though it likely didn't matter considering how wet she felt against me, it still made me feel like a virgin fumbling through my first time. And just as I went to move my hand between us to ensure she was ready, she dug her heels into my ass cheeks and pulled me closer until I was inside her.

Taking the lead, I rolled my hips, completely filling her. I was so deep that my balls rested along her ass, yet that didn't stop me from continuing to grind into her as if my entire cock wasn't already buried inside her heat. I just needed a moment, not only to acclimate to her tightness—as I'm sure she needed to adjust to my size as well—but also to burn this moment into the back of my mind, never wanting to forget a second of it.

"Corbin..." Like before, my name was filled with a hearty moan, except this time, there was no question about the meaning behind it. She wanted more. *Needed* more.

So that's exactly what I gave her.

I slowly dragged my length almost all the way out, stopping with only the head of my dick inside, and then just as slowly pushed back in, stopping at the last inch. I needed to see her reaction, so I leaned my head back enough to watch her expression and then slammed the last inch in.

Her reaction definitely didn't disappoint.

Her eyes were closed, but her brows rose. She dug the back of her head into the pillow and arched her spine, her mouth wide open as a sharp gasp filled the room. It was the most beautiful thing I'd ever witnessed, and it made me want to see it again.

And again. And again.

Each time I hit her with that last inch, she grew tighter and tighter, and I knew she was close to coming. Hell, I was close, so I needed her to be as well. The last thing I wanted was to finish before she did, and that's when I realized something—this wasn't about my pleasure; it was all about hers. For the first time in my life, having sex wasn't just about sex. It wasn't just about getting off and finding release but about Brooklyn's needs being met.

As strange as that was to realize, it filled me with a sense of purpose and excitement.

I pushed up with my arms until I was seated on my knees, clenched my teeth, and thrust into her again, watching as my entire length disappeared into the most beautiful pussy I'd ever had the pleasure of seeing. With this new angle, my pelvic bone met her clit and caused her to whimper. It also caused me to do it again.

Between her heat, how tightly she gripped my shaft as I

moved in and out of her, the sounds that escaped her lips, and the sight of my cock filling her, I couldn't hold back any longer. And it seemed neither could she. With one final thrust, she cried out at the same time I let go of my control, pumping every last drop of cum into her.

I must've blacked out for a moment, because one minute, I had a death grip on her hips, slamming wildly into her, and the next, I was hunched over her body, desperately fighting to catch my breath. I wanted to kiss her, but until we both calmed down, it would likely end up feeling more like CPR than kissing. So instead, I pulled away and pressed my lips to her forehead before collapsing next to her on the bed. She turned her body toward mine, her leg still curled over my hip, and lazily traced invisible lines on my chest with her fingertip.

"I'll go get a washcloth and glass of water in a sec, once I can breathe properly." I sounded like I'd just finished running five miles in the middle of the hottest day of the year.

"That's okay," she panted, intently studying whatever she was drawing on my chest. "I need to go to the bathroom anyway. Once I calm down; I doubt my legs will carry me that far at the moment. But I can do that while you get us something to drink."

"Deal." Except I didn't want to leave the bed. I didn't want to leave the comfort of her body, even though I knew I'd eventually have to. But rather than dwell on what I couldn't change, I decided to focus on what I could do instead.

And that was to keep her here long enough for round two.

After another couple of minutes, she untangled herself from me and rolled to the side to get out of bed. As if that wasn't bad enough, she began to search the floor for what I assumed were clothes. I admired her backside while I could, but I knew if I had any hope of keeping her here longer, I had to make sure she didn't get dressed, so I jumped up and grabbed my T-shirt from the pile of discarded clothes and tossed it to her.

"Here, put that on," I said while stepping into my boxers.

I then waited until she slipped it over her head and disappeared into the bathroom before I located her panties and discreetly shoved them under the bed. I hadn't done so to keep them like some wonton pervert who enjoyed sniffing underwear. I'd only hidden them for the time being, until she was ready to leave—well, until I was ready to let her leave.

While she busied herself in the bathroom, I headed toward the kitchen. At first, I only meant to fill two glasses with water and take them to the bedroom, but once I got there and stood in front of the fridge, I realized how much of an appetite I'd worked up. I only hoped she felt the same.

"Are you hungry?" I asked when she rounded the corner, still wearing only my T-shirt. It looked way better on her. Especially the way it barely grazed the tops of her thighs. It was one of the sexiest things I'd ever seen.

"Starving!" she exclaimed with her hand over her stomach.

I chuckled and lifted her to sit on the island. "How does an omelet sound?"

"It sounds amazing."

"If you continue to moan like that, I'll ditch the eggs and eat something else instead." I eyed her and then turned around to pull the ingredients out of the fridge before I did just that. While I had all intentions of enjoying round two, I was a man, which meant I needed a moment to recoup before I could satisfy her all over again.

But when I turned back around, my arms full of eggs, milk, cheese, and diced ham, I caught her toying with the hem of the shirt across her thighs and nibbling away at her bottom lip. Either she really was starving, or she had something on her mind and didn't know how to get it out.

"Are you okay?" I asked, hoping to prod it out of her.

She glanced up, eyes wide as if she'd been caught, and then shook her head. "Yeah, I'm fine. Just thinking how weird this is. You know?"

My heart lodged itself into my throat, cutting off my air supply. Instead of giving away the panic that filled me, I swallowed hard, went about getting a frying pan, and as casually as possibly, asked, "What's so weird about eating after sex?"

She giggled, which was a good sign. "No, not that. Us...what we just did."

I glanced between the door to my bedroom and her a few times, feigning dramatic confusion. "You think *that* was weird? Damn, girl...what kind of sex have you been having if you think missionary is weird?"

She rolled her eyes yet continued with the conversation. Thank God. "I guess I don't know what all this means, and I have a tendency to overthink things. I don't want to do that with this—with *you* I mean. And while I know the last thing you probably want to do is talk this to death, I worry that if we don't discuss it, we could potentially fuck everything up." Her raw honesty did nothing but make her even more beautiful to me.

Laughter bubbled up in my chest, but I held it in—other than the smile that burned my cheeks. "Bridge...I've been trying to get you to talk for a week. Trust me, I don't have a problem whatsoever talking to you about anything you want to discuss."

She rolled her eyes to the ceiling and lifted one shoulder the tiniest bit, as if to say *you've got a point*. "I can't help but feel like I'm betraying my best friend, and it's not a feeling I'm used to or comfortable with. But I'm also not content with ignoring you. I did that all last week, and it made me miserable. And I guess considering what we just did, I'd say it was a wasted effort."

I set the pan on the stove and went back to the fridge for the butter. "I get it."

And I did. I truly did understand the war that waged inside of her, because there was a part of me that had fought that same war. Except, I wasn't worried about Nellie's feelings; my concern was that if she found out, Brooke would be the one who'd lose.

"So, what do you want to do? What options do we have?" I went about making us something to eat while avoiding eye contact, not because I didn't want to look at her, but because I didn't want to make a bigger deal of this than there had to be. Nonchalant was my approach.

"Well, it's not like we can rewind time and change what's happened."

I cut off a couple squares of butter and put them in the pan, and while I waited for the burner to heat up, I gave her my attention, needing to see her face when I asked, "Do you wish you could?"

"What? Go back and change what's happened? No. Not at all."

I all but sighed, my shoulders dropping with relief.

"I just think we should really know what we're getting into before *actually* getting into it." She giggled and shook her head. "I mean, more so than we already have."

"Um, I hate to sound like a moron here, Bridge…but I thought we already discussed what we're getting ourselves into. I thought we're trying to see what this thing is between us. Maybe I'm confused about what you're trying to say."

With her legs crossed at her ankles, she swung them slightly while keeping her attention on the floor. "Well, since I have no idea what's going on with you and your ex, I guess I need to know if this is a temporary thing, or if you're trying to see if you can move on from her. I also have no idea what this will do to the plan with Chase and his new girlfriend. If I'm going to sneak around behind Nellie's back, I need to know it's for a good reason. That way, if she finds out, I'll have a valid excuse that she can't argue with."

That made sense.

I cracked the eggs and began to whisk them in a bowl, along with the other ingredients, while keeping my eye on her. "Things between Lindsey and me are over. If we both had taken a step back years ago, we would've known this was coming. Neither of us have been willing to put the other first, and it doesn't take an expert to know that's not conducive to a healthy relationship."

"When did you come to that conclusion, because a few weeks

ago, you were saying that you two will get back together, that you always do." She had a valid argument.

"I guess you can say I've been slowly coming to that realization, but it really hit me last weekend when I accidentally sent her flowers. She just started seeing someone else, and apparently, he was upset about the bouquet. Which I totally understand; I'd probably feel the same way if Chase sent flowers to you."

She was quiet for a moment, her lips twisting to the side in thought. "Then what does that mean for us? Are we *seeing* each other? As in seeing where things go? Or do we go into this with a plan in place? To be honest with you, Corbin…the thought of just winging it with you leaves me unsettled."

"I couldn't agree more." I poured the egg mixture into the pan and then moved to stand in front of her, situating my body between her legs. "I don't know how I feel about setting a time limit on it, but I definitely think that we need to go into this with as much communication as possible. If either of us get to the point where we don't see it going anywhere, we need to trust that something will be said."

My chest constricted at the thought of her calling me up one day to tell me she wasn't into me. But that was a chance I'd have to take if I wanted the opportunity to have the opposite happen. Honestly, I couldn't foresee the future, but I knew enough to know that there was something special about her, and I wouldn't be able to figure it out if we kept each other at arm's length.

"And if we realize that there is something between us worth holding on to…then we need to figure out a way to tell your sister. Because I don't want to sneak around longer than necessary."

I smiled as I kissed her lips, and then groaned when she pulled away to say something else.

"Oh, and she said she's worried about losing me." Brooke amazed me at how well she could stay focused on what she was discussing while my lips and tongue teased her neck and shoulder. "So you can't get upset with me if I choose to spend time with her instead of you, or if I have to bail on plans to be there for her."

I pulled away and held her stare while my hands roamed along her thighs. "Until we make things official and we tell her what's going on, I will keep my hurt feelings to myself if you drop plans with me to hang out with her. But once we go public, she'll have to figure out how to share you with me." With a hearty grip on her thighs, I pulled her legs further apart. "Now...enough talking about my sister."

The omelet sizzled in the pan as I lowered myself and leaned forward, getting my face closer to her pussy. I'd been too side-tracked to do this earlier, and I'd be damned if we got through the night without her coming on my tongue.

"What are you doing?" she squealed while laughing. "I'm going to fall!"

"I won't let that happen," I growled and then pulled her bottom closer to the edge of the granite.

She conceded and leaned back, propping herself up on her elbows. Just before I dropped my head to take the first lick, her head fell back, and she hooked her knees over my shoulders. I swear, the heavens parted and angels sang at the first swipe of my tongue through her folds, and I began to suck in search of more. My tongue darted around her sensitive nub, and she bucked her hips, desperate for more.

I moved my mouth down so I could thrust my tongue in and out of her opening, coating my tongue with her juices. She began to cry out and arch her body so high I worried she'd catapult herself off the counter. This wasn't the most comfortable position to be in, but I didn't care. I'd walk around hunched over all week if it meant making her come on my tongue.

And that's exactly what I did.

Less than a minute after getting my first taste of her, she came undone, writhing against my mouth while she held herself up on the kitchen island. All the while, the eggs crackled and sizzled on the stove a few feet away, their aroma filling the air yet not doing a damn thing to mask the scent of Brooke's arousal.

Nothing smelled better than that.

I sucked her lower lips one more time before standing up and taking her face between my hands. Never in my life had I wanted a woman to taste herself on me this badly. Then again, I'd never done so with someone as eager to suck her own scent from my lips as Brooke was.

Any man who'd let her go was a fucking fool.

The sizzling turned into popping, catching both of our attentions. She gave me one last kiss and then pulled away to look at the pan on the other counter. Pointing to it, she said, "You might want to do something about that before you burn this whole building down."

After finishing the omelet, I split it in half and put each piece on a plate. She grabbed the two cups of water I'd originally gone into the kitchen to get and then followed me into the living room, taking the spot next to me on the couch.

"So…about the plan," she mentioned between bites. "It's still on, right?"

I nearly choked, but thankfully, I was able to play it off that the food was still too hot. The last thing I wanted to do was lie to her, but considering I already had, I was more or less between a rock and a hard place, so I decided to follow up her question with one of my own. "Do you still want me to go along with it? Even though we're trying to see if there's anything between *us*?"

She bobbed her head side to side as if contemplating how to answer. "Well, it's not like we're serious yet or anything. And I'm not asking you to actually do anything with the woman." She shrugged and added, "So I guess I don't see anything wrong with keeping it going for now. It shouldn't take you too long to succeed, right?"

"You don't see anything wrong with following through on a revenge plot against your ex while trying to *date* someone else?

Not just someone else, but the same guy who's playing the lead role in said plot?"

She remained quiet while finishing the food on her plate and staring across the room, deep in thought. Finally, she set her plate down and turned to face me. "How about we keep it going for now. Like I said, if you're planning to get her out for drinks this week, then it shouldn't take long to see it through. For all we know, this thing between us is nothing more than pent up sexual energy, and once we get it out, we go our separate ways. So if we put a stop to the plan now, I'm basically ensuring that he'll never know what it's like to have his heart broken the way he broke mine."

I couldn't argue with her point, but that didn't mean I wanted to continue playing along. Oh, who the hell was I kidding? I hadn't played along since the beginning. So really, I could simply continue with what I'd been doing all along, and once we admit that there's something serious between us—because I wholeheartedly believed that was a real possibility—then I could just "give it up" then.

After taking my last bite, I set my plate on top of hers on the coffee table. "Okay. So we keep it going until we decide enough is enough, or until it's fulfilled, whichever comes first."

"Yup." She smiled and then shifted on the cushion, moving closer to me. "So, tell me, Corbin...when did you realize you liked me?"

The way she asked, as if she were in middle school, made me laugh. It was adorable and cute while turning me on at the same time. "If I had to pick a moment, I'd say the second time we met for drinks—the time after I met up with you and Nellie when you guys roped me into this scheme of yours."

She squealed when I took hold of her hips and moved her to straddle my lap.

"What about you?" I asked, relaxing into the back of the couch so that she had to lean over me, causing her hair to fall over her shoulders. "When did you start to see me as more than Nell's older brother?"

Her eyes lit up with her smile, even though she shrugged as if to say she wasn't sure. She was. Her eyes had given her away. "Probably the first time we met up for drinks…the time Nellie and I roped you into our *genius* plan."

"Really? That soon?"

She glanced over my shoulder and then returned her attention to my face. "Well, I guess at that point I still saw you as my best friend's brother, just a really hot one."

"You didn't think I was hot when we were younger?"

"I'm afraid not. Maybe that's because you used to tease us all the time, or possibly because I always thought you hated me. But you can't be upset about that. It's not like you found me attractive all those years ago, either."

"Of course not…you were a kid."

And just then, she rolled her hips, reminding just how much she'd grown up.

I slipped one hand between us, to test the waters so to speak, and before pushing my fingers inside her, she was practically dripping with desire. "Damn, Bridge…you're so fucking wet. That's such a turn-on, such a boost to my ego."

"Well, how's this for an ego boost…" She steadied herself with her palms against the cushion behind my head and brought her lips to my ear. "No one has ever made me as wet as you do."

Her body stiffened, and I could tell that admitting that had set off her insecurity bells. Not that she was an insecure person, but from what I'd gathered about her, I assumed she lacked a lot of experience with men—especially if she'd stayed with her ex, the douchebag, for as long as she had.

Feeding into her confidence, I growled and pumped two fingers insider her, just enough to make her take the lead and ride my hand. But she didn't let it go on for long before pushing away. Just as I started to worry that she was putting an end to this, she surprised me by putting her hand between us, freeing my throbbing cock from my boxers, and lining it up with her entrance.

Releasing a slow and steady exhale, she lowered herself onto me until she impaled herself with my erection. I wanted to drag this out, but she had other plans. As soon as she sat fully seated on top of me, she began to buck her hips in urgency, lifting herself up and down over my cock. I enjoyed her assertiveness immensely, but I could only let it go on for so long before taking some of the control. With a firm grip on her hips, my fingertips digging into the bare flesh of her ass cheeks, I started to rock back and forth, lifting her and then slamming her onto my dick so that we were meeting thrust for thrust.

"Oh, God. I'm so close." Her cries turned to whimpers as she rested her head in the crook of my neck. Her hand snaked between us, and she began to rub herself frantically, her breathing growing more ragged.

Her muscles tightened around my shaft and made it nearly impossible to hold on much longer. Thankfully, I didn't need to worry because she took that moment to let go and come. Her entire body spasmed, and that, along with her vocal enjoyment, enhanced my orgasm.

I'd wanted to sit like this, keeping myself inside her while we both came down from the high of round two, but she pushed away and wiggled off my lap, regardless of my obvious protests.

"Wait," I begged and reached for her hand. "Let me look at you for a minute. I can't get over how beautiful you are."

She shifted on her feet, drawing my attention to the mixture of our cum slipping down her inner thigh. It was obvious it made her uncomfortable, but I'd be willing to bet she wouldn't feel that way if she knew what a turn-on it was.

"I wish I was an artist; I'd capture this moment forever on canvas, though I doubt there's a single color that could do you justice. Or hell, if I had any skill with a camera, I'd snap a picture and frame it. You, my dear, are a work of art."

Suddenly, a wave of laughter rolled through her, breaking me out of the spell she'd put me under. I wasn't sure what she'd found so funny until she said, "I'm sorry, but that just gave me major flashbacks of the movie, *Titanic*."

"Oh, you've seen it? I was hoping that was before your time." Honestly, that hadn't crossed my mind, but at least it saved me from looking like a silly sap, talking about turning her into a work of art.

"Corbin, *Titanic* is like *Ghost* or *Dirty Dancing*...they're timeless. I'm just surprised you're a fan of the movie."

I stood and stretched, not caring that my now flaccid dick still hung out of my boxers. "Why wouldn't I be? Like you said, it's a classic." Then, I took her hand and pulled her toward my room. "Come on, gorgeous, let's go clean you off in the shower."

CHAPTER 16

BROOKE

MY MUSCLES WERE sore and my body exhausted. But I wouldn't have changed a single second of last night.

Well, maybe I would've changed one thing—sneaking out of Corbin's bed at two in the morning. I hadn't wanted to leave him that way, but he had looked so peaceful that I couldn't bear to wake him. We'd had prior conversations about wakeful nights, and I knew sleep didn't come easily for him. His mind would wander, mostly about work and the numerous things he'd left unfinished. I doubted staying up so late with me had contributed in a positive way to his sleep situation.

My mind was all over the place today. I'd hardly been able to pay attention to the students' antics—a fact they'd fully taken advantage of. They had run all over me, and I'd let them. It had been a day, and I was so thankful that it happened to fall on a Monday, which meant I got to meet the girls for drinks.

I'd arrived early, since my school got out before most of their work schedules; that's the way things usually went. So to kill the time, I decided to scroll through my texts with Corbin from earlier. I couldn't believe we'd hooked up last night. And to make matters worse, I hoped it would happen again.

Me: Hi. Sorry I left this morning without saying goodbye. I'm also sorry that it took me so long to text. It's been a hectic day.

Corbin: Are you wearing panties?

Even though I'd read through these texts numerous times, flames still licked up my neck, arriving as red-hot heat in my cheeks. I couldn't believe he asked me that. The truth was, I'd had to go home sans panties because mine had disappeared sometime after Corbin had taken them off me last night.

Me: Um, yeah. Now I am. LOL

Corbin: That was a pleasant surprise to wake up to this morning...you were gone, but left your panties behind.

Me: Yeah. It was a cold ride home. Are you still at work?

Corbin: Yup. All work and no play for me. When are you going to claim your panties?

I had to put my reminiscing to rest when Julie showed up. After the last time we all met up, I'd learned to keep my phone at the bottom of my purse for fear something else would happen to it. I doubted it'd be another drink; just my luck, Mady would chuck it across the room.

Somehow, I managed to remain normal while exchanging pleasantries with Julie and Mady. But when Nellie showed up, it was a game-changer; guilt ate me from the inside out. She knew me better than anyone, and I'd convinced myself that she'd know I'd slept with her brother within ten seconds of sitting down.

After going around the table, greeting the other two, she leaned into me, kissed my cheek, and said, "Hey, girl." So far, so good. But the second her bottom met the barstool, I began to count.

Ten.

"Has Dandy come to take our order yet?" She glanced around the bar, looking for our usual waitress, whose real name was Dandelion.

"Yeah," Julie answered for the rest of us. "She should bring them over any minute now."

"Thank God, because I need it. I've had *quite* the day." As long as Nellie kept her nose in the menu, she might not catch the scarlet letter gleaming on my forehead. "I'm thinking it's a fries-and-ranch kind of night. What do you all think?"

Nine.

"After all the drinks last night? Hell, yes," Mady chimed in.

Julie rolled her eyes. "I'd agree, except *someone* limited the number I had."

"Hey, don't blame me. The jerk deserved it for grabbing my butt."

The girls laughed—I didn't, because I remained frozen in fear.

Eight.

"Mady…he didn't actually touch you."

"Oh, yeah, that's right." She shrugged, causing more giggles to erupt around me. More giggles that I couldn't participate in. My attention remained glued to the saltshaker in the center of the high-top while the impending doom hung over my head and threatened to suffocate me at any moment.

Just then, Dandy stopped by with our drinks and took our order for a basket of fries and bowl of ranch, offering me a momentary reprieve from my anxiety. And then I gulped half the glass of wine, needing another moment to compose myself before my life fell apart. My hope was that the more I drank, the better I'd be able to conceal my guilt.

"Slow down, girl." Julie moved my glass away from me. "Keep that up and you won't be able to drive home."

"I took an Uber here. My car still isn't working."

"Oh, yeah." Nellie turned to face me, and my stomach flipped. "How'd you get to work?"

Seven.

"One of the other teachers picked me up and then took me home."

Her eyes narrowed.

This was it. My life was over.

Six.

But just as quickly as she'd brought the conversation to me, she moved on. "Mady, do you mind if I borrow that little black dress? I have a date tomorrow night, and I want to impress him. Nothing says *my legs would look amazing around your neck* better than a classy yet sexy black dress."

That was enough to make me choke...on thin air. It would've been better had I been drinking at the time, but I wasn't. I didn't even have anything in my mouth, other than a giant ball of betrayal, caused by the memory of *my* legs around Corbin's neck the night before in his kitchen.

Nellie patted my back and studied me with concerned eyes. "Are you okay?"

Five.

I couldn't do anything other than nod, my ability to speak gone.

Luckily, Mady saved me by saying, "I'd totally let you borrow it, but I'm taking it with me on my trip. I leave in the morning for that work retreat, remember?"

"Aren't you going to some dude ranch?" Julie asked, brows arched high on her forehead. "What the hell do you need a black dress for in the middle of the woods?"

"You never know who might be there. It's always best to be prepared in any situation. That's what my mom always said, at least. She'd tell me, 'Mady, you need to make sure you're taking your birth control every day on time. You don't want to learn the hard way like I did and wait until the asshole forgets to pull out before realizing you weren't prepared.'"

Julie snickered. "Um, Mady, I think she was talking about being *protected*, not prepared."

"No, that's not what she meant. She specifically told me what a major lesson that was to learn, because it taught her just how un*prepared* she was to be mom. She didn't need to explain the importance of protecting myself; in this day and age, with all the different hook-up sites like Tinder, every woman should be using *something*, or at least have condoms in their purses."

"Well, that's true. We're all on birth control, right?" Julie asked, glancing around the table. Then she flicked her wrist in my direction. "Not like you need it. You're not having sex."

Four.

Again, I started to choke. But this time, I was able to blame it on the mouthful of wine I'd been in the middle of swallowing. Nellie started to pat my back, but I shrugged her off and glared at my friend on my left. "In case you've forgotten, I was in a very long-term relationship not that long ago. I didn't stop taking it just because he broke up with me."

Julie held up her hands in apologetic surrender at the same time our fries were brought to the table. Dandy pointed to my nearly empty glass, and I nodded, silently asking for another. But when she pointed to the other's, Julie shook her head, saying, "No more for me, thanks."

Nellie was surprised. "Just one glass? That's it?"

"I picked up an extra shift at the hospital, so I'll be working twenty-four hours straight, which means tonight will be an early one for me," Julie stated with a half-shrug.

"So...it looks like you might get bent over a haystack at a dude ranch this week." Nellie pointed at Mady with a gleam in her eye, and then pressed the tip of her finger to her chest. "If all things go well, I'll have beard-burn between my legs tomorrow night, and"—she pointed at Julie across from her—"you'll be sucking off some hot doctor in the supply closet."

"How many times do I have to tell you...*Grey's Anatomy* isn't real!"

Apparently, I'd spaced out—and lost my mind—because the next words out of my mouth didn't only surprise me, they shocked the hell out of the other girls. "How does one give a good blowjob?"

Three.

"Whose dick are you planning on sucking?" Nellie asked with wide, incredulous eyes.

Two.

My cheeks flamed with heat, but I answered her anyway. "I'm single now; who knows when I might meet someone and want to give it another go. And like Mady's mom said, I should always be prepared. I mean, it's not my fault I hate blowjobs." I sighed and picked up my drink to polish it off.

"Don't feel bad, Brooke," Julie said while giving me a sympathetic pat on the shoulder. "There are lots of women out there who can't do it."

"Or *won't* do it," Mady chimed in.

I pointed to myself and joined in on the teasing. "Or don't know how to do it."

We all laughed again.

When Dandy came back with our second rounds—minus Julie —I leaned in and got serious. "So give me some tips."

"Look who's putting herself back into the dating pool." Nellie shoulder bumped me before stealing another fry.

"I wouldn't say that. I'm more or less dipping my pinky toe in." That was fair to say. Even though I'd dipped far more than that, they didn't need to know the specifics.

"Oh, yeah?" Nellie appeared very interested. "With who?"

And one.

I held my breath, waiting for the lightbulb above her head to flick on.

When it didn't, I exhaled and pushed my luck. "No one in particular."

Thankfully, Mady came to my rescue, saving my life for at least another minute. She swatted at Nellie and said, "Leave her alone. When she's ready to tell us, she will. Right now, the girl needs tips on...well, *the tip*." She wagged her brows, easing my tension a little more. "My advice, Brooke, is it's best to practice with a popsicle."

"Nah, that's too frickin' cold. A banana is better," Julie suggested.

"You're both wrong. A dildo is best. It doesn't turn to mush, *and* it's not cold. Plus, it's the most realistic size-wise." Nellie would know. She had the most experience. She wasn't easy, per se, but she had a healthy appetite where sex was concerned.

"That's all nice and everything, but *how* do you do it?" I asked again.

The girls took turns giving *actual* advice.

"I think it's best to twirl your tongue around it, kind of figure out where your boundaries are."

"Yeah, and you can watch his face to see which places he likes best. Once you get him going, you'll totally get into it and won't want to stop. It's all about being in control. I bet you'll really like doing it once you find someone whose pleasure turns you on."

I just sat back and listened, taking mental notes on the subject. At least it kept me from counting down again. As long as I had Nellie talking about sex, I could enjoy the rest of my evening with the girls without worrying about her suspecting anything.

"MISS BROOKLYN, WATCH ME!"

I was on recess duty, which meant it was the end of the day. Thank God! I was dead on my feet after staying up late texting Corbin. I just wanted to be in bed, texting him again. Only one more hour until I could do that—as long as I could stop daydreaming about our steamy conversation long enough to keep these kids alive.

"Slow it down, Garrison," I warned, walking closer to the monkey bars.

"I can do it, Miss Brooklyn! I can go high like Superman!" He began to swing his legs and leap from bar to bar.

Oh shit! He's going to fall and break his neck.

I held on to the main pole and reached out to steady him. Then, out of nowhere, *whack!* Stars danced above my head, and I heard voices. Maybe angels were singing?

"I killed her!" a tiny voice screamed. "Miss Brooklyn died. I'm so sorry, Miss Brooklyn. Please come back to life."

When I finally came to, only succeeding at peeking open one eye, I found Garrison holding my hand, crouched over me with tears lining his chubby cheeks.

"I'm okay. Just give me a minute," I mumbled.

"Stand back. Give her some air." It wasn't until another teacher came over that I realized I'd garnered a crowd. Either they all raced over as soon as I fell, or I'd been knocked out longer than I thought. "Garrison, you need to go back to class. Recess is over. Don't worry, Miss Brooklyn will be fine. Nurse Betty will fix her up in no time."

"She just needs a bandage?" he asked, his little face full of hope.

I sat up with a groan. "And maybe some ice; I'll be fine."

Garrison threw himself into my arms and almost succeeded in knocking me down again, but thankfully, I had put one hand behind me for support. "I thought I killed you." He spoke with a lisp because of his missing tooth, and it sounded like *kissed you*, which made me smile.

"You didn't. I'm going to be fine. It will take more than that to put me out of commission." Well, I'd managed to make it through *most* of the day unscathed. Not bad for two nights in a row without much sleep.

A couple of the teachers helped me to the front office, and the nurse did the normal precautionary tests to see if I had a concussion. We cracked jokes back and forth before she gave me an ice pack. My head began to pound, so she told me to lay down for a few minutes. Someone stayed with me despite my persistence that I was fine. I guess because I lost consciousness, it made things worse.

The school nurse refused to let me go home. In fact, she insisted that I go straight to the emergency room to get checked out. This was ridiculous, especially because I was without transportation. I'd gotten a ride to work again this morning, since my car was still parked uselessly in front of my house. I'd planned to just take an Uber home, but that tidbit of information sent the nurse into a tizzy. I would've laughed if the situation wasn't so frustrating. I hated the thought of being trapped and I didn't have any options available to me. My independence had been taken from me with one swift kick to the temple, all because of a stupid playground accident. Tears started to form, and I attempted to sniff them back when my co-teacher came in.

"Oh, honey. It's okay. These things happen. Especially with those rambunctious kiddos. Don't let this get to you. We've all had incidents like this, and we bounce back, then we move on. In a few weeks' time, this will just be a blip on your radar, and you won't even remember all these details and things you're going through at the moment." She handed me my purse and tote bag, which held my laptop and papers that needed to be graded. She patted my hand before asking, "Do you have someone to call? The day is going to be over in fifteen minutes, so I can drop you somewhere."

I nodded and wiped my tears with the back of my hand. "That would be great."

"As long as you're dropping her off at the hospital and not home." Nurse Betty was a watchdog; nothing slipped past her. I had to find a way to get out of going to the emergency room. I felt fine and had no nausea.

The idea of spending hours in a waiting room did not sound appealing whatsoever.

I SAT in my hospital bed with a flimsy sheet that shielded me from the outside world. All the tests had come back fine; I only had a slight concussion but should heal and be fine in a day or two. My quandary was that the hospital wouldn't release me unless someone picked me up.

The hospital staff were as bad as Nurse Betty and absolutely would not bend on the issue. Per policy, calling a cab was not an option. And my explanation of living with someone, so I wouldn't be alone, was a no-go as well. They wanted someone to physically come and pick me up in order to listen to the directions and things to watch out for. I guess there was a chance I could combust in the middle of the night.

My eyes hurt. They felt laden with sand, not to mention, my right eye was housed beneath an ice pack and swollen shut. I could barely open it enough to see out. They'd given me ointment for it, which only served to further impede my vision.

I'd texted Nellie first, but I hadn't told her what happened, just fished for what she was up to. I knew she had something planned, but for the life of me couldn't remember what.

Me: *Happy Tuesday! Hope your day was better than mine. How are things going on your end?*

Nellie: *I'm making a mad dash to my apartment to change for my date. Then we're heading out to dinner.*

Me: *Have a great time! I hope things go well.*

Nellie: *Are you okay?*

Me: *Yes, I'm fine. Just checking in. Text me when you get home and let me know how it goes.*

Nellie: *Oh, you know I will!*

I had no doubt in my mind that if I had explained what happened, she would've dropped everything and rushed over to be with me in a heartbeat. But she hadn't been out on a date in forever, and she'd been really looking forward to this one.

Unfortunately, Julie worked at a different hospital, or she could've pulled some strings, and Mady was out of town. *Crap!* How was it possible that *all* of my friends had plans on the exact same night? A night I just happened to need one of them, too.

Corbin.

I closed my one eye and leaned my head back into the gurney pillow before letting out a big sigh. He would, undoubtedly, still be at work. I hated to inconvenience anyone. This was one of my faults. I'd been raised by a single mother, which meant I could be too independent most of the time. I never knew when it was okay to ask for help, because I always tried to do everything on my own, which in turn, ended up making things more complicated. So my two choices were to contact Corbin or call Nellie and make her choose me over her date. Corbin would have to choose me over work, which was just as bad. To him, nothing came before work.

Phyllis, the lady I lived with, wasn't in any position to drive. She could take a cab here, pick me up, and then take me with her back home. But there was a good chance she would get lost along the way or forget entirely where she was headed. The orchestration it would take to make that happen was beyond my capabilities at the moment. She wasn't to the point that she needed full-time help, but she'd get there sooner or later. My job consisted of making sure she had stuff in the fridge to eat and her bills were paid.

I drew in a deep breath before typing out the text.

Me: *How was your day? Are you still at work?*

I could see the bubbles bouncing and it made my heart skip a beat. Thank God he wasn't in a meeting or something. He was answering right away.

Corbin: Yup. Just finished my last meeting for the day. Trying to decide if I should pick up dinner or go straight home. Are you hungry?

Me: Actually, I was going to ask you for a ride. I'm still without a car.

Corbin: Sure! Are you still at school?

Me: no…I'm at the hospital. I'm totally fine. Just got in a minor accident with a student.

My phone began to ring, which startled me and almost caused me to drop it.

"What the fuck do you mean, you're at the hospital?" Corbin roared into the phone as soon as I answered.

"I'm fine. I swear. It's just a little bump on the head. They won't release me without someone coming to get me, and Nellie's busy." My voice trailed off because I didn't know what else to say.

"I'll be right there. Tell me where you are."

I rattled off the name of the hospital. "If you check in at the emergency room desk, they'll bring you to me."

"I'll be there in fifteen minutes, tops."

The urgency in his tone made me regret asking him, because I didn't want to add stress to his plate. I should've just called Nellie. If she ever found out I didn't, she'd totally kill me. Not only had I slept with her brother, but now I'd called him instead of her to come get me. The guilt just continued to pile up.

I carefully got dressed and only had my shoes left when the curtain whipped open.

"*My God…*" Corbin stood there with his hand over his mouth, his reaction worrying me.

Was my face that terrible? I hadn't seen a mirror since the incident had happened. I must've looked like utter shit.

"What happened to you?" He rushed to me and tenderly scooped the good side of my head into his chest. The moment his arms wrapped around me, I finally relaxed. My shield tumbled away, and my anxiety decreased. Everything would be right in the world.

"I'm okay."

"No offense, Bridge, but you don't look all right. Not even in the slightest." The concern that etched his brow and widened his eyes made me wonder if I'd grown another head.

"Well, I will be." I winced when I leaned forward in an attempt to put on my socks and shoes.

"Here, let me help with that." Corbin took the sock from my hand and sat on the bedside chair. He took my naked foot into his lap and effortlessly slipped my sock over my heel, then my shoe. He followed suit with the other one.

"Well, it looks like you had someone to call after all." Nurse Ratchet returned to the room and gave me a pointed stare. She was one of those people you didn't mess with. She had the death glare down pat.

"Yeah," I mumbled.

"I'm Corbin Fields." He stood and shook her hand. His stance held authority, and I could tell even she was impressed by my rescuer. Ladies would ogle him; it was a given. He was handsome, but more than that, it was his demeanor that made him sexy.

"You're going to need to watch this one." She pointed at me. "She'll try to get away with whatever you let her. Did you know that she was planning to call a cab to pick her up? Nope, not on my watch. Lord have mercy! I would've been fired."

"I completely agree. Don't you worry, I won't let anything like that happen."

"She needs to be monitored for at least twenty-four hours and cannot return to work for at least two days. She should also follow up with her physician before being released back to work. If she starts getting confused, experience nausea, cannot be roused, or has no appetite, bring her back immediately. Do not pass go; do not collect two hundred dollars. Come here pronto. Got it?" The entire time she explained the instructions, she didn't once glance in my direction. She spoke about me as if I wasn't even in the room.

"I understand. I promise to take good care of our patient."

"Mmmhmm. I'm sure you will." She looked him up and down so feverishly, it made me blush. "But no hanky-panky. Bedrest means just that. Bed and rest."

Corbin chuckled to himself; he must've thought her comment was hilarious. I thought it was borderline rude.

I couldn't wait to get home. I needed my bed and sleep more than anything else.

Well, unless Corbin was under those sheets with me.

That would be nice.

CHAPTER 17

CORBIN

THE SIGHT of her had caused this fierce protectiveness to come over me.

Bridge looked like something the cat dragged in. Like she'd been chewed up and then spit back out. The right side of her face was all shades of red, black, and purple. I'd never seen anything like it, and I'd been in my fair share of testosterone-fueled brawls. I had no idea why she'd decided to call me to come get her, but I found it flattering all the same.

I glanced over at Brooke curled up in my passenger seat. She'd started to nod off the minute I buckled her in. The nurse had stated that she could sleep, but she needed to be woken up every two to three hours during the first night, then she should be in the clear after that. It was well after eight in the evening, so she had to be tired. Especially since we hadn't gotten much sleep the last two nights.

After pulling into my underground parking spot, I tried to shake Brooklyn awake. She got kind of upset and tried to swat my hand away, which I thought was cute. "Brooke, we're here. It's time to wake up."

"Whatchu talkin' about?"

My internal alarms began to sound at her confused mumbling,

and I debated heading back to the hospital, but when she spoke again, she was clearer, more alert, which was enough to calm me down.

"We're here?" She sat up with a groan and quickly pressed her hands to both sides of her head.

"Hold on, let me help you." I opened my car door and swiftly made it around to hers, hating that I had to take my eyes off her for a second. "Here we go. Up and at 'em."

She was like a rag doll; her limbs were wobbly due to the pain shot they'd administered to her before leaving the hospital. They'd hoped it would also help reduce the swelling of her eye. I'd been given instructions on ice packs as well. It would be a full-time job this evening, but I didn't mind.

"Where's my home?" she mumbled before turning into the crook of my neck. I swung her legs around and lifted her into my arms. I'd decided carrying her was my best option at the moment.

"We came to mine instead. I thought it would be easier to keep an eye on you, hope you don't mind." I held her against my chest and shoved the passenger door closed with my foot. The elevator and my place were operated by a key fob, so all I had to do was wave the fancy teardrop-shaped keychain in order to gain access.

Technology these days did come in handy when carrying a beautiful woman in your arms.

"Huh? I thought you were taking me home. You don't need to carry me." She seemed to be gaining more awareness of her surroundings, which made me feel better. Also, her tone was stronger and her words clearer. But that didn't mean I was ready to let her loose just yet—or anytime in the near future.

"Well, we're already here, so there's no need to walk now." I laughed at her dubious glare.

Once we were inside my place, I took her straight to my bedroom and smiled. The thought of Bridge in my bed for twenty-four hours sounded like heaven. It didn't faze me that we couldn't fool around; I already knew we got along—with or without clothes.

I set her on her feet, still not letting go, and pulled back the covers so she could sit.

"Really, all this fuss isn't necessary."

"I don't mind, Bridge. We all need someone to look after us from time to time." What I really wanted to tell her was that she meant something to me, but since we were still trying to figure out what this was between us—as well as her having a concussion —I decided not to push just yet.

"Thank you." She grabbed my hand and gave it a squeeze. "My head is still foggy, but I'm actually starting to feel a little better." Her stomach took that moment to rumble.

"And a little hungry?" We both laughed as I kneeled in front of her and began to remove her shoes. "Here, why don't you lie back while I go whip us up something quick to eat?"

"I'm okay, but thanks. I think I just need some rest. It's been a day." She stifled a yawn while drawing her sock-clad feet onto the bed and got comfortable with a pillow behind her head.

I pulled the covers over her and took a seat on the edge of the mattress. So far, all I'd gotten were instructions on her care and what to do if something went wrong. I still had no idea how she'd ended up in the hospital to begin with.

I carefully touched her cheek and asked, "What happened?"

"Well, I was on recess duty when I noticed one of the boys swinging wildly on the monkey bars. He declared he wanted to be Superman and went for it. Unfortunately, it was at that same time I stepped in to catch him to keep him from falling, and I'm assuming his foot collided with my face." She shook her head but kept a small smile on her lips. "The next thing I remembered, I was flat on the ground with everyone hovering over me. I definitely know what it means now to see stars."

"Damn. He really got you good, Bridge." With my finger beneath her chin, I turned her head to the side to take it all in. "You're bruised from your temple to your nose. I bet you'll have a nice shiner once the swelling calms down."

She groaned and pushed my hand away. "I don't even want to know what I look like."

Rather than remind her that she'd already seen her face after getting in the car, I said, "They gave you something for the pain before we left the hospital, so you should be good for a while. But do you need anything else? Maybe some water?"

"Yes, please. My tongue is dry and feels thick in my mouth." She stuck out her tongue and tried unsuccessfully to look at it with one eye.

"Okay, I'll be right back." I went into the kitchen to get her a glass of water and decided to include a packet of saltines. The nurse had warned against having her eat anything too heavy, so I didn't want to give her anything that would upset her stomach, but I didn't want her to be hungry, either.

In the less than two minutes I'd been gone, she'd fallen asleep. I didn't want to disturb her, so I set the items on the bedside table in case she woke up before her allotted time ran out. I noticed her phone on the corner of the table and decided to plug it in to keep it from dying while she slept. The screen lit up, signaling that the battery was being charged, and something caught my eye. A text. Normally, I would've ignored it, but when I saw Chase's name, I couldn't simply put it down and walk away—not without seeing what he had to say.

Chase: *Are you okay? I just got your message. Why the hell were you in the hospital?*

So, I hadn't been the first one she'd called after all.

———

"BROOKE, YOU NEED TO GET UP." My tone came out harsher than I'd intended, but finding out that Chase had been her first call had hit me hard. Harder than I thought it would. I knew she'd initially reached out to Nellie, but she wasn't competition. Chase was.

I'd spent the last two and a half hours staring at the ceiling while obsessing over his text. It was ridiculous. It wasn't like he'd gone to get her—I had. But still, it left me feeling like I'd been her last option before having to spend the night in the hospital for observation.

It was good to see where I ranked.

I shook her again, trying my best to bite back my frustrations. "Brooke, come on. It's been over two hours. You have to get up."

"Corbin. Help me!" Her distressed tone made all thoughts of introducing Chase to my right hook move to the back burner. Her arms shot out in her sleep, grabbing at anything in reach. But the second I had her cradled against my chest, she immediately settled.

"I'm here, Bridge. But I need you to wake up so I know you're okay." I rubbed her shoulder, and she moaned, which did things to my body that weren't okay when holding a woman whose eye looked like a raw steak. "Bridge, babe. You need to wake up."

She finally opened one eye. "I'm okay," she grumbled.

"Good try, but I'll need more than that. What's your name and, where are you?"

"My name is Brooklyn Bridge. And I'm being held captive in Corbin's bed. Oh, and I hope he does naughty things to me in my sleep. Goodnight."

I leaned back against my pillow, pulling her closer with my arm around her. "That's not funny, Bridge."

"Seriously, I'm fine. I need to sleep, that's all." She cuddled closer and settled into my chest with a contented sigh, so I let her be.

It was already after midnight, and I'd pretty much decided to call in sick. If the last couple of hours were any indication on how much sleep I'd get—none—then it was safe to say I would be of no use to anyone at the office tomorrow. I'd only ever called in sick once before, and that was when I had food poisoning so badly I spent the day on my toilet in fear of being too far away from it.

Brooke wouldn't be going to work anyway, so I figured I would stay with her and make sure she took care of herself. It was unfortunate the situation wasn't different, or we could've spent our time together playing doctor.

I decided I'd give myself one day, and when she was well, I'd let her go back to Chase if that's what she wanted. The longer I thought about it, the more pissed off I became. He hadn't been there for her when she truly needed him. But as I stared at the shadows on the ceiling, listening to Bridge sleep, I had to accept that I didn't have a dog in the fight. I honestly had no idea how they were before the breakup. There had to be a reason she'd stayed with him for so long, and I couldn't imagine she'd have been so heartbroken if he'd been the asshat I'd painted him out to be.

We'd spent a handful of times together and slept together once —well, technically twice. If that was all I'd have with her, I had to be okay with it. But I told myself at around three in the morning that, if she allowed us to continue seeing what we had, I'd give it my all.

BETWEEN MY ALARM going off every two and a half hours to wake Brooke and Chase's text message set on repeat in my head, I hadn't gotten much sleep. Not that I needed much to survive, but I still had a bare minimum and that hadn't been met.

The sun began to rise, and I decided to stop fighting the inevitable. I pulled out my laptop and started the inordinate task of answering emails. The number of emails I received daily was ludicrous, and there weren't many of my colleagues who could keep up that pace. The only reason it worked for me was because of my lack of any personal life.

"Hi."

I turned to find Brooke laying on her side facing me, her pillow hiding her injuries. "Hi, yourself. How are you doing this morning?"

"Pretty good! I can open my eye." She pushed up onto her elbow to show me.

"I see that." I chuckled, because it was hardly larger than a slit, but it did look a lot better than yesterday. The swelling had mostly gone away, thanks to the icepacks I rotated throughout the night. I wondered if Chase would've done the same. Probably not, because pretty boy needed his beauty sleep.

"I think I might attempt a shower," she said with a yawn. "Do you mind?"

"Help yourself." I then wondered if Chase would be so giving with his personal space. Fuckhead. The thought of her with *him* made me sick.

I had to let this Chase shit go, or it would put a black cloud over my entire day with her.

I busied myself with a couple more emails before Brooke came out wrapped in a white towel. That's when I had to put the computer away, because nothing else existed. God, she was beautiful. She took my breath away. Just the sight of her, even with her puffy eye that was now a little more blue than purple.

"I feel so much better. Thanks for letting me use your soaps and stuff." She'd washed her hair, and I swore those soaps never smelled half as good on me. I wanted to lick every inch of her body, which was strictly against the rules given to me by the nurse.

"Of course," was all I could offer, considering all my blood had headed south.

"Shouldn't you be at work by now?" Her lips stretched into an easy smile as she came to sit on the side of the bed where she'd slept last night.

"I decided to take a sick day." I shrugged as if it were no big deal.

"You?" She looked at me like I'd developed malaria. "I

thought I was the one with the concussion. Why are you home sick?"

I opened my laptop, not that I'd be able to concentrate, but at least it gave me something to do other than stare at each and every drop of moisture on her delicate skin. I realized if I didn't do something now, I'd likely break all the rules regarding her care, starting by licking her dry—*everywhere*.

"Well, someone has to keep an eye on you, and I doubt the woman you live with will be much help, especially after you had to get ahold of your neighbor last night just to make sure she'd eaten dinner."

"Oh…well, thanks. Although, I honestly think I would've been fine on my own. I'm sure the worst of it is over." She shifted on the mattress, turning away from me. "Speaking of Phyllis, I should really check on her and see how she's doing. She's fine by herself, otherwise I wouldn't be able to go to work every day. I'm sure the neighbor has already popped in; she usually does shortly after I leave in the mornings."

She grabbed her cell from the side table, and my heart nearly stopped.

I guess it was time to put me out of my misery.

CHAPTER 18

BROOKE

I PICKED up my cell from the table next to the bed, and my blood ran cold. Why the hell had Chase texted me? I hadn't contacted him.

"This is so weird," I mumbled, more to myself than Corbin.

"What is?" Corbin asked without taking his eyes off his laptop.

Ever since I'd come out of the shower, he seemed tense, maybe even a little distant. I didn't know if calling in sick had stressed him out or what. But if that was the case, he didn't need to stay home on my account. I was perfectly fine to be alone. Not to mention, I never asked him to sacrifice a day of work to babysit me, so really, he had no reason to act so cold toward me.

"Chase texted me." I turned and pulled my knee onto the mattress so I could see him. Just because he didn't want to look at me when he spoke didn't mean I felt the same. "I haven't heard from him since last week when I returned his text—which, as we now know, he'd sent in a drunken stupor."

"What did he want?" He glanced my way long enough to point to my cell in my hand. "In his latest text, I mean."

I read it to myself again. "He said he got my message and

asked if I was okay. But I don't understand. I never left him a message. So how'd he know I was in the hospital?"

"That's a good question. You sure you didn't text him? Maybe you did but don't remember due to your head injury." Still, Corbin's attention remained on the opened computer screen in front of him, yet it didn't seem like he was actually doing anything on it other than staring at it.

It started to make me self-conscious about wearing nothing but a towel in front of him. I'd wanted to be sexy—well, as sexy as possible with a black eye—but maybe the sight of me turned him off instead.

I held the towel closer to my chest and said, "I wasn't that out of it. I would remember if I texted someone or not. And I don't at all remember contacting him in any way, shape, or form. I didn't suffer memory loss."

"Well, there's got to be an explanation," Corbin mused.

Suddenly it hit me. "Oh, I bet I know what happened. The school had asked me about my emergency contacts. I bet they called him because I never took him off the list. I need to change that ASAP."

"That's the reason?" Finally, Corbin faced me, looking elated like I'd handed him the biggest present with a bow on top.

"It's the only thing that makes sense." I shrugged and went back to my phone to reach out to Lourdes, the woman next door who kept an eye on Phyllis for me. After all, that had been the entire reason for grabbing my cell to begin with.

I quickly tapped out a text and sent it, not bothering to wait for a response before turning to face Corbin again. I was just happy he seemed to have shaken out of his mood.

"Are you hungry? If you let me wear some of your clothes, I can make breakfast for us."

He closed his laptop and threw the covers off his legs before heading into his walk-in closet. When he came back a few moments later, he handed me a folded pair of boxers and a T-shirt he likely pulled off a hanger, taking a seat beside me. "Listen, I'm sorry I was out of sorts. Let me make us breakfast while you get dressed. Okay?"

I nodded and busied myself with putting on the clothes he'd given me. I finally gave up on trying to get the boxers to stay in place and settled on wearing only the T-shirt instead.

MY EYES SHOT open and I panicked, momentarily forgetting where I was. Then I felt the warm surface beneath my cheek move and remembered...*Corbin*. Somehow, he'd convinced me to spend another night with him, even though the twenty-four-hour period had passed.

I snuggled into his shirt, deciding to take full advantage of his delicious smell while he slept. We'd had an amazing day together. We watched countless movies, ate until we were full, and talked until our voices were hoarse. But he hadn't made one sexual inuendo or tried anything whatsoever. I'd been friend-zoned and had no idea why. I'd thought for certain he'd try something when we went to bed, but nothing had happened.

The shirt beneath my palm was soft and comfy. I'd already become addicted to his chest and never wanted to leave. Which was ridiculous because I'd only spent two and a half nights with him. How could I already be ruined to the point that the mere thought of spending nights alone felt daunting?

My hand moved lower to the waistband of his boxers, and my breathing hitched slightly. I almost pulled away and got cold feet. Almost. But I knew what I wanted, more than anything, and I wasn't going to allow a case of cold feet deter me. My hand trembled slightly and then moved lower until I reached what I'd been after.

A completely hard cock.

Tingles went up my thighs, and I instantly felt moisture pool between my legs. All from the realization that he had a boner. And as far as I knew, it was a reflex and nothing more. What guy didn't suffer from hard-ons during sleep? But that didn't matter. For some reason, Corbin had a different effect on me. Anything he did, even if it was a simple knee-jerk reaction, was sexy as hell.

I held my breath as I slipped my hand farther inside his boxers, and I didn't begin to breathe again until my forefinger and thumb had encircled his shaft. He was so endowed that my fingers couldn't even reach the entire width of him. This should've deterred me, but it didn't. I was going to give him a blowjob, even if it killed me. My assumption was that the best time to practice was when he slept. That way, if I screwed up, I could say it was a dream.

Yeah, anyone would believe that.

Sleep talking? Not me. Sleepwalking? Never. Sleep fellatio? *All the time*.

I slowly tried to pull down his boxers, but I couldn't really see because it was early in the morning and still a little dark, and the last thing I wanted to do was wake him up. Then I remembered—there was an opening in the front. I carefully worked the button loose without stirring him and then freed his thick, heavy cock.

I wasn't sure how he managed to stay asleep through all that, but he did.

And I wasn't about to complain.

I scooted under the covers and climbed over his leg to crouch between his thighs before starting my mission. I gulped. Then I took a deep breath. And gulped again.

I cautiously encircled his thick, heavy, and rock-hard shaft with my fingers—or should I say, *tried* to. Then I tentatively licked his crown. It wasn't bad. So I licked him again, but this time, I swirled my tongue around the head of his dick and then put it between my lips. I bobbed my head up and down before pulling him from my mouth, which produced a pop. I instantly stopped breathing and studied Corbin, positive that would've woken him up.

But he was still asleep.

So I continued.

I tried to take his entire length into my mouth, but there was no way. Although, that didn't stop me from trying. At one point, I gagged, which had been my biggest fear going into this, though it wasn't as big a deal as I'd thought. I didn't die from it. And oddly enough, I found myself slightly more aroused because of it. Feeling a little more brazen, I started going lower and lower, taking more and more of him into my mouth while learning to fight past my gag reflex. Once I got the hang of it, I found it much easier than I remembered.

I also found it much more enjoyable, too.

I released him from my mouth to look at him, marveling in what I'd accomplished. But my mental pat on the back came to an abrupt end when he groaned, "Jesus, Bridge. You're killing me." I jumped and tossed the covers off my head. There, basking in the glow of the early morning sun, I found Corbin staring at me with intense desire burning in his eyes. I'd gotten so into it I hadn't even thought to see if he was still asleep. Then again, I *had* been aware of his melodic moans and the subtle way he'd thrust his hips as I sucked him. But rather than alerting me to the fact that he was awake, they'd heightened my excitement and urged me on.

"Bridge, you okay?" he asked, panting the words more than speaking them. The laughter in his tone wasn't lost on me. And if I weren't so mortified, I likely would've found the humor in it as well. I mean, he did just catch me performing sleep fellatio on him.

I pulled the covers back over my head and cowered between his legs. "No. I died."

"Why the hell did you stop?"

"Because you woke up."

He laughed, hooking his arms beneath mine and dragging me up his body. "Was I supposed to sleep through that? Bridge...I don't know what guys you've been with, but if *anyone* can sleep through what you were doing, they've jacked-off too much and lost vital sensation where it matters most."

I tucked my chin toward my chest and covered my face with my hands.

"Come on, babe. Talk to me." He wrapped his thick fingers around my wrists and pulled my arms away, forcing me to look at him. "I don't understand. Why are you embarrassed? Please, explain it to me."

"It's just…" I either had to word vomit, or I'd just plain vomit, which would only serve to make matters even worse. So, I took a deep breath and went for it. "I've never done that before. I mean, I *have*, but only once. And it was a long time ago. And I hated it. But I wanted to try it again to see if I even could. Or if I even liked it."

"What the fuck? Are you kidding me?" His eyes widened in disbelief, and after staring for what seemed like seventy-seven years, he said, "That's impossible. There's no way you've never done that before."

"You're just saying that."

He threaded his fingers through my hair to push the hanging strands away from my face. "Listen, Bridge. That was unbelievably amazing. So amazing that I had to hold back from coming. You had me so close numerous times, but I didn't want you to stop, so I held back."

"Really?" I studied his face to see if I could detect a lie, but I couldn't. All I found was sincerity.

"Seriously." He pulled me closer and then whispered, "Come here."

My lips met his, and when his tongue entered my mouth, I moaned and arched my back to deepen the kiss. He gripped my hips and rolled me over his erection, lining up the head of his dick with my entrance, but I pulled away.

"I don't want to be in control."

"But you're so good at it," he pleaded.

I believed him, but I'd had enough vulnerability for the time being. "It's not that I don't want sex, so please, don't think that's what I'm saying. I just prefer to be more…"

"Submissive?" He moved my hips again, getting himself into position once more, and then slowly sank into me, giving my body time to adjust to his size and welcome him. "That's okay. Just sit there and enjoy yourself, Bridge. I'll top you from the bottom."

Holy hell. That was...*hot*.

He rolled his hips in a way that made his pelvic bone hit the right spot. And it didn't take long before I fisted his shirt and met each of his thrusts with wild abandon.

"Are you in control now?" His voice was hoarse and sexy as hell.

"No."

"Do you like it?" he asked with each thrust of his hips.

Instead of responding with words, I let my climax answer for me. Strangled cries ripped from my chest as wave after wave of pleasure rolled through me. His frantic movements told me he was close, so I fell to his chest and panted, "Come in me, Corbin. Please, come inside me." It didn't take long after that for him to finish. And as we laid there, trying to calm down, I began to nip his neck between kisses.

I swear, I couldn't get enough of him.

"If you keep that up, we'll have to go again," he murmured and rolled me onto my side so that I was nuzzled next to him.

I wanted to lay here all day with him inside me.

Just like this.

I WOKE up with something between my legs. It took me a moment to realize it wasn't something but some*one*.

However, I wasn't at all scared or shocked. If it's possible to wake up fully aroused, that's how I'd describe it. Corbin's body was between my thighs, his tongue thrust deep within me. I arched my body to meet his mouth, until he switched tactics and began to suck on my clit. He went between swirling his tongue over my lips to flicking it between them.

I had his hair clenched in my fist as I tried to dictate what to do next. But Corbin wouldn't allow me to control his movements. He knew exactly what he wanted to do to me. He brought me to the brink of an orgasm, over and over again, but just as I got to the proverbial cliff, he moved on to do something completely different, stopping me short of reaching my goal every damn time.

I groaned in frustration and tried to move my legs away from him, but he held on tight. I reached between my thighs to give myself a good flick, but he blocked every effort I made to take matters into my own hands. After several failed attempts, he growled, "You said you don't want the control, so I'm taking it from you. Stop fighting it."

And with that, I gave in and let him dominate me with his face between my legs.

Finally, he pushed two fingers inside me, ensuring that each thrust and "come hither" motion hit the spot I needed to come apart. I'd gone my entire life without experiencing something so powerful. It was the orgasm of all orgasms. And then I came so hard I saw stars for the second time in one week.

CHAPTER 19

CORBIN

IT'D BEEN LESS than thirty-six hours since I'd last seen Bridge.

And I couldn't wait to see her again.

She'd gone back to work this morning after taking the last two days off. I thought it was silly to return to work on a Friday rather than just take the rest of the week off, but she claimed she needed to be there since the school was closed all next week for spring break. I kind of understood that, but her returning to work meant she had to return to her house, too. Which meant our sleepovers had come to an end.

Ultimately, that was where my problem was—my bed felt empty without her.

But at least it was Friday, and she had all of next week off, so I had every intention of making the most of the time I was given with her. Now that I knew for certain she wasn't back with Chase, I'd made it my mission to not only figure out if we truly did have something great, but to also make her realize the same thing. I refused to drag my feet with this.

The closer I drove to her house, the more impatient I became, which was ridiculous since we'd only been "seeing" each other for less than a week. But I guess I'd gotten used to having her around, so when she wasn't there, my days seemed longer and my nights lonelier.

When I'd dropped her off yesterday morning before heading to the office, she'd offered to take an Uber, but I refused to let her go home alone. It was bad enough that she didn't have her own transportation due to her car still not running. I hated thinking that she couldn't leave the house to run a simple errand, especially considering she was supposed to be helping Phyllis by taking her places. So as soon as I got to the office yesterday, I'd made a few calls, and before noon, I'd gotten a buddy of mine to tow her car to his shop and fix it. I don't know why I hadn't thought of that earlier.

Maybe because she'd kept me occupied for a couple of days.

I left work a little early tonight so I could take her to pick up her car. I'd been assured that it was in proper working order, which made me feel marginally better. If she weren't at my place with me, where I knew she was safe, at least I didn't have to worry about her being stranded on the side of the road somewhere. Still, I would've preferred her to stay with me, but that was something we'd have to wait to discuss—until we were both confident that our connection went beyond the honeymoon stage.

Every time I pulled up to the curb in front of the house Brooke was staying at, my heart broke a little more. It was sad that she had to live in something so rundown, but even more sad that there were people out there, like Phyllis, who didn't have any other option. Between dropping Brooke off yesterday morning and now, the outside had seemingly fallen apart even more. Aside from the overgrown weeds that littered the front lawn and dilapidated shutters on the front windows that had been like that since my first visit, the soffit had begun to fall, drooping from the eaves along the front of the house.

I could only imagine what kind of shape the back yard was in.

Before I could take note of any other damage, Brooke came bounding down the driveway, practically skipping toward me.

Her excitement to see me put an instant smile on my face. Or maybe it was already there. Maybe I'd been wearing it since leaving the office, knowing I was on my way to see her.

"Is there no one to do any work on this house for her?" I asked after giving her a quick kiss when she got in the car. "She can't let it keep falling apart or it'll be condemned."

Brooke glanced out her window at the house. "No, unfortunately not. She has relatives, but they aren't local. They visit every year or so and keep the inside updated and in working order, but there's never any time left to address the outside issues."

"You did an entire renovation on your school, and you're telling me there's no way to help this woman with her home?" I pointed past her to the house, the low-hanging sun only serving to highlight the peeling paint, showcasing just how rundown it was. "A few nails, a couple screws, a lawnmower, and some paint is all it'll need."

That was a total lie.

It needed so much more than that. But I figured if I approached it like it wasn't a big deal, then maybe she wouldn't fight me on this as hard as she had the car situation. Then again, her main issue with that was I'd paid someone to fix her car. I doubted she'd object to letting *me* help her with the house. I'd seen the insane amount of work that had gone into the school beautification day and then witnessed the amazing transformation. I didn't see why the same couldn't happen here.

Did I seriously just volunteer for another manual labor project?

The things I did to create excuses to be around her.

"You're sweet, Corbin, but trust me, it's bigger than a two-man job. Plus, I don't know the first thing about fixing any of that." She hitched her thumb over her shoulder toward the house while keeping her pistachio-colored eyes on me. "Just my luck, I'd start to rehang a shutter and the roof will fall off."

I couldn't help but laugh. This was a woman who approached the world like there was nothing she couldn't handle, yet here she was, scared of a minor cosmetic project. "Bridge, you were raised by a single mother. I'm willing to bet she had to climb on a roof once or twice to clean out the gutters, crawl beneath the sink to fix a leak, and learn how to patch drywall in the house. And she would've had to do all of that without the help of YouTube videos."

"And your point is…?" She narrowed her gaze on me. "It's not like I can call her up and ask her how to do any of this. She can't help me. She's dead."

I hated seeing the shimmer of tears in her eyes. Even though it'd been years since her mom passed away, there were times when Brooke reacted like it'd happened yesterday. I couldn't fault her for that. I imagined losing a parent wasn't something you got over. Ever. I only wished I could make it better for her, or at least make it hurt less. Anything to stop the pain that seemed to strangle her without a moment's notice.

Taking her hand in mine, I waited to speak until I had her attention. Once her eyes met mine, I softly said, "All I was trying to say is…you were raised by one of the strongest women who has ever lived. There's nothing you can't do, because there was nothing *she* couldn't do. You had the best role model anyone could've asked for, so if anyone is beyond capable of fixing this place up, it's you."

She blinked, and a single tear slipped free.

Lifting our joined hands, I swiped the soft skin on her cheek with my knuckle. "Lucky for you, though, I'm not suggesting you do it alone. Not that you couldn't, but at least you don't have to. I'll get the supplies, and possibly a few extra hands, and we'll tackle it together next weekend. How does that sound?"

Brooke sniffled and then ran her finger beneath her eyes, making sure there weren't any more evidence of her pain. "You'd really do that?"

"For you? Of course I would."

"But you hate manual labor. And it's not even for me; it's Phyllis's house."

I adjusted myself in my seat and shifted the car into gear to pull away from the curb. "Except you live there, so really, it is for you. The place is falling apart, and I'd feel much better about you staying there if I knew it wouldn't collapse on you while you're asleep."

Barking laughter broke free and filled the car with her contagious amusement. "See? I knew it wasn't for me. You're doing it for yourself, to feel better about where I live so *you* can sleep better at night."

"Bridge, I sleep so much better when you're next to me. So if my motivations were truly that selfish, I'd let her house continue to fall apart just so I'd have an excuse to keep you in my bed every night. In fact, I'd probably find ways to speed up the deterioration process."

She was quiet for a moment, and when I chanced a glance to my right, I found her staring at her hands in her lap with her lips twisted to the side. Over the last several weeks, anytime I'd caught her doing that exact thing, she'd been in deep contemplation, usually regarding something serious. I tried to replay my words in my head, but for the life of me, I couldn't figure out what I'd said that made her retreat behind her walls.

"Bridge? Everything okay?"

It was like I'd snapped my fingers, freeing her from a trance she'd been under. Her shoulders rolled back, she removed her hands from her lap, and her wide, surprised eyes landed on me. "Huh? Yeah, I'm fine."

Even if this was the first time meeting her, I would've been able to tell she was lying. The biggest red flag was that she never questioned why I'd asked if she was all right. If there truly wasn't anything wrong, my worry should've confused her, causing her to wonder what had led me to ask in the first place. But she never did.

If I'd learned anything from her silence last week, it was that pushing got me nowhere. Abduction did, but I figured it was best to save that tactic for emergency situations. So far, this didn't seem to be an emergency. So, I let it go and hoped that if something truly was bothering her, she'd open up about it when she was ready.

In the meantime, I prayed like hell it wasn't anything serious.

I HAD a massive smile plastered on my face as I walked to work this morning.

Normally, I spent my journey running over my schedule and the pitches I'd studied for our team meetings. But this time, I blocked all that out and only thought of Bridge. Of falling asleep with her in my arms last night and waking up next to her this morning—her in my T-shirt lying across my bed, one leg peeking out from beneath the covers.

Fuck!

It nearly did me in. If I hadn't already been late, I would've totally ripped that shirt off her and taken her once again. Technically, I was right on time, but considering I'd spent my entire career at AdCorp arriving a solid hour before everyone else, this was as good as a tardy. And the worst part was, this was the second time this week.

That wouldn't be too bad if it weren't Tuesday.

But as long as my day started with Brooklyn in my bed, I wouldn't be at the office before eight. The same went for the evenings as well—if I had plans to see her, I was on my way out no later than five.

For the first time in my life, work didn't come first.

"Morning, Em!" I greeted my assistant as I rounded her desk.

"Good morning." Skepticism filled her tone.

Ignoring Emily's scrutinizing stare, I walked past her and headed into my office. I set my briefcase on my desk and went through the motions of my morning routine. It was something I went through every day, every single morning, without fail. And it was boring as fuck.

I chuckled to myself as I thought of the ways Bridge seemed to be changing me.

Yet I had not one complaint, because for the first time in my life, I felt like I was doing more than merely existing. I felt like I was *living*. The scariest part of it all was the thought of this thing between us *not* working out. Not that I didn't think it would, but it wasn't like we'd discussed our feelings since the night of the parade when we'd decided to see if we had something.

"You look weird."

I glanced down at myself and then back to Emily, who stood in the doorway with her legal pad clutched to her chest and pencil behind her ear. "Do I? How so?"

"You look happy. I mean, it's not a bad look on you…just weird."

Ignoring the smile that remained on my face, I rolled my eyes and ignored her.

"Anyway, the team is already in the conference room. Want me to tell them you're on your way?" Now the legal pad against her chest and the pencil behind her ear made more sense.

Shit. While I was mentally prepared for this meeting, I didn't have the actual presentation put together. Luckily, I was the team leader, so I didn't have to worry about being called out for my disorganization. Unfortunately, walking into a meeting unprepared didn't do much to convince the rest of the team to trust me.

Oh well. At least I knew what I wanted to say. So be it if they didn't have my notes projected onto a wall. Maybe this time they'd actually have to listen to what I had to say rather than relying on a PowerPoint presentation to save their asses.

"No need, I'll follow you in." I grabbed my briefcase off my desk, not even having opened it since setting it down, and walked with Emily down the hall to the large conference room. She attended every team meeting and took notes from the back of the room.

"Good morning, everyone," I greeted the room as I made my way to the head of the table. "I'll keep it short and sweet this morning; we all have lots to do before the end of the quarter." I set my briefcase on top of the table and popped it open, then immediately shut it, glancing around the room to see if anyone had seen what was inside. When I felt safe that no one had, I cleared my throat and took a step toward the door. "I, uh...I actually left the details report in my office. I'll be right back."

Emily stood and waved me off. "I'll grab it for you."

"As much as I appreciate that, it'll be much faster if I get it. I know exactly where it is."

The truth was, I hadn't forgotten the report. It was right inside my briefcase, along with the summary report and contract logs for the entire team. But papers weren't all I had in there. It seemed Bridge had left me a surprise, something I wished I had known prior to opening my briefcase in the meeting.

When I made it back to my desk, I quickly pulled out the pair of panties she'd had on last night, balled them up in my fist, smiled at the memory of taking them off with my teeth, and then shoved them into my top drawer.

I was a goner.

Everything she did intoxicated me and left me yearning for more. Just the thought of her made me hard. Over the last couple of days, I'd found myself walking around with an erection most of the time. It was like I'd become a born-again teenager. I'd always had a healthy sex drive, but this last week, I couldn't get enough. *Of her.*

And it seemed she couldn't get enough of me, either.

I grabbed my cell from my pocket and quickly typed out a message.

Me: *You're a bad girl, Bridge.*

Her response came just before I'd made it back to the conference room.

Bridge: *Who? Me? I have no idea what you're talking about.*

216

The purple devil emoji she added at the end begged to differ.

CHAPTER 20

BROOKE

"YOU'LL NEVER GUESS what I saw in my brother's office yesterday."

By the look on Nellie's face, I would've guessed heroin, possibly an orgy. But I knew neither of those could be true—I'd spent enough time exploring Corbin's body, so if he'd had track marks, I would've seen them. And I knew the orgy was out of the question because...well, if he had time to play with a group of people, then I clearly wasn't doing my job. Not to brag or anything, but I was *definitely* doing my job.

"If I'll never guess, then why do you always make me try?"

"Because it's no fun if I just tell you." She shrugged and put the linen napkin in her lap.

Since I was off work for the week, and she wasn't, she thought it was necessary to have lunch dates every day. I didn't mind, because at least it gave me a chance to see her without feeling guilty for all the time I'd been spending with her brother...*behind her back.*

"For heaven's sake, Nellie, just spit it out already. What did you see in Corbin's office?"

She leaned forward, cupped her hands to the sides of her mouth, and whispered, "Women's panties in his desk." A smug smile curved her lips as she sat back, but I couldn't move from the hunched position I was in. "Gross, right? I wonder whose they are. I bet they're dirty."

Feeling like I could choke on my tongue any second now, I reached for the glass of ice water and began to gulp it down. When I was ready to speak, I asked, "So you have no idea who they belong to? Like, no clue?"

Nellie's gaze narrowed on me, and her brows pulled together the slightest bit, but it didn't last long before she waved me off. "How should I know? My only two guesses would be Lindsey or Emily, his assistant. But honestly, I doubt they're Emily's."

"Why would you say that?" At this point, I didn't care whose panties she thought they were, just as long as she didn't suspect that they were mine.

Mindlessly browsing the menu, she said, "Well, I was in there looking for a pen to leave him a note because he wasn't at his desk, so of course, I pulled them out to see what they were."

"Of course." As if that was the natural thing to do. Seriously, what else could they have been?

"Anyway, they wouldn't fit Emily. It's not like they were big or anything, but she's a really small girl, so it was fairly easy to tell that they'd be too big for her."

If that didn't make me feel like shit, I didn't know what would.

Lucky for her, she didn't know the panties were mine.

"Oh!" I snapped my fingers, hoping she hadn't caught the offense on my face. "Maybe he scored with Heather."

"Nope, he came back to his office before I left—but *after* I returned the soiled thongs—and I asked where he was on the plan, because I had the same thought. If they are hers, then he's lying about his progress, and I don't see why he'd do that. Lying wouldn't benefit him at all."

They were cheekies, not a thong. But that was a moot point.

"Where did he say he was on the plan?" For some reason, he hadn't mentioned anything to me about Heather. I'd assumed he hadn't made much progress since I'd seen him nearly every night —with the exception of Sunday, which he was at his parents' house, and last night because I had laundry and cleaning to catch up on.

"He said they had plans to get drinks last night, but since I saw him before his supposed date, I don't have any other information. I guess he's been busy with work, so that was the first opportunity he's had to do anything. So yeah, they weren't hers."

I doubted he would've met her for drinks without telling me, but it wasn't like I knew that for certain. However, the more I thought about it, the more suspicious I became. The few nights we hadn't been together, we'd stayed up late texting. But last night, they were quite sporadic. At the time, I hadn't thought anything of it because I was busy picking up around the house. But now, I couldn't shake it.

"Okay, so that leaves Lindsey?" I needed to keep talking, or she'd definitely know something was up.

Nellie closed the menu and set it aside. Really, there was no reason for her to have even opened it. This place was right next to her parents' office building, so she frequently ate here. And she was the type to always order the same thing for fear of trying something else and hating it.

"It's possible. Not likely, but possible. Although, it'd be amazing if they were hers." She let out a long sigh. "My parents love her and have already accepted her as part of the family. I would love to have her as a sister. We just need Corbin to straighten himself out, but he will. They always end up back together."

My chest constricted, and her words hit me like knives to the heart. I cleared my throat before continuing. "Well, is it plausible that he met someone online, and she stopped by for a midday quickie?" Even I didn't believe that one, but I couldn't think of anything else to say.

Once the waitress left with our food order, Nellie put her

elbow on the table and perched her chin on her fist. If only her mom could see her now... "So what's been going on with you?"

"What do you mean? I've met you for lunch every day this week."

"Yeah, but we've been a bit preoccupied with my drama. I realized on the way here that I haven't really asked you how *you're* doing. How's your job? How are you handling the Chase situation?"

"Job's good. Nothing new on the Chase front." I wanted to tell her I'd be a lot better if we stopped talking about me, but that wasn't exactly an option.

"I'm still pissed at you, by the way. I totally would've come to get you at the hospital if you'd told me you were there."

"I know you would've, Nells. But you had a date, and I wasn't about to ruin that."

"Yeah, but still, you shouldn't have to rely on your neighbor to drive you home. She's what...seventy?" Nellie was under the impression that she would never get old.

"Sixty-two I think."

"Eh, close enough." She was lucky that she came from money so that when the time came, she'd be able to afford all the plastic surgery to keep her from looking a day over twenty-nine.

"Anyway, it's over and done with. Let's stop bringing that up."

"Deal. So why don't you tell me what you've been up to this week?"

Dammit, I thought we were moving away from me! "Not much, just relaxing and taking care of Phyllis. Same thing different day, but with the exception of not having to go to work. Oh, and having lunch with you every day. But other than that, nothing new. You know me...boring, boring."

I finally drank more water just to shut the fuck up.

But her words about Lindsey stung and refused to go away.

WITH MY ARMS over my head, I stretched out my entire body. It was the good kind that reached every muscle. I needed that extra moment, because today would be grueling work.

I finally talked myself out of bed and padded to the kitchen in my socks to start the coffee. Phyllis must've still been asleep because her door was firmly closed. She usually slept until nine or ten in the morning, so we'd start without her. Knowing her, she'd come out to contribute, so I made a note to myself to leave the easy jobs she could manage.

As I entered my bedroom, my phone beeped with a text message.

Corbin: On my way, gorgeous. See you in fifteen or so! Xxx

Me: Sounds perfect. Jumping in the shower now.

Corbin: Naked?

Me: Is there another way to take a shower?

Corbin: No...dammit. That image caused something to stir. Why couldn't you have said you were doing laundry...never mind, that still made me hard and think of you naked. Xxx

Laughter bubbled through me as I read his texts one more time before jumping in the shower. I'd never been known to evoke that sort of reaction or think of myself as sexual in nature. Yet he encouraged those feelings in me like no one ever had. Our chemistry was undeniable, and even the thought of him in that way did things to me. I enjoyed it. These newly sparked sensations left an impression on me, but sometimes left me confused.

Once I finished my shower, I began to straighten up the living room and kitchen. There wasn't much to do. With just the two of us living here, things were kept pretty tidy, but I had nervous energy. I hadn't seen Corbin in a few days, and the excitement of him coming over made butterflies dance in my stomach.

I jumped at the knock on the front door, even though I'd been expecting him.

"Hi," I greeted him, shyly.

"Hi, yourself." He kissed me softly, and I nearly melted in his arms. The feel of his lips always did me in—and automatically made me want to take things further.

I opened the door wider to silently invite him in. "I can't believe we're doing this."

"I brought us sustenance. We're going to need it." He grinned like a little boy on Christmas morning, which didn't match our current predicament. We had this gargantuan project hanging over us, which was stressful, yet he seemed giddy.

"Thank you. And I made coffee."

"Perfect."

We silently ate our sandwiches at the kitchen table, but it wasn't an awkward silence. It was familiar and safe.

"Which tasks should we tackle first?" I finally broached the daunting projects that awaited us outside, knowing he'd had it all scheduled out. That was his thing—organizing. So rather than pester him all week about the plans for the house, I'd decided to wait for this morning.

"I actually have a surprise for you. I've got several guys coming to help. They should be here in a few minutes." Corbin shot me a tentative glance while he waited for me to answer.

"Seriously? What will that leave us to do?" Excitement practically bubbled over at the thought of having help. I'd spent all week imagining that we'd be doing all the work. "I mean, that's amazing."

"I had a buddy of mine—well, he's actually an old client from years ago—come out last week to evaluate the condition of the house, and it turns out it's a lot more extensive than I originally thought. So, I hired his crew to help us with the structural stuff. It shouldn't take them long, but I'd rather things were put back accurately versus leaving us to guess what to do."

"Oh my God, Corbin! That's too much!" I'd gone from grateful to guilty in a matter of seconds. When I'd agreed to his crazy idea of cleaning up the outside, my one stipulation was that he couldn't pay anyone to do it. It was hard enough to bite back my pride and let him spend money on the supplies—the paint alone wasn't cheap. "I told you I didn't want you paying for labor."

He smiled, as if my irritation was cute. "It's not a big deal. We either let a few professionals handle the bigger stuff, or we do it and risk creating more issues…which would require us to have someone come out anyway. I figured at that point, it might cost more money, because not only would they have to fix the original problem, but all the shit we fucked up trying to do it ourselves as well. Think of it as a time and money saver."

"I appreciate it, but I'm still upset that you went behind my back and did what I specifically asked you not to."

"Be honest…if I'd mentioned it to you first, would you have gone along with it?"

"Hell no." I shook my head and smiled, realizing his point without him having to state it.

Just then, someone knocked on the door. Corbin stood to answer it, leaving me at the kitchen table to finish eating. There was something so domestic about that simple action, and it'd sent me into a daydream of what my future with him would look like while he dealt with the workers at the front door.

When he returned, I stood and kissed his cheek. "Phyllis will be so happy. Thank you."

"No need to thank me, babe. I fully plan to collect payment when this is all said and done." He chuckled and patted my butt before returning to his seat at the table.

Since he'd prearranged to have a crew come to work on the structural projects, and those needed to be done before we could paint—or do any other cosmetic work—we took our time going over his plan of action.

When we finished eating, I got Phyllis settled on the sofa in front of her daily soap operas, and then we set off for a hardware store to pick out plants for the yard. I'd allowed him to get everything else, but my one request was that he'd let me choose the flowers—a contingency he'd willingly agreed to.

The contractors were almost finished by the time we made it back from the store—to give them extra time, we'd visited a few nurseries as well. The transformation took my breath away. The shutters had been removed and neatly stacked on the side of the house. All the peeling paint had been sanded away, and even though there were areas that still needed work, it already looked a hundred times better. Someone had stopped by to mow the grass, so all that was left was the weeding, painting, and planting. It was such a relief that so much had been done. The project would still take a good amount of time, but now, it didn't feel so daunting.

Phyllis came out in the early afternoon and insisted on helping, so I set her up on a stool in the shade pulling weeds from a planter while Corbin and I dug up the flowerbeds in the blazing sun. It didn't take long before I was completely drenched in sweat. There was no way in hell I looked even the slightest bit attractive.

"This is disgusting." I lifted the hem of my shirt to wipe off my dripping brow. "I'm getting hungry, so maybe we should finish this last one and stop?" We'd successfully weeded the walkway and were on the last planter box.

"Brooke?" Phyllis called out and then shuffled over to where we worked. "I think I'm done for the day. This is more work than I've done all month." She chuckled to herself.

"I know. But it's going to look so good once it's all finished." I got up to help her inside. "I can't wait for you to see the final product."

She stopped me for a moment and turned to face Corbin. "Do you like Chinese food?"

He smiled widely and nodded. "Yes, ma'am."

"Good, because that's what we're having for dinner. I suspect you'll want to stay around for a bit and relax after all the work you two have done today." She took my hand and continued toward the front door, waiting until we'd reached the top step before saying to me, "Let him know he's welcome to stay over with you." She patted my hand and then let herself into the house.

She'd taken a liking to Corbin.

And she wasn't the only one.

Yardwork had its pros and cons—the pros being all the time it lent to thinking. And I'd spent all day thinking about Corbin, contemplating how I felt about him and our situation. I'd allowed my mind to wander while sorting out the things I never had time to process otherwise.

I had come to care very deeply for him. We'd started spending a lot of time together over the last several weeks, and I honestly couldn't imagine a life without him in it. But after lunch with Nellie the other day, it was clear that her family didn't see anyone else but Lindsey in Corbin's future.

We'd definitely reached a crossroad. Either we stopped things now and tried to salvage what was left of our friendship or carried on with what we were doing. I wouldn't lie, after all we'd shared together—especially these last two weeks—it'd be hard to remain friends, but it could be done. We'd simply go back to the way things were before we'd slept together. I'd hardly see or hear from him, but that would be best, especially if he went back to Lindsey.

That thought tore me apart, which led me to contemplate our other option: continue things as they were and see where it led. But if I took that fork in the road, my friendship with Nellie would suffer, and I couldn't imagine a world without her in it, either.

It was an impossible situation, which was why I rarely let my thoughts go rogue. I hated to think about the future—or lack thereof—because both options killed me. There was no way to win in the end, and that would only happen if Corbin and I had what it took to last. Which, considering the odds, was a bit of a gamble.

"You look deep in thought," Corbin mused as he shoveled through the last corner of dirt.

"Yeah. That tends to happen when I garden. My mind begins to drift to things I'm able to suppress during the normal day-to-day grind." I attempted a smile, even though I knew it came out half-assed.

"Is something bothering you?" His brow creased as worry set in.

"Honestly, nothing worth mentioning." I leaned over and kissed him.

Luckily, Phyllis chose that moment to stick her head out the front door, stopping him from continuing the conversation. "I just ordered Chinese. It will be here in twenty minutes."

"Thank you!" I smiled at her and then began to gather our tools to put them away.

"Looks like we're finished here." Corbin groaned as he got up from his crouched position. "I may need a massage later."

"Oh, yeah?" I teased. "Is that your payment for today?"

"No, that's just because you like me. Your payment will be way more than that." He grinned at me so wickedly my face burned.

"Then I guess it's your lucky day, because Phyllis let me know earlier that she doesn't mind if you stay the night." My stomach flipped with nerves. I'd stayed over at his place countless times, yet the thought of him being here caused heart palpitations. There was something intimate about having someone share your personal space, like letting them inside your walls. It took a lot of trust to be that vulnerable. "You know...if you want to."

He smiled while putting the last of the tools in the box. "I'd love to."

I wanted to offer excuses for why it made sense that he'd sleep here—earlier start in the morning, less driving—but I couldn't form any words that would take away from my honest desire to have him next to me…in *my* personal space.

"Come on." He broke me from my thoughts by grabbing my hand and tugging me toward the front door. "Let's go get washed up for dinner."

Today had been nearly perfect. I'd never had someone take care of me before. I mean, when I was little, I had my mom. And she was the best and showed me what unconditional love truly was. But I'd never been in a relationship where I'd experienced that sort of thing.

Chase had never demonstrated that level of love; our relationship had been very one-sided. I had fully supported him in every aspect of his life, and even though he'd argue that he had done the same, I'd never seen the proof. Hell, he'd never once visited my school. Granted, anytime I wanted to do something—hang out with friends, become a teacher—he never stood in my way, and I guess I'd confused that with support.

Yet somehow, in the short time I'd been with Corbin, he'd shown me what is was like to truly be supported. He'd succeeded in every area Chase had fallen short. And for the first time in my life, I began to believe that unconditional love wasn't solely reserved for parents—it was obtainable in a romantic relationship as well.

I'd given Chase my heart and soul; he was my everything. And when he dumped me, I was left with nothing. He'd taken everything with him. Our future, mutual friends, his career that we'd nurtured together. Everything had disappeared in the blink of an eye. Life as I'd known it had been erased.

But with Corbin, I had a life again. One I could call my own. One that I cultivated and nurtured. One that I felt comfortable in. Corbin didn't take over my world—he added to it. He didn't invade my space or smother me. If anything, he encouraged me to grow and become more. Become me. By myself. So that when we were together, doing things as a couple, it was because we *wanted* to.

For someone so independent, I'd somehow become *co*dependent with Chase.

Letting down my walls was a different thing entirely. I just couldn't bear to let someone in and give them the power to demolish me again. I couldn't bear the thought of being that reliant on another person again.

Maybe my crossroad wasn't as confusing as I thought.

Maybe I'd already knew what I wanted.

But how could I have that if I couldn't ignore the fear of losing myself again?

CHAPTER 21

CORBIN

PHYLLIS WAS A SWEET LADY, and I could instantly see what Brooke saw in her.

It was easy to see why this situation worked. I guess Brooke had gone to college with Phyllis's granddaughter, and when she'd learned of how dire Brooke's situation was, she offered Brooke her old room at her grandmother's house. It was a win-win for everyone involved.

She was in the final stages of moving away to do her post-graduate work, and her grandmother's caregiver had bailed. Having Brooke stay with Phyllis eased the worry over finding someone to keep an eye on her grandmother, and it kept her from having to stay home and put her education on pause, while offering Brooke a place to stay rent free.

Brooke had really lucked out, because not only did she get a free place to stay in exchange for a few chores and the occasional errand, but Phyllis was easy to get along with. She was also funny. There were many times during dinner when she'd say something mildly inappropriate, but considering her age, it had us in stitches.

After the food was put away and the kitchen was clean, I waited on Brooke's bed while she finished her shower. She had a decent-size room, and her bed was comfortable. I could've easily drifted off to sleep, but thoughts of Brooke's soapy, wet, naked body kept me awake. I'd thought, more than once about sneaking into the shower and surprising her, but the bathroom was right next to Phyllis's room. It just seemed wrong.

I'd already taken my shower, and thankfully, Brooke had a T-shirt and pair of boxers of mine that she'd worn home one morning last week. So at least I had clean clothes to wear while mine were in the wash. I'd told Brooke it was pointless to run them in a load tonight since I'd just be getting them dirty again tomorrow, but she insisted.

It was just one of the many things she did to take care of me.

"Hey, sleepyhead," Brooke whispered with her mouth incredibly close to my ear.

I rolled over and wrapped an arm around her, pulling her closer into my chest. "I must've drifted off. I swear I tried to stay awake for you."

"It's okay. We're both exhausted." She nuzzled into my neck while stretching her legs down the length of mine. "It feels so good to finally be horizontal!"

"I can't argue with you there." I settled onto my back so that her head rested comfortably on my chest, the way we'd fallen asleep together countless times. It felt right. She fit perfectly. The closeness I experienced when lying with her this way was something I'd never known.

I utilized the silence in the room and the calming sound of her soft breathing to ponder my relationship with Brooke. I wanted her. All. The. Time. But not just sexually, even though that was a given. I wanted her there with me. In every aspect of my life. After spending time together that first week, I never wanted to go back to the way things were. I wanted this—*her*—for as long as she'd let me keep her.

I knew what I wanted, but I wasn't sure Brooke had come to her own conclusion yet. We'd promised each other that, when one of us knew what we wanted, we'd talk about it and make a decision on where we'd go from there. But even though *my* mind was made up, I worried about broaching the subject too soon. The last thing I wanted to do was push her away before giving her the time to truly discover her feelings for me. There was no way she'd be able to make a decision on where to go from here if she were still ten steps back.

So now, all I could do was wait.

"I CANNOT BELIEVE you blackmailed me into attending Sunday dinner. Again!" Brooke huffed and crossed her arms while we stood in the circular drive, waiting for her to finish with her tantrum.

"I don't know what you mean." I worried that my tongue-in-check comment would earn me a smack, so I was happy when all she gave me was the death stare.

"You led me to believe that I'd be paying you back with sex. Had I known you'd collect by making me come to dinner at your parents', I never would've agreed to those guys working on the house." It seemed the drive here only heightened her anger toward me.

Since I couldn't very well drive her here without raising suspicions—we'd dealt with enough of those from my sister—I had to follow her, knowing she couldn't be trusted to meet me here on her own. So after finishing up in the yard, I'd gone home to change, and then met her back at her place to collect her debt.

"I told you I'd take you out for dinner. Well, here we are." I held out my arm to gesture to the house, Vanna White style.

She scrunched her nose, which only made me laugh harder. "It's not fair, Corbin."

"Come on. You can see Nellie and my adoring parents. It'll be fine."

"That's the point. I don't want to see Nellie while *with* you. That girl can read me like a book. It was hard enough being around her without you there." She groaned and stomped her foot on the brick driveway. "We're so fucked."

"Hmm...interesting." I cocked my head and studied her like she were a painting in a gallery.

"What's interesting?" At least she'd dropped some of the attitude.

"I didn't realize that if you spent most of your time with bratty kids, you'd turn into one." I stepped away from her scowl and headed to the front door, snickering. "I certainly hope it's not contagious."

Thank God she didn't turn around leave. I hadn't had the fore-thought to take her keys from her when we arrived. Although, just because she stepped inside when I opened the door didn't mean she did so with a smile on her face. Her feelings were very obvious as she begrudgingly followed me down the hall to the dining room. I just hoped she had enough wherewithal to mask it in front of my parents and Nellie.

"There you are." Mom kissed my cheek. "I thought I heard you pull up a while ago."

"How have you been, son?" Dad patted my back heftily in greeting.

"Brooke, what are you doing here?" Nellie managed to call everyone's attention to Brooke, who had barely taken two steps into the room.

Mom seemed confused when she turned to my sister. "I invited her. Is there a problem?"

I held my breath, worried Nellie would ask more questions, until she finally said, "Oh, no. I just didn't know she was coming. Why didn't you tell me?"

Brooke shrugged. "It was last minute. I thought I'd surprise you."

At least that seemed to calm my sister. She smiled brightly and finally gave her friend a hug. "Well, it's certainly a nice surprise. Did you guys come together?"

I didn't miss the scrutiny in her glare as she looked at me. It was enough to piss me off. Keeping any worry or guilt from invading my voice, I said, "No, I actually pulled up right behind her."

"Well, I'd say it was perfect timing." Mom ushered us all to the table. Once again, Bridge was seated next to Nellie, and I had to fight the urge to move her next to me where she belonged. "They're ready to bring out the starters, and we wouldn't want the main course to get cold."

Like clockwork, once bowls of soup had been placed in front of everyone and we all had a glass of wine, it was time to dive right into intense conversation topics.

"You all will be attending our annual Easter egg celebration, correct?" Mom glanced around the table, making eye contact with the three of us.

Nellie nodded and finished swallowing her food before answering. "Of course. I wouldn't dream of missing it." Sarcasm filled her tone, but beneath it all, I knew she'd meant it. There wasn't a holiday Nell didn't love. "Brooke and I were thinking about dressing up as chicks."

"You *are* a chick, dork." I couldn't resist.

She sneered in my direction and rolled her eyes. "Not that kind of chick, dumbass."

"I think that would be adorable. I'm sure the neighborhood kids would love that." Mom clasped her hands together in excitement. "And watch your language, Penelope. You know the rules."

"That's not happening, Nellie." Brooke shot my sister a look that clearly asked what the fuck she was thinking.

"Oh, come on! At least think about it."

"We'll see." Brooke shrugged, but based on her body language, it was obvious that this topic would not be revisited.

"Have you heard from Lindsey?" Mom's question snapped me out of my amusement, which was good, because the thought of Bridge in a chick costume entertained me in more than one way.

"Um, not in a while, no." That would hopefully put an end to the conversation.

Out of the corner of my eye, I saw Nellie perk up and study Brooke. It made me a little uncomfortable, so I could only imagine what was going through Bridge's mind. Between the two of us, she was definitely the most paranoid. She claimed she had more to lose, but I begged to differ. I risked losing *her*, and in my book, there was nothing worse than that.

Mom, once again, spoke up and pulled me from my thoughts. "I really do wish you'd work things out with her, dear." She wiped the corners of her mouth with her linen napkin before returning it to her lap as if we were in some five-star restaurant.

"That's extremely unlikely, Mom."

"I don't get it, son. Lindsey fits perfectly in every aspect of your life. She supported your work ethic and never batted an eye at your late nights. She never questioned where you were. Do you have any idea how rare it is to find someone like that? I've seen promising careers get tossed aside due to jealous wives making ultimatums—the family or the job. Lindsey would never do that to you. She also comes from a very affluent family, and with their backing, you could write your own ticket. The two of you could eventually take over and run the family business."

My dad had always loved everything about Lindsey. Both of my parents did. They'd made it no secret that they wanted us to work things out. But their reasons were based on things I no longer desired. Being career-driven individuals themselves, they saw our dynamic as a positive trait, but in reality, they were negative and borderline toxic. We constantly chose work over each other. We never chose to spend time together unless we were both caught up on emails and spreadsheets and pitches, and even then, our conversations revolved around work. How could I explain to them that I never wanted to go back to that? Not after experiencing what it's like to actually live my life versus merely existing.

"It's not that simple, Dad."

"Sure it is." While his voice was stern, I knew it was simply because he felt passionately about it. What he and my mom had together worked for them, but that didn't mean I wanted the same. "She won't be in another state forever, son. Long-distance relationships *can* work providing both parties put forth the effort. Your generation and your need for instant gratification… You can either make sacrifices now and reap the benefits down the road, or you can take the easy way out and suffer the consequences later. The choice is yours."

"Thanks, Dad." I lifted my glass in a mock toast. "I'm glad you realize that it's *my* choice."

Brooke remained quiet with her eyes locked on her plate during the entire exchange.

Nellie, being the meddling nuisance that she was, decided to add her own commentary rather than let the conversation die. "Why don't you at least call her?"

If I could, I'd drown her in her bowl of soup.

"Seriously?" I glared at her from across the table. "I'll date who I want, when I want. End of conversation."

Throats were cleared and silverware clanked during a tense few moments of silence.

"How did your weekend go, Corbin?" Mom asked sweetly for no other reason than to lighten the mood. "Did you manage to finish that community service project you were working on?"

I nodded while shoveling another spoonful of soup into my mouth to keep from having to speak. The faster she moved on to questioning someone else the better it would be for all of us.

Nellie curled her top lip and narrowed her gaze at me. "You're doing *another* community service project? What's it this time?"

Unfortunately, since I'd kept my mouth full of food, I couldn't respond, leaving my mom to answer for me. "Oh, he's been helping an elderly woman fix up the outside of her house. Been working on it all weekend. Isn't that nice of him?"

"How convenient…" Nellie turned her attention to Brooke. "Weren't you doing the same at your house today? Hmm. What are the odds?"

"Penelope, sweetheart, lots of people do yardwork on the

weekends." Mom took a sip of what was at least her third glass of wine. There was a chance all of this would go straight over her head if Nellie would simply drop it.

But she wouldn't, because that would be too much to ask of her. She settled her accusatory stare on me and asked, "Are you going to deny it? Are you going to try to tell me you weren't at Brooke's house all weekend helping her?"

Refusing to answer her, I glared back, as if we were in the middle of a staring contest.

Mom set her wine glass down and waved my sister off. "Calm down, honey. He was working on an older woman's house, not Brooke's."

"Except Brooke *lives with an old lady*, Mom." Nellie's entire face had turned red by this point. Much longer and she'd be purple. "So, Corbin, are you going to deny it?"

I glanced at Brooke, finding her staring down, likely wringing her hands together in her lap. My heart hurt for her, but there was no getting out of this one. Lying would only make it worse. My only option was to tell the truth—well, not *all* of it.

I shrugged to make a point that it wasn't a big deal. "Yeah, so? I've been helping Phyllis fix up the outside of her house and clean up her yard. I guess I don't see what the problem is."

As if our parents weren't in the room watching this all unfold, Nellie turned in her seat to face Brooke. "Why didn't you tell me?" Even I could hear the betrayal in my sister's voice.

"I didn't?" Brooke's acting skills needed polishing. "I thought I told you."

Feeling compelled to save her, I asked, "Why is this such big deal?"

"Because *my* best friend did something with *my* brother yet failed to mention it." She slammed her fork on the table, making Brooke jump in her seat. "Even though we had lunch together every day last week."

"Look, it was something that came up last minute. I'd mentioned it to him in passing, and he offered to give me a hand.

It was a big job; no way would I be stupid enough to turn down the help, no matter who it came from. You're making this into something it's not," Brooke whispered.

"Fine." Nellie picked up her fork and took a bite of her meat, chewing slowly. A fire had been lit behind her eyes, which only meant one thing. She hadn't believed a fucking word either of us had said. The wheels were beginning to turn, and if we didn't put an end to it, she'd soon figure everything out.

If I thought Brooke was mad at me for dragging her to this dinner in the first place, I bet it was nothing compared to how she'd feel after this disaster. The entire table finished their meals in silence. My dad probably kept his mouth shut because he loathed the drama, and my mom was more than likely too tipsy and confused to know where to begin. Luckily, it didn't take us long to finish eating, and as soon as they were done, they excused themselves from the table, like this was no different than any other Sunday dinner.

"How'd your date with Heather go?" Nellie asked once our parents were out of earshot.

Fuck! That little bitch. She knew exactly what she was doing, and if she didn't, she would after taking one look at Brooke, because her face had completely drained of color. We hadn't discussed the plan in at least a week, so I didn't see the point in telling her anything. I hated lying to her.

"We went out for drinks. She got drunk, and I took her home. End of story."

Brooke's mouth fell open and then closed again. She didn't know any of that because it really didn't happen. But I had to give Nellie something.

"Did you take any selfies together? Steal her panties?" Nellie quipped.

"God, no!"

"Then whose panties did I find in your office?"

"I have no idea what you're going on about." I did, but playing dumb was much easier than trying to explain why I had a pair Brooke's underwear. "And why were you going through my desk anyway?"

"You obviously know what I'm talking about because you knew they were in your desk. I didn't tell you where I found them. So, if they aren't Heather's, then who do they belong to?"

"Yes, I had a pair of women's panties in my desk last week. But it's none of your business who they belong to. I don't ask you how many dicks you've sat on and who they belong to."

"That's low, Corbin." Nellie grew quiet. "Even for you." Her chair scraped along the wooden floor when she stood. "Excuse me, please."

Brooke stayed seated while watching her best friend walk out of the room. "What just happened?"

"I'm not sure." This whole evening had started off wrong and ended completely worse.

"You went out with Heather?" She finally looked at me, and when I saw her eyes, my blood ran cold. They depicted storm clouds instead of pistachios or rolling green hills like usual. I'd caused her pain, and I never intended to.

"Hear me out."

Brooke didn't give me a chance to explain before following my sister.

And there was nothing left for me to do but to leave.

CHAPTER 22

BROOKE

TONIGHT HAD GONE from bad to insane. And I'd almost ended up completely alienated from the two people who meant the most to me in the world.

I'd managed to mildly repair things with Nellie, but she still didn't believe that I wasn't hiding anything. And why would she? I'd never had the ability to lie, especially to her. I felt like a despicable, conniving human being and could not understand how things had taken such a drastic turn.

After sitting in the Fields's kitchen talking to Nellie for at least an hour, I'd left and headed to Corbin's to deal with him. We needed to have a discussion, which would end with us taking some time apart. I needed to regroup and have some time to contemplate things. I'd basically jumped from Chase to Corbin. Now it was time to slow things down.

My knuckles met his door, producing a firm knock. I waited a few seconds before lifting my hand to try again when it opened.

Corbin stood before me, clad in nothing but flannel pajama bottoms, naked from the waist up. My mouth went dry at the sight of his gleaming chest. He was beautiful. Even though that wasn't usually an appropriate adjective used to describe someone masculine, it fit.

My mind went void of all the words I'd prepared during the drive over. My bravado began to slip and fall. I couldn't do this. My breathing hitched, and my voice became caught in my throat when I tried to speak.

"Bridge." Concern laced his voice, and worry filled his eyes as he took a step toward me. I started to retreat, but he lifted his hand and rested it on my cheek. "Please, don't. Don't turn away from me."

All the emotion that had eaten at me all evening came crashing down at once, leaving me completely overwhelmed. I was angry at him for lying to me and disappointed in myself for not being honest to the one person who'd always been there when I'd needed her most. I was sad that my relationship with Nellie now hung by a thread when we'd always been super solid.

My friendship with her was the one thing I wholeheartedly believed in.

But standing before me was the man I'd grown to care deeply for, more than I thought possible. He meant so much to me, his presence in my life just as important as Nellie's only in a different way. The conflict was too much to bear alone. I needed him. My body fell forward, and I allowed myself to collapse in his arms.

"Corbin," I half-sobbed, half-gasped. "I need you." My mouth met his with urgency, but his kiss seemed to match in intensity.

Once he had me inside his place, I spun us around and pushed him against the door, causing it to slam shut. I feverishly kissed his mouth and then trailed my lips down his neck. Needing more, I began to lick my way down his chest until I was on my knees in front of him. When I reached the waistband of his pants, he pulled me back up and into his arms. I'd seen evidence of his desire, so I knew he sought the same thing I did. I wanted to be as close to him as humanly possible.

We stumbled toward the living room, and when we'd made it to the back of the couch, he turned me around so that I was facing away from him—the leather sofa in front of me, the hard planes of his chest against my back. He didn't bother removing my clothes, just lifted my skirt and pulled my panties to the side right before sliding into me.

We'd had lazy sex before, desperate sex, passionate sex, and we'd even made love in the middle of the night. But this was the first time he'd ever *fucked* me. Yet even as he slammed into me from behind, hitting the perfect spot only he'd managed to find, I knew this was no different than any other time we'd been together. His grip on me might've been firm, but there was no doubt in my mind how much he cherished me.

His hips thrust forward, and I let out a pent-up groan I'd held back. The way he felt deep inside me was so delicious it should be illegal. I arched my spine and met each powerful push, knowing it wouldn't take long to reach my goal. With him at this angle, my G-spot had started singing before he'd even found his rhythm, and now, with the momentum building, I wouldn't be able to stop it.

"I'm going to come, Corbin. Oh, God!" My eyes squeezed shut and my toes curled.

He took one more forceful plunge forward, pushing me off the cliff of ecstasy, and by the sound of his guttural groan, I knew it had done the same to him.

AFTER CLEANING UP, we sat, facing each other, on the very couch we'd just fucked against. I had no idea what had come over me, but nothing had gone as I'd planned.

"I'm not sure what to say," I started.

"You don't need to say anything. I'm the one who does. I have a lot of explaining to do." Corbin scooted closer to me and took my hand in his. "I don't think any of us expected what happened tonight, but it did. And because none of this would've happened had I not forced you into going with me, I'll take the fallout. It's not your fault."

"What do you mean it isn't my fault? It's entirely my cross to bear. I lied to my best friend, and I'm fucking her brother behind her back. Plus, it's evident your entire family wants you and Lindsey back together."

"That's not going to happen." He shook his head emphatically. "Never. Even if you and I didn't work out, I wouldn't go back to her."

"Okay," I responded in an attempt to urge him to keep going.

"We were never a good fit. The only reason we ever thought we were is because of how it looked on the surface. Take anything at face value and it'll look stellar. The truth is, we've never dug deeper with one another, probably because we both knew we wouldn't be able to survive it if we did."

I nodded but kept quiet. What he said made sense.

"As far as you lying to your best friend…you haven't lied. You just haven't disclosed all the details about us, but that doesn't mean you've told untruths. I may be naïve, but I think your relationship can grow stronger after this. What did she do when you told her about us?" Corbin's eyes looked full of misery.

"Tell her about us? I didn't tell her anything!" I covered my face with my hands. "I couldn't. It would kill her."

"So what did you say when you went after her?"

I shrugged and then met his sincere gaze. "Nothing we haven't already said—she's making a bigger deal out of this than there needs to be, and how I didn't tell her because I knew she'd overreact. She reiterated her reasons for not wanting you to be with any of her friends, but most of all, me. I apologized, we hugged it out, and that was it."

"Why 'most of all' you?"

"Because I'm her best friend, and she's worried she'll lose me like she did when I was with Chase. She feels like you've always gotten everything, and I'm the one thing she can say is all hers, that you don't have any part of. It scares her to think of coming second to you in my life."

"Well, I can understand that."

I covered his hand with mine on the cushion between us. "You need to fix things with her. You nearly killed her tonight."

"That's a tad dramatic, Bridge. But I know I do, and I will. We've made it through fights worse than this. We'll be fine, don't worry." He kissed the tip of my nose and said, "You have the cutest nose."

Which caused me to wrinkle it. "It's crooked."

"It's perfect."

I rolled my eyes, yet I couldn't help but swoon on the inside.

"Now…can we talk about this date with Heather?" I tried my best to sound unaffected by the thought of him with another woman, but the truth was, it crushed me, and I refused to analyze the reasons for that at the moment.

"I didn't go out with her, Bridge."

I so badly wanted to believe him. "Then why did you tell Nellie you did?"

"Listen, she came to my office on Wednesday, and I was having a shitty day. I was disorganized, and my mind was all over the place. She was literally in my office when I came back from a meeting with my boss—a meeting that hadn't gone over too well thanks to a member on my team completely botching a deal at the end of the quarter—so I told her whatever I could to get her to leave so I could catch up on paperwork."

"So you haven't met her for drinks yet?"

"Babe…I've been with you almost every night. When would I have had the time?"

I couldn't argue with that, except there was one flaw to his alibi. "I wasn't with you Wednesday night, and we barely texted each other that evening."

"Yeah, because I was at the office until after seven, and then I took the rest of my work home to finish there. I knew you were busy, so I figured I'd take advantage of the opportunity to get caught up. That way I could have the rest of my evenings free to see you."

Well, if he were lying, at least it was a good one.

MONDAY, Funday.

I made sure to get here early tonight on purpose, hoping to catch Nellie alone. Last night, Corbin had promised he would reach out to her today and apologize. I just hoped he had; that way, things could go back to the way they were. Before the fallout at dinner last night.

"Brooke." I instantly recognized Nellie's voice before her face came into view.

"Hey." My voice wobbled a bit, thanks to the nerves that had set in.

"What are the specials tonight? Did they change?" The questions and her tone were normal, but something felt...off.

"Yup. Same ol', same ol'. Just how we like it." I giggled in an attempt to lighten things up and test the waters.

She perused the menu and debated what drink to order before finally putting it down and turning to me. "Corbin called me today. Everything's fine," Nellie stated. Yet everything didn't *feel* fine. Either she was hiding something, or she was still pissed at me.

"Are you sure? Last night got pretty hairy." I wanted to believe her so badly that I almost let myself, but something was still amiss. I just couldn't put my finger on it.

"Yup. You know how siblings fight. Well, you don't have siblings, but you've seen us over the years. This wasn't anything out of the ordinary. Tempers flared and things were said. Now it's time to move past it."

"Okay." Even though Nellie said all the right things, I couldn't seem to get over her mood. And as much as I wanted to accept what she was saying, I couldn't. "I've got to be honest; you still seem angry."

"Honest? *You*? Really, Brooke?"

"I don't know what you mean, Nellie."

She knew. She had totally figured it all out, and now, I was toast and left to face her all on my lonesome. I gulped in preparation of what would come next. Did I outwardly lie my ass off and deny, deny, deny? I had no clue what to do.

"Hearing that you and Corbin have been hanging out so much behind my back took me by surprise. I mean, you never mentioned that he was helping with the house renovation. And it's a big deal because it's not the first time you've been around him without telling me. I understand why you didn't—I get that you were worried I'd freak out—but how else do you expect me to react when I find out the truth? Do you honestly think you and Corbin can do things together *without* me finding out? He's my brother, Brooke. And you're supposed to be my *best* friend."

That stung, and I doubted I'd been able to hide my reaction. "I *am* your best friend, Nellie. Not *supposed to be*. I am."

"Then act like it."

I gripped her hand tightly in mine, as if trying to convey exactly how important she was to me. "I can't bear to have you mad at me, Nellie. Your friendship means everything to me."

"I know, because you mean the same to me. Let's not fight anymore," she suggested.

I instantly agreed, and then we hugged it out.

Mady and Julie hadn't even shown up yet, and I was already drained and ready to go home. It was going to be a long night ahead.

CHAPTER 23

CORBIN

WITH IT BEING Friday and most of the higher-ups in a conference, a lot of the support staff had opted to take the day off, which left the atmosphere relaxed. That meant it was a good day to get caught up on work.

Except I couldn't manage to stop daydreaming about Bridge. Everything seemed to make me think of her. The green folder on my desk reminded me of her eyes. The chocolates Emily ate while typing up my notes were the exact color of her hair. And I swear, someone walked by wearing her favorite perfume. I'd become fixated on her, and nothing was able to distract me.

So I finally decided to text her, hoping that by doing so, I'd be able to move on and concentrate on my actual job.

Me: How's your day going so far? Thinking of you. xxx

I knew she wouldn't answer me until her lunchbreak, so I placed my phone on my desk and tried—for the third time—to finish the profile sheet in front of me.

Less than twenty minutes later, when I heard the familiar chime of my texts, I excitedly reached for my phone, but it wasn't from Bridge. And my excitement quickly turned to annoyance.

Nellie: *Hey bro, how's it hanging?*

I groaned; this was *not* the distraction I was hoping for. Then again, I really shouldn't have been looking for *any* distraction, but oh well. That didn't change the fact that dealing with my sister wouldn't help matters.

Me: *Status quo. You?*

Nellie: *Last I checked I don't hang, but I'm doing well. How are things going with the plan?*

For the life of me, I couldn't figure out why my sister was so damn interested in my progress with Heather. I realized she'd been the one who initially roped me into it, but ultimately, the details were between Bridge and me. Aside from the fact that this whole *"plan"* was for her best friend, she didn't have any part to play in it.

Me: *Good. I went out with her last night and we made plans to see one another again next week.*

Nellie: *Have you told Brooke yet?*

Me: *No, I haven't spoken to her.*

Although now, I definitely planned to discuss it with Brooke, just to ensure Nellie didn't say anything first. I couldn't put my finger on it, but she was up to something. And I'd be damned if she tried to cause trouble between Brooke and me again.

Nellie: *Have a good weekend.*

Me: *You too!*

Usually, when Nellie contacted me, it was for a reason, one she never made me wait too long to discover. Which meant, this conversation had been nothing but a fishing expedition. She would probably text Bridge and tell her the news; if I didn't hurry up and tell her myself, I'd be questioned the next time we spoke.

I spent the next ten minutes debating about sending Brooke a second text. She still hadn't read the first, so I didn't want to come across pushy or needy, worrying that might turn her off, but at the same time, I needed to say something before my sister took it upon herself to whisper in her ear about Heather.

Pushing aside my fear of annoying her, I sent one anyway.

Me: Just heard from Nell. Call or text when you get a break. I'm in my office all day.

And then I set about *trying* to finish my work.
Emphasis on "trying."

It took me less than forty-five minutes to accept my utter failure, though. I'd only managed to get through the first page—out of eleven—in that time. It wouldn't have been too bad if it weren't the first of *nine* profiles I had to deal with today. At this rate, I'd be here all weekend, which couldn't happen. Not only did I have full intentions of leaving on time today to spend the evening with Brooke, but it was also the weekend of my parents' Easter party. They wouldn't care if I missed it due to work, but I would. For the first time in my life, I actually found myself looking forward to one of their parties.

Realizing that I needed to get *something* done, I put that profile to the side and grabbed the next in the stack, hoping I'd be able to get through this one faster and just save the other for last. But again, I stalled out before finishing. Although, I'd at least made it to the third page this time.

This profile was from a company who was in search of a way to market their products to lower-income shoppers. While their products weren't considered high-end merchandise by any means, they were gadgets that weren't needed—meaning, they wanted a marketing strategy to sell useless crap to people who, not only couldn't afford it but also, didn't need it.

Honestly, it pissed me off.

Which had been the entire reason I'd stopped going through it.

It made me think of Phyllis and the families at Brooke's school, like the little boy's mom who'd cried tears of sincere gratitude for the few dollars Brooke had given her. Sure, I could come up with many ways to convince them to spend fifty bucks on an air freshener that can be controlled by an app, but that would mean I'd be taking money out of their already-tight grocery budget or gas bill. Which did nothing but make me sick to my stomach, because I used to do just that. I couldn't recall how many accounts I'd procured over the years by creating ads aimed at convincing low-income or middle-class shoppers to spend money they should've saved on things they didn't need.

Rather than finish with the profiles—*any of them*—I grabbed my phone and scrolled through my contacts, realizing now more than ever what I needed to do. It'd been on my mind for a while, but it was time to do something about it.

BRIDGE and I had spent pretty much every night together for the past two weeks. Either I stayed at her place or she came to mine. Phyllis had totally accepted me, thanks to the renovation, so she didn't have a problem with me being there overnight. Although, I can't lie…it still felt a little weird, like having your mom down the hall.

I never got tired of having her around. Actually, it was quite the opposite; anytime we *weren't* together, I wished we were. For over three weeks now, I wouldn't get to the office until eight, and I'd be out the door every day by five, not a minute after. Unless, of course, it was a rare night I didn't see Brooke. But today, after the issue I'd had with that profile, I finished all the calls I needed to make and left shortly after four.

I just couldn't wait to start my weekend.

That wasn't my typical mindset. Normally, weekends did nothing but bring me down. While most people went out or made plans with friends, I'd watch movies with my computer in my lap. I'd go to the store for food or whatever else I needed, but aside from that and family dinners on Sundays, my weekends were lonely and boring—something I hadn't truly realized until about a month and a half ago. That's when my life had come to a screeching halt, forcing me to take a good look at myself and where I was headed. Ever since Brooke had entered—or should I say, *re*-entered—my life, there had been subtle changes. In me. For the good.

Such as not living in my office.

My parents had drilled into us at a young age that work came first. Always. No matter what. When I was two, I'd fallen and needed stitches; it was my nanny who had taken me to the hospital and held my hand. I, of course, couldn't remember any of that, but the story—as well as many others—had been told to me. I'd grown accustomed to my parents' absence, because it was the way things were in our household.

And for the first time in my life, I realized how abnormal that was.

Looking at Brooke now, curled into my chest with my arm around her, it made me contemplate her upbringing. It wasn't like I'd never thought about it before; I'd always known about her mom and the struggles they'd had to face. But now, it was like I was looking at it through a different lens.

I didn't feel sorry for her. I didn't pity her. I *admired* her. But at the same time, I felt angry—mostly at myself. I'd known her since she was twelve. Granted, I was sixteen or seventeen, so it wasn't like I'd had the wherewithal to help, yet that didn't stop the frustration that burned inside over the fact that I *hadn't* done anything. Not when she was a kid, not when she was in high school dealing with her mom's diagnosis, and not a few years later when she had to bury her only parent.

While I knew how unreasonable it was to be upset with myself for such things, it didn't change how I felt. I'd technically known her while she dealt with all of that, and to make matters worse, I'd known it was happening. Nellie used to talk about it when she'd call to check in with me after I moved away for college. I guess that was the part that pissed me off most—the fact that I was aware of her situation, *knew* her personally, yet I never did anything to help or protect her.

That realization hit me hard, because as I stared at her, her attention glued to the movie that played on my big screen, I wanted nothing more than to protect her from anything bad ever happening to her again. It could've been the fact that we were watching a Marvel movie, full of superheroes and villains, but I doubted it. My need to hold onto her and keep her safe was honest and genuine, not some silly idea I'd gotten from Iron Man or Thor.

Just then, she lifted her chin to look at me. With a smile so bright it lit up the room, she asked, "Why are you staring at me? Do I have something on my face again?" She pushed up on her elbow and began to wipe her hand down her face.

It made me laugh, reminding me of the marker she'd worn to dinner that one time.

"Nah, I was just thinking about something."

"Oh, that's vague." She moved to sit up more, wagging her brows. "And intriguing. Tell me more, Mr. Fields. What were you thinking about?" She knew what it did to me when she called me *Mr. Fields*.

"Do you remember that time Nell broke her leg? I think you two were, like, thirteen or something." I laughed at the confusion that marred her face. "You guys were doing something you weren't supposed to, she got hurt, and I had to drive her to the hospital."

"Yes, I remember that. I guess I just don't know why *that's* what you were thinking about."

Normally, I had an iron stomach, but after seeing the bone protruding from my sister's shin, I'd wanted to vomit. It was bad. But that hadn't been what stuck out to me the most; it wasn't the reason for that specific memory coming to me just now. The reason had been Brooke.

I brushed a strand of hair off her cheek and smiled. "That was the first time I ever held you, and having you in my arms right now made me think of it."

"Oh, great," she said with a soft laugh, rolling her eyes. "Cuddling with you makes you remember the time you had to console me because I was crying that Nellie had to have surgery? You're *so* romantic."

Brooke had taken charge and remained calm…until Nellie was taken into surgery. Then she broke down. I hadn't even realized it until I'd noticed her shoulders violently shaking. When I glanced over to see what she was doing, she'd had her arms crossed over her chest—as if holding herself—while silent tears streaked down her face.

I laughed with her, even though I didn't really find anything funny. "I'd always thought you were so strong, Bridge. Hands down, one of the strongest people I ever knew, and you were four years younger than me. Until that moment, the thought never crossed my mind that you'd need someone to comfort you. I guess I always thought you never needed it."

I'd never had anyone comfort me in times when I'd needed it, and even at such a young age, I'd felt like she and I were a lot alike. Although, I doubted I'd been able to fully process that thought at the time. We were young—I was only eighteen, so she had to have been thirteen or fourteen. I'd known enough to feel a connection, but not mature enough to understand what it was. Now, I could look back at that moment and know, without a doubt, that us being together made more sense than anything else.

"Wanna know a secret?" She sighed and crossed her arms over

my chest, resting her chin on top. "You're the only person, aside from my mom, who's ever been able to console me like that. You made me feel safe that day."

"Well, I'm glad." I traced her brow with my finger and smiled at her. "Although, I doubt you've needed much of that in your life. I wasn't lying when I said you're the strongest person I know. You're resilient and tough."

Her gaze fell from my eyes, landing on my chin or neck or chest, I wasn't sure. And when she glanced up again, I couldn't ignore the heavy emotion that darkened her irises, turning them from two meadows to two avocados. "Wanna know another secret?"

Unable to speak, I simply nodded and waited for her to share with me.

"When my mom died, I thought about that time—you comforting me in the waiting room at the hospital. I kept thinking...*if he were here, I'd feel better*. Don't take that the wrong way; it's not like I *liked* you, or anything. I just remembered how safe you made me feel, and without my mom being there to hold me, I couldn't help but wish you were."

The pain in her eyes reignited the anger I'd felt earlier when thinking of all she'd been through in her life. And it once again had me hating myself for not having the forethought to reach out. I couldn't help but think that had I called to check on her, not just rely on Nellie's updates, she could've told me all of this, and then I could've been there for her.

Then again, that was assuming she would've told me.

And knowing Brooklyn, she more than likely wouldn't have.

"The only reason I'd made it through those first weeks and months was because of you," she continued, gratitude shining in her eyes.

I was about to say something, question how I could've possibly gotten her through those times when I hadn't even been there, but she beat me to it.

Offering me a sad yet appreciative smile, she added, "There

were nights I cried so hard I couldn't breathe, and my heart felt like someone was squeezing it. Those were the nights my pillow would be drenched in tears. But as soon as I closed my eyes and thought about you holding me, it all stopped. I'd imagine we were back there in that waiting room, your arms around me, and *instantly*, the tears would dry up, like someone turned off a faucet. My breathing would return to normal as if I hadn't just been hyperventilating, and my heart no longer felt constricted."

And just like that, the burning anger was extinguished.

CHAPTER 24

BROOKE

I COULDN'T BELIEVE I'd just admitted all of that to him. Must've been the wine.

Being that vulnerable and candid wasn't something I was used to, except with Nellie. But for some reason, the words had just tumbled out, my brain too caught up in memories to stop it from happening.

Honestly, I was surprised he'd even remembered that day. Sure, his sister had broken her leg, and he'd been the one who had to drive her to the hospital. I didn't expect him to forget that, but the rest of it? Holding me while I cried? Never in a million years would I have thought he'd remember that.

It just made that moment even more special to me.

"You could've called, Bridge. I know I wasn't in town, but it's not like you couldn't have gotten ahold of me. Had I known, I would've been here."

I rolled my eyes dismissively and let out a soft giggle. "Easier said than done, Corbin. Nellie had taken it upon herself to be my keeper; calling you would've made her feel like I didn't want her around. Not to mention, you know damn well she never would've given me your number. Anyway, it's fine. It's not like you knew—or could've done anything about it—and in the end, you were able to get me through it. Even if you had no idea you were."

He ran the pad of his thumb along my cheek, and it sent heat racing through my body. If we hadn't just had sex less than an hour ago, I would've totally acted on it. Not only because his touch instantly aroused me, but because it would've been the perfect way to put an end to this conversation.

I lifted myself just enough to kiss his lips and then pushed away until I was sat on my knees between his body and the couch. "I'm thirsty. Want anything from the kitchen while I'm up?"

Corbin sat up as well. He pressed his incredibly soft lips to my forehead before standing. "That's all right. I'll get us something; I have to take a leak anyway. You stay here and keep my spot warm. Water?"

I nodded and then smiled when he winked. Once he was out of the room, I snuggled into the couch where he'd been lying and pulled the soft blanket up to my chin. His absence was enough to remind me of just how warm he was when we snuggled, because without him, there was a chill I couldn't seem to fight off no matter how hard I tried.

We'd pretty much been inseparable over the last several weeks, not including work hours. But about a week ago, it really hit me—I didn't want this to end. Ever. However, even though I felt that way, I still had reservations about what we were doing.

When I thought about my relationship with Chase, I realized there had always been something missing. While I had no doubt that we truly cared for one another, I couldn't deny the writing on the wall—I had been more in love with the *idea* of love than love itself. And there was a part of me—albeit, a small part—that made me want to put on the brakes for fear of rushing into this with Corbin, only to walk away with the same conclusion.

And as if my history with Chase wasn't enough to battle, I also had to deal with the stigma of Lindsey. I trusted Corbin when he said they were over. There'd been a bit of a question mark over their relationship in the past, but I fully believed him when he said that, regardless if we were together or not, he had no desire to be with her. However, that didn't stop his *entire* family from rooting for them, and that was something I just couldn't compete with.

When Corbin came back with two glasses of water, I moved over to make room for him on the sofa. And once again, I was warm and safe. Even though the movie still played, I was more interested in talking to him. It was something Chase and I never did much of. Well, I'd done a lot of talking, but looking back over the course of our relationship, he never listened or interacted the way Corbin did. So with one leg curled over his, I crossed my arms over his abdomen and propped my chin on top of my hands to look at him.

"You never did tell me about your conversation with Nellie today. You told me to call you when I was on break, but when I did, you didn't answer. What was all that about?"

"Oh, yeah. I'm sorry, babe. I was on the phone for most of the day trying to take care of a few things for work. By the time I finished with that, it was already after four, so I just left." He dragged his finger down my nose. "And as you know, once you got here, the *last* thing I was thinking about was my sister."

My face flushed at the memory of what we'd done right here on this couch. "No, silly. I wasn't asking why you didn't answer the phone. I meant, what did Nellie have to say? You made it sound important."

He took a deep breath, causing my head to rise with his chest. I didn't think anything of it at first, but as soon as he lifted his gaze over my head, I stilled and paid attention. That was usually a good sign that he had to contemplate his response, which had me a little worried.

"I don't know, Bridge…it was just weird. She texted me out of nowhere and asked how the plan was going. Then she asked if you knew, and when I said I hadn't spoken to you, she quickly ended the conversation. It felt like she was fishing for something, but I don't know what."

"Well, what did you tell her?" I asked and then held my breath.

"That we had plans to meet up next week."

"Do you? Have plans, I mean."

When his eyes met mine again, I began to relax. "No. Honestly, Bridge, now that I'm not spending every waking hour in the office, I'm finding myself much busier when I am there. Finding time to go downstairs to hit on someone I really don't care to talk to isn't high on my priority list. I'm sorry. I know how much you want to get back at Chase, and trust me, I really want that for you, too."

When Chase had broken up with me, I wanted him to hurt as badly as I had, and while I still felt that way on some level, I began to question how important that was. After going days believing that Corbin had had drinks with another woman—despite it being someone I'd told him to hit on—I was no longer sure how I felt about the plan. Yes, I still wanted Chase to know what it felt like to be cheated on. But in my heart of hearts, I had to trust that his day would come, and that I didn't have to orchestrate it for that to happen.

I'd actually spent some time contemplating this over the last couple of weeks, but it wasn't until right now that I realized I no longer wanted Corbin to pursue Heather in *any* capacity. Except, I wasn't sure how to tell him that, and since he'd made no real plans to meet up with her, I figured that conversation could wait. At least until I'd worked out my feelings for him and where I wanted our relationship to go. Which would have to be after the Fields's annual Easter egg hunt this Sunday; I didn't need any added stress in my life. Once that was over, we could sit down and discuss where we were in regard to our feelings now that we'd been "together" for a month.

"What are you thinking about?" Corbin ran his fingertips up and down my bare arms, creating gooseflesh in his wake.

"Nothing much." I grinned up at him.

"That's not fair. I told you what I was thinking about when you asked." He tried to act offended, but it didn't work. I could read him pretty well. That, and he was a horrible actor.

"Fine…I was thinking about your parents' shindig this weekend. I know I've been to their house with you since we started hooking up, but this just feels different."

"What do you mean? Different how?"

"I guess I'm just so used to being flirty with you that I'm worried I'll do or say something, not thinking, and it'll call attention to us before we're ready. I mean, we've got so many inside jokes and things we do unconsciously. What if your parents pick up on it, or heaven forbid Nellie catches on? It's honestly stressing me out." My hands began to fidget beneath my chin at the mere thought of it.

"Everything will be fine, okay? You're worrying about nothing. Don't sweat it, or you'll end up calling attention to yourself anyway by acting weird." He held my face between his hands and leaned forward to kiss me.

Don't sweat it. Yeah, easy for him to say.

EVEN THOUGH I'D woken up next to Corbin this morning, I was on my way to his parents' house alone. He'd practically begged me to get ready at his place, but I couldn't. I'd been filled with nervous energy ever since last night, and if I had any hope of making it through the day around his family and friends—and, apparently, half the city—I needed a moment to myself.

And by "a moment," I meant three hours.

The event—yes, *event*, because Corbin's parents didn't know how to do anything on a small scale—didn't start until eleven. Corbin and Nellie had to be there early, which meant I had to drive myself. Well, it wasn't like I could've arrived with Corbin without it being scandalous, but at least this way it got me out of having to ride with Nellie.

Things between us had been a little...*off* lately. I wasn't sure what was going on, and while the paranoid side of my brain thought she might've known about her brother and me, the rational side believed her excuses—*all* of them. Anytime I had tried to make plans to hang out, there was always a reason she couldn't. A date, a headache, work. But the one thing that kept gnawing at me the most was her lack of texts. Last month, it would've taken hours to get through a couple days' worth of messages, but now, I could scroll through an entire week in less than a minute.

I decided not to freak out about it until I had a real reason to. I figured I could feel her out today and go from there. Even if she did still suspect something was going on between Corbin and me, it was only a matter of time before I confessed everything anyway. So really, I didn't have anything to worry about.

I checked my phone while sitting at a red light. Corbin had asked me to text him when I left my house and then again when I arrived at his parents'. I'd sent the first one before pulling out of my driveway, yet he hadn't responded nor read it. I hoped that didn't mean anything. Luckily, the light turned green before I could obsess too much about it.

That was such a lie.

I obsessed over it for the rest of the drive.

But once I rounded the corner, the infamous *Field of Dreams* coming into view, anxiety took over. My chest tightened, and my entire body began to vibrate with nerves. Cars lined one side of the street, but I knew there were many more coming. It wasn't quite eleven yet, and most people showed up just after the start time. Hopefully, that meant I'd be able to hide in the crowd.

Easter Sunday wasn't for another week, but Corbin and Nellie's parents didn't want their party to conflict with family gatherings or church, so they always held it the weekend prior. I couldn't help but wonder how many people would come if they'd actually done this on Easter day. If I were to guess, I'd say all of them.

I parked across the street, suddenly embarrassed about my car. It had been well-taken care of, not a beater or clunker by any means. And ever since Corbin had graciously gotten the alternator fixed, it'd been running like a champ. But that didn't mean it fit in with the likes of what lined the street. I imagined it would be the equivalent of one of my students walking into a private Catholic school on this side of town.

Needing a moment to compose myself, I adjusted the rearview mirror to check my face. Thanks to a few YouTube tutorials, a visit to Ulta, and a bag of bolder makeup than I was used to wearing, my eyes appeared bigger than normal. It wasn't necessarily the look I was after, but knowing how much Corbin loved my "big eyes," I'd decided to keep it.

I double checked my hair to make sure it still hung perfectly straight—which it did, all thanks to the seventy-seven passes over every strand with my flat iron—and returned the mirror to its previous position. This was it. Do or die. Or was it *ride or die*? Either way, it was go time.

That's it! It was *go time*.

After sending Corbin another text to let him know I was here, I opened my door and stepped out, flattening the skirt of my new dress before locking my car. With the key. It was that advanced it didn't even have a working key fob. And then I walked across the street, careful not to fall and twist an ankle. Between the brand-new pair of wedges I'd purchased to go with my dress and my wobbly legs, there was a good chance I'd kiss asphalt before ever making it to the party.

"Fancy meeting you here," I heard as I stepped onto the brick path that led to the back yard, where the guests were already starting to mingle by the sounds of it.

When I turned to find the familiar voice, I saw Nellie and smiled. "Hey."

The hug she offered wasn't out of the ordinary, other than the fact that she seemed to hold on just a little longer than normal. I chalked it up to her missing me, considering we hadn't really spent much time together in two weeks, and returned her embrace with equal enthusiasm.

She pulled away but held me still for a moment to assess my outfit. "You look cute. Is that new?"

Holding the skirt that hit me mid-thigh, I did a couple half-turns to show it off. "Yeah, it is. Do you like it?"

I hardly ever splurged on new clothes, and this ensemble had taken up a good bit of my budget, but it was worth it. I wanted to feel confident today, and in this dress, I would. It also helped that I had on Corbin's favorite body lotion, which made me feel invincible. And if that wasn't enough armor to make it through today, I'd even bought new lingerie. Although that had come from the clearance rack. I smiled at Nellie, thinking about how she would probably say my thong was huge. I'd never forget that comment, even though I now found it funny.

"Love it." She smiled brightly at me and then nodded toward the back of the house. "Come on, let's get in there before my mom sends out a search party. I've been hiding from her for the last thirty minutes."

"That doesn't surprise me." We giggled. "Is Mady or Julie here yet?"

"No, but they're on their way," she said as we made our way to the back yard.

There were no words to describe how relieved I was to see her and know that everything was okay. I'd really missed her, and even though there seemed to be something going on with her, I assumed it had to do with the guy she'd recently started to date and trusted that she would open up to me when she was ready.

My thoughts of Nellie and our friendship quickly evaded my mind the second we stepped into the back yard. It was a wonderland of festivities, decorated with people in fancy clothes. Even though they had extended an invitation to me every year, this was the first Field of Dreams egg hunt I'd attended, and I had to admit, the stories didn't do it justice.

The trees were adorned with tinsel, and all the colors screamed spring. There were things to do and games to play in every corner of the yard. And we aren't talking about a normal yard. No, Mr. and Mrs. Fields owned almost two acres, so there was enough room to wander between the various tents, booths, and egg-themed activities.

Every detail had been addressed and outdone.

A tall, attractive blonde came toward us, and Nellie greeted her with a hug. But I was too busy taking everything in, paying attention to every wonderous detail, to hear anything they were saying. I assumed it was a family friend that I'd be introduced to once I stopped walking around like a kid in a candy shop.

And then I spotted Corbin, who had the ability to snap me out of my awe.

Butterflies danced in my stomach at the sight of him. It reminded me of the realization I'd come to this morning as he stirred me awake with his tongue. I'd made up my mind. I knew exactly what I wanted. And I couldn't wait to get back to his place tonight after the party so I could tell him everything.

A smile tugged at the corners of my mouth but quickly faded when Nellie waved him over, shouting, "Hey, Corbin! Your girl-friend's here!"

What the hell?

CHAPTER 25

CORBIN

BOOTHS FOR CRAFTS, games, and food adorned my parents' back yard. We usually had a couple hundred people show up, so there had to be enough food and drinks for everyone—it would be the end of the world if we ran out of something.

On top of having a good work ethic drilled into us from an early age, my parents also taught us to never disappoint when planning festivities such as this. The egg hunt was slated to start after lunch on the east lawn. The green hills rolled as far as the eye could see, and some poor soul had been tasked with hiding the eggs, which now adorned the landscape like colorful confetti. Some were laid out and easy to find for the little ones, and others were hidden and more difficult. But in addition to that, my parents always had another hunt set up for the adults on the west lawn. Those eggs held lottery tickets, money, and other trinkets that were fun to find.

Several of my friends planned to attend today, but no one had shown up yet.

I finished talking to an older gentleman who worked for my dad, Leo I believe his name was, when I decided to check my phone. Bridge had texted me a little bit ago, letting me know she was on her way, but I was waiting for the one letting me know she'd arrived.

Heading toward the far side of the lake, I decided to take a moment to myself, because once things began, chaos would ensue. I walked along the bank and reminisced about the time Brooke and I had experienced our first make-out session. It had taken me by surprise, in more ways than one.

Several minutes later, the text alert on my phone broke me from my thoughts, and the message on my screen made me smile bigger than a kid on Christmas morning.

Brooke: *I'm here!*

Excitement bubbled in my chest at the thought of seeing her. I couldn't walk fast enough as I made my way toward the vine-covered archway near the back of the house, the same break in the bushes I'd chased Brooke through the night Nellie had interrupted us after dinner. And as soon as I turned the corner, I saw Brooke. I couldn't miss her. She shined brighter than the sun in her yellow dress. And *my God*! Her legs went on forever. I began to think of viable excuses I could use to steal her away while no one was looking, and then contemplated all the things I'd do to her once I had her alone.

My mind was full of Brooke and nothing else until Nellie called out, "Corbin, your girlfriend's here!" Instantly, all the color drained from Bridge's face. It made me turn my attention to my sister, who stood between Brooke and Lindsey.

Wait. *Lindsey*?

I studied the leggy blonde in a white form-fitting pantsuit and hot-pink heels on the other side of Nell for a second, and sure enough, it was none other than my ex. Only a few feet apart from my current girlfriend. With my sister, and her devious smirk, between them.

What the fuck is she doing here?

If I didn't think I could walk any faster before, I'd just proven myself wrong. I stormed the several yards that separated them from me and grabbed my sister by the arm. "May I have a word with you, please?" I gritted out through clenched teeth.

"Jeez, Corbin, you don't have to be so rough with me. I've got extremely delicate skin. I'll probably have a bruise there tomorrow, in the shape of your fat fingers."

"Shut up, Nell." I stopped when we were far enough away to be heard. "What's she doing here? Did you invite her? Why do I have the feeling you're behind this somehow? Or that you knew about it ahead of time."

She held up her hands in a dramatic display of surrender. "I don't know. I swear. I was just as surprised as you were to see her walk in. Well, no…that's a lie. I *was* surprised, though. But I was also happy, and you don't look very happy about it."

"Of course I'm not. Why would I be?" I ran my fingers through my hair, not caring if I'd just messed it up. At this point, I didn't care if my entire appearance seemed disheveled; at least then my look would match my mood. "Who invited her?"

"She said Mom and Dad did. Seriously, they should've been your first guess. Not me."

Without properly excusing myself like we'd been raised to do, I stepped around her and headed back to the two women who both stood in what appeared to be uncomfortable silence. I attempted to cool my horses and slow my pace, not wanting anyone to sense my anger, but I didn't have to see myself to know I'd failed miserably.

While I wanted to address Brooke first, I couldn't—thanks to my sister, who was, apparently, hot on my heels after our little chat. She grabbed Bridge's hand and said, "Come on, Brookie. Let's leave these two alone. I'm sure they have lots to catch up on." She wagged her brows, and her voice was saccharine sweet. So sugary, in fact, that it almost gave me a cavity, which only served to sound alarm bells in my head.

"Hi, Corbin. Bye, Corbin." Brooke offered a small wave and a meek grin as she allowed Nellie to drag her away.

I followed her with my eyes just in case she turned around. I needed her to know that this wasn't planned, that I never would've led her into the lion's den. Well, at least not knowingly. After the last time she was here, I doubted she'd believe me, but I needed to try anyway.

Unfortunately, she walked away without a backward glance.

And then it was just Lindsey and me.

"Hey, Corbin. You don't look too pleased to see me." Lindsey had always had the gentlest voice. It was the first thing I'd noticed about her in our economics class freshman year of college. Always soft-spoken, making her sound innocent and polite.

Although, I'd learned the hard way that it was her secret weapon—after we'd both been hired at the same marketing firm while in grad school. Needless to say, that was the first and last time we ever worked together.

"Please forgive me, Linds, but I wasn't exactly expecting to see you here."

She pulled her shoulders back and lifted her chin, proving just how tough she was. It made me think of Brooke, except where my ex was all hard lines and straight edges, Bridge was soft curves and sleek slopes…and I hadn't been referring to their bodies.

Although, even that aspect was drastically different as well.

"I didn't intend to piss you off. Honestly, I thought you'd be happy to see me."

"Happy? Why would I be happy to see you?" With my hands on my hips, I dropped my head back, closed my eyes against the harsh midday sun, and sighed. "I'm sorry, I didn't mean for it to come out like that. I guess I just don't understand what you came here expecting."

"Can we talk?"

I glanced around and then met her stare once more. "Sure…talk."

Her smile used to do things to me—nowhere near the things Brooke's did to me—but now, I realized just how predictable it was. It didn't matter how much makeup she put on her face or what color she painted her lips. Hell, it didn't even matter what clothes she wore. She was a stunning woman, I couldn't deny her that, but in comparison to Bridge? She now looked ordinary.

It was amazing how being with someone new could affect your eyesight like that.

Lindsey touched my arm, giving my bicep a little squeeze, and I fought the urge to yank my arm away. "Corbin, there's so much to say to you, and I don't want to say any of it while standing ten feet away from the exit. There's got to be somewhere we can go. Some place we can sit and talk for a bit."

A bit. That meant she wanted to have a full-blown conversation.

Flicking my gaze to the entrance behind her, I asked, "Is your boyfriend here?"

Her light eyes softened. "No. That's actually what I wanted to talk to you about."

I glanced behind me, trying to find the goddess in the pale-yellow dress, but I didn't see her. I needed to find her and make sure she was okay, and the last thing I wanted was for her to spot me chatting away with Lindsey. I knew how her mind worked by now, especially regarding my ex and her ties with my family. But I also had no desire to drag this out with Lindsey. I wanted to get it over with so I could move on, and if I took the time to hunt down Brooke now, it would just prolong the conclusion of this conversation.

I nodded toward the lake. "Follow me."

We crossed the yard in silence, and somehow, we'd managed to make it to the backside of the lake without getting stopped. A small gazebo sat on an old floating dock that had been there since I was kid. It was far enough away to talk in peace, but if I wanted to ensure we wouldn't be found or interrupted—or spied on—then we had to take the paddleboat that sat covered in the grass near the edge of the water.

"I'm not getting in that thing," she protested with her arms crossed and a scowl on her face. "It's probably dirty, and in case you didn't notice, I'm wearing white."

"I did notice, but thanks for pointing that out." I unlatched the hardcover and removed it, unveiling the two fiberglass seats and bike pedals used to propel the boat. "See? Clean as a whistle. You've got nothing to worry about. But if you'd like, I can always go inside and grab you a towel. Although, I'm sure that might garner some unwanted attention."

"Why can't we just sit there?" She pointed to the built-in wooden seats in the gazebo.

"Well, we could, but I'm willing to bet that's a lot dirtier than this thing. The rain and dirt and—"

"Okay, fine. But don't tip me over."

I laughed to myself while sliding the two-seater boat into the water. "It's not a canoe, Linds...it won't tip. Trust me, okay? Have I ever led you astray?" I held out my hand to help her in, which she took. But when she started to step off the dock, I stopped her and pointed to the blinding-pink high heels on her feet. "You might want to take those off."

"No way. My Jimmy Choos are staying put."

I shrugged and said, "Fine, suit yourself."

As soon as she got settled into the seat, I climbed in after her. And with a harsh push off the side of the dock, we on our way to total privacy. Lindsey could've wanted to talk about the weather for all I cared; there was no way in hell I'd give anyone the opportunity to tell Brooke what was said before I had the chance to tell her myself.

"Lindsey...you need to pedal if you expect us to go anywhere." I demonstrated what to do with the set of foot pedals located on my side. And when I noticed her struggling, her shoes making the task almost impossible, I couldn't help but laugh. "Will you listen to me now and take them off?"

She grunted her frustration, yet she kicked them off anyway. "Why must you always be so damn impossible?"

"The better question is...why would you choose to come all

the way back here to see someone who's so damn impossible?" I used the lever on the console between us to guide the direction of the boat, taking us around the curve of the property where absolutely no one would be able to spot us.

"Well, if I'm being honest, I didn't exactly come back to see you." She focused on pedaling while she talked. "I came to see the rest of your family. I mean, yeah, there are things I'd like to say to you, but the entire reason I accepted your parents' invitation was to see them one last time."

She definitely had my attention there.

The sun bounced off the lake and forced her to squint as she tried to look at me. "I've come to this event—and so many others —every year for nearly a decade. Coming back one more time is a little bittersweet, and I think I needed to do this so I can finally let go."

"This isn't the first time we've broken up, Lindsey. You've never acted this way before, so what's going on now?" For some reason, the first thought that popped into my head was that she was dying, and this was her final goodbye.

Her brows pinched together as deep creases lined her forehead. While I understood the sun probably made it hard to see, I couldn't shake the feeling that her expression went beyond one's natural reaction to bright light.

"Well, Corbin, as you know, I've been seeing someone. I told you that not too long ago when I had to call you about the flowers." She swallowed harshly and squinted even more. "There's something different about him."

"Like what? He's a serial killer?" I needed her to get to the damn point.

She softly backhanded my bicep and rolled her eyes. "Not like that. I just mean that while we've both been with other people during our times apart, I feel like we've always kind of had this silent pact to keep things light because it just went unsaid that we'd get back together eventually."

I suddenly understood the taut pull of her brows and drastic *V* marring her forehead between them. Pity. Sympathy. She believed that whatever it was she needed to tell me would hurt me. I opened my mouth to stop her, to assure her that she didn't need to handle this with kid gloves, but what came next stunned me into silence.

"But not this time, Corbin. He asked me to marry him…and I said yes."

All I could do was stare at her and blink, my mouth hanging open to keep me from choking on my tongue. Truth be told, my shock had nothing to do with our history together or any lingering feelings between us. I guess I was surprised by how fast she'd gone from leaving me to getting engaged to someone else—not that it bothered me or anything. It simply surprised me.

"Which is why it was so important for me to come back this one last time to see your parents and sister and the few remaining friends in town. I hope you can understand, Corbin. You rushed off the phone when I told you that I was seeing someone else, so I just want to make sure you're okay with this. Well, I'm not expecting you to be okay, but at least respect my decision."

That's when the gaping mouth and blinking stare turned to belly laughs and knee slaps.

"What's so funny?" And it seemed her pity had morphed into irritation.

"Nothing. Nothing." I calmed down and cleared my throat to speak normally. "That's seriously the best news you could've told me, Lindsey."

Again, her eyes squinted—creases in brow, the whole nine yards—but this time, she regarded me with puzzlement in her stare.

"I've also started seeing someone, and while we're not at the diamond-ring stage yet, it's definitely something special, something I want to hold onto and never let go of. So I understand. It's really nice to know we're both at the same place, at the same time, ready to finally put an end to this merry-go-round we've called a relationship for the last nine years."

"Good. Me too."

Ready to head back, I adjusted the shifter to turn us around.

The return ride was a lot smoother and more comfortable than our departure. We were able to let go of the fear of hurting the other person and just enjoy one last laugh. And after getting the boat back on shore and covered, we were also able to give each other one last hug, and one final goodbye.

"I don't plan to hang around long. I honestly only came to see the family and enjoy the atmosphere a bit. I guess I just needed a memory to take with me, you know?" She smiled as I nodded, and then she patted my arm and put one heel behind the other. "Take care, Corbin."

"You do the same, Lindsey. And I mean it…congrats on the engagement."

And now that I'd made peace with my past, it was time to find my future.

I took my time making my way from the far side of the lake to the back of the house. If anyone saw me, they'd simply think I was casually making my rounds through the groups of friends and neighbors, when really, I was searching for Brooke. It seemed that most, if not all, of the guests had arrived, so I knew if I rushed through my search for her, I had a higher chance of missing her in a crowd.

But once I'd made it to the back porch, satisfied that she wasn't in the yard—and that I hadn't simply overlooked her—I snuck inside. She had to be here somewhere. And considering the house, there were only a few places she could be. I started with the kitchen, then checked the bathrooms she frequented when here, and when I didn't find her in any of those places, I moved toward the stairs, suspecting she might've been hanging out in Nellie's old bedroom.

"Oh, honey…there you are." Leave it to Mom to stop me before making it to the staircase. "Lindsey's here. Have you seen her yet?"

"Yes, Mom. I actually just finished talking to her."

"Good. I'm glad you two had a chance to catch up." Either she hadn't spoken to Lindsey yet, or their conversation had gone very differently than the one I'd had with her on the lake. "What are you doing inside? The party's in the back."

I huffed, tired of being coy. "I'm looking for Brooke. Have you seen her?"

"I actually just ran into her outside. She was sitting all alone beneath the pergola on the side of the house." Mom had a natural ability to acquire fancy things and insist they were called by their proper names.

Lucky for me, I knew exactly what she was referring to. Except in my vocabulary, it was known as the pavilion. Granted, that technically wasn't what it was, but considering it was made of four columns holding up rafters that were covered in vines and various-colored flowers that offered anyone beneath it shade, to me, it was a pavilion.

"Why are you looking for her?" she asked, although not at all suspiciously. At least there was one woman in my family who didn't immediately jump to conclusions. Then again, it wasn't like Nellie hadn't jumped to the *right* conclusions, but that wasn't the point.

"I wanted to catch her before she left. I, uh…I had a few more ideas of things she could do to her house that would improve the, um…the curb appeal." Damn, I really needed to get better at coming up with things on the spot.

Thankfully, she didn't question it and offered a loving smile in response.

I took off through the side door, hoping she hadn't left that spot before I got there. And as soon as I caught the sight of her yellow dress through the foliage that had wrapped itself around the wooden columns, I felt like I could breathe again, realizing I'd pretty much held each breath since she'd walked away with Nellie. And that had been more than an hour ago.

"Thank God you're still here. I couldn't find you anywhere." I took a seat next to her on the wrought-iron bench. "I was getting worried that you might've left already."

She turned to face me, and I couldn't have been any happier to see that her eyes were the color of limes, and as far as I could tell, there weren't any signs of tear tracks through her makeup. Good lord, she was stunning.

"No, I didn't leave. I'm not going to run away with my tail between my legs. I didn't buy this dress or spend hours this morning getting ready to only get fifteen minutes of enjoyment out of it. I told myself I'd stay for at least two hours." Her smile may have been guarded, but it was beautiful all the same.

"Well, for what it's worth, you took my breath away when you first got here. Hell, you're still taking it away." I made a show of my chest heaving, as if I were fighting for air. "You're by far the most gorgeous woman here."

Casting her gaze onto the lawn, she asked, "I take it you spoke to Lindsey?" Her voice was so soft it nearly got carried away in the gentle breeze that drifted through the pavilion. Yet it was loud enough to hear the trepidation in her tone.

"Yeah, we had good talk."

"I bet your parents are thrilled with that."

I shrugged, even though she wasn't looking my way. "Maybe, but I'm sure once they find out what we talked about, they won't be." That earned her attention, her wide eyes swinging to me mine, and I had to fight against the smile that yearned to play on my lips. "She's getting married, which means it's over for the both of us. It doesn't matter how badly my parents or Nellie want us to work things out, it's never going to happen."

Peace and relief blanketed her and left hope shining in her eyes.

I held her hand and turned my shoulders to face her. "Listen, Brooke—"

"I'd love to see how you guys plan to lie your way out of this one." Nellie interrupted me when she stepped out from behind the shrubbery with her arms crossed, catching us red-handed. I must've been too focused on Brooke to notice any movement or hear her footfalls as she approached.

Both of us just sat still, staring up at her, unable to speak…or move.

"So that's it? No one's going to bother trying to tell me that I'm making a bigger deal of this than there is?" She pointed to Brooke and asked, "You're not going to look me in the eyes and swear that there's nothing between you? The least you guys could do is come up with something. I think I deserve a little entertainment at this point. Can't one of you at least attempt an explanation as to why you're holding hands?"

Brooke slipped her hand out from beneath mine and laced her fingers together in her lap. I'd never experienced such painful rejection in my life. Everything that had taken place over the last hour or so felt like one giant sucker punch. One major curveball out of left field. And I had started to doubt my ability to handle it all.

"So were you really the one who invited Lindsey?" I asked, staring point blank at Nellie.

"No. I'm not like you, Corbin. Or Brooke. I'm not a liar. Mom and Dad invited her, like they do *every* year. Trust me when I say, if I had known that she was coming, there would've been fireworks."

"Why?" Brooke glanced up, her eyes shimmering with tears though none had taken the plunge. "Just because you hadn't asked her to come or knew ahead of time that she'd be here doesn't change the fact that you just admitted that if you had, you would've gone out of your way to hurt us. Why, Nellie? Why would you want to hurt us?"

"Because you've done nothing but lie to my face. How can you stab me in the back and then expect me not to react? Don't treat me like I'm the one who betrayed you. Remember who did the betraying first. And you have no right to be upset with me for something I only wished I had done yet never did, while defending yourself for *actually* doing something."

"Can we please talk about this?" she pleaded.

"No. You had your chance, and you chose to lie instead. The time to talk about it has passed." Nellie shook her head and took a step back. "You know, until I walked over here and caught the two of you, I didn't have proof that anything's been going on between you. I've suspected it. I've assumed it. But until this very moment, I wasn't entirely sure. I *wanted* to believe you, Brooke."

I stood and put myself between my sister and Brooke. "Nell, that's enough."

"That's rich, Corbin." Her laughter was borderline methodical, and it matched her crooked grin. "You guys have snuck around behind my back for God knows how long, and yet you stand here and tell *me* when it's enough?"

"We understand that you're mad."

"Well, good. I'm glad you *understand*, dear brother. But understand this…I wanted to believe that nothing was going on between you guys. I actually felt bad for doubting you two. Pathetic right? But something just kept eating at me, so I dug a little deeper."

Rather than respond or entice her to keep talking, I simply stood in front of her with my arms crossed over my chest, clenching my teeth as I desperately held on to the last strand of my patience. She was upset; I got that. But there was a time and a place to handle this properly—like adults. And hiding out on the side of our parents' house while their guests mingled less than twenty yards away was *not* it.

"Imagine my surprise when I discovered that you've been lying about the plan." She leaned to the side to see around my form. "Both of you."

Brooke finally pulled herself off the bench and moved to stand by my side, just one tiny step behind me. "I never lied about that. I just didn't correct you."

"Um, *no*, Brooke. You lied. To my face. Countless times. What else would you call it when you tell me the plan is still in effect, even though there's been absolutely *no* progress since the beginning?"

Brooke took two more steps, moving to now stand in front of me, and turned her attention my way. Yet I didn't look at her. I couldn't. The heat from her stare was enough, and I knew I wouldn't be able to handle looking into her eyes, knowing that I'd lied to her for two months now.

Giving up on gaining my attention, she turned back to Nellie and whispered, "I don't understand."

"What's there not to get, Brooke? This whole time, the two of you have told me—as well as Mady and Julie—that he was making progress with Heather. He's told me that they've gone out a couple of times. Are you trying to tell me that you didn't know that?"

"Well, no. I mean, I knew he hadn't actually gone *out* with her. But how do you know he hasn't done anything at all about it? He's gone down to her desk to see her, ran into her in the hallways a few times, talked to her at the office. Just because he hasn't met up with her outside of work doesn't mean he's done *nothing*."

I so badly wanted to put an end to this, but I couldn't move. My mouth wouldn't even form the shapes to make sounds, my lips refusing to part while I just stood there like an arsonist amongst the crowd watching as my building burned to the ground, the flames taking everything I cared about with it.

"Brooke, sweetheart…" That patronizing tone was almost enough to snap me out of my trance and strangle her, but the words that followed kept me locked in this steel box of panic. "I called and spoke to Heather a couple of days ago. She's never even met him. He literally hasn't made one move toward the goal. Not one."

This time, when Brooke turned her attention to me, I met her stare. The sheer betrayal in her eyes was enough to make me crumble. I'd done that. I'd caused her that pain. And on top of the hurt that Nellie had just dished out, it was very clear that she'd reached her limit.

She glanced between Nellie and me a few times before quietly saying, "Excuse me," and walking away.

I wanted to go after her, chase her down, explain it all to her, but I couldn't.

Because my parents had chosen that moment to drag Nellie and me to the back yard for the adult egg hunt. The only thing that got me through was knowing she wouldn't be able to hide from me. As soon as I finished dealing with my sister and figured out what I needed to say to Brooke, I'd go after her. And we'd get through this together.

I believed that with my whole heart.

CHAPTER 26

BROOKE

I'D STOOD there in a state of shock, convinced I had heard her wrong. But no matter how badly I wanted to believe that, I couldn't, because even when I offered Corbin a chance to correct her, he didn't.

And when I could no longer stomach the thought of him lying to me this entire time, I walked away, needing a moment to compose myself. But as I stepped closer to the back door, making my way inside to use the restroom, I realized I didn't need to stay. I had no obligations to hang around until the end.

I could leave anytime I wanted.

So that's exactly what I did.

I'd planned to talk to him tonight about how I felt and the status of our relationship, but now, I no longer knew what I wanted. Today had been a whirlwind—hell, these last two months had been one massive vortex of lies and secrets and broken trust. My life had been turned upside down, and I had no clue which side was up at the moment.

I needed to clear my head and think.

As weird as it felt to get in my car and drive away without telling anyone bye, or even thanking their parents for inviting me, I was happy for the easy escape. Things were awkward between all of us now, and I had no idea how long it would be before they would calm down. A swift exit worked out for the best.

Nellie's face kept playing on repeat in my head. She'd looked so *disgusted* at the mere thought of Corbin and me together. Had she seriously thought I'd known all along about the lack of any sort of progress on the plan? Did Corbin honestly think that would never come out? Then again, I had no right to be upset with him for that. After all, I'd done the same to Nellie, knowing that at some point, our entire relationship would get out.

God, I had a lot to think about.

As I approached the traffic light just outside of the subdivision that Corbin and Nellie had grown up in, I began to slow, preparing to turn left down the country road that led to my house —well, Phyllis's house. Shit, I didn't even have a place I could call my own. While I knew that Phyllis had thought of it as *our* home, and had even said so many times before, it didn't change the fact that I literally had nothing.

Aside from the car I drove and the clothes that hung in the closet, I had nothing. And that was a depressing realization to come to. I was more than thankful for all that Phyllis had ever done for me. I truly was. There was not one part of me that was ungrateful for the help I'd received along the way. However, the fact still remained that I had no parents, no family, no valuable possession that I could call my own.

For fuck's sake, I didn't even have a paying job.

Instead of turning left at the light, I decided to keep driving. I had no idea where I'd end up or how far I'd go, but I just needed to drive. I needed to roll down the windows, silence the world, and get my head straight.

And by the time dusk had begun to set, I came to the realization that I'd had enough soul searching for the evening. I pulled into an empty parking lot two towns away and grabbed my phone from the passenger seat, where I'd tossed it after turning off the ringer.

There were a dozen texts and even more missed calls from

Corbin. But I couldn't be bothered with reading his messages. I only glanced at the last one—mainly because it was short and didn't require much thought to comprehend—and noticed that he'd asked if he could come over tonight to talk. I guess it worked out for the best that I'd taken my impromptu road trip.

I quickly tapped out a reply and pressed send.

Me: I'm really tired, so maybe we can meet up tomorrow instead? Please respect my decision. I don't have anything left in me tonight.

Then I turned on the *do not disturb* function and headed home.

FIRM KNOCKING WOKE me out of a dead sleep. I laid there for a moment, still unsure of what had actually awoken me. I slowly blinked my eyes and then glanced around. I didn't see anything. It was Monday, so Phyllis had gone with our neighbor to play bridge at the local senior center.

At the realization that it was Monday—and based on the amount of light seeping through my blinds, I knew it had to around midday—I sat up straight, nearly jumping out of bed in a panic that I'd missed work. But just as I was about to whip the covers off me, I remembered that it was a teacher duty day—the schools were closed.

I didn't even get to fully relax before another set of harsh knocking resounded from the front door. They weren't the thuds that resulted from pounding, but more like heavy knuckles impatiently beating on wood. Then again, they could've been frantic of fearful knocks.

Either way, it was enough to pull me from the confines of my bed. But I didn't hurry. Just because they were impatient didn't mean I had to be as well. And by the time I'd made it to the front window and peeked past the curtains, recognizing Corbin's car parked along the curb in the space he'd dubbed his reserved spot, my speed managed to decrease even more.

I turned the deadbolt and swung open the door, holding up one finger to silently communicate that I needed a moment before he started talking. Then I picked up the pace and ran to the bathroom to brush my teeth, pull my hair back, and wash my face. When I was done, I found him in my room, sat on the edge of my bed with his head in his hands.

It'd be a lie if I said my heart didn't break a little at that sight.

"What are you doing here, Corbin? Aren't you supposed to be at work?" I walked past him and grabbed my cell from my nightstand, remembering that I hadn't taken it off *do not disturb*. Aside from the countless missed calls and texts from Corbin, I also saw the time. It was eleven in the morning—I hadn't slept this late since I was a teen.

"I needed to see you." His eyes bore into mine, and in them, I saw nothing but fear and pain—although I had not a clue what had caused him pain. I hadn't lied to him.

"So you just left work before lunchtime to come see me?" I understood that I was making this harder than I needed to, but I was still upset and confused and half-asleep. It was all I could do to sit and talk to him right now.

"Yes. You weren't answering any of my calls, and you weren't reading your messages. I've been trying to get ahold of you since you left my parents' house. I even came by last night, but your car wasn't in the driveway. I've been losing my mind, Brooke. So yes, I left work before lunchtime because I *needed* to see you. I had to know that you're all right, even if you're still angry with me."

"I'm not angry, Corbin." And I wasn't. Hurt and upset? Yes. Mad? No.

He shifted on the mattress to face me. "Please tell me I haven't lost you."

I had to look away, the terror in his eyes made my heart hurt. "No. You haven't lost me."

He threw me by surprise when he leaned forward and, with

one hand cradling my face, covered my mouth with his, kissing me deeply. It was intense, but he didn't use his tongue or make it sexual; it was more than that. Which only served to completely confuse me once again.

After a moment, he broke the kiss, yet he didn't let me go. He dropped his forehead to mine and asked, "Can we talk?" His emotions radiated through me and I tried to keep them separate from my own, but it was hard.

"Yeah," I whispered, and with a sigh of relief, he dropped his hand into my lap and pulled away so that we could comfortably see one another without needing a chiropractor. "I'll be straight with you, Corbin...I'm confused. And before you ask me about what, the answer is, *everything*."

"I completely understand that, and I'm really sorry, Bridge. I'm so fucking sorry."

"I know. I knew that yesterday, too. But there was just so much going on, so many emotions swirling around, that I couldn't make sense of any of it. If I'm being honest, I still don't think I'm able to make sense of it."

He nodded and regarded the rumpled sheet between us for a moment before asking, "Do you think it's possible to discuss where we go from here?"

I nodded, but my heart pounded so wildly in my chest that I wasn't able to speak.

Yesterday morning, I'd known exactly what I wanted, and I had every intention of going after it. Corbin hadn't made a secret of his feelings since the beginning, so it wasn't like I had any worry that he'd turn me down or surprise me by saying he didn't want the same things. I wasn't scared to tell him how I felt.

But the last twenty-four hours had changed so much.

Yes, I still knew where his head was at. I didn't question or doubt his feelings or what he wanted with me going forward. And yes, I still wanted all the things I had prior to walking into his parents' back yard yesterday. My confusion was more or less tied up in all the messy pieces we'd left loose—or should I say, that *I* had left loose when I walked out on him and Nellie.

"You lied to me," I whispered. "About the plan. You never did anything. Why did you tell me that you had?"

"When I originally agreed, I'll be honest…I didn't want to do it, but I figured that if I was able to work it into my schedule, then why not. But soon, you and I started hanging out, and instead of putting energy into someone else, I wanted to put that energy into you. At first, I lied about it to give me excuses to see you. To talk to you. Even if they were just text messages. But then we started actually seeing each other. I never wanted to entertain Heather. I just wanted to be with you."

That wasn't something I could argue with. "Well, since we're being honest with one another…I can't be upset at you for that. I thought I wanted you to follow through with the plan, but that was because I was so stuck on wanting to get revenge that I didn't fully think it through. And by the time I did contemplate what that would mean, I realized I no longer cared if Heather cheated on Chase."

"Why the change of heart?"

"I decided to stop worrying about what happens to him and start focusing on what I have in my own life. Not to mention, without him breaking my heart the way he did, I never would've gotten the chance to be with you. Once I stopped focusing on the anger and started looking at all the positives that came from it, it was a lot easier."

"Then why didn't you tell me that when you realized it?"

"I guess I didn't know how without explaining *all* of my feelings, and at the time, I wasn't ready to do that yet. My mind was still all over the place, so I figured I'd wait until I had a better understanding of my feelings before discussing it all with you."

He placed his hand on my thigh, making me take note of my wringing fingers, which called my attention to my nervous habit of nibbling on the inside of my cheek. But when his eyes held mine, he had my undivided attention.

"I care for you, Bridge. So damn much. You've imbedded yourself into my life without even trying. Everything is so easy with you, so effortless, exactly the way things *should* be." He took a deep breath and let it out slowly.

"Easy? Effortless?" I laughed and then playfully rolled my eyes at him. I had a habit of using humor to deflect during uncomfortable situations, and this conversation was the epitome of uncomfortable. "I don't think I'd use either of those words to describe us, Corbin."

"You're right, it hasn't been easy in some ways, but I don't think that's anything against *us*. If it had only been us, just the two of us, things would've unfolded so much differently. But instead, we had my sister, and the plan, and my parents, and Lindsey… We had so much stacked against us, but look at how well we did."

He made a very valid point. Not that I hadn't believed him prior to that speech.

"We have so much in common, Bridge. And more importantly, we have *fun* together. Our sexual chemistry is off the charts, and if I'm being honest, I don't think we've even scratched the surface. All of these things make me optimistic about the future."

"I get that. But you're failing to acknowledge some very important details. Such as the fact that Nellie hates the idea of us being together. Our relationship has pretty much destroyed your entire family dynamic! That's pretty huge, Corbin. If we're together, does that mean you can never see your family again? How would that even work?" I realized that I'd started twisting my hands in my lap again, but no matter how hard I tried to make it stop, I couldn't, which only served to increase my nervousness.

"Nellie and I had a long conversation yesterday."

Well, that piqued my interest. "Does she hate me?"

"She loves you, and I think that's why this is so hard for her. She feels like you're choosing me over her, but that's because she's only considered things from *her* point of view. So we talked about broadening her horizon and putting herself in your shoes. And mine."

I nodded. What he said made sense, but I needed more.

"You've basically grown up like sisters, except you weren't raised with the same family dynamic, so you process things very differently. Give her some time, and I swear she'll come around. Your friendship is stronger than this. Have some faith in it."

I decided to put the Nellie situation on the back burner for now, because his words made me feel better and gave me hope. But also, because it was time to concentrate on the dilemma that we had right in front of us.

"Listen, I don't mean this in any malicious way, but maybe you need to think of the other position, too. Just like you advised Nellie to do, maybe you need a moment in the other shoe."

His gaze narrowed and brow furrowed, confusion darkening his eyes.

"If you take a step back, you'll recognize that I'm not good for you. You're Corbin Fields, the self-proclaimed workaholic who's turned into leaving early and arriving late. Here you are, in my room at eleven o'clock in the morning on a workday. That's not you. You've spent weekends and evenings with me, doing mindless activities instead of putting in the hours at AdCorp."

I could tell he wanted to cut me off, but he didn't. He allowed me to continue my rant while sitting there and taking it all.

"You don't play hooky or skip meetings. You're absent from daily life, and work is your priority. Yet ever since you started seeing me, your work ethic has gone to shit. And you can't deny that it's all because of me."

"Isn't that a good thing? Being present in daily life, making the people I love a priority over my job? Isn't that what we're *supposed* to do?"

I ignored the giant purple elephant in the room—the *L* word—since it wasn't necessarily directed at me and continued to make my point. "But that's not what *you* do. What if you're just fitting into my life? Giving up your dreams for me? That's an awfully big burden to bear. Not to mention, your parents—your *entire family*—loves Lindsey. They all want you to be with her, not me."

"Do you seriously think I'm that impressionable? That I'd spend a month with someone and suddenly start thinking like them? Not to mention, what's so wrong with taking a page from your book? For the first time in my life, I'm *living*. So what if *you* taught me that? All that should matter is that I feel alive." He paused and shook his head. "And I've already told you…it doesn't matter if the entire world wants me with Lindsey. I want you. Only you. No one else. End of story, because I won't repeat myself again."

Well, that certainly was an effective way to shut me up.

"Don't you see, Bridge? I'm finally present in my own life. The other day, I stopped by my parents' and had dinner with them out of the blue. Then my dad and I played chess, something we haven't done since I was a kid. I'm not giving up on my dreams. Not even close. I'm finally fulfilling them. I was lost until you found me and showed me the right direction. You're not a bad influence. Quite the opposite, really. You *saved* me."

My eyes filled with tears, and every time I tried to speak, my voice broke, so I gave up.

He brought my tangled hands to his lips and kissed them. "I love you, Brooklyn Bridge."

My eyes widened. I'd been able to successfully ignore the slight mention of love a few moments ago, but there was no way I'd be able to pretend I hadn't heard him say that. Instead, I didn't say or do anything. Just stared at him.

"I really do, Brooklyn. I cannot for the life of me imagine a day without you in it. Every day we're apart, I spend it thinking and planning of what we'll do, excited for when we're together again. You belong *with* me, by my side." Each word spoken was full of raw emotion, it was clearly etched in his face and body language.

But I was scared to voice how I felt—how I *truly* felt about him —so I decided to start small. "I care about you, too, Corbin."

"Well, that was like a knife to my heart," Corbin joked, though he couldn't hide his true feelings. It'd hurt him not to hear it back, but I had to go about this at my own pace.

"No, I'm serious. I really do, probably more than I've ever cared for anyone else—Nellie included. I'm on the verge of losing the most important friendship I've ever had...for *us*. But more than that...for *me*. Because it's what *I* want. I do want to be with you, but I'm scared. I'm terrified that if I put myself out there, I'm going to get hurt. I'm petrified that if I give you my heart, you'll stomp on it like Chase did. I endured Chase doing that because I didn't really love him. But if you did it, there's no way I'd survive. Does that make sense?"

"Yes," he said quietly.

"When Chase left, my whole world had been flipped on its head. I'd planned our future, nurtured our relationship...but it was all *me*. Not him. I realized I drove the relationship and set the tone, but I never really made sure he was on board with everything. I was in love with the idea, not the reality. But you..." I released a drawn-out sigh. "Being with you is different. I do love you, Corbin Fields. More than I even wanted to admit."

Without pause, he took me into his arms, and I hoped he'd never let go.

This was what I wanted. As soon as the words had left my mouth, peacefulness set in, and it served as confirmation that I'd made the right decision. I'd finally had the courage to share my heart, mind, body, and soul with him.

I'd battled the fear.

And won.

It wouldn't influence this decision. And I'd start working on not allowing it to affect the other choices in my life, either. The next one on my list to tackle was Nellie. That would be a hard one. But no matter what happened, Corbin would be by my side, and we'd weather the storms together.

That was all the encouragement and support I needed.

CORBIN and I had made plans to see each other once girls' night was over, and then he'd gone back to work. Which meant I'd had nothing else to do all day but obsess over my impending conversation with Nellie. And I didn't need to overthink it one more time. I was ready to confront her head-on. Not in a negative way, but to finally come clean with what had happened and apologize for not being up front with her.

I finished my third soda while continuing to drum my fingers along the table.

"What up, chicken butt?" At least Mady's greeting was enough to put a much-needed smile on my face. "How are things?"

"That's kind of a loaded question," I confessed.

"Yeah, sorry. I don't even know what all happened yesterday. Nellie came out for the adult egg hunt, all sorts of pissed at the world, and you were nowhere to be found. Julie and I left shortly after that. Nellie kind of made it awkward for everyone, to say the least."

"I don't doubt that, but I'm hopeful we can get through this." When my refill was brought to the table, I took my straw from the empty glass so Dandy could take it with her and then turned my attention back to Mady. "Do you know if Nellie's coming tonight?"

"No idea. I haven't heard from her since yesterday."

"Haven't heard from who?" Julie gave us each a one-armed hug in greeting before taking her seat to my left, leaving Nellie's usual seat to my right empty. "Who are we talking about?"

"Nellie," Mady answered. "Have you talked to her?"

"Yeah. I finally got ahold of her about an hour ago to see if she was coming. I wasn't sure after what happened yesterday—which I still don't have all the pieces to. She said to order her usual drink, that she'd be a few minutes late."

My stomach turned into knots. I did everything I could think of to untangle the uncomfortableness, but nothing worked. I'd just have to do my best and get through what lay ahead while keeping my head held high. There was no telling what all she'd said yesterday after I left, and I didn't think it would be right to put the girls in the middle of it by asking—although, after tonight, they'd most certainly be in the middle of it.

"Hello, everyone." Nellie finally made an appearance. She greeted us as a group, and even though she didn't hug or greet me personally, she seemed okay. That was, until her eyes landed on me. Then a coldness took over that nearly had me running.

I couldn't do this. *Maybe I should let things lie low for a while.*

There were a few tense moments while everyone placed their orders, but once Dandy walked away, it turned into awkward silence. No one knew what to say, or even where to look.

Finally, Julie broke the ice. "So, how is everyone?"

Nellie shot me a look, but otherwise stayed quiet.

"I'm good," Mady finally answered, because no one else did. Then, in her usual bubbly candor, she added, "Come on, guys. It can't be that serious!"

"Oh, trust me. It is. How would you feel if your best friend fucked your brother?"

"I honestly don't know." Mady shrugged. "I don't have a brother. But what I do know is that you guys are the glue in this group. Don't let this be the end of our foursome!"

"The only reason I even came tonight is because I didn't think *she* would be here," Nellie spat.

"Look, I know I hurt you. And for that, I'm truly sorry, but—"

"No!" She pointed her finger at me, her face the color of an overripe tomato. "Don't you dare follow up an apology with a *but*. You're either sorry or you're not. It's an apology or an excuse; you can't have it both ways, Brooklyn."

Brooklyn? If that was the worst she could think of to call me, then we'd be all right. Using my given name rather than issuing hateful ones was a good sign that we'd be able to work things out.

"I'm not really all that surprised at my brother's part in it. Most men don't know how to keep their dicks in their pants. But the part you played? Surprised the fuck out of me. Want to know why?" She set her stare right on me and said, "Because I never thought you were a slut."

Strike that. Name calling had ensued.

"Maybe you should let her speak, Nell. Will you at least hear her out before slinging mud?" Julie suggested gently.

Nellie thought about that for a minute and then nodded at me.

"I hated lying to you, but I did so out of fear over losing you, because you are *that* important to me. I was scared to death that if I told you how I was feeling, you'd cut me out of your life, and I can't imagine a world where we aren't friends."

"I can't, either!" Mady exclaimed. "I imagine the four of us growing old together and complaining about things only old people complain about."

"Mady, let her finish!" Julie admonished.

"It's not coming out right." I lowered my head into my hands and took a second to breathe before dropping my arms, meeting her eyes, and trying again. "I'm sorry. I screwed up! I've grown up watching dirty skanks pretend to be your friend and then spend all their time at your house following your brother around. And I guess I didn't want you to think that I was just as bad as they were—*or worse*. I wanted to prove that I was better than all of them. So yes, I hid it from you. It wasn't planned. It just happened —literally. And I can't even blame him, because I'm the one who initiated things to begin with."

"See?" Nellie glanced between Mady and Julie while pointing at me. "Slut."

"That's not cool, Nellie." Based on Julie's expression, she was dangerously close to speaking her mind, and it didn't look like it would be something Nellie would appreciate hearing.

But I was capable of fighting my own battles.

"I'm *not* a slut. And you know that. You, of all people, know what kind of person I am. I'm a *good* person who happened to have made a mistake. I allowed fear to control my decisions. I was so afraid to lose you that I kept things from you, things I knew would hurt you instead of giving you the benefit of the doubt—instead of giving our friendship more credit."

At least she wasn't interrupting me or calling me names. I'd call that a win so far.

"I'm sorry for lying to you, Nellie. But I'm not sorry for being with him, because I love him. Never in a million years did I expect this to happen, but it did. I love him, and I'm a better version of myself because of him. So please, Nellie, I'm begging you, *please* don't let this be the end of us. Because for the first time in my life, my future feels so fucking bright and promising, and I can't imagine not having you in it." I sniffled and wiped my nose with my napkin.

She took a minute to wipe her eyes too, and then cleared her throat before speaking. "I just never thought you'd lie to me. And I wasn't even prepared for how much it hurt."

"I know." People I cared about had lied to me, like Chase, and it hadn't felt good. In any way, shape, or form. "Trust me, if I could go back and do things differently, I would."

"I'd suspected that you and Corbin had something going on, but I never considered the possibility of it being serious, or that you loved each other. That never even crossed my mind because you were so secretive about it. I assumed that if you were hiding it, it must not be real."

"I understand." And I did. Hearing her point of view made complete sense. We'd both made assumptions and had presumed the wrong thing. "Are you still my lobster?"

She rolled her teary eyes and waved me off with a genuine laugh. "Duh. Don't you know? Once two lobsters lock claws on the ocean floor, they're besties for life." We hugged each other, holding on a little bit longer. "I'm sorry, lobs."

"I'm sorry too, lobs!"

"Aww! The lobsters have found each other again!" Mady clapped excitedly.

"You'll always be my lobster, Brooke. No matter what!" Nellie beamed.

CHAPTER 27

CORBIN

MY HEART POUNDED WILDLY AS I shifted the car into park in front of my parents' house.

I had a big announcement—well, *two* big announcements—and I wasn't sure how they would react. Truth be told, I didn't care how they felt about my news, but I had to tell them anyway, so I figured there was no better time to do that than Easter Sunday.

"Are you sure about this, Corbin?" Brooke asked from the passenger seat, concern dancing in her eyes as she studied me. It seemed she could sense my trepidation. "You know you don't have to say anything today if you're not ready."

I was confident in my news, excited even. But at the end of the day, I was still a boy who hoped to have my parents' approval. Not that I would change my mind if they didn't give it to me, but still, I sought it all the same.

I squeezed her hand and smiled. "Nah, I'll be okay. As long as I have you by my side, I can't lose."

Over the last week, I'd been working on making my dream a reality—with Brooke's help. If not for her, I never would've realized my potential or found my passion. I owed so much to this woman, and I was happy to have a chance to repay her every day for the rest of my life.

She gave me a quick kiss and then opened the car door, preventing me from stalling even longer. She was right; I had to get this over with, knowing that once the cat was out of the bag, we could all enjoy Easter lunch.

Brooke gave my hand another squeeze as we walked into the house. I wasn't sure if she'd done so to calm herself or offer me support. Either way, it settled my nerves as I made my way down the hall to the dining room. I had to admit, walking into my parents' house while holding her hand gave me a sense of power I'd never experienced before. There was something about having the support of someone I love that made me feel untouchable.

"Look who's here," Nellie said with a smile when I rounded the corner to the dining room.

Mom beamed when she turned around, but once she saw Brooke behind me, and then dropped her attention to our linked hands, her excitement fell. Not that she was *un*happy about what she saw, just taken by surprise.

Dad shook off his confusion quickly and came over to pat me on the back in his typical greeting. "Happy Easter, son." And then he nodded at Brooke. "Good to see you again, young lady."

"Well, this is certainly a surprise." Mom gave Brooke a small hug and then moved to me. "When you said you were bringing someone, I thought it would be Lindsey." Of course she did, because for some reason, no one in this family was capable of letting that go.

The biggest reason I hadn't informed my parents about my relationship with Brooke and wanted to wait until now was because I knew them. No matter how much they disagreed with it, they'd never let that be known, and I wanted Brooke to see their acceptance—even if it was only for show. And I really wanted to give them a chance to see us together. Like, *really* together. I figured if they got to see us interact naturally—as in not having to pretend that we were only acquaintances—they'd come around a lot sooner.

"Mom, Dad…you guys have made your opinion known. There's no question in *any* of our minds that you both wish for Lindsey and me to work things out. But I need you to know—*no*, I need you to *accept* that it's never going to happen. On top of me not wanting it to, Lindsey's engaged…*to someone else*." I had to add in that last part to ensure that neither of my parents would assume, for whatever reason, that I'd meant with me.

Dad plastered a wide grin on his face and said, "Well, regardless, we're happy to have you, Brooklyn. You know you're always welcome in our home." And then he extended an arm toward the table, gesturing for us all to take a seat.

Seeing the extra place setting next to where I always sat made me giddy. I'd endured two dinners having to sit across from Brooke, and finally, I got to have her next to me. I couldn't have been happier.

"Things are already changing," Nell whined as she plopped into her seat, her bottom lip poking out like she were a child. "I don't even get to sit next to my best friend anymore. This is so unfair!"

Taking her seat next to me, Brooke giggled. "How about we alternate? Next time I'll sit next to you."

"Deal." Well, that was easy.

Maybe the rest of this meal would be just as smooth.

I almost laughed at myself for that ridiculous thought.

"Does this mean you two are dating?" Mom asked after taking a sip of her wine.

"Yes. We've been seeing each other for a month now. We haven't said anything to anyone about it because we wanted to see if we had anything before…making it official, I guess you can say. But now we're ready to take it to the next step."

Mom gasped and held her napkin over her lips. "Are you getting married?"

Brooke laughed nervously next to me, but I ignored that to

answer my mom. "No, we're not. There are other steps that need to be taken first—such as realizing that we want to be more serious than just *seeing where things go*. Trust me, you'll know when I'm ready to pop the question."

Truth be told, I already knew I wanted to spend the rest of my life with Brooke, but there was no need to rush it. We both wanted to do things the right way, considering we hadn't done so until this point. I trusted that she felt the same way as I did, so there was no reason to skip the important milestones. But I couldn't lie...I doubted I'd be able to wait long before moving her in with me. We just had to figure out how to deal with the Phyllis situation before that happened.

"Go ahead"—I gestured to my parents, knowing their minds were swirling with thoughts they weren't sharing—"say what you want. This is your time to share your opinions, comments, or concerns, because once we leave here, your opportunity will have passed."

They glanced at one another, and then my mom turned to look at Nellie. "How do you feel about this, Penelope? I assumed out of the three of us, you'd be the one with the problem. After all, isn't she *your* best friend?"

Leave it to my mother to put the burden of objecting onto someone else.

Luckily for us, Brooke and I had spent a good amount of effort this past week working things out with my sister. She'd even created a plan of her own, one that ensured that she would still get to see Brooke as much, if not more, than she always had.

Nell's brows knitted together as she glanced around the table, somewhat offended and maybe a little confused. "My best friend and my brother? Why on earth would I object to that? I've always thought of her as a sister, and now she actually gets to be one! What's there to complain about?"

"Well, I just meant if they break up. I'm sure that would put you in a bad position."

"No it won't. If they break up—which I *highly* doubt they

will, but if they do—it won't affect my relationship with Brooke. It'll just mean Corbin will be dead to me." She winked at me in jest.

When my dad cleared his throat, I knew he was about to say something that would either upset Brooke or piss me off. "I think I can speak for the both of us when I say we're happy for the two of you. As long as you're happy, we're happy. But I also want to make sure you're aware of what you're getting into."

"Dad, I appreciate your concern, but this isn't my first relationship. I'm well aware of what I'm *getting myself into*."

"That's not what I mean, son. You've really only been in one serious relationship, and that was with a woman who didn't need to be taken care of. She didn't have to rely on you for anything. This relationship will be very different from that one."

"I don't mean to be rude, Mr. Fields, but I've been taking care of myself for years. I was seventeen when my mom was diagnosed with cancer. So not only did I have to rely on myself, but I also had to care for my mother. By the time I was twenty, I was all alone. I didn't have anyone to come to my rescue. I supported myself. I *relied* on myself." God I loved this woman—her strength, her determination, and the way she could stand up for herself with offending anyone.

In fact, if anything, her words had seemed to leave my dad embarrassed. "Oh, no. My apologies. That's not the way I'd meant that at all."

Lies. That was *exactly* what he meant.

"With all due respect, Mr. and Mrs. Fields, I love your son. I understand that you're only looking out for his best interest, but so am I. I may not have a six-figure salary, but that doesn't mean I don't live and breathe my job the same as the two of you. I'm responsible for eighteen six- and seven-year-olds. Just because I don't have a corner office doesn't mean what I do isn't important. In fact, some might argue that what I do is *more* important, because I'm responsible for molding future generations." She glanced between my parents and added, "So please, believe me when I say I'm just as invested in your son's best interests as you are."

"You don't have to worry about that, Brooklyn." Mom smiled, and there wasn't a piece of me that doubted how genuine and sincere it was. "We believe you."

"Just as long as you don't come over and announce you've quit your job, we'll be okay." Dad might've thought he was being funny, but that didn't stop Brooke from choking on her water, or Nellie from kicking me under the table.

"Well, there is something else I want to tell you guys." There really was no easy way to put this. My only option was to just spit it out. So, after a deep breath, I grabbed Brooke's hand in her lap and blurted, "I've decided to leave AdCorp."

Dad stared at me with wide, bright eyes. "Does this mean you're coming to work for us?"

"Uh, no. Not exactly."

His excitement quickly fell from his face. "Then where are you going?"

I'd spent years dreaming of doing something else, but it'd always felt like a pipedream, something I'd never be able to materialize. That was, until Brooke. That dream began to get bigger and louder and brighter after the beautification day at her school. And ever since then, I hadn't been able to ignore it. Finally, a little over a week ago, I'd spent all day on the phone making plans instead of doing my actual job. I'd done all of this without even discussing it with Brooke, so no matter what my parents had to say about it, they couldn't blame her.

Brooke squeezed my hand in a much-needed show of support and then said, "He's starting a non-profit organization that'll offer better work and education opportunities to those who need it most."

Last week, when Brooke had come to my place after making up with my sister, I told her everything. I'd been excited to discuss the early details with her, but I had wanted to wait until I knew, without a doubt, that I'd be able to move forward with my idea. And earlier that day, after I'd returned from confessing my love to her, I'd gotten the call letting me know that I'd gotten the greenlight.

I still found myself unworthy of her reaction when she'd found out exactly what I had orchestrated. Her love and support were all I needed, yet she'd offered so much more than that. She'd given me enthusiasm, praise, but most of all, she'd given me a purpose.

"I don't get it, Corbin." My mom studied me from across the table. "Your passion is corporate marketing. You've been working toward making the switch from AdCorp to our firm so that, one day, you'd be the one running the company."

"Those were *your* dreams—yours and Dad's."

"Don't put this on us, son." Apparently, Dad didn't appreciate being called out. "We never forced you into anything."

While that was debatable, I chose not to use this time arguing with him. Pointing out all the grooming he'd done my entire life would only be a waste of time. Instead, I decided to speak from the heart and hope he understood. "Do you really want to know what I want?"

They both sat silently and nodded.

"I want to be happy going to work every day. And while I enjoy the creativeness of what I do, coming up with marketing strategies for big companies to make even more money doesn't make me happy. It feels like a waste of my talent, my time, and my energy."

"So how does this new venture fit into your need to fulfill that in your life?"

"Easy…it allows me to help the less fortunate rise above the limitations life has set on them. I can help them reach what society has told them is impossible. Do you have any idea how many underprivileged youths don't attend college simply because of financial reasons? Even with a scholarship, they're less likely to attend a four-year college, or finish, because they can't support themselves *and* focus on their workload at school at the same time. I can help with that."

Silence filled the room while I sat there holding Brooke's hand. My parents looked at each other as if reading their minds, and Nell smiled at me from across the table, offering support I hadn't really sought yet was more than grateful to receive. And Brooke remained by my side, where she had promised she'd always be.

Finally, Mom turned her pride-filled eyes to me. "That's a truly honorable thing to do, sweetheart. I can't say we're not disappointed that you won't be taking control of the family company, but that's simply because we're sad to be losing someone as smart and talented as you. Hopefully, by doing this, you'll be giving others the chance to take your place in the marketing world."

"I agree," Dad added. "We wish you nothing but the best."

"Thanks, you guys." Their acceptance allowed me to breathe again.

In the end, it didn't matter if they approved of my choices or not. It was time to live my life for me, and that meant making decisions that I could live with. I wanted to accomplish more than just ticking off boxes on some master plan my parents had choreographed for me. And more importantly, I needed to march to the beat of my own music. Not theirs. But that didn't mean that their acceptance wasn't fully appreciated.

Nellie clapped and said, "Now that we've gotten that out of the way...let's eat!"

EPILOGUE

Brooke

CORBIN'S PARENTS held a party for every holiday, but Fourth of July was my favorite.

We'd been dating for almost a year and a half, so I'd officially attended every celebration they held during that time. And the fireworks over the lake was hands-down the best. Granted, they did something similar on New Year's Eve, except it just wasn't the same. There was something about the warmer weather coupled with the bright colors in the sky and crickets chirping in the distance that completed the entire evening.

"They're about ready to set them off," Corbin said, coming up from behind me and catching my attention. "Come on."

I shrugged at my three best friends, trying not to read too much into their smiles.

Corbin had never been much of a holiday person...until we started dating. Even still, while he enjoyed attending parties at his parents' house, he hadn't shown much enthusiasm for the events. However, over the past month, it was like he couldn't wait for this one, which we'd all found a little odd. So strange, in fact, that all three girls had become convinced that tonight was the night Corbin would pop the question.

That thought excited me, but I didn't want to get my hopes up. Plus, we were so happy. An engagement wouldn't change anything except enhance it. It wasn't necessary for him to prove his commitment to me, but it would be fun to plan that next part of our lives together.

Over the last several months, there had been a couple other instances where we'd all thought the same thing, yet he hadn't proposed any of those times. So this could very well be the same. And if I were being honest, I didn't know how many more times I could get my hopes up without actually feeling let down if it didn't happen.

I wanted to marry Corbin more than anything. It was something we'd discussed a handful of times at the beginning of our relationship, yet it hadn't been mentioned since. I'd felt positive he'd revisit the idea after I moved in with him, which had happened shortly before Christmas after Phyllis opted to live in an assisted care facility.

But still, nothing had been said about marriage—or the future at all.

Then again, we'd both been busy with preparing ourselves for a future. I finally became a real teacher at the school I'd assisted at, and Corbin had busied himself with his non-profit organization, which had taken off and surpassed either of our dreams.

My assumption was that he was simply happy to have us living together, that he didn't feel rushed to make it down the aisle. Which I was okay with, just as long as I didn't continue to get my hopes up for a proposal that would never happen. If tonight turned out to be like all the others—meaning it'd end without a ring on my finger—I'd have to man-up and initiate a conversation. For no other reason than to know where his mind was.

"Good luck," Nellie whispered while giving me a hug.

Corbin laughed. "We're not leaving. No need to say goodbye."

"Oh, then where are you taking her?" Thank God for Mady's ability to play dumb. She'd done it enough times that even when she knew the answer, it was believable that she didn't.

I rubbed her small belly and smiled at her in the moonlight that lit up the entire yard. "We're going to watch the fireworks from the dock. It was a little too loud last year, so Corbin wants to sit far enough away to enjoy the show while still being able to carry on a conversation."

"What kind of conversation does he want to have while watching the fireworks?" Mady wouldn't let up, likely trying to prod Corbin into answering for himself.

Which she got when he said, "Nothing specific, but if I want to talk about the colors or point out which ones I like best, it's hard to do when my ears are ringing and I've got about a hundred people gathered around. Not to mention, I got eaten up by mosquitos last year from sitting in the grass, so I'm trying to avoid that happening again."

Mady rolled her eyes and shooed us away. "Fine. Go on, then. Enjoy your *conversation*."

Julie grabbed my hand and squeezed my fingers. "Have fun."

I nervously laughed them off and followed Corbin through the back yard toward the dock. The lake curved around the back of the property, and where he wanted to go was the furthest point away, which offered nearly complete privacy. However, it wasn't the first time he'd opted to take me there, be it during a party or after dinner on a random Sunday night. So really, his desire to sit out there didn't necessarily mean anything.

"What's up with your friends?" he asked while holding my hand, leading me around the curve of the lake. "They were acting weird."

"They always act weird." And they did. It really wasn't anything unusual.

"This is true, but they're just... I don't know, worse than normal tonight."

I hummed to myself, refusing to answer his question. He was right, though. The girls were acting obvious, but I couldn't exactly tell him why. If they were right, it might keep him from following through with the proposal. If they were wrong, I wouldn't want him to think there was pressure on him. In the end, humming seemed like the best response.

When the dock came into view, my breath caught in my chest. Twinkling lights were strung about inside the gazebo, and from what I could see, a bottle of champagne sat in an ice bin on the bench. At some point, he must've come out here—probably while I was with the girls—and spread out a blanket on the floating dock, a lone candle flickering from the center.

As hard as it was, I needed to keep my hopes at bay. He was a hopeless romantic, so this didn't necessarily mean anything. But it would be a lie if I said my stomach didn't flip with excitement at the thought of being proposed to beneath fireworks on my favorite day of the year.

"Wow, Corbin…what's all this for?"

"We never get much alone time together during *any* holiday, and I know how much you loved Fourth of July last year, so I wanted to do something special this time." He released my hand and took the few steps to the gazebo to grab the bottle of champagne.

Pointing to the paddleboat, I asked, "Why don't we take that out and watch the fireworks from the water? I can't think of anything more romantic than that."

He glanced at the covered boat and then back to me, the moonlight highlighting the creases in his brow. "You want to go out in that? It's dark, and there's no telling what's in the water."

I was well aware of his objections when it came to the boat. He'd told me once a while ago that he'd gone out on it with Lindsey at last year's Easter egg hunt, and he didn't want to taint our experience with that memory. But it had been over a year since that happened.

It was time to make new memories.

"I'm not concerned about what's in the lake. I'm not asking to go swimming in it. I just thought it would be nice to be surrounded by the colorful reflections of the fireworks on the surface of the water."

"What about your clothes? You're wearing a new skirt; I wouldn't want it to get dirty."

"Corbin…I know how to do laundry." I laughed. "If my skirt gets dirty, I'll wash it. But if you don't want to—"

"We'll go. If that's what my baby wants, then that's what she'll get." He kissed my forehead, set the champagne bottle down at my feet, and then trotted into the grass to remove the hard cover on the two-person paddleboat.

Once he had it pushed into the water and pulled up to the side of the dock, he held my hand and helped me in. It was a little wobbly at first, but as soon as he had himself settled into the seat beside me, it evened out.

"You might want to—" He glanced at my bare feet on the pedals and chuckled beneath his breath. "Never mind…I see you've already taken off your shoes."

"Well, yeah," I said, practically singing the *duh* tune.

"You fucking amaze me, Brooklyn Bridge."

I didn't understand why he'd said that, but I didn't ask. If taking off my shoes amazed him, then I wouldn't question it. Instead, I linked my arm with his and rested my cheek on his shoulder. We hadn't gone out too far, but we were far enough away from the dock to enjoy the colors littering the night sky. They'd only just started the show, and based on last year, it would last at least half an hour.

"Shit," he muttered beneath his breath, catching my attention.

I pulled away to look at him. "What's wrong?"

"I brought the champagne, but I forgot the cups."

"That's okay. We can just drink from the bottle. Your parents aren't around to see us, so we should be safe," I teased. It was a good thing he saw the humor in his parents' rigidness; it'd become a bit of an inside joke between us, as well as with Nellie.

He popped the cork and held the bottle over the side to keep himself from getting soaked by the overflow. Then he passed it to me with a smile. "We can't exactly cheers each other, since we can't drink it at the same time, but regardless...*cheers.*"

I brought it to my lips and took a sip, enjoying the feeling of the fizzy liquid on my tongue. The entire time, I kept my eyes on his. The moonlight blanketed his face, which allowed me to take in his gorgeous features. He hated it when I used words like *pretty* or *beautiful*, but that's exactly what he was—as well as hot and sexy.

"I love you," I whispered as I passed him the bottle.

He took it from my hand, though he didn't drink from it. Instead, he held it in his lap and stared at me. "I love you, too. Where did that come from?"

I shrugged and glanced up at the glittering colors in the sky. "Nowhere. I just wanted to tell you how I feel. And this moment seemed like the perfect time to do it, sans cups and all."

He leaned forward and kissed my cheek. "Feel free to tell me as often as you'd like, my love. I never get tired of hearing it."

We enjoyed the rest of the show while polishing off the champagne. Well, technically I finished it off. Corbin only had a few sips, but considering he was driving, I didn't think too much of it. The only problem was that since I'd had the majority of the bottle, I was a bit tipsy by the time we made it back to the dock.

And *tipsy* meant loose lips.

"Looks like I just made fifteen dollars," I said, laughing to myself.

Corbin finished dragging the boat onto the grass and flipped the cover on top, ready to latch it closed. "How'd you do that?"

"The girls made a bet with me." Somewhere, in the back of my brain, a small voice told me to shut the hell up. Yet I didn't listen to it. Instead, I kept talking and threw all caution to the wind. "They were convinced you were going to ask me to marry you tonight. I, of course, didn't think so, so I took the bet. And it looks like I won."

He dropped his head back, stared at the sky, and howled to the moon like a coyote high on marijuana. When that finally subsided, he put his hands on his hips and faced me. "Why on earth would they think I was going to propose?"

"Hell if I know. Pulling me off to the side for a bit of privacy beneath the fireworks." I shrugged again. "They're girls…they overthink every romantic situation."

"But you didn't?" He stared to walk closer. "Tell the truth, Bridge. Did you think I was going to pop the question tonight?"

Well, shit. I didn't think he'd turn it around on me. Then again, I didn't know what the hell I expected him to do or say to that. And considering all the alcohol I'd just consumed, there was no way I could come up with anything before I blurted out, "Maybe a small part of me did."

"Babe, I can assure you that when I do ask you to be my wife, it will be when you least expect it." He winked at me and then continued to latch the cover on the boat.

I couldn't say I didn't feel a little sad at that, but not enough to bring down my mood. There wasn't a doubt in my mind that we'd spend the rest of our lives together. If it took him ten years to marry me, then so be it.

Corbin grabbed my hand and kissed the corner of my mouth.

"Aren't you going to pick up all this stuff?" I asked, pointing to the unused blanket and now extinguished candle that still remained on the dock, as well as the empty bottle of champagne in the gazebo.

"Nah. I've got someone to take care of that for me."

Must be nice, I thought to myself as I followed him toward the back yard where everyone else was gathered. The fireworks had ended, which meant the guests would likely start to make their way home. Some lived in the neighborhood and had walked, while others had driven. So I assumed we were heading back to start saying our goodbyes.

However, that didn't happen.

Corbin led me past the crowd to the other side of the property, which wasn't as desolate as the dock, but there weren't many people around. I was about to ask why he'd taken me to this side of the lake when he stopped, took my face in his hands, and covered my mouth with his, effectively silencing my question.

And after thoroughly kissing me, he silenced me again.

By getting down on one knee.

I hadn't seen him pull a ring box out of his pocket—nor had I ever seen him put it *in* his pocket to begin with—but there he sat, on one knee, an opened ring box in his hand, and his eyes shining in the bright-white light of the moon.

"You kissed me for the first time right here in this spot. So it's here that I'm asking you, Brooklyn Miller, if you'll please make me the luckiest man alive and be my wife."

"But…" I covered my mouth and shook my head in shock. Then I realized what shaking my head might've looked like to him. "I mean…" Again, I struggled for words.

Thankfully, Corbin knew me and just laughed under his breath. "It seems I succeeded in asking when you least expected it, huh?"

At that, I nodded. But then I followed it up with, "Why did you drag me all the way to the dock and do all of that over there if you were planning to ask me *here*?"

"I had every intention of asking you over there, but *someone* insisted we watch the fireworks *on* the lake. *In* a boat. And I can't get down on one knee in a boat, so I had to come up with another plan."

"You mean I ruined your proposal?"

He laughed again, though this time, it was much louder. "You're about to if you don't give me an answer."

That was enough to snap me out of my shock. I covered my mouth with both hands and nodded, crying out a muffled "Yes!"

"Thank God. You had me worried for a second there, Bridge." He took my left hand and slid the most gorgeous diamond onto my ring finger. Then he stood, held my face one more time, and kissed me like it was our first time all over again.

I used to get embarrassed anytime I thought about the move I made on him in this spot. But now I couldn't stop celebrating my brazenness that night, for that had led to this. And I couldn't imagine anything better than *this*.

"Looks like you didn't win that bet."

"That's okay. I won something so much more."

LEDDY'S NOTES

It feels like it's been forever since I last sat down to write one of these. And while yes, in a way it has, the real reason it feels that way is because *so* much has happened in my life since then. In fact, the last time was for *The Reality of Wright and Wrong*. Looking back on it now, I can't believe I've actually made it to this point— writing another Leddy's Note.

I like to write these to explain my journey through each book. And while it started as something to let you, my readers, have a bit of an "inside look" into the process of that particular book, over the years, I've discovered that it's just as much for me as it is for you. Because it lets me go back and physically see how far I've come. And I've got to say...between the last book and this one, I've come SO far.

After finishing *The Reality of Wright and Wrong*, I took some time to myself. I spent a lot of time with my kids, friends, and family. I was struggling with a lot in my personal life, and for the first time ever, I had no desire to write. I felt lost without characters in my head or a story I was working through, but I just didn't have it in me to write anything. I know now that I needed that time, because it allowed me to find happiness. And I can honestly say, I'm in the best place of my life. I've never been happier, never felt more positive. Which was why I started this book.

I'd heard a song called "I Hope" by Gabby Barrett, and it inspired this story. But rather than focus on the angry, vengeful side of the song, I decided to concentrate on the hopeful aspect of it all. And the more I thought about it, the lighter and more fun the story became. By the time I finished the first chapter, I was excited to keep going. Which was a *big* deal for me, considering how badly I had struggled for months prior to that.

If anything, this book shows me just how far I've come, from crying and not wanting to look at a computer to being excited and eager to publish something new. I may have gone through hell and back, but I can honestly say I'm in the best place of my life, and I never want to go back.

Thanks to the love and support of everyone in my life, I've finished my eighteenth book. When I wanted to give up, they wouldn't let me. And for that, I'll forever be grateful for them. I can't wait to keep going and see where this new chapter in my life leads.

I love you all!

HEY YOU!!

I couldn't have made it through this without my family. My three girls push me to better myself on a daily basis, and if it weren't for them, I probably would've given up by now. I owe everything to them.

I also wouldn't have gotten through writing this book without these people...

Lobs: Without you, I'd be in a corner either drooling or crying. Likely both. I couldn't have finished this without you holding my hand. Actually...there's no way I would've made it through this year without you. You truly are the best person I've ever met. Thanks for not being a crab!

Sean: Keep supporting my ideas and dreams and I'll never let you go. Then again...that's kinda my plan HAHA!

Mimo: You are now Hannah's BFF. That's forever.Which means you're stuck with me!!

Amanda: When are you coming back to me???

Best Friend: Thanks for always having my back! ITS for life!

Emily: You're one of the few people in my inner circle who've never given up on me. I can't thank you enough for that. I'm back, and I'm ready to make you proud...again. I love you!

Autumn: Thank you for not firing me for always forgetting to do what you asked me to LOL!

Robin: You've once again given my book an amazing cover! You're the best!!!

Angela: I can't thank you enough for giving me whatever time you can spare. I love you, girl!!

Sarah: I'm SOOOO thankful to have you back in my life again! You complete me!

Dani: You're my angel! You've saved me more times than I can count!

Aliana: I'm so happy I've found you! You can't get rid of me now!

All the girls in Leddyisms: You all have shown me so much love and support. I seriously have the *best* group ever!!

Kevin: Thank you for inspiring Chase. Really, I couldn't have created him without you.

My two "best friends": Thanks for showing me your true colors. You both really deserve each other.

Readers: Whether you enjoyed Corbin and Brooke's story or hated it, I can't thank you enough for giving me chance. It means the world to me!

Bloggers: You all are hands-down my heroes. I'm so appreciative for each and every one of you for all you do. Without bloggers' help, I'd be nothing. I love you all!

ABOUT THE AUTHOR

Leddy Harper had to use her imagination often as a child. She grew up the only girl in a house full of boys. At the age of fourteen, she decided to use that imagination and wrote her first book, and never stopped. She often calls writing her therapy, using it as a way to deal with issues through the eyes of her characters.

She is now a mother of three girls, leaving her husband as the only man in a house full of females. The decision to publish her first book was made as a way of showing her children to go after whatever it is they want to. Love what you do and do it well. And to teach them what it means to overcome their fears.

ALSO BY LEDDY HARPER